Mystic Awakening

The Mystic Series Book 1

J.L. Lawrence

Jumpmaster Press
Birmingham, AL

Copyright Notice

Mystic Awakening, a novel by J.L. Lawrence
Copyright ©2021 all rights reserved. No part of this book may be used or reproduced by any means, graphic, electronic, or mechanical, including photocopying, recording, taping or by any information storage retrieval system without the written permission of Jumpmaster Press™ and J.L. Lawrence, except in the case of brief quotations embodied in critical articles and reviews.

This book is a work of fiction. The characters, incidents, and dialogue are drawn from the author's imagination and are not to be construed as real. Any resemblance to actual events or persons, alive or dead, is entirely coincidental. Registered trademarks and service marks are the property of their respective owners.

Cover Art copyright: Rae Monet

Library Cataloging Data
Names: Lawrence, Jennifer
Title: Mystic Awakening / J.L. Lawrence
5.5 in. × 8.5 in.
Description: Jumpmaster Press™ digital eBook edition | Jumpmaster Press™ Trade paperback edition | Alabama: Jumpmaster Press™, 2018 - 2021. P.O Box 1774 Alabaster, AL 35007
info@jumpmasterpress.com

Summary: The Mystic must maintain the balance of all realms and save the world in an ultimate battle. However, the new Mystic has been born in the human realm. Kate is not only unaware of her unique destiny; she avoids anything outside the scope of normal. The magical community is on edge while searching for their lost weapon against the dark. Xander is the Guardian of the Mystic. He's in a race against time to find and protect the being who can save the world and himself.

ISBN-13: 978-1-949184-97-6 (eBook) | 978-1-949184-59-4 (paperback) |

1. Mystical 2. Demons 3. Realms 4. Portals 5. Swords and Sorcery 6. Strong Heroine 7. Magic

Printed in the United States of America

The Mystic Series Book 1

J.L. Lawrence

To Papa, the greatest man I've ever known.
You always saw the creativity inside me
and taught me to chase my dreams.
I'm incredibly blessed to have had you in my life.
The strongest source of power on this planet is love
and you gave it in abundance.

Prologue

"Julie ..." Kate hugged her friend. It was the night before graduation, and their excitement was hard to contain. "That looks amazing."

"Dad had it delivered." She displayed the large picture frame. "He bought it for our new apartment. The photo we took earlier today will be perfect. I can't wait for our new lives in Nashville to begin."

"Amen, sister." Angie wrapped her arm around Julie's shoulders. "After tomorrow, we start a whole new phase, and I couldn't wish for two better people to share that adventure with."

Kate wholeheartedly agreed. Her life before freshman year in college always seemed a little blurry, but the last four years had been a blast. She wouldn't trade a moment of it.

The three of them had met in the unlikeliest of circumstances. Julie's dorm roommate had plummeted out of the window and barely survived. Through Julie's belief in her friend, she had convinced Kate and Angie that it hadn't been suicide. Instead, it had proven to be an attempted murder. They had barely figured it out in time to save the girl before the second attempt.

After that first case, Kate, Julie, and Angie had decided to use their skills to help others. Julie was the numbers girl. She could solve any numerical problem and see inconsistencies in a heartbeat. She'd be starting a forensic accounting job in a few weeks.

Kate turned to catch Angie making faces at something Julie had said. She smiled and shook her head. Angie had a lot of training in martial arts and a highly intuitive mind. Kate admired her tenacity and utter confidence in anything she attempted. She had no fear and would make a great police officer. Her academy training started next week.

"Earth to Kate." Angie waved her hand on front of Kate's face. "Where you at girl?"

"Just thinking about how each of us got here today." Kate shrugged. "Also, thinking about the road in front of us. It seems a little overwhelming at times."

"You're not getting any of those hinky feelings, are you?" Angie joked but there was a note of seriousness in her voice.

Julie glanced up. Her smiled faltered and concern filled her eyes.

"Stop it, Angie." Kate glared. "I'm just nostalgic and a little apprehensive. Nothing else."

She felt Angie search her mind for the truth and Kate allowed her to see her thoughts. One of the strangest discoveries with Angie, had been their strong telepathic link. Over the years, it had strengthened, and they could slip in and out of each other's minds at will. It had proven to be a gift and a curse.

Kate had cultivated a few other gifts along the way like camouflaging her appearance to project what she wanted others to see, and she could use her voice and compulsion to help guide people to her way of thinking. She used her talents sparingly and only in intense situations. Otherwise, she tried to stay as normal as possible. Julie and Angie had helped her find the balance, and she'd be forever in their debt. She had found a productive future with their support.

Angie sat down beside her on the floor. They had boxes stacked everywhere in preparation for their move to Nashville. "I still can't believe you're not coming to the academy with me, or at least joining one of the other agencies constantly recruiting you. Kate, you were born to investigate crimes."

"Not this again." Kate groaned. "With all my mental abilities, I want to focus on the human mind and what makes it tick. I can catch just as many criminals being a consultant and helping those with other mental issues along the way. I don't want a life constantly surrounded by danger and having to fight for survival."

"But the last two summers in the training camps, you were always at the top, and you're a highly ranked martial artist. You've trained me over the years." Angie reasoned with her.

"I remember. I was there." Kate sighed. "They have all recruited me. They want me to be an undercover operative and focus on all the bad in this world. I'd never have a life, and I can't go down that path. I can't explain why I know this, but I do. Yes, I want to provide justice and protect innocents. But I want to do it my way not theirs."

"Enough of that, Angie." Julie cut off Angie's retort. "Graduation is tomorrow, and we are set with jobs, an apartment, and a wonderful outlook on life. Angie, Kate's life is her own. If she's meant to be in law enforcement, then it will happen in its own time. The point is, we all will make a difference in this world. We'll make an everlasting impact. I feel it."

"You're absolutely right, Julie." Kate smiled. "We have a party to get to. Our last as college students, so I vote we start working on that lasting impact tonight." Kate wiggled her eyebrows, and all three erupted into laughter.

"You're right about the time. I didn't realize it had gotten so late." Julie jumped up and pulled Kate to her feet. "Let's get dressed and dance our butts off."

"Is Hank meeting us there?" Kate asked Julie. She and Hank had been dating for the past year. His new job was in California, so they had decided to part ways after graduation. Neither wanted to be weighed down by a long-distance relationship.

"Yep. His parents flew in and they're having a late dinner, then he'll meet up with us."

"Great," Angie interjected. "Then, we have some girl time before he arrives."

They blasted music and laughed while they got dressed, totally feeling the excitement of what was to come. Kate's heart remained full of hope and happiness as they headed to the party.

They danced for several hours until Kate's legs ached. Sweat had erased most of her makeup and her hair had begun to frizz. She looked like a hot mess and felt like it, too.

She and Angie found Julie and Hank sitting outside. Kate cleared her throat to announce their arrival because she didn't want to intrude on the couple. She had checked in on Julie's thoughts, so they didn't end up interrupting a steamy moment. Julie was trying to make the most of their last night together.

"Hey girl," Angie said. "I think we're heading back to the apartment. You coming?"

Julie shook her head. "I'm going to walk with Hank back to his place and then head home. There are still plenty of people out, so I'll be safe."

"Call us when you're on your way." Kate didn't like the idea, but she wasn't her mother and couldn't tell her what to do. Maybe she and Angie could walk really slow and give her time to catch up.

"Okay, *Mom*." Julie winked. Hank took her hand and led her down the street.

Kate and Angie purposely took a long time saying their goodbyes. And when they finally left the party, they walked as slow as possible.

"She's on her way." Angie hung up the phone. "So, if we keep this pace, she should catch up in a couple minutes."

"Yeah." Kate rolled her eyes. "She won't suspect a thing."

"Do you care?" Angie countered.

Kate shook her head. "Not in the least. Slow it is."

White hot pain ripped through Kate's side as a shrill scream launched into the night.

"Julie!" Kate and Angie both screamed and took off running in her direction.

Kate couldn't fight the dread weighing heavily on her heart. Her lungs fought for air as she ran faster than she ever had.

Kate's heart stopped when she saw Julie pinned to the ground and blood spilling out beneath her. A large man had both her arms pulled over her head. Time froze and Kate gasped for air. The horror turned to rage as Kate's training and love for Julie cleared her focus. She had to save her. Nothing else mattered.

Kate flew in with a kick, knocking the man several feet back. He fell to the ground with a thud and held his chest. She'd probably cracked some of his ribs. He rolled to his side and got to his feet.

"Angie, he's running!" She knelt by Julie's side. She had to keep her attention on Julie, or she'd probably kill the man. She might still.

"Not for long." Angie took off after him and wrestled him to the ground.

Kate focused on Julie and the gaping wound in her side. The man had stabbed her with a knife to subdue her. Kate tried to stop the bleeding, while Angie called for an ambulance. Deep in her heart, Kate knew it would never make it in time. She tried to speak and reassure Julie, but the words wouldn't come. She had a giant lump of emotion stuck in her throat and didn't know how to fix it.

Julie moaned in pain. Kate blocked some of it and absorbed the searing agony. It stole her breath. She connected with Julie's mind and could see her consciousness fading fast. She took all of Julie's memories of the attack and stored them away.

Julie's shocked eyes met hers. "Everything will be fine," Kate crooned, over and over.

"I'm not so sure about that," Julie stammered.

"Of course, it will," Kate lied. Tears streaked down her face. Why had this happened? She never should have let Julie walk alone.

"You can't lie to me, Kate." Julie attempted to smile. "I know you."

Kate fought to hold back the panic and speak in a calm voice. "Just hang on. The paramedics are almost here. You can hear the sirens."

Julie's sad eyes met hers. "It's my time, Kate. I don't feel much pain anymore."

"No, it isn't. Kate is helping you block the pain." Angie bent over her and held her other hand. "Just keep breathing. You can do this."

"I love you both so very much," Julie whispered. She struggled to breath and coughed up blood.

Kate had a feeling Julie's lungs were filling with blood. All she could do was prevent her friend's pain and hope for a miracle.

"We love you, too," Angie reassured her. "Don't try to speak. Save your energy."

"Why is this happening, Kate?" Julie gasped for air "Why me? I feel so cold." Another gasp. "Don't leave me."

"I don't know why." Kate's heart shattered. "But I'll never leave you. Sisters till the end, remember?"

Julie tried to smile. "Don't lose faith. Either of you. Fight for those like me. I love you..." Her eyes drifted closed.

Kate's sobs filled the night air as she felt the light drain from Julie's body. The pain quickly turned to fury when she looked at the man Angie had tied to the tree. He was smiling, proud of his handiwork.

Kate stood and walked to him. Her entire body shook with vengeance and anger. It literally radiated around her like a living entity.

She punched him in the face as hard as she could. Blood spurted from his lips. "Not smiling anymore, are you? You're a coward and a worthless piece of shit. I should kill you now and make the world a better place."

She lifted her hand to deliver a death blow.

"Kate!" Angie yelled. "Stop."

Angie switched to their mental link. *This isn't the way, Kate. You know it. Julie wouldn't want his blood on your hands. Control the hate and remember who you are.*

Kate's hands trembled as she tried to gain control of her emotions. Pain, anger, and fear were at war within her. She wanted to kill him. To see his life drain away the same way Julie's had. She met his crazed eyes and decided to look inside his mind to see his motives.

He had no remorse and had killed countless women. The loud party had drawn his attention when he'd been driving through the area to avoid the interstates. Julie had simply been unlucky. There was no rhyme or reason to his choices. Evil covered every thought. He considered himself to be the devil's spawn. She almost believed it.

In the following moments when the police had taken the maniac, and the paramedics had taken Julie, Kate understood what Angie had been telling her all along. You can't change evil by analyzing it, you have to remove it. If she sat on the sidelines, she'd never protect the innocent from these crazies.

The next day proved to be one of the worst in Kate's existence. A rose had been placed in Julie's chair at the graduation ceremony, and Julie's parents were asked to accept her diploma. Facing them as they struggled to understand why their daughter had died would be forever etched into her brain. She didn't have answers.

She promised herself that no parents would feel that pain if she could stop it. She would dedicate her life to ridding the world of evil. Something inside her heart shifted and her focus became crystal clear. She'd be joining Angie at the police academy, after all.

1

Kate lunged for the phone, restraining her inner urge to put a bullet through it. She wanted to just toss it out the window. This number was a dedicated line and its insistent shrill meant another girl had died. That made five in the past few months. She had failed again, and one more death rested on her shoulders.

It had been over six years since Julie's death, and every time this happened, Kate felt like she'd let her down all over again.

"Agent Smith speaking. What've you got for us?" *Another victim.*

At her office desk, she opened her computer and flipped through the file that the local authorities had emailed her. She grimaced; this victim was less recognizable than the last. So much blood and violence; parts of her body torn to shreds.

Kate rose from her chair slowly and faced her team. They had received this case a month ago. Her team specialized in the weird, brutal ones. She had been with the FBI for four years and had been lead agent of this specialized unit for two. They handled the cases no one else wanted — or could stomach.

The screams of the victims tore through her head, and their last gasp of air tightly seized her own lungs. The triumph of the killer assailed her as he forced the last breath from his current conquest. He tortured them and wanted them to feel ultimate pain. The more pain, the more satisfaction.

Kate hadn't asked for the psychic abilities that plagued her night and day, but she was stuck with them. And that was a good day. On a bad day, every cut, bruise, and fear of these poor women invaded her. It was as if she was living through it. She had always been able to turn it off until this case started. Her anxiety continued to escalate daily, as did her temper. She had snapped at her team at least twice this week. She'd never lost her cool before. Something was different about this case, and she intended to figure out what. For now, she had to get them moving. Their flight to St. Louis left in an hour.

Hope no one had any plans. Or a life.

"Our perp has struck again. Grab your gear. We leave in an hour, so don't be late. I'll send out the file, and we'll review on the plane. Let's move!" Despite her being younger than most of her team, they didn't question her. She read their thoughts and knew they respected and feared her. The way she channeled and understood the killers made them uneasy. She wasn't too happy about it herself. She grabbed her gun and backpack and headed out the door.

Once they were in the air, she surveyed the people surrounding her.

Angie was her connection to sanity. She pulled Kate's long blond ponytail as she sat down beside her. "You always remind me of a Barbie Doll." It had been a constant joke between them since college. Angie had been there when Kate had tried to look more professional and decided to cut and dye her hair. She woke up the next day with her hair back at its original length and color. Not long after, they also discovered that they were telepathically linked. When Angie hadn't run screaming for the hills, Kate knew she had found a friend for life.

Chris dropped in on her other side. "I keep telling her she's way too hot for this line of work. Although, she has some killer shades. Are those new Oakley's?" If she was Barbie, then he was Ken. He had a slight crush on her, but she did *not* return any of those feelings. His observation skills and detective work were unsurpassed. So, she'd deal.

"I wouldn't be a proper FBI agent without them. They make me look like a hard-ass, right?" She laughed along with them. The truth was simply that they would be totally freaked out by her real eyes. The multiple shades of blue literally swirled in them. Even contacts couldn't completely hide it.

She rubbed her temples. The files sat open on the table in front of her. The women were in her head and begging for her to bring them justice. The voices swirled and their cries intensified. She pushed everything into her mental compartments. The one thing she was grateful for was the ability to feel numb. The killer had outsmarted them every time, and Kate was starting to suspect that he might have certain talents like her. It would explain a lot, including the intensified backlash.

She shook her head and focused back on her team. Would they all survive this one?

Mike, the resident nerd, typed away at his computer. His skills were unsurpassed when it came to gaining information. Recently he had shared that he and his wife were trying to adopt a child. Kate had gladly filled out the recommendation paperwork. In addition to being a great agent, he had a kind heart, worked great with children, and had a genuinely fun-loving spirit. She envied his ease with others at times. He'd be a great dad.

"Anything new so far?" she inquired.

"Not really. I'm plugging everything into our matrix to create a profile. This one is harder than our previous perps. He's insatiable. Maybe it's a traumatized childhood thing, but I'm not sure. This one feels different." Didn't she know it. She couldn't have said it better herself.

Teri spoke up next. "There has to be a pattern or a trigger that hasn't been uncovered yet. In all the cases we've worked, there's always a method to madness. We just have to figure out what it is he craves. Then we can nail his ass." Kate trusted her opinions. She was soft spoken and reminded Kate of a porcelain doll.

She smiled internally. *Yeah, a porcelain doll with a spine of steel and a nasty right hook.*

"I don't know," Randy said. "Some people in this world are plain crazy. They don't have a good reason. They feed off of others' misery. Maybe our guy is a sicko with no logical reasoning. Or maybe he craves the control. So many wars have started from false truths and hunger for power. He needs to be eliminated. That's the bottom line."

Randy had a valid point, too. And he would know. He had been on so many secret military operative missions, the ghosts would haunt him forever.

She'd been given an amazing crew. They all had excellent points. However, if they couldn't *track* the killer, they'd never *catch* the killer. They had to hope Teri was correct and there was some sort of trigger or desire.

The anxiety in the air overwhelmed Kate. They were all afraid this time. Afraid more women would be murdered. Afraid they wouldn't live through this one.

It's on me. I've got to catch this SOB. She just had to keep them alive long enough to figure it out.

"When you finish the morbid obituaries in your head, you might want to pay attention to the case." Angie's voice echoed in her head. *"Kate, you've got to quit obsessing over the things you can't control. Find the killer. Save lives. That's what you do and you're damn good at it. The team will stand by your side and time will move on. Teri just brought up a good point about why the killer is targeting victims."*

Kate leaned forward, kicked Angie lightly in the shin and grabbed the file to look it over again. Blood. Gore. Mutilation. Right up her alley. No wonder she had nightmares every night.

She cleared her throat and shuffled in her seat. Heat rose in her cheeks. It wasn't often that she was caught daydreaming. "Sorry, Teri, my mind wandered off. Would you mind repeating what you were saying?"

Teri repeated her analysis.

Kate nodded. "I agree. The motivation for choosing the victims doesn't make sense." She went over the details again. They were all female and brutally raped, so the killer was undoubtedly male. He had to be in good shape to abduct and kill the women, especially adding in how fast he disappeared from the scenes. The worst part — he took their eyes. Why? Why did the eyes matter so much? Were they simply trophies? She didn't think so, but what else?

Five faces swam in front of her eyes. Lives cut short, and there would be a hell of a lot more if she didn't do her job.

"The women are all similar in their size, shape, and age," she said. "They also had either blue or green eyes. Maybe our killer is trying to recreate something that he's lost or punishing these women because of someone he hates. It doesn't take much to trigger a serial killer. Let's work more on that theory and create our profile. It's a place to start." She tapped her pen against her paper. A piece was missing. What else did these women have in common?

The plane landed and interrupted her thoughts. Their first stop was the medical examiner. If the pictures had not been graphic enough, the play-by-play of everything the victim suffered made her physically sick. No one's life should end like that. What kind of depraved man were they tracking?

Kate gritted her teeth. Several weeks had passed and they were no closer to solving anything. More women had paid the price. Now, they were in New Orleans still chasing him.

"How are we supposed to apprehend a phantom? It's not exactly like he's going to wave me down and say, *take me, I give up.* He's always one step ahead, and we have another victim to clean up. Nine women have now died." Kate paced across the crime scene, ranting over the fact they had missed the killer again. His victim hadn't been so lucky. She had been beautiful and young with auburn hair, pale skin, and blue eyes, at least, according to her pictures. It was almost impossible to identify her now. Such a waste of an innocent life.

They wouldn't be able to hold off the media much longer. Stories had already been released and it wouldn't take much to cause widespread panic. The only thing helping them keep it quiet was the fact the killer moved from state to state. Plus, she kept a tight lid on the details, but after eight months, people talked.

"Let it go, Kate." Angie said and put her hand on her shoulder. "You have to let it go or it's going to consume you. We need you focused. We'll get him the next time. And before you say anything, I realize we didn't save her. Think about the ones we *will* save once we catch and kill this son of a bitch. Because between me and you, he's not coming out of this alive."

Kate glared at Angie, not exactly comforted by the words. "The next time isn't good enough. He has killed nine women in the past eight months. The next one will put us in double digits. *Double digits!* We still didn't even catch a glimpse of him. He's been gone for at least an hour. I don't know what to do."

She had been born with gifts that she spent most of her time and energy trying to hide, but with this job they could be useful. She was extra sensitive to certain scents and she could smell this dickhead a mile away. Hence the problem, he was always miles away. If she tried tracking him, his trail would vanish about five miles out from the victim's location. How was that possible? He couldn't vanish into thin air.

She worked the scene, closing down her emotions and letting her instincts take over. She believed they had him this time, but when they approached the building, his scent weakened. He was gone. At least she had figured out he was stalking music festivals. All of his victims were singers with a very distinct throaty voice and blue or green eyes. It had been the missing piece in their profile. Her only hope had been that they interrupted him, and he hadn't killed yet. No such luck.

What bothered her more than the death itself was what he did to them before he killed them. The victims had bruises, cuts, and bites from head to toe. They had been violently abused. The women were basically *shredded*.

Kate's stomach turned every time she inspected one of the victims. The coroner always confirmed the women had endured the sexual acts before they died. Victims less damaged were the ones who were lucky and died quicker. It was a pathetic world when a quick death made you one of the fortunate ones. She couldn't comprehend the level of insanity that must exist for anyone to commit these acts.

Through profiling, they had determined the killer enjoyed the torture, and possibly even considered it *fun*. It was all part of the thrill. After being brutalized, the women were drained of almost all their blood. And it hadn't been done at the crime scene, because there was almost no blood anywhere around the victims. Their eyes were always removed. It was sickening to say the least.

Kate wanted vengeance for these women. She wanted the perp to suffer like his victims had. Even so, she kept those thoughts to herself with the exception of Angie who could read all of her emotions and thoughts regarding the case.

Turning away from the young woman, Kate raised her eyes to meet Angie's. "We have to find a way to bring this on our turf and gain some control of the situation. We can't keep losing innocent lives, especially like this. Their bodies are so mangled that their families can't even look at them one final time." And she was always the one who had to notify them. Informing someone that a family member had died was bad enough, but to also tell them that they could never see the body and *why*, was brutal.

Kate walked over and placed her hand on Angie's shoulder. Angie tried not to vomit as she finished examining the body. Her mental gagging reflex made Kate's stomach turn. Although, no one else on the team would know what hid behind Angie's stoic façade. Kate helped her control the emotions, so she could keep that image intact.

Angie was rock steady, and Kate depended on her more than she would ever admit.

"We get the damn place right every time, but he still beats us." Angie straightened her shoulders and pushed her long auburn hair back from her face. "It's so frustrating." She sighed deeply, looking defeated.

This case had driven Kate's team to the very edge. This was the kind of case you had to close, or you didn't sleep at night. Hell, none of her team had slept well since this case began, and today told them how much longer they had to go. Not something she wanted to phone into her boss, who was not going to be pleased that they'd failed again.

How do you catch a freaking ghost?

Turning toward her team, she realized they functioned as a solid unit without much direction from her anymore. Chris was talking with the ME, Mike was typing away in his computer, trying to find reason in the insanity. Teri and Randy were finishing the photographs and gathering the evidence. Angie had collected fingerprints, but she already knew the results: not in the database.

"All right, wrap it up," Kate said. "We need to get back to the hotel and try to sort all this out." They hadn't been home in months.

Before Kate could join them, she had a meeting with a young officer in the French Quarter. He seemed a little young to be handling a case of this magnitude, but Kate acknowledged she probably appeared the same way to most.

A handsome man with dark hair and warm brown eyes stood up to greet her when she entered the small café. She guessed his age to be mid-twenties, but his eyes held intelligence and caution. This was a man who'd survived something horrible. Kate stopped herself from prying into his head and focused on her case.

"I'm Agent Kate Smith." She extended her hand. "Nice to meet you."

"Nate." He accepted her hand and shook it. "Have a seat."

Kate sat in the chair closest to her. "What can you tell me that's not in a file or at the scene?"

"What do you mean?" Nick replied, not quite meeting her eyes.

"You asked me to meet you at a place of business and not your precinct. You also requested just me and not my team. That leaves me to assume that there's something else you want to say, but don't want anyone else to hear. Am I wrong?" Kate signaled the waitress and ordered some tea.

Once the waitress left, Nate responded. "I see you're very perceptive. Yes, there are a few things that don't add up for me. I did my homework on you and discovered that you lead a team that specializes in very unusual cases like the one you're tracking now. My fellow officers and supervisors couldn't wait to hand this off to you and pretend everything is normal.

"Why would they do that?" Kate sensed his intelligence and wanted to know more.

"Because they're afraid." Nate sighed. "New Orleans is known for some freaky stuff and we have seen our fair share of crazy and downright disturbing. This case is different. The officers who found the victim said they could feel evil in the room watching them, waiting. I don't think our perp is a regular human." He paused and met her eyes waiting on her to rebuke him. "Yes, I know I sound crazy, but that's how I feel."

Kate sipped her tea while trying to digest Nate's assessment. He had a valid point. This perp did seem above average in the human department. However, that didn't make him some freak of nature. She had enough to worry about without adding supernatural elements. People always searched for an easy answer, so they didn't have to face the depravity that can exist within any human.

"I'm not quite convinced that we're looking for a *new species*," Kate said calmly and without sarcasm. Though the idea of a non-human seemed way out there, she still wanted to show respect. "However, your observations have merit and we are looking for someone with rare, but I think, *human* abilities. Have there been any other victims?"

"No, whoever or whatever this thing is, he seems to have left my city. No offense, but I'm glad it's *your* problem and not mine."

She smiled. "Yeah, I hear that a lot."

"What led you into this line of work?" Nate leaned forward. "You don't look like a typical agent."

"I guess looks can be deceiving." Kate hesitated and then told him about Julie and some of the cases during college that had led her down this path.

"Wow." He whistled softly. "That's a lot to handle."

"We all have our cross to bear and our calling." Kate forced a smile. "It's not a glamourous life, but someone has to be there to stop the crazy people in this world."

Nate nodded. "Then, I'm glad it's someone as dedicated as you. If you ever need anything, let me know. Before you leave, I was wondering if you could tell me about some of the other cases you've solved over the last few years. I'd like to know what to look for and when to give you a call."

His tenacity and genuine desire to help others impressed Kate. So, she spent another hour in the small café telling him about some of her most bizarre cases since joining the FBI. He had visibly paled by the end of it. Most couldn't handle all the depravity she'd witnessed over the years.

"Thank you." He touched her hand. "For all the good you do in this world that most will never hear about. I hope we get to work together again someday under better circumstances."

Kate stood and shook his hand. "If I'm called in, I can guarantee the circumstances will be dire. It's the *only* work I do." She tried to keep the defeated tone out of her voice. "Best of luck to you."

They exited, and she caught a taxi back to her hotel. Until that moment, she hadn't realized how depressing her life had become. For the first time, she admitted to herself that she would probably never find the normal life she craved. Maybe she should accept the hand of the stranger in the mist that haunted her dreams each night. He couldn't possibly bring her *worse* luck.

2

As her team gathered their stuff and headed down to the vehicles, Kate pulled Angie into a stairwell. "What about a trap? We know he's following the music and what type of voice he goes for. Let's get to the next festival first and give him a singer he can't refuse. Traci can handle the correlations and find us the most likely place his ass will show up to."

Angie suddenly looked wary. "And what exactly are you scheming in that head of yours for this little escapade? I certainly hope you don't mean you're going to be the bait."

Kate hurriedly drug Angie down the stairs. "Look, you know I can control the pitch of my voice to match the other women. No one else can do that. If we do this right it might be our only shot. It's not my favorite idea ever, but we have to put this to rest or lose our team to a mental institution."

Angie switched to their private mental link as they met up with the rest of their team. *"Are you freakin' crazy? Do you not see what he does to these women? You do not want to be on his radar."*

She pushed Angie toward the car. *"Then come up with a better plan. We're running out of options. We've chased this thing from California to Virginia. Where will he show up next? What if he leaves the U.S.? Then what?"* Kate felt herself practically shouting in her head, but she knew Angie would eventually understand. They were both tired but also felt something even worse could be coming.

Angie interrupted her thoughts. *"Could we not find a singer that matched and not use you?"*

Kate glared. *"Oh sure, I want to put another innocent life on the madman's radar so that I won't be at any risk. Because we definitely have a great record so far. Please!"*

She finally noticed that they had been staring each other down for over five minutes, and the other team members were starting to get a little freaked out. Angie slid into the car. *"We'll talk about this later, but don't think I'm agreeing. There has to be a better way, but I do agree we need to get to the next festival first."*

Angie blocked her out the rest of the ride to the hotel. If Kate wanted to, she could break through the barrier, but she respected Angie's privacy, so she'd never do that. Not when Angie had made it clear she needed space. Kate used the time to review the evidence collected and give Angie time to cool off. Kate understood her anger. She would feel exactly the same in her shoes. They had found out the hard way how fragile life could be and how much evil existed all around them. Still, Kate could never allow someone else to be the bait. Angie would come to realize it, too, once the shock wore off.

The car stopped at the hotel entrance, and Kate dragged her weary body up the stairs. She carried this backpack every day, but today it seemed to weigh a million pounds. Her thoughts weighed more. They were the real problem. Her mind wouldn't stop spinning, and she hadn't been able to sleep in weeks.

She pushed in her room key card and went inside, then put her gear down on the bed before meeting up with everyone in their momentary conference room. She was tired of the office on the road.

Thinking about her conversation with Angie earlier, she called her supervisor, Myers, and went over the idea. It didn't go well at first, but as the conversation progressed both agreed that they were down to their last options. Between the media and increasing fear of the public, they needed to solve this case *yesterday*. After a lot of convincing, he agreed to the plan and said he'd make the arrangements when she had a location.

Kate headed down to the room and turned toward her team members with resolve. They had been her team for two years, though some had been on the team longer, like her and Angie.

With sorrow and determination, Kate addressed her team. "I'm disappointed we weren't able to catch him this time. We all worked hard and did everything we could. This is no one's fault." Even as she said the words, she saw the doubt written on their faces. They all felt responsible for yet another innocent's death. "Angie and I think the best chance we have is to figure out where he's going next and get there first before he attacks his next victim."

"Kate, none of this is your fault," Mike interrupted. "But if we go with this new tactic, what if we pick the wrong festival or city? How many will die for something that's our mistake?" Mike was great with his computers, and he also had a soft heart. His sincerity washed over her.

Chris tended to follow orders but had no problem speaking up about this plan. "So far, we've picked every place *right*, so our odds look good. Besides, even when we've known the places, we haven't exactly stopped or prevented anything. I say we take our chances and do a preemptive strike. I agree with Kate on this one."

She turned toward Teri and Randy. This would have to be a decision her whole team could stand behind.

"I'm in," Teri said. "We have to do something different. Change the pace. We're getting our asses handed to us so far." She glanced quickly away from Randy as he brushed past her. They had been hiding a relationship for quite a while now. Kate understood their need for secrecy and had even hidden it from Angie until she had discovered it for herself. This job was hard with insane hours. She didn't begrudge them any happiness. Neither of them realized how deep their feelings ran, and those emotions overwhelmed her psychic circuits.

"I agree," Randy said. "So, what have you got in mind? I know you, Kate, and you're definitely up to something. Let's have it." He gave a brisk nod in his usual uptight military style. She always half expected him to salute.

Angie sneered. "Oh just wait, you'll love what she's got in store for us."

Kate jerked her head toward Angie. "Shut up or go home," she snapped. In her mind, she expanded the reprimand. *"I mean it. You know this is our best bet, so deal with it. I need you to support me so we can end this and go home and sleep at night. Myers approved it, by the way."*

Angie stepped forward and apologetically put her hand on Kate's shoulder. "Sorry guys, I guess I'm more on edge than I thought." Through their link, she added, *"I'm always here for you, Kate. I'm just scared for you. We're dealing with something different, and you know it."*

Kate nodded and smiled. "Here's the deal." She told them the plan she'd shared with Angie earlier. Major objections broke out the moment she was done. They all simultaneously voiced their anger at the plan.

"No. Freaking. Way. Kate," Chris angrily said between clenched teeth. "I need some air." He stormed out of the room.

Kate ignored him and addressed the rest of the objections. "This is our best chance. If it works, we get the bastard. If not, you get me the hell out of Dodge, and we continue to do our job and fight another day."

They discussed the plan in depth and all the resources that would be needed. After a few moments, the team began to settle and focus on the task at hand. Kate looked toward Angie as Chris came back through the door. His face was no longer red, and he appeared in control of his emotions. "Contact Traci and have her do her thing and tell us where this sicko is heading next," Kate instructed Angie, then switched to their mental link. *"I can feel him heading north and should be able to narrow it to at least a handful of cities."* Angie stepped out to make the call.

Mike moved forward to stand beside Kate. "Are you sure about this? We've seen what he can do in a very small amount of time. And he is obviously very unstable."

Kate looked directly into his eyes. "I'm sure this has to end, and we are all ready for a vacation."

Mike nodded.

Kate's cell phone rang, and Traci's name popped up on the caller ID. "Hey girl, that was fast, so tell me some good news."

"I'd actually already been working on it. I don't know about good, but if we're looking at the northeast, it looks like he's probably headed toward Rhode Island. They're having a big music festival next week. It's the Newport Music Festival. Otherwise, the next big festival in that direction is about a month away and his escalation pattern suggests he won't wait that long."

Kate nodded, thinking to herself and working on logistics. "That sounds good, so tell me about the festival, and by the way, I can tell you have doubts on this one, so spill it."

Kate patiently waited. Something must really be eating at Traci. She was always confident and the master of forensics and technology. Finally, Traci took a deep breath and began to speak. "According to the data, that's where he should be heading."

"Okay, so what's the problem?" Kate countered.

"The music collections at the festival don't match the other festivals exactly. It's more concert music and opera. He may go to this festival, but I don't think he'll find what he's looking for and move on."

Her agitation rapidly increased, and Kate wished she would get to the point. "So, what are you getting at?"

"There's a hotel club in Providence just thirty miles north of Newport, and they're having a big showcase around the same time as the festival to attract extra attention for themselves. I recognize some of the performers that will be there and one of their singers is a dead ringer for the victims' voices, not to mention all of the victims' eyes have been blue or green, never brown. The lead singer has bright blue eyes. I can't help but think this is where he'll strike and find his victim."

Kate paced the room. She had picked a hell of a day to wear a skirt, but her favorite pair of black pants had ripped yesterday while she was doing some recon work which had been a colossal waste of time. They were already taking a risk and needed to be damn sure of where they were going.

"Traci, what exactly are you saying? I'm tired and we can't be wrong this time."

"I know, Kate. The computer says the Newport Music Festival, but my gut says he'll be in Providence. I'm sorry."

"I need more than a gut feeling this time. Send me some clips from the bands in Providence. I'll see if I can get a read on them. Make it quick! We've only got a few minutes to decide the whole course of this investigation."

Traci sighed and sent the music files. "I can't explain it, but I think I'm right. I really do."

"I'll listen to the music and get back to you." Kate turned off her phone with much more force than necessary. She could *not* afford to break any more phones.

Angie walked up. "So, what's the word? Where we headed?"

Kate growled. "Not sure yet. Of all days, Traci has chosen today to have a gut feeling that goes against her computer info. I'm going to study it myself before I make a decision. Let's head back to the room. We're done here. Make sure the team gets everything packed and ready to move out."

Angie nodded, giving Kate space. "No problem. We'll be ready to follow your lead within an hour. Just my opinion – give Traci her due. She hasn't led us wrong yet and neither have you. Your gut instinct is your claim to fame. Why don't you go for a run? It always clears your head."

Angie placed a hand on Kate's arm and met her eyes. "Your mind works a mile a minute, but the team can't always compute at your level. Plus, the rest of us could use some extra sleep. You have an enviable energy source that we don't all share."

"I know. I just can't quiet all my thoughts. A long run might work, but I have a few things to finish up first." Kate rubbed the back of her neck.

"Fine. And while you do that, I'm gonna take a long *nap*," Angie warned. "So don't be waking me up if you get hit by some brainy revelation. I need my beauty sleep. Not all of us get to wake up looking like *supermodels*." She bumped Kate's shoulder and smiled.

Kate rolled her eyes. "Some of us are just lucky I guess." She flipped her hair over a shoulder in a mocking gesture.

Angie hmphed and trudged back to her room.

Kate walked back to her own. Thoughts started spilling into her mind again. She tried to sort it all out and get her brain moving in the right direction.

3

Kate sat down and stared at her laptop. With a tired sigh she started it up. The computer whirred to life and she flushed her emotions into compartments she'd created long ago. She pushed all of her anger, doubt, and sorrow away so she could concentrate without the pain of her failure. It was her greatest asset. Any emotion she didn't want to feel — especially if it was painful — she could just push aside and lock away.

Maybe a run wasn't a bad idea. She accessed the files Traci had sent and forwarded the music to her phone. First, she listened to the Newport selections and found herself agreeing that it didn't really fit the profile. Next, she listened to the band that would be in Providence. They were called *Innocence* and just like Traci had said, the lead singer was a dead ringer for the voices of the other victims, enough so that Kate's stomach literally turned, and she could see her as the next target.

Kate did some investigating into the band and found they were quite popular. She also found several other media outlets that were also advertising them. She had no doubt once the perp heard a sample of the music, he'd be there. They were also going to be promoting at the Newport Festival.

As a last measure, Kate closed her eyes and let her instincts take over. She focused on the killer and traced his movements. It was one of the quirks she'd been born with. Traci was right; Kate felt it all the way to her bones. This was it. This was where they would make their stand. She only hoped she would survive it.

She headed out for a run and let her mind clear. A fresh start and a new plan gave her hope.

The stab of pain in her side brought her back to her surroundings. She'd been running hard for an hour. It was a rare indulgence for her to walk through memories of her past. Her thoughts centered on the dreams she'd had all her life. Every night she would see a man half hidden in the shadows. He beckoned her to follow him. He seemed safe, but Kate never had the guts to follow him into the mist. The one thing she could always see clearly was a tattoo on his arm. It resembled a shield protecting an angel with symbols etched into a sword going down the center of the entire image. She wanted so badly to see the man's face, just once.

A powerful connection existed between them. She had worked hard to put it behind her and stop searching for a dream man. The doctor she'd been dating recently was kind, generous, and *normal*. They could have a happy life. Couldn't they? She didn't need or want the man in the mist. She pushed it aside. On the bright side, she had come up with a plan. It was time to get moving.

Kate rushed back to her room and packed all of her belongings. She sent a quick text to her team, giving them the departure details. She kept her mind occupied with the specifics of the plan. Mistakes would be deadly.

She ran down the stairs as her team waited at the doors. She didn't have to read their minds to know they were ready to follow her and that they trusted her decision.

"You know, they do make elevators," Angie remarked as Kate hit the last step.

"Yeah, but I need the exercise and time to think. Wouldn't hurt you to join me some time." Kate raised an eyebrow.

"You wrestle me into enough of that crap back home. So, where we heading?" Everyone turned and stared at Kate. Their eyes were haunted, but their expressions showed fierce determination. The tension in the air told Kate they expected this to be a final stop.

"We're heading to Providence, Rhode Island," Kate responded with confidence. "I've listened to the music and did some investigating. Traci's right. I'm sure he'll go after this band's lead singer. If we can get there first and convince the band to let me sing a song or two, I can match the pitch and lead him our way. Let's go. We have a party to crash."

Kate switched to her link with Angie and reviewed the plans as they walked out of the hotel. *"If I can take the girl's place for a song or two, I can match her pitch perfectly and inject a compulsion to latch onto my voice. I will ease the compulsion at the end of the songs so the crowd will latch back onto Jessie, the lead singer. The perp will still follow me, because I'll make sure he is addicted to the compulsion and won't let go. I hope so anyway."*

Angie agreed and continued using telepathy. It was a great weapon between the two partners and useful at times like this. It also allowed them to hide Kate's gifts, so she didn't become alienated, feared, or ridiculed. *"We'll need two teams just in case he doesn't follow you and* stays focused on the other singer. If he does follow, they can drop back and be our reinforcements."

"Sounds like a plan." Kate paused, trying to figure out how to word the other thoughts running through her mind. "Angie, I'm getting a different feeling on this one. I don't know exactly what it is, but something isn't right. The preternatural speeds, the camouflaging ability, the absurdities of the crime itself, and he never fears us being on his heels. I never sense fear, just enjoyment. And that is scary as hell. Also, I'm picking up traces of other people like followers, but their attachment is one of total servitude or devotion. They even have a part of his stench. I've never witnessed this type of behavior before." Kate leaned back in her seat to rest for the remainder of the flight. She was going to need plenty of energy for this fiasco she'd gotten herself into.

"I know, Kate. I feel it, too, but what can we do but see it through? I hear all the questions floating around in that expansive mind of yours. Why didn't we sense them before? Will they be an issue or are they admirers or worshippers? Who knows? Kate, you'll drive yourself insane if you keep focusing on the unknowns. By the way, I also saw that Myers thinks our scheme is brilliant — in his own childish way."

Kate smirked at Angie's mental sarcasm. "Yeah, he's usually not so theatrical. I guess he's feeling the pressure, too. He wants the case solved but he feels the potential danger like we do."

Myers had nearly come through the phone when she'd informed him of her plans for Providence. He yelled, swore, and even stomped his foot in defiance. So much for dealing with mature adults. He'd made plans to meet them in Providence and orchestrated all the arrangements with the band. They had worked out a smooth transition for Kate to sing a couple songs, then slip back out.

Right before she drifted off, she looked over at Angie who was listening to her iPod and reading her latest murder mystery. "Angie."

She took out an earbud. "Yeah, Kate?"

"Wake me up when we get close to Rhode Island. They have no idea of the terrifying things coming their way and hopefully they never will."

Angie nodded and went back to reading as Kate drifted into a dreamworld of unrest, and justice, and that relentless tattoo.

J.L. Lawrence

4

Fog swirled around her feet, guiding her toward the dark forest. The man hidden in the shadows held out his hand. He silently begged her to take the next step, to find him. His tattoo glowed in the night, beckoning her to follow. The shield was medieval with angel wings around it. A sword sliced through the middle. She wanted to believe she could find peace here. Find her destiny here. But she was afraid. She didn't know what waited for her deep in the night. Once again, she turned away from the man in the mist.

And right into another vision.

She'd never been in this place before, but she recognized the landmark. She stood on the Cliffs of Moher looking over at the ocean. The wind whipped her hair into her face. She braced against its strength to keep her balance. It swirled faster. She lost visibility. What was she doing here?

A soft voice began to speak. She turned, but no one was there. Straining, she tried to hear all the words being spoken.

"Kate, my child, your destiny is upon you. Fate must be followed despite the path taken. The power inside you should not be feared. Embrace your future. So much

exists in this world that you refuse to believe, but you will. In time, you will know all. Find peace, my daughter. We shall meet again at the awakening."

What the hell did all that mean? Her father was still alive so who was this joker? The things he spoke of couldn't possibly exist. It made no sense. Maybe this was simply a regular dream and not a vision.

Then she saw it.

Out over the ocean, she saw a symbol that had plagued her since birth. She could never figure out its meaning and hoped it would just go away. Phoenix wings spanned the width of her vision. Two swords appeared and crossed in the middle. Blue and red flames surrounded them. Ivy wrapped around the blades. She squinted to see the center. Ancient symbols — Celtic in origin — formed a circle in the center of the green vines. They glowed and hummed with power.

The Phoenix rushed forward and shot through her body. The last thing she heard was the voice telling her that it was time.

The fog swirled once again. She landed hard on her backside in the middle of a luscious green meadow. A stream flowed in the distance. Children's laughter surrounded her, but she couldn't find the source. A man cleared his throat. She jumped up and spun around.

"Who are you?" Kate demanded.

"My name is Cassius." He smiled. His swirling blue eyes mesmerized her. They had tiny silver flecks. It reminded her of staring into the depths of a raging sea.

Just like her own eyes. "Are we related?"

"In a manner of speaking." His mouth twitched like he was hiding a secret.

Kate sighed. "What does that mean? My visions usually don't involve actual people."

"They used to." He spoke in a mysterious voice.

She began to feel like they had met before, but she would have remembered him. She couldn't take much more.

"Tell me what it is I need to know or let me return to my somewhat peaceful sleep," Kate demanded.

The man didn't pay her much attention. He walked over to the stream and sat down on a large boulder. His large muscular frame seemed a little less imposing once he sat. He motioned for her to sit beside him.

She hesitated, then walked over.

He stared in the distance for several seconds and finally turned to face her. "Kate, there are so many things in this world that you do not know. I'm unsure where to begin."

She narrowed her eyes. "What do you mean, many things?"

"Other realms for instance."

"Don't be absurd," she interrupted. "There's only one world."

"And yet, here you are." He met her eyes. "What would you call this?"

"A very bad dream," Kate muttered.

His laugh sounded musical and calmed her. "My dear girl, you haven't changed much over the years."

His comment brought back the panic. They had met before, so why couldn't she remember?

"You can't remember because I didn't want you to. Your destiny is not what you think. It's much greater. You are meant to fight for the innocents but on a much grander scale than this human life you've created."

When he spoke the words, human life, her heart froze. She didn't want to hear what came next. She'd worked too hard to carve out a near-perfect life for herself. It had taken years for her to cultivate a normal image.

"I'm sure you mean well, Cassius." Kate gritted her teeth. "But I've got the life I want. I won't listen to any of your fairy tales."

"Fate doesn't seem to care what we want in life." Cassius' tone held a bitter edge. "Believe me, I know."

"Then, you understand?" Kate asked.

He sighed. "I understand your fear and reluctance, but it does not matter. Your destiny was written before you born, and even before my own birth. I'm here to guide you to that path. Listen to me. I will tell you where to go, and you will find happiness in time."

"No!" Kate stood and faced him. "I will never give up my life. No one can make me. I don't care how many people are sent to haunt my dreams. You speak of other worlds, but that can't be. My world is real. I track down bad people and save many good ones. I couldn't save a friend of mine, but I will prevent her fate for as many as I can."

"Ah … Julie." He frowned. "She was a beautiful soul. You miss her a great deal."

The blood drained from her face and she felt faint. "How could you know that?"

"I know most everything about your life." He walked over to her. "I've watched over you since your birth."

"Enough of this." Kate tried to find a way to wake up from the vision.

He moved so swiftly, Kate didn't have time to react. His hand jerked up her chin, and he stared deep into her eyes. Kate could feel his disappointment and a little fear.

"It appears my timing is off." He held onto her face. "Your mind is closed tighter than ever before. Deleting the memories of your past did more damage than I envisioned."

"What are you talking about?" Kate demanded. "What memories?"

Cassius stared into the distance, ignoring her question.

She grabbed his arm. "Tell me."

He turned. "You chose to delete many memories from your past to attain the normal life you so covet now. Once, you understood much more about this world. Now, your mind has narrowed."

"I don't understand." Kate sat back down. "Why would I delete memories?" As she asked the question, missing moments and blurred occurrences popped into her mind. Hadn't she felt that pieces were missing from her past many times over in the last few years?

Cassius kneeled in front of her. "At the time it was a coping mechanism that has turned into a handicap."

"Can I get them back?"

He frowned. "Not for a while. The mind is a funny thing. Nothing is ever completely gone, but you don't have the power at this time to retrieve them, and it's not my place."

They remained silent for a bit. If she had made the choice, there must have been a good reason. She wanted to return home and forget about all of this.

As if hearing her thoughts, Cassius stood again and reached out his hand. "You won't remember this vision or me. I see I came too early. Your mind isn't yet ready to see the world around you and embrace all that can be. However, it won't be long until you have no choice. Only your guardian can awake the dormant power inside you now. While it is a different path than I originally foresaw, it will still guide you back to us."

"I don't understand." Kate stared at him. Her heart hammered and dread filled her mind. "What is it you want from me?"

"In time, you will know all." He began to walk away from her.

Part of her wanted to grab him and make him tell her everything. The other part wanted to say good riddance and return to her normal life.

"Why me?" she yelled at him.

He faced her. "That's a question I've asked myself many times without answer. We are all given a destiny. Some great and some small. Yours is the greatest of them all. In time, you'll see, and we will meet again."

He walked to her once more and touched her head. "The only thing you need to know for now is that change is coming my child, and it is useless to resist. The countdown has begun."

She tried to speak to ask more questions, but he had silenced her. "Until we meet again, Cadence Hope Smith."

He kissed her cheek, then whispered in her ear. "The time has come. Wake up, Kate."

She gasped as she opened her eyes. *Time for what? Why couldn't she get rid of all these stupid dreams?*

Angie reached over and tapped her shoulder. "We're here. You okay?"

"I'm good." *And may never sleep again.* "Let's get started. We have a lot to do in a short amount of time." She'd figure out how to get rid of the visions when this case was over. She didn't care who she had to ask for help at this point. She would find the path to a nice normal life.

"Providence is beautiful this time of year." Kate continued to stretch as they got out of their vehicle in front of the hotel. She turned to her team. "Unpack, set up, and rest for today."

Her team set up headquarters and laid out the maps of the club and surrounding areas. Kate glanced at each of them and had a horrible feeling in the pit of her stomach. She brushed it aside. They had to be prepared for this one. There could be no mistakes.

Kate cleared her throat. "Late tonight we start working all possible scenarios with both teams. I want nothing left to chance, all equipment checked a million times, all weapons inspected, and get some sleep tonight. We only have two days until, as a wise man once said, *the shit hits the fan*. Be ready for anything. We all know this is different, and it's possible he may be ready for us and bring backup of his own. He has help for sure."

They all headed to their rooms to get situated and try to find a way to relax.

Kate went to her own room with Angie following close behind. "What are you not telling us? I get the secrecy, but you never keep facts from me."

Kate felt stress taking over her back and shoulders. She rubbed the back of her neck. "I don't know, Angie. I just can't shake this feeling that this is going to be much more than we bargained for." Tension knots were a bitch, and she was getting them a lot more often since this case began.

Angie stretched her own neck as she sat down on the end of Kate's bed. "I know, I see the conflicts in your mind. The constant unrest. The fear it's not quite human." Angie voiced the feelings out loud for the first time.

"That's the problem. It's just plain ridiculous. It has to be human. What would I say to our team? What else is there? A vampire? The Boogey man? A deranged power-hungry psycho?" Her restlessness made her extremely uneasy, and she began to believe her instincts. That made it worse. "I mean, really, what else? I know there are things in this universe that I don't understand, but I have no reason to believe in strange creatures that have suddenly come out of hiding."

Angie shook her head. "You, the queen of paranormal romance and suspense, don't believe? You know there's more out there. It's inside you, no matter how much you try to hide it and whether you want to believe it or not. You need to accept it and be prepared for anything. Hell, for that matter, look at yourself. You're not exactly the paragon of all things normal. Maybe you're right and it's just an extremely sick and twisted pervert, but you better be ready if it's something else."

"How the hell do I do that? We don't know what or who it is, and by the way, everything you read doesn't have to be true. Yes, I love to read the stories and watch the movies, but other than a few unique talents, tell me what proof you have ever seen to make any of it real?" Kate grabbed her computer and flopped down on the bed. Angie shrugged and headed to the door to go to her own room.

Stopping at the door, she turned to Kate, "I don't know, but I truly believe only you have the ability to figure it out. You've always been special. Whether you own up to it or not, doesn't change the facts. Who would believe you can do all the things you can do? I know because I've seen them, but others would call us crazy. Don't be blinded by your obsession to be normal. It could cost another life. Maybe even *yours*." The door closed with a soft click.

Angie was right, but Kate didn't know what to do about it. What if someone had the same powers as she did? If they were used for the wrong reasons, is this what could be created?

However, Kate *did* know this case and had a plan to take this SOB down. It was her job, her mission. She opened her computer and started running scenarios and getaway plans until her eyes burned. As for the supernatural stuff, if there was such a thing, she just had to hope her instincts would see her through.

Uh-huh, that always worked.

The afternoon quickly approached. Kate and her team ate a relaxing early dinner at a local Mediterranean restaurant. The food had been excellent and the atmosphere quiet. They all needed this break and a chance to reconnect with real life. For several months, they had eaten on the run, jumped from one place to another, and talked about this case until they were ready to explode.

Kate skimmed the faces of her team and realized just how much she cared about them, especially Angie. Maybe she cared too much. A definite issue in the weakness column. She obsessed about keeping them safe day and night.

Trying to clear her thoughts she inquired, "How about a walk around the town? We still have some time to kill before our meeting starts."

Everyone agreed, but the expressions of shock that flew across their faces as they traded looks with one another nearly made her laugh.

What, she wasn't a tyrant?

Angie stepped up beside her. "I can't believe you're letting us have time to just walk around wasting time." She bumped Kate's shoulder and smiled.

"Yeah, well, maybe that's what we're missing. We've been so focused, so frustrated. We've forgotten who we're fighting for. Look around us, the families, college students, everyone. They all depend on people like us to keep them safe from nightmares. We need to see them. Remember their faces. Remember what we're fighting for."

Chris leaned forward against the rail. "We remember. You don't let us forget. But it does make a difference to take time to see all the positive that still remains, and how many good people there are trying to survive and simply have a happy life."

They continued walking, and the silence was deafening. Kate couldn't pretend that they didn't all feel something was going to happen this time. The buildup was unbearable, but the climax could be deadly. She headed toward the park across the street, and her team followed silently.

The park was small but beautiful with a gorgeous fountain in the middle. The benches were full, and several people were laid out under the trees or on blankets: some eating, some relaxing. Kids played, laughed, and ran. All innocent. Kate was determined no other victims would lose their lives to this – *whatever*.

A woman's frantic yell jerked her from her melancholy. Kate pivoted toward the sound.

A toddler headed for the busy street full of late afternoon traffic. The youngster waddled, her body teetering back and forth. Her mother moved toward her with an infant in her arms. Time slowed and Kate knew the mother would never make it.

Kate sprinted toward the toddler without a second thought. She heard Angie's footfalls behind her, receding in the distance. Her sole focus latched on the child. The little girl, blond curls bouncing, skipped toward the oncoming traffic.

Her mother shrieked in terror somewhere nearby. Kate pushed herself to go faster until her muscles burned. Her lungs could barely pull in oxygen. *Almost there!* She took one final step and launched herself toward the child.

Horns blasted. Tires squealed.

She twisted her body in midair and landed hard on her back. She slid across the asphalt, feeling her clothes rip and the skin underneath grated. She never relinquished her hold on the small girl.

The child wiggled free from Kate's grasp and flung her arms around her neck. Her soft brown eyes met Kate's. "Whee! Fun." She pulled on Kate's hand. "Again?" The innocence and joy in the small child's expression spoke volumes.

Kate patted her head and stood up. "Not today little one." She scooped her up and tickled her. Then, she returned the girl to her mother.

The lady kept thanking Kate for saving her child while at the same time fussing at the little girl out of pure fear.

She grabbed her daughter in a bear hug filled with relief and immediately went back to reprimanding her again. A mother's love. It had to be the strongest emotion Kate had ever encountered. A mother was willing to give everything to protect her child. Even die, if need be. Her own mother had saved Kate from falling off a cliff once and saved her life. Despite their strained relationship, her mom had proven the strength in that parental love.

Kate encountered people every day willing to sacrifice themselves to create a better world. Her team would choose to give their lives to save these women who would become mothers. Sometimes she struggled to understand a love that ran so deep. She locked away so many emotions. Maybe she had locked up some of the good ones, too. This was worth fighting for. She dusted herself off and patted the woman's shoulder, then rustled the girl's curls and told her to be careful and listen to her mother.

Watching them leave, she was hit by an intense internal yearning for a normal life. All she really wanted was a nice husband, a house, and children to fill the home with laughter. *Was that too much to ask?* Instead, she was a protector of the innocent and it was her cross to bear. She admitted to herself that she might never have the life she dreamed of, but she could at least give others a chance to have it.

She led her team back across the street. They all remained quiet, afraid to break the spell and momentary peace. Seeing lights up ahead, Kate headed through a tunnel covered with colorful tiles. All of them were beautiful and seemed to be decorated by children. Her breath caught as they emerged from the tunnel. She read the sign. They were created by children in honor of 9-11.

Hope seemed to be in the very air tonight. She prayed that was a good omen.

On the other side of the tunnel they stepped into another world. A stunning display greeted them. Barrels were in the water and on fire, creating an awe-inspiring scene. All around them were street vendors and live music — the truest reminder of human survival and celebration, despite any odds.

Wars may be fought, but life continues on. Goodness and light always endure.

Tears came to Kate's eyes as she watched the miracle of living life unfold before her. Always the spectator, never the participant. Always in the shadows.

She closed her eyes, took a deep breath and smiled. Maybe they would win and score another point for the good guys. Maybe. Straightening her shoulders and facing her team, she knew it was time to begin. "It's time. We've got a score to settle."

They returned to the hotel for an intensive strategy session.

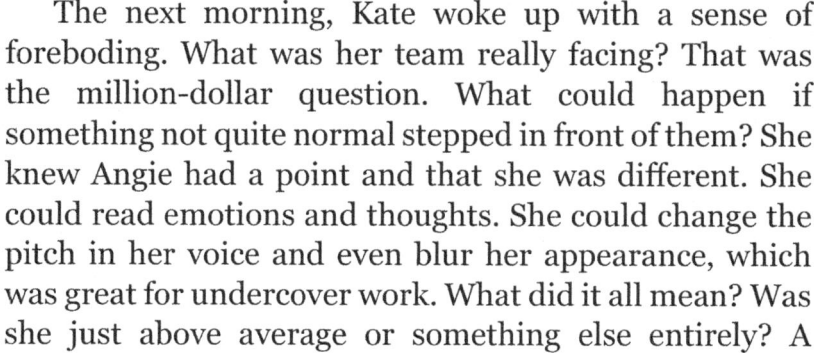

The next morning, Kate woke up with a sense of foreboding. What was her team really facing? That was the million-dollar question. What could happen if something not quite normal stepped in front of them? She knew Angie had a point and that she was different. She could read emotions and thoughts. She could change the pitch in her voice and even blur her appearance, which was great for undercover work. What did it all mean? Was she just above average or something else entirely? A question that had plagued her entire life.

She dressed in her black tactical pants and pale blue blouse, threw her hair back into a ponytail, and packed her papers and computer. She focused her mind back to the task at hand and headed down to where Angie had set up their headquarters. In a few hours, she had a meeting with the band to arrange a place in their show for her to sing two songs. This should give her enough time to create the compulsion for the killer and take care of business before the band even finished for the night.

Myers had done an excellent job setting the scene with the band manager. He had simply told them that there had been some trouble at some showcases in other states and asked if they would allow one of his agents to sing a couple songs to scope out the scene. Their only question had been concerning her talent because they did *not* want to scare away their fans. Kate had spoken briefly with their lead singer, Jessie, on the phone to go over a few details. Jessie had seemed down to earth and fun to talk to. She was extremely talented and probably had a bright future with her band. Angie had already downloaded several of *Innocence's* songs to her phone.

She turned and looked out of one of the huge windows facing the downtown area. Providence was a beautiful city, and she would have loved to be visiting under different circumstances. Someday, she promised herself, she would return as a regular tourist. *Someday.*

5

Kate entered the room and faced her team and another set of individuals she knew only by an e-mail sent yesterday afternoon. "Hello all, I hope you had a good night's sleep because there won't be any tonight." She looked straight into their eyes, wanting them to grasp the severity of this assignment, especially the new team members. She exuded a confidence she didn't truly feel.

"Here's the deal. Tonight is, in all likelihood, our only shot to catch our killer. The next stop is probably New York and there are too many clubs, music festivals, showcases, venues, etc. to even begin a decent search. We won't be able to track him and my guess is, he knows it. He's been playing a cat-and-mouse game with us. After New York, Canada is probably next, and we lose. We lose the perp, the case, and many more innocent lives." Kate nodded toward Angie to pick things up.

She stepped to the table where they had mapped out all the scenarios. "All right everyone, listen up!"

Angie went through all the possible options and backup plans. Kate answered questions until she felt like exploding. Words were not enough. They needed to experience it.

"Let's head out into the field," Kate suggested. "We can answer more questions after everyone is familiar with their position and expectations."

Angie shook her head. Her eyes were full of doubt. Kate wanted to reassure her that everything would be fine. If only, she believed that herself.

Mike, Chris, Teri and Randy caught on pretty quick. Kate's team was solid and flowed seamlessly through the drills. The backup team – not so much.

Chris snarled as he rounded the corner toward Kate. "What! Did they send us every newbie on the freaking planet, or do they just come this dumb these days?" His hands flew in time with his words and Kate tried to avoid getting hit by them. "They are never where they're supposed to be, they miss the marks, and are we even sure they can fire weapons?" He continued toward the hotel to probably cool off and grab some lunch.

The rising pressure and tension seemed to be getting to everyone. Kate sighed. Angie walked up, sweat glistening across her brow. "He has a point. This other team has no experience with this level of crime and are not taking it as seriously as they should."

Kate nodded. "I know, but they wanted to include locals who have a lay of the land and a decent relationship with the local authorities to keep them out of our hair or call them in if we need them."

Angie grimaced, trying to hold her tongue, but was unsuccessful. "Let's hope they stay out of our hair as well and don't accidentally shoot us." She paused, then, giggled. "Or wet themselves."

"Hush, Angie." Kate's blood began to boil as her agitation grew. "They may not be ours, but we'll still show them respect like they've been showing us. They won't shoot us and who knows, once we actually see this thing face to face, we may all need a change of clothing. Stuff the arrogance. We need them. Bottom line." She walked toward their team leader to clean up the mistakes. Though she didn't admit it out loud, she was worried about them being ready, too. It was her life on the line after all.

The night came too fast. Only two hours until show time. Everyone crammed in the small room for a final meeting. The tension suffocated the air around them. Everyone wiped sweat from their face. Not the look of confidence Kate hoped for.

She forced her nerves under control. Her stomach and chest resembled a carbonated bottle someone had shaken one too many times. Her belly gurgled and roiled, and if things got any worse, she feared she might vomit.

Despite the fear, she stood and commanded everyone's attention. "We're at the finish line. Whether we win or lose is in our hands now. I've already told you how important it is to nail him tonight, and there are no second chances. We know he has many followers based on previous evidence. We don't know how many he may have with him tonight, but rest assured he won't be alone. Do not underestimate him. Never lose focus and don't become complacent."

Nodding toward her team members, she added, "and don't be too cocky."

Angie smirked. Chris laughed. Mike harrumphed with his arms crossed, while Randy and Teri passed a knowing look. Together they were unbeatable. Together they would win this and end a nightmare. Tonight was their night.

Kate stared at the mirror for the millionth time. "I am so not wearing this."

Angie rolled her eyes and handed her the makeup bag. "You're a singer with a band, not an agent with a gun and badge. You have to look the part, or it will be a dead giveaway no matter what you do with your voice."

On another kind of occasion — like a party or a night on the town — she'd have to admit that she looked kind of amazing in the red sequined sleeveless top. It snugly wrapped her upper body with a couple inches of midriff showing, and the black leather pants fit like a glove. But this wasn't one of those occasions. She'd worked so hard to be taken seriously, but no one would *ever* view her as the tough agent looking like this. Her long dark blond hair flowed halfway down her back — something else most every male over the age of twelve appreciated, and she was pretty certain her eyes shined bright blue with nerves and anticipation. She could inspire lust in the happiest of married men, but she chose not to. That was one more power that she never wanted. Other than the rare occasion of going to a club or an undercover assignment like tonight, Kate always hid behind her black suit and badge with her hair neatly tucked away. She was nicknamed the Ice Queen for a reason.

Angie worked a miracle with her makeup. Her eyes had a smoky eye shadow effect and her mouth seemed to have a constant pout; full and sensual. Her whole face radiated a sensuous glow.

"I can't believe I voluntarily got myself into this," Kate muttered.

Angie smirked and patted her on the back. "Well, it was your idea, so suck it up. And while you're shaking that ass up on stage for all your co-workers, just remember I told you so."

"And why are you my best friend?" Kate laughed and looked over her song selections. She jerked, nearly dropping all the music. She sat up straight and caught Angie's eyes. "He's here. I feel his emotions and he is definitely hunting."

"One piece in place." Angie checked her gun and put it back in the holster. "You finish up and get into position with the band. I'm gonna go make sure everyone is ready and tell them the good news. I'll be backstage with your weapons. You'll at least have enough time to slip on a jacket over the holster to get to the rendezvous point."

Kate gave Angie a quick hug. "We're gonna do this. We'll use our telepathic link most of the time to keep the channel clear. We need to know what we're dealing with before everyone rushes in." She rarely ever wore an earpiece. Instead, she always relied on Angie to keep the team contact and kept in touch through their mental link. It kept her from actually hearing their voices; feeling their emotions helped her stay more focused.

Angie nodded. "You got it. Now it's showtime for you, girl. Go do your groove thing." She smiled, and Kate caught some of Angie's smug thoughts. Angie loved giving her a hard time. It helped justify her existence in life.

"Yeah, yeah, I'm going and I'm never going to live this down," Kate groaned as she walked through the door to the backstage area.

"Nope, but you'll be a hit at the next Christmas party." Angie laughed and ducked around the corner, so Kate couldn't hit her with the bottle of water she launched.

Jessie walked her from the dressing room to the backstage area. Emotions from the crowd poured into her mind. She had left it open to assess the perp, but the constant barrage of neediness, sexuality, and loneliness made it very hard to concentrate.

She tried to home in on his energy source without tipping him off. She could feel him, but his thoughts were centered on the hunt but not what he intended to do. Teri had been right. The music or voice must be some type of trigger that created the extra layer of evil within him. Either that or he had psychic powers, too.

The band took the stage to do their warmup number. Kate's nerves were a mess. She rubbed her hands against her pants to remove the sweat. Her heart raced. She forced her breathing to return to normal. She'd spent her whole life hiding in the shadows. She didn't want the spotlight, nor did she want anyone else to die. That last thought helped her gain control over the fear. She pushed the unwanted emotions into her compartments.

Once again Kate focused her energy and cleared her mind. She brought the notes, pitch, and words together and stepped out on the stage. She'd been brought in as the guest act and was supposed to start off the night with two songs and then turn it over to Jessie, the band's real singer.

She felt the perp in the crowd reaching for her, and her stomach lurched. Darkness rose up and surrounded his aura. He was evil incarnate. Negative black energy pulsed around him, saturating anyone near him with fear and despair. Gathering her nerve, she focused on the notes in her head and added the perfect amount of compulsion to attract a serial killer. That was a mental statement she hoped to never make again.

6

"Show's almost over," Angie whispered into the mike, "boys and girls. Everyone, be ready — " she sucked in a breath, "for anything."

Kate came off the stage, strapped on her holster, checked her gun, and then put on her black leather jacket. "I can feel him tracking me," she told Angie. "He's so focused on me he doesn't even hear Jessie."

Good for Jessie, but not so much for me.

She had talked with the singer. Jessie wanted to make a living doing what she loved, and she worked with several charities determined to give back to the community. Kate hadn't known any of the other victims — not while they were alive. She *had* to win tonight. She could not bear for Jessie's lifeless body to be seared in her mind. She had enough painful images there already to last several lifetimes.

"Great," Angie said, following Kate. "Can't beat being obsessed over by a serial killer."

"Is everyone in place?"

"Of course," Angie smiled and embraced the cliché, "and raring to go."

"Angie, be careful out there tonight. This guy is more than what he seems, and I'm feeling the presence of others, which means he brought back-up."

Kate met Angie's gaze. Through their mental link, a memory of their close friend, Julie, popped into their thoughts. She had been their third musketeer in college until she'd been murdered the night before graduation. The memory gave them both a bad feeling about tonight. "I'll be careful, but you're the target, Kate. So, you're the one who better watch her ass."

Chris piped through the earpiece and Kate could hear him through Angie's mind. "I thought that was my job, and after tonight, I plan to watch it very closely from now on." His laughter ran through her head.

Angie smothered a laugh as Kate muttered, "Shut up and man your post." Then she addressed the entire team. "Here we go, we're stepping into the side lot."

Her boss had worked it out so they could have a large area to bring the perp in the open without onlookers. The team carried standard Glocks fitted with suppressors. Kate assessed the area. *With the loud music, I doubt the crowd would hear gunshots anyway.*

It was eerily silent as Kate and Angie walked through the side lot. *"You feel that? All the hairs are standing on the back of my neck."*

"I feel it. Can you locate it?" Angie stayed watchful, observing every direction. Everything sat unnaturally still. She felt eyes watching her, but they seemed to be coming from every direction.

"I can and you're not going to like it. This is bad, Angie. We're surrounded and their perimeter is bigger than ours. It's basically an ambush. He was ready for us. He used our scents to discover our perimeter and went

beyond it. Call in the backup team. As much as it bothers me to say it, they may be our only hope to create a diversion and allow us time to get back on an even kilter."

The air shifted, and she braced for the attack. *"Angie, here it comes, stay at my back."* Just as she prepared for him to appear, sirens sounded in the distance. *"Team B came through, after all. That's our distraction and more reinforcements. Shit, he knows who I am. He knows I'm psychic. I can read some of his thoughts, but they're distorted. That rattled him. He's going to make a run for it. We'll lose him if we don't move quickly."*

"Here we go, they're making their move," Angie whispered into the transmitter.

Chaos erupted. Thirty or so crazy-looking men and women poured in on top of them; their eyes black and bloodshot. Tattoos covered most of their bodies. All were bald, including the women. They charged the pair, their movements strange and stiff. Most didn't bother with weapons, relying on impressive strength. They tossed garbage cans and barricades aside without slowing.

Who are these people? Kate mused. If she didn't know better, she'd say they weren't human.

Mike and Chris advanced from the shadows near the stands. The crowd swatted them away like flies. The others appeared, weapons in hand. Kate watched the pistols buck in their hands. Muzzles flashed; the muted reports echoed in the night. Her team fired round after round, taking down as many as they could. The stench of blood, sweat, and gun powder permeated the air.

They would run out of ammo before they ran out of people to kill. Slides clicked back; the pistols empty. The agents, overrun by the advancing horde, switched to hand-to-hand techniques. Their attackers were stronger, quicker, and damned hard to kill.

Angie ducked a punch from the thug in front of her. She grabbed his head and jerked down hard. Kate heard the bone crack from the force. Angie turned to join Kate, but the guy with the broken nose made a grab for her from behind.

"Angie!" Kate yelled. "Behind you."

Kate tried to reach her, but Angie took care of herself. She grabbed her attacker around his neck just as he towered over her. Using all her strength, she flipped him over body. When he hit the ground, it became obvious that she had snapped his neck due to the weird angle. At least it put him out of commission, so they knew one way that could stop them.

"Radio the team." Kate ordered Angie. *"They need to know how to decommission these assholes. Tell them to break their necks. I know it's not protocol, but it's all we've got for now. It takes too many bullets to incapacitate them."*

"What's happening, Kate? I've never seen anything like this."

"I don't know. Whatever drugs these idiots ingested has made them batshit crazy and superhuman strong. All we can do is hold our ground and hope we outlast the effects."

The reinforcement rescue squad moved in with more magazines and more manpower. Unfortunately, within seconds they had joined their colleagues on the ground and were tossed around like rag dolls.

Kate could barely make out her own team members in the dark and chaos.

Using her psychic senses, she zoned in on each team member. Chris hit the ground, flipped back to his feet, and knocked the legs out from under his opponent. When the guy tried to regain footing, Chris leaned in and twisted his neck. He had moved onto the next one before the man hit the ground.

Randy caught Teri as she was thrown into the air. They both toppled to the ground. Teri's arm pinned underneath her body, and she screamed in pain. Randy picked her up and hid her behind the dumpsters. He stayed close to protect her.

All of her agents appeared to be holding on, but they couldn't last much longer. The strain and fatigue etched across their faces. Kate could feel their energy waning.

She looked at Angie. *"We're losing him. His trail is getting cold. I can't hold onto him much longer, especially if I have to keep killing his pawns. He sent them to die as a distraction. Probably pumped them full of drugs."*

Their numbers started to dwindle as many began to flee. Her team took control of the scene. Fury raced through her body. They had screwed up and missed their chance. He'd been in her grasp. She saved Jessie and she would have to hide for a while. But she would live. How many more women would die because she messed up? His final message to her had been the impression that they would meet again. Then he vanished. She was definitely on his radar now.

"Kate." Angie's voice was soft and full of pain. Kate felt sorrow emanating off her.

"What is it?" Kate feared the answer.

"Mike." Tears streaked down Angie's face. "He didn't make it. His neck was broken." Angie barely got the words out. Kate read it in her mind.

She also saw that the rest of her team had survived. Some injured, but alive. Most of the other fatalities were from the reinforcements who'd had less training. Two of the members from the rescue squad had died as well. She underestimated her opponent. Her grand plan had been an epic fail, and she'd lost a dear friend.

Kate wanted to howl and scream in fury, but she couldn't. She had to lock it away and clean up the scene before it got out of control. The patrons and performers were hiding in the club because they didn't know what was happening.

At least that was one thing they had done right. They had posted guards at all the doors to make sure no innocents came outside, so no one but the agents and local law enforcement got caught up in the fight. Panic radiated inside the building, but they didn't realize what was going on outside.

The remaining agents helped the injured until more medics arrived. Close to twenty bodies of the assailants had been stacked up so far and many more were strewn over the lot.

Turning toward her team members, she tried to keep her voice under control. "Pull all the good guys clear and start gathering what evidence you can find. It's fixing to rain so the fires shouldn't be a problem. It's not perfect, but it's the best we got. We need to finish processing the scene, so we can do right by the ones who have fallen tonight."

Kate wanted time to grieve over Mike, but there would be time later. She had to protect her team as a whole first.

As usual, all her emotions were pushed into their boxes and she moved forward. They wrapped up everything as quickly as possible, but it seemed to take forever.

Back at the hotel, she glanced around at her team members who were wounded, grieving, and shocked. Randy had his arm wrapped around Teri, while she wept into his shoulder. Chris stood by the window looking out with vacant eyes. Angie stood beside Kate providing mental support, but her heart had broken into a million pieces. No one had packed or moved anything. The room hadn't changed in the hours that their life had turned upside down.

"Mike was a great agent and a wonderful man and friend." Kate's voice cracked. "We will always honor his memory and know to the depths of our hearts he would be proud of each one of us and our continued fight for justice. No, we didn't win tonight, but we saved an innocent woman. That's a step in the right direction. We'll finish this and win. We'll honor Mike and all that he stood for." They bowed their heads briefly for a moment of silence to remember Mike. Kate couldn't allow the memories to flow or she might lose control. She kept her mind blank.

She straightened her shoulders. Gaining full control, she addressed the survivors of the battle. "We still have a fight on our hands. We leave in a week, after the funerals. He's headed down to the Pittsburg area next according to papers left at the club. We got lucky. At least he didn't go to New York."

In actuality, he had sent her a challenge. That's why he changed his pattern. He was ramping up their game of cat and mouse. He enjoyed the rush of the chase. She could only hope he still wasn't attached to the image of her singing.

Several days later, Kate sat at Mike's memorial service. Seven other funerals were taking place today or tomorrow. Telling Mike's wife had been the hardest thing she had ever done. She lost her husband and the child they had been trying to adopt all in one fatal blow. The devastation hulled out Kate's heart. She watched Mike's family heartbroken, weeping, and asking why. She couldn't give them the answer they sought. She didn't know what this crazy killer was capable of or how to stop him. She did know it was *not* an average human, but how did you explain that to someone's grieving family? So, what else was out there? How many more of these possible psychic killers could be in existence somewhere in the world? What was her role in the whole scheme of things? How would she restore the gaping hole in her team?

A lot of questions, but no answers. As the service came to an end, she laid a white rose on Mike's casket and said her final goodbyes. She made him a promise. Kate vowed to find those answers to provide the safer world that Mike had given his life trying to protect. She would track and kill the son of a bitch that had taken his life and so many others. No matter how long it might take or how frightening it could become, she would find the truth. She wouldn't rest until this menace was removed from this world. She intended to be the one to kill him.

It's a well-known fact; the truth can set you free. It's the journey to discovering the truth that's the hardest part of all. Dangerous or not, this was her new personal mission. She would not fail. She'd follow the voice that mesmerized a killer. She would protect the innocent. Even if it meant embracing the very gifts that she had spent a lifetime trying to forget.

7

Kate dove behind the car, bullets hitting the pavement to her left and right. She had tracked her latest serial killer for almost a year, starting in California and ending in this little town outside of Pittsburg. Every nerve in her body stood on alert. Sunlight blinded her as she searched the locations of the shooters.

Where the hell were they?

She dropped to all fours and peered under the car to get a clear look at the building. She desperately searched for a way into the apartment complex. The gunmen were merely a distraction. Somewhere inside, an innocent woman fought for her life against a brutal murderer hell-bent on taking it.

She fought the panic and frustration escalating in her mind.

Deep breath.

Focus.

Perspiration trickled down her forehead and back. She fired several rounds, trying to draw out the shooters. The woman's screams echoed in her mind, the psychic backlash nearly split Kate's head in two. She shook the pain away. In a matter of minutes, the woman would be dead.

She had to make her move or the psycho her team had been tracking for months would once again escape. With another deep breath, she cleared her mind and pushed all emotion aside. She sure as hell wouldn't fail now. It was time to take a risk.

Signaling to her partner, Angie, to cover, Kate made a run for it. She projected the image that she wanted others to see using the mental skills she'd had and hated all her life. It provided camouflage when she needed it most. She blended her appearance with the nearby scenery, becoming a blur as she ran the last fifty feet and slipped through a side door. Hopefully, no one had noticed, or she'd end up in the psych ward. At least she'd made it inside the building.

Time was running out.

She raced up the stairs two at a time. Her calves burned, and her lungs strained with the effort to breathe. She jerked open the door to the sixth floor. Pulling her weapon, she cautiously edged down the hallway.

Her stomach dropped and her chest tightened. Her psychic connection disengaged. The woman's screams turned to eerie silence.

Kate followed the residual energy of the connection and stopped in front of the apartment. She grabbed the knob, surprised when it turned under her hand. She threw the door open, and with her gun extended, entered. "FBI! Drop your weapon!"

Her team caught up and came into position behind her. She dodged behind the kitchen counter located off the front door, expecting gunfire, but more silence greeted her.

The smell of copper assaulted her nose, and the weight of death threatened to overwhelm her. Some people might see her abilities as a gift, but at times she wished she could return them. She felt the backlash of the victim's fear and brutal demise. It sickened her. She used as much energy as she could spare and closed the mental connection.

She didn't have to be cautious anymore. Her team moved forward into the formerly white living room now streaked with red. The son of a bitch was gone, and the woman was definitely dead. Her executioner had escaped but left behind the broken remains of a once-beautiful woman.

They cleared the apartment and returned to the victim to maintain protocol. Tears filled Kate's eyes and clogged her throat. The woman had been beaten and tortured and lay in a pool of her own blood.

Kate passed by a large mirror and table in the hallway, where the woman had tossed her keys and purse. She opened the wallet to see if there was any clue identifying the perp. Instead, she saw the girl's life and shattered dreams. Victoria Green was her name.

Kate closed her eyes and took a deep breath, desperate to get a grip on her emotions. She wiped any trace of sentiment from her face. The pull of her dark blond hair wrapped tight in a bun helped to keep her focused. She relied on her outside appearance more than she cared to admit. Her polished black, standard suit and black boots protected her like armor.

She fought to master the three-ring circus inside her mind. The mask she often hid behind slid into place and calm descended. She'd become the master of emotional disguise. No one could see the pain and sadness behind the walls she'd perfected over the years except Angie.

This particular case had become a media nightmare, and she'd failed again. Kate closed her eyes, and images of the victims flashed through her mind. Her stomach churned at the thought of the viciously raped, disfigured women with their eyes cut out. A horrifying vision they'd spared the family members from seeing. *But they weren't able to say goodbye.*

Kate pushed all of the unwanted emotions into her blessed mental compartments. One of the few psychic gifts she did not hate and used often to deal emotionally. "Angie, was anyone arrested from the lot?"

"No, it was the weirdest thing. All fire stopped when you entered the building, and we couldn't catch a single one of the shooters. They disappeared. Did you see him?" Angie's tone indicated she meant more than seeing him *visually*.

The medical examiner and crime scene unit arrived, and with the additional people on site, Kate pulled Angie to the side for a little privacy.

"No, I didn't see him." Kate pushed her fingers through her hair in utter frustration. "He wasn't here and hasn't been for several minutes. I'm going to guess the medical examiner's report will say she died anywhere from thirty minutes to an hour ago. The shooters were meant to buy him more escape time. He wasn't in the building when we arrived. I don't understand."

The rest of her team spread out in the apartment to process the scene. The ME finished her initial examination, agreeing with Kate's prediction.

Kate walked around the room searching for answers. They were dealing with some*thing*. This perp was *not* an average human. What the devil were they up against? Despite denying her own gifts, she embraced the fact that the serial killer must have psychic abilities, too.

Kate switched to a mental link she shared with Angie. She quickly filled her in with her new line of thought.

"He's been gone for over thirty minutes. Somehow, he created a cover for himself, managed to mess with my head, and delayed the victim's screams. It's not a normal human. I know it."

Angie dusted for prints to keep appearances. They managed to keep their connection hidden over the years by being vigilant and careful. *"Since you're the only one who actually hears the victim's screams, and he deliberately messed with your head, do you think he might be targeting you?"*

Soft opera music played in the background and groceries lay out on the counter. It looked as though the victim intended to cook dinner and have a relaxing night; instead, she'd become the dinner for a monster Kate had failed to catch. Again. She pressed her fingers against her temples.

She didn't have to ask. She already knew that she was the reason for his current obsession. He'd changed the game. Now it was about the chase.

Heated anger flashed from her chest all the way up her neck. *"I don't know what the hell it is, or what it wants, but I know what it will be. Dead!"*

Two weeks later, Kate found herself rushing after the same madman again. They tracked him to Boston. She intended to make it her last stand. Live or die. The end of the line.

Kate and Angie rushed into the dark alley. Her fellow agents followed without question. She felt a moment of hesitation and briefly paused. Was she risking too much? They were her family, and she was the leader they depended on to survive. They'd already lost Mike. She glanced back over her shoulder, taking in each one. Chris, the jokester with a slight crush on her. Teri, the behavioral psychology genius, and Randy, the weapons specialist and former Marine.

No regrets. She moved forward.

Anticipation hummed in her veins as she drew nearer to the suspect. His presence crackled in the air. Something seemed different tonight. He'd changed his pattern. Desperation, rage, and pure evil emanated through his energy field.

"I want him dead." Kate glared at her team with a look no one would challenge. Right or wrong, she didn't care.

They moved in close enough she picked up on his thoughts and feelings.

You're not running because you want me.

A sinking feeling hit her stomach. Just like she could sense him, he could probably sense her.

Great, I've managed to attract a serial killer with mental abilities probably stronger than mine.

The team crept forward. The alley widened behind a popular nightclub and led into a deserted gravel lot. The hair on Kate's neck stood straight up, and chill bumps broke out over her entire body. She could feel his breath on her skin.

She spun around but found nothing. He was toying with her and using her mind against her. She reinforced her mental blocks, then sensed he had not come alone. He had dozens of followers waiting on the outskirts. An ambush.

"Take cover," Kate whispered urgently into her mic. "He's here and not running this time."

"Kate, we have movement on the left," Chris's voice came back.

"Movement on the right," Teri confirmed.

Kate paused. *She* was the real target. If they were going to live through this night, they'd have to split up or risk getting ambushed. It looked as if the SOB would be all hers and Angie's.

"Check it out," she ordered. "Be careful. Angie and I are moving forward."

Her team dispersed, and the monster she tracked for months stepped out of the shadows.

"Oh, shit, he's ugly." Angie took a step back. "What is it?"

"I have no freaking clue, but we can't stand here and wait for the answer to strike us." Should she believe her eyes?

The ugliest creature she had ever seen stood before her. Over six feet tall with grayed-out, hollow eyes. She momentarily thought he might be blind. Skin fell off of his face and arms, but she could hear his heartbeat — or at least it sounded like a heart. His sharp teeth reminded her of a shark going after its next meal.

"Well, shoot it!" Kate barked.

Angie sent three rounds into its chest. It looked at them and laughed–*well you might call it a laugh*–sounding a bit more like wheezing.

"*Okay, double shit!*" Her partner's thoughts screamed louder than words. "*Bullets didn't even faze it. I think he actually enjoyed it. We're pretty screwed unless you have a brilliant idea up your sleeve.*" They both slowly backed up.

Kate frowned. *"Me? Take cover while we try to think of something. We're out here like sitting ducks. Get over there to the cars."*

She looked around. They were seriously getting their asses kicked. Her entire team struggled with the entourage the beast had brought along. With suppressors attached, guns fired with minimal sound, fists hit against flesh, and bodies flew through the air. It didn't look good. They were definitely losing.

"Focus, Kate. The team can handle themselves; we need to think. We'll find a way." Angie flew in with a jump kick. Both feet landed in the beast's chest. Angie landed hard on the ground, but popped back up. The horrid creature merely staggered back a step and smiled.

Maybe there isn't a way. Kate thought to herself. Now they were both fighting the beast, while Kate tried to keep tabs on everyone else.

Director Myers had made sure they had more backup for this mission, not that it mattered. Her team and rescue squad reinforcements went down fast against the pure strength of the opponents. They crushed guns in their bare hands and threw the agents several feet away. What seemed to last forever had only been a few minutes. A battle they couldn't win.

The man-beast kicked Angie. She hurled through the air and landed a dozen feet away. A half-full dumpster stopped her slide across the pavement.

"Angie!"

"I'm okay," she responded. She slowly picked herself up from the alley. *"Watch out!"*

Kate turned her head to see a massive fist aimed at her chest. The impact tossed her into the air and she smashed into a nearby car. Glass shattered. She groaned in pain.

That's gonna leave a bruise.

She crawled over to Angie. "We could try a retreat, but we're surrounded, and he'll never let us go. For some reason, I seem to be his main target."

"I know." Angie nodded and slapped a fresh magazine into her pistol. "We have no choice but to keep fighting."

They both launched at him. He backhanded Angie and knocked Kate to the side. Angie pulled Kate to her feet, and they ran toward him once more. He picked up Kate like she was a small child and threw her hard against the pavement. Angie had spun around and attacked from behind. He simply caught her over his shoulder, lifted her over his head, and tossed her beside Kate.

Kate's bones rattled, and pain launched up her entire spine. They couldn't give up. Once again, she landed on the ground with a thud, then rolled over and quickly scrambled to her feet. As she started to stand, Angie plowed into her, and Kate hit the gravel again.

Her skin bled in several places, and her leg wounds were filled with gravel and dirt. The pain in her side radiated and indicated bruised ribs in the mix as well. A piece of glass sliced through her lower left leg, and her right ankle throbbed. She compartmentalized the pain and reached down to help Angie to her feet.

Kate wiped at the blood trickling into her eye. "Considering he doesn't seem to have a scratch, or tiring in any way, I'm going to say we're losing. Even if bullets *did* work, he crushed your gun with his bare hands."

"I get it. We're screwed." Angie held onto her. They walked backward to gain space. Most of her injuries were similar to Kate's, so they were in no shape to fight. "Any ideas?"

"What choice do we have?" Kate used what little energy she could spare to block the pain in both of their minds. She'd probably die, but she sure as hell would take that piece of shit with her.

She started to advance again. Someone grabbed her and pulled her quickly behind a dumpster, while another figure seized Angie. She threw her hands up to defend. Two men dressed all in black quickly flashed a badge. *Too* quickly. Both looked as if they had stepped out of *GQ* magazine, and yet carried an air of pure danger. "Who the hell are you and what are you doing?"

"Federal Agents. I'm Agent Xander Montgomery, and this is my partner, Agent Gregory Pierce. We've been following this case and your team. Let's just say the two of us tend to get the weird ones."

Montgomery held out a badge again and nodded to his partner. "We'll take care of it from here. We've wasted enough time. We have a demon to kill."

"A what?" The air rushed out of her lungs.

The two men left Kate and Angie on the ground. They ran toward the beast.

Kate called out to warn them. "Hey, you don't know what you're dealing with."

They didn't even turn. *How odd.* Why had he called it a demon? Was it his term for this thing like she called it a beast? They weren't the least bit surprised by the impossibly strong monster. She didn't she believe their story, but at this point she wouldn't turn down assistance. She didn't trust him, yet she didn't sense evil in him either.

The two men leapt into a heated battle. Montgomery punched the creature in the jaw, while Pierce sent a low kick to its knees. It howled in pain but didn't go down. The two men took turns with their assault. Their moves were unnaturally fast, but Kate became mesmerized by their strength and agility. The beast's followers rallied to help. Pierce stayed focused on the beast as Montgomery turned to face the new opponents.

He held out his hand, and a sword appeared. Kate's heart stuttered in shock. How was that possible? He literally pulled it out of the air. No way he had that stashed somewhere on his person.

Montgomery drove back the followers and returned his attention to the beast. The full moon reflected off the sword. A single stroke severed the monster's head, and it hit the ground with an ominous thud. His followers froze in shock then most began to flee. Some stayed to fight the two mysterious agents. Swords sliced through bodies and turned them to smoke and ash. The constant flames erupted all around them.

Kate's heart still pounded from the adrenaline. She could definitely learn a thing or two from these two agents.

She looked at Angie; her face frozen in shock and disbelief. "You're writing the report on this one, 'cause I don't want to be locked up in the looney bin."

Their eyes met. "Well, I'll be damned," Angie stuttered. "No, you are *definitely* writing the report. I don't even know where to begin with unkillable beings, strangers appearing out of nowhere, and our perps turning to ash all on their own. We're gonna be in psychiatric evaluations the rest of our careers."

Kate nodded in agreement as she slowed her heart rate and focused her mind to gain her bearings.

"Check on our team." Kate slid down against a car and tightly grabbed her leg with her hand to stop some of the blood pouring out.

Angie spoke into her mic, listened for a moment, then turned to Kate. "They're sorting through everything and gathering evidence. The rest of his groupies ran away when he died. We lost a few local officers, and Teri has some severe injuries, so that'll have to be addressed. I told Chris to take point while we deal with our new friends." Angie squatted to help Kate wrap her leg, but Montgomery kneeled and pushed her aside.

"Let me take a look. I'm good with wounds." He reached toward her and placed his hand over her injury. The pain immediately faded. In its wake, an awareness filled her — so acute, she struggled not to gasp aloud. Her skin tingled. Her heart rate jumped. He pulled her into him and formed some kind of connection.

What is he doing to me? His energy swept through her.

She gathered her resolve, pushed him away, and stood to find her balance. "Thank you, but I'm fine now." She limped over to Angie. She had leaned against a car to keep herself upright. They needed to get cleaned and bandaged up. First, she wanted to know more about what they'd just fought and the two men who'd mysteriously appeared and saved the day.

"Listen, who did you say you worked — " She gasped.

They vanished.

She'd only had her back turned for a few seconds. This was impossible, even for highly trained agents.

Her instincts told her they'd meet again. Something had started tonight. She could feel the connection lingering. It was an inner voice that vibrated through her entire being, whispering that her time had come, over and over. The time for *what* scared her the most.

Kate woke up at first light and rolled out of bed. Two days since they faced the serial killer in the alley and her body still ached. The medics had patched her up: bruised ribs, a sprained ankle, and various cuts and abrasions. She stretched out her muscles, but they screamed in protest, so she made her way into the bathroom and immersed herself in a warm bath.

She leaned her head against the cool cast iron and let her mind slip away. She had been born with many unexplainable gifts and spent a lifetime hiding them. Reading thoughts, emotions, and auras, while unusual, did not actually trouble her. Many psychics professed they could do the same thing, although she never sought their counsel.

No, it was her ability to control others' thoughts and perceptions, use her voice as a weapon, and move objects with a simple thought, that scared her. They made her doubt herself.

Am I good or evil?

She devoted her whole life to proving her goodness and rarely used her gifts.

She considered blurring her appearance and creating mental compartments her two greatest weapons. She could store and lock away information on every case and never feel the emotion, and she could blend into any surroundings, which made her perfect for undercover operations. These gifts had led to her current role. She still doubted her abilities, with the exception of her telepathic link to Angie.

Angie always stabilized her. They met at college during their freshmen year and shared an instant connection. A first for Kate. She spent her whole life shutting people out until that point. Within a couple months, they realized their telepathic link, which saved them both many times over the years, especially since joining the FBI.

Hiding her abilities took tremendous effort; she often came home exhausted from her job. She hated keeping her secrets hidden from those closest to her. Her own family had not accepted her. Why would anyone else?

Kate's body relaxed; the warm water relieved the aches in her bones. She pushed her worries aside and let her mind drift to a more peaceful world. Something tickled her leg. She brushed it away, and her mind and body once again relaxed. It touched her a second time, firmer, then grabbed her ankles and dragged her under the water. She tensed but couldn't wake up or fight.

Her heart thumped in her ears like banging drums. She forced her adrenaline under control and took a slow breath. She wasn't actually drowning, but her chest remained constricted. Once the fear subsided, she became aware of her surroundings. Darkness swirled around her like she was traveling through time. A powerful vision swept over her.

The fog cleared and revealed a beautiful, luscious green field, with a small brook that ran through it. A gorgeous woman, with long, flowing brunette hair and two twin girls with bouncing blond curls, played in the distance. They giggled as they chased the woman, then collapsed in a patch of flowers.

A man she hadn't noticed before walked toward her. Kate only felt love within him, so she hoped he didn't mean her any harm. His hair was also brown, but lighter than the woman's. His bright smile radiated happiness, and his sapphire eyes looked similar to her own.

He stopped directly in front of her and hesitated for a moment before giving her a quick hug. "Welcome. We meet again."

"Where am I exactly? I don't recognize this place," Kate responded.

He reached for her hand and led her to a large boulder beside the water, motioning for her to have a seat. The trickling creek caught her attention. She never had a vision seem so real. The warm breeze caressed her face, and the scent of wildflowers filled her nose.

"You're in Ireland, my child. Though it may not still look this way in your time, this is my homeland. You are my descendent."

She wasn't sure how to respond. You didn't often meet grandparents this many times removed. She tried to hold everything in but wanted to ask a million questions. She started with the most obvious. "Why me? Why have I been burdened with these abilities that I don't understand? Why are you here?"

The man watched the children splashing in the water. He turned back to meet Kate's eyes, his own filled with sadness and regret. "You, child, are my future, my hope. We are currently in one of my fondest memories, before I lost everything. It took place only months before my death. My name is Cassius."

She started to speak, but he held his hand up for silence. "I'm sorry, but I do not have much time. I used a spell to connect us, but it has limitations. As your power grows, I may be able to answer more questions for you. For now, I must tell you only what you need to know.

"You will soon embark on an incredible and terrifying journey. In order to maintain civilization as you know it, many battles have been fought and many have died. Please understand that everything I did was to give you a normal life, a chance at true human happiness without the weight of the world on your shoulders. Destiny is a path we all must follow, and unfortunately, yours is a great, but sad one."

He stood and extended his hand toward Kate. He took her into his arms one last time and squeezed tight. "We have done much to protect you. Now the time of the *Awakening* has begun. Embrace it. Live your life. Find love. I am so proud of the woman and leader you have become."

He gestured toward the girls rolling in the meadow, but his eyes held great sorrow. "They are your past. The beginning of who you are and what you will become. You will not be alone. Look for your guide. I will always be with you. Be brave, my child."

His hand lovingly brushed her cheek. She felt his pain, but also his love and acceptance. His eyes bore into hers. She gasped for air. Pain stabbed through her body. She awoke in her tub. Everything returned to normal.

She pulled herself up and splashed water all over the floor. Her movements were lethargic, and her mind felt consumed in a fog. She struggled to clear her head and remember all the details of her vision. She had never experienced anything this powerful before. How was it possible to talk to a dead person? Then again, how was any of this possible?

She grabbed a towel, caught a glimpse of her body in the mirror, and froze.

She braced her hand on the wall and stepped closer to her full-length reflection on the bathroom door. All of her cuts, bruises, and pain were gone, like they never existed. The jagged cut on her leg hadn't even left a scar.

What the heck? She stared in amazement and shook her head. It had to have been the pain in her vision, when Cassius had sent her back. He somehow healed her.

Angie's going to be so pissed.

Kate sat down on the edge of the tub, rubbing her forehead. None of this made any sense. In the past few weeks, her abilities had increased to the point she had trouble controlling them, and she discovered that demons or some type of evil creatures were possibly real. Now, to top it off, she experienced a vision that completely healed her.

Wrapping her arms around her chest, she rocked back and forth. What was this new destiny he spoke of? What the hell did an awakening mean? And why did she need to be brave?

8

"Xander, why didn't you knock her out and grab her? We could be well on our way to the Meadows by now. Your powers aren't recharging, and that tattoo on your arm is glowing like a damn beacon. I hate to say it, but maybe it's time to call that absent brother of yours." Gregory paced to the window.

Xander rolled his eyes. "His name is Xavier."

"Yep. That's the one. Now see what he has to say, if he can come out of hiding long enough to bless us with his opinion."

Gregory's agitation started to rub Xander the wrong way, regardless of his supposed good intentions. He shook his head, closed his eyes, and began the connection.

His twin brother should have been on this mission with him, but Xavier's wife died at the same time the Ancient Council detected the Mystic's birth. The loss drove him to insanity. Protecting the Mystic fell to Xander without the help of his second in command.

Luckily, his best friend had volunteered to step in. Who knew it would take nearly thirty years to find her? That's why he cut Gregory so much slack. They were both stuck in hell.

Xander couldn't blame Xavier for choosing to live in a place where his emotions could be muted, and the Shadow Realm gave him that. At least it still provided them with portals to give them access to each other anywhere — even in the human realms.

Xavier finally connected. *"What is it? I'm trying to keep an eye on your charge while you come up with another grand plan to introduce yourself, Agent Montgomery. Like she can't figure that one out."*

The tension was so thick, Xander doubted his sword would make a dent. Eventually, they were all going to have the *come to Jesus* meeting that was always nipping at their heels. He started to retort but decided to see it as a positive omen that his brother showed more signs of emotions. *"I've got something happening to me that Gregory and I can't figure out. I don't want to encounter the girl again without knowing if I have some kind of demon-tracker or spell following me."*

"What are you talking about? There's no such thing for a Guardian." Xavier's demeanor shifted, but irritation still remained in his voice.

What did his brother have to be frustrated about? Last time he checked, Xavier hadn't given up thirty years of his life searching for a needle in a haystack.

Gritting his teeth, Xander took a deep breath. "Why don't you pop your ass over here and look for yourself?" he said out loud. Gregory spun around and smirked.

A slight electrical charge filled the air and caused the hairs to raise on Xander's arms, then his identical twin stood before him. It was always a shock to see himself in his brother, since they were apart for so many years at a time.

"Let me see it," Xavier demanded. Xander held up his arm. His brother inspected the tattoo that proclaimed him as the Guardian. The image appeared the moment the Mystic had been born.

Xavier casually flicked a glance toward Gregory. "Doesn't he have the answer since he thinks he knows everything?"

Gregory flew off the couch and landed a few inches from Xavier's face, ready to fight, but Xander shoved him away. "We don't have time for these petty differences right now. The fate of the world is on our shoulders, remember? Keep your heads straight." Facing Xavier, he added, "So, do you know why my tattoo is glowing like a Christmas tree?"

"When did it start?"

"The night we helped the Mystic kill the demon."

Xavier sighed. "I'm not sure what's going on. The tattoo usually only lights up when the Mystic is activated, but she's still human at this point. I'm going to have to consult Rowena on this one." His brother turned, then hesitated. "You know, at some point, you're going to have to start speaking to her again." He vanished in a flash of light.

Xander ran his hands through his hair, walked to the window overlooking the city and placed his head against the cool glass. He'd wasted the past thirty years looking for this woman and now that he'd found her, she had no idea of her destiny. Without convincing evidence that his message was truth, she was unlikely to jump on board and say, *Sure, I'd love to face a battle controlling the fate of all humans that will probably kill me.* Doesn't everyone want to do that?

He growled in frustration. Twenty-eight years ago, the Ancient Council, governing body of the Magical Realm, announced the Mystic's birth, but powerful magic protected her identity. They refused to give him any more information. He hadn't been in contact with them since, with the exception of a few meetings he'd been forced to attend.

Xavier finally learned from Zane, leader of the Shadow Warriors, who guarded the in-between realm, that the previous Mystic cast a spell to protect the identity of the future Mystic. An unbreakable spell, because she was of his bloodline. No one knew exactly how he had pulled it off before his death, but it had worked. Nearly thirty years later, they had found her, but she was still mostly human. How the hell would a *human* save the world? *She better be something truly special.*

Kate was strong, he gave her that. He decided he should probably start using her name. Before they appeared in the alleyway, he'd watched her fight a pretty tough demon. If she understood what she was fighting, she might have been able to defeat him on her own. Despite the fact she had taken several hits, he'd been impressed that she kept getting back up. She would need that tenacity. He reminded himself again. *She is still human.*

Humans tended to be weak, needy, and pathetic. He had met few honorable humans in his lifetime. Most ran at the sight of trouble and would throw their own friends or family under the bus to escape. The more time he spent with them, the more he despised their species. However, he was not an idiot. He'd felt the immediate spark between the two of them. He wasn't sure what to do. Should he foster the emotional bond or stay away from it?

She would have to choose to cross the threshold of her own free will.

Xander felt a tingle in his shoulder blades. His brother flashed back into the room. It hadn't taken that long, so maybe that meant good news. Then he saw his brother's face and the way his eyes darted away from his, and he knew something was wrong.

Xavier motioned them toward the couch. "You better sit down. I checked with Zane and the Council, and they both came to the same conclusion. They believe you inadvertently started the Awakening process ahead of schedule."

"Holy shit." Gregory sat across from Xavier and for once didn't make one single nasty comment. Not good.

Xander rubbed his palms across his thighs, trying to sort through all he knew about the Awakening. "How is that possible? The Awakening doesn't start until she's in the Meadows, safe within the magical realms. There's a full ceremony, then she'll arise as the Mystic. They must be wrong."

"I don't think they're wrong, and neither do you. It has to be because she was born as a human and hasn't transformed yet. Different rules are applying this time." Xavier reached forward and touched Xander's tattoo. "You've triggered the Awakening and therefore, the Rising has begun. We only have a matter of months to prepare her. Zane believes it occurred when you healed her leg. If I'm not mistaken, you had a cut on your hand from blocking a knife. When you healed her leg, you accidentally began the blood bonding process. After the Mystic is awakened by the Council and granted powers, he or she is then bonded to their Guardian through a blood ritual for eternity."

"Are you shitting me? I didn't perform a ritual. I barely touched her!" Xander didn't wait for his response. Somewhere inside, he already knew the answer. It explained the weird pull to go to her, and the sudden spike in sexual tension. He forced himself to focus and felt the pulse of their connection. *Great.* "We haven't officially met the Mystic yet, and I've already screwed it up. What now?"

Xavier reached forward and grasped his shoulder. "You didn't complete the bond. It was only sparked, but that's enough to set things in motion sooner than anticipated. And there's more that I need to tell you." He hesitated. "Because you created the bond before you entered the Meadows and partially awakened the Mystic within her, your energy field and essence are binding to her human half."

"And that means what exactly?" Xander uttered through gritted teeth.

"It's the reason you feel the drain on your powers and can't recharge. It's already hard enough for our kind to maintain energy in this realm for long periods of time, but your energy source is turning human. It will eventually drain all of your power and prevent you from re-entering the Meadows." Xavier paused "You must find the girl and convince her to cross over."

Xander stared at him. His chest seized up. His fists tightened and he hurled the coffee table across the room. Gregory quickly intercepted it and returned it to the floor. Xander, breathing hard, pushed him out of the way and punched the wall.

Xavier froze him with a wave of his hand to calm him down, but he had no difficulty spewing anger from his mouth. "Are you telling me that I'm turning into one of those pathetic, sniveling humans that cursed us into hiding in the first place?"

"Not exactly. You can still get to the Meadows and maintain your power and energy. Then you can reconnect to the full Mystic and be back to normal." Xavier sat down for the first time, and Xander finally came to his senses as he felt the pain and emotions of his brother.

Xander tried his best to control the rage swirling inside him. His entire livelihood was threatened because of this one stupid human *savior*.

Yeah right.

He forced himself to breathe normally and stay focused. "How much time do I have?"

Xavier shrugged. "According to Zane and the Council, probably around two weeks, depending on how much power you use along the way. And two days have already passed. One more thing you need to understand is that this is not just you losing your powers. If you turn human, your real age will take effect. Humans do not live one hundred and fifty years."

Anger once again boiled to the surface. Gregory tried to help but something ruptured inside Xander. His chest heaved and his vision turned red. Enraged energy escaped from his tightly coiled body. Gregory created a shield to deflect it and Xavier kept it from destroying the room. He despised that FBI agent for putting him in such a predicament. She should be embracing her powers and preparing for battle, not playing cops and robbers.

He calmed after several minutes. "So, what we're facing is that I will lose my powers and *die,* if she doesn't willingly cross into the Meadows within two weeks. Let's say ten days to be on the safe side. Does that sum it up?"

Gregory stood in complete silence, a rarity. If he didn't have a smart comment to make, they were definitely in trouble. Their timeline had taken a massive shift for the worse. How could they convince a total stranger to follow strange men on a crazy quest that she might have to trade her life for? What was the alternative?

We're screwed. I'm dead.

Xavier faded back into the Shadows, most likely to give Xander space and find more information. They also had demons to track. The good guys weren't the only ones searching for the Mystic.

Xander walked to the kitchen table and fell into the nearest chair, laying his head in his hands. He now had a death sentence hanging over his head, with less than two weeks to make miracles happen.

He brought a picture of Kate into his mind. He would not outright deceive her, yet he had no choice but to make her fall for him. In her line of work, she would have to trust him first. He could work with that. If she fell in love with him and depended on him, she wouldn't question crossing over.

Guilt consumed him as he devised a plan that would eventually cause her pain. He certainly didn't want to feel love for her in return. This could easily end in misery for them all.

He grunted in disgust, then slapped himself on the forehead, disgusted with his depressing inner monologue. Time to man up.

He faced Gregory. "I need you to stick close to us at all times. We'll depend more on your magic, since mine is in shorter supply."

"But I won't be able to recharge effectively in this dimension." He clasped Xander's shoulder. "I promise you this. We will get Kate to the portal, and she *will* cross. I won't leave you or her. You will not die, especially not as a human."

"Thanks, man. Grab a map. As humans, we can't flash in and out of places, so we'll have to travel in the traditional human methods. That will save more energy, anyway. Demons will be tracking us, so we need to be vigilant and careful with our route." Xander paused and felt a twinge of guilt for his next request. "Listen, I need you to promise me one more thing."

Gregory nodded. "Anything."

"No one tells her about this ticking clock going on inside me, understand?"

"What? If you tell her, she'll willingly cross. Problem solved. It's probably programmed into her DNA. We've watched her for days. It's who she is. She'll want to protect you." Gregory shook Xander's shoulders. "Don't go stupid on me."

Xander swatted his hands away. "I'm not. She's the key to saving the world whether we like it or not. Without her, all of our realms plunge into demon reign. She is who you say and would cross over to save me. I believe that, but that is not a choice born of free will. That would be her sacrifice. Maybe it wouldn't matter, but are you ready to test the theory and risk the entire world?" He watched the man who had been his friend for nearly sixty years come to the same realization. His silence spoke volumes.

"Me either. As my closest friend, Gregory, I'm asking that you protect this secret, even if my life is on the line. If something should happen to me, make sure she crosses over safely." Xander held out his hand and waited patiently for him to make the choice.

Gregory reached forward with his right hand and grasped Xander's right forearm. "I swear to uphold my oath to maintain the secret of your transition to humanity. Should I fail, I forfeit my own life as penance." He laid a tiny silver bowl on the counter in front of them and brought out his ritualistic double-edged dagger. He used the extremely sharp athame to make a small cut straight across both of their arms. "Our mixed blood seals this promise." The blood bubbled for a few seconds and then evaporated into the air, binding his oath.

Gregory left the room, leaving Xander time to process his possible fate. Reaching toward his neck, Xander brushed the Celtic-knot necklace his mother gave him as a child. He wondered what Kate's childhood had been like. Did she have hopes and dreams that he was going to destroy? Would she hate him for it?

None of that mattered now. She would have to embrace her new world. They needed each other, and he would do well to remember it. They didn't have to love each other, but respect went a long way. He dropped his necklace and began planning. He had ten days to save his own life.

Kate still felt dazed. She walked into the kitchen. She couldn't figure out what to make of the vision, or what it meant for her future. She was beginning to have a normal life and wouldn't give it up without a fight.

She paused for a moment to consider the friend she often took for granted. She was beautiful inside and out. Angie's wavy auburn hair flowed down behind the chair. Unlike her own, she didn't keep it restricted. Angie was a few inches shorter than Kate, with a rock hard, athletic frame that made Kate a little envious at times. Angie's eyes seemed hypnotic at times and one of her most notable features. They were a warm chocolate brown that could trick anyone into confiding in her. It had worked on many criminals over the years.

Angie glanced up from her iPad. "What's up? You look like you've seen a ghost." Her eyes popped wide. "Where the crap did your freaking bruises go?"

"I had a visit from an old ancestor while I was taking a bath."

"Kinky, do tell." Angie laughed.

Kate sent her one of her death glares. "When I laid my head back against the tub, I received a vision." She mentally transferred the whole experience to Angie. She showed her the spots on her legs that should have at least had scars but were clear.

"Could you ask him to pay me a visit? I'm still in a lot of pain over here. Seriously though, what does it mean?"

Kate shrugged and sat down across from her friend. "No clue. I guess some life-changing event is headed my way. Honestly, I don't care. I'm not considering anything to do with my psychic stuff, or whatever it is. I finally have my dreams within my grasp. Trey's been hinting at marriage, and I'm up for that promotion at work. My friends accept me, and my life is normal, *completely* normal." Kate wanted normal to become her everyday reality, more than she wanted air to breathe.

"Uh huh, except the part where you have visions, speak to me telepathically, and have several other powers. Oh, and don't forget that we fought a demon just yesterday." Kate started to interrupt, but Angie bulldozed forward. "Let me talk. No one knows you like I do. I have literally been inside your mind. So at least do me the honor of not spouting all this bullshit. Those are not *your* dreams. Those are merely representations of your desperate desire to fit in and be accepted."

Kate's mouth fell open. Angie cleared her dishes and stomped into the kitchen. She hadn't realized her friend felt so strongly about the life choices she'd recently been making.

"What do you mean?" she called after her. "You know I've wanted a husband and family for a long time, without any interruption from my psychic issues."

Angie returned, warily shaking her head, and stared straight into her eyes. Kate caught a glimmer of pity before Angie cleared her emotions. "Look, I know you want a family, and that is a genuine desire, but that's where your head and heart take two different roads. Take Trey for instance. He's an amazing neurosurgeon that you rarely see. You two have a comfortable relationship and expect the marriage to be a partnership — you *will* have your perfect children and white picket fence. The problem is, you don't love him. I can see into your thoughts and feelings.

"Did you really think I can't see the truth? You're substituting acceptance for love. In your heart, you know I'm right, and you're looking for the true love found in fairytales and great love stories. A love that goes beyond acceptance to embrace everything you are and to even help you build your abilities. Don't sell yourself short, Kate. I only say all of this because I'm your friend and I love you. Settling for second best is not you." She sighed. "We can talk more later. I'm going to take a shower."

Kate sat at the table for several minutes processing everything her roommate and best friend said. Was she right? Was she just wanting Trey because he'd never be home enough to figure out who she was or discover any of her gifts? She'd never been accepted by her own family. Some feared her and others tried but never understood her. She'd finally learned to rigidly control all of her gifts, to have any semblance of normal, but then something would happen, and she'd be the outcast again.

Her grandfather had been her solace — accepted her completely. In retrospect, he'd probably shared a few of her gifts. Since his death, she'd searched endlessly for that same love and acceptance.

After several painful relationships over the years, Angie became the only other person to accept her fully. Hiding her gifts seemed to be the only way to find affection that at least came close to love. Maybe Angie did have a point, but she'd take her chances and embrace what happiness she could find. *Fairytales, my ass. That kind of love doesn't exist.*

Kate heard the water cut off and headed toward Angie's room so they could continue their conversation. Angie was her rock and reminder of who she was deep inside. Sometimes she didn't recognize the person staring back at her in the mirror, but Angie always brought her down to reality. If only she could make her understand her reasons for dreaming of a normal, uncomplicated life.

She started to knock on the door, but she heard Angie's muffled, "Come on in." She sat on the bed while Angie was still in the bathroom and anxiously patted the sheets as she searched for the words to help her friend understand. Finally, Angie came out dressed in her ratty, long robe from their college days. It had been a gift from Julie, so its condition didn't matter.

"Hey, maybe you *do* have a point, and that's all I will admit. But I *have* searched for *true* love, you know I have. And you've also seen the results and how horribly many of them ended. I have a real shot at happiness with Trey. It may not be perfect, but it's better than spending my whole life searching, and at the end of the road, being empty-handed. Gifts or no gifts, I deserve the chance to move forward."

Angie's embrace gave Kate the answer she needed.

"I'll be there for you, Kate, no matter what. I'll be your constant dose of reality. But promise me one thing. Think carefully before making any big decisions. You had that vision for a reason. For now, let's move on and focus on the present. Due to our current injuries, or at least *my* injuries, we have a few weeks off." She made sure Kate saw every bruise on her body.

"You're such a baby." Kate rolled her eyes. "Your point?"

"I'm thinking since we have some time off, we need to recapture some fun in our lives. Spending a year tracking a serial killer put a major downer on my love life. Let's go dancing and do something spontaneous. I might be sore, but I need more fun in my life. Plus, we promised Julie we'd go at least once a year and keep tradition. This case prevented that. It's time to celebrate and blow off some steam. You do remember what having fun is, right?"

Angie's challenge lit a spark in Kate. She threw a couple pillows and hit her in the face. "Of course I do, you wretched witch." Laughing, she ran to her room before Angie could return fire.

After an hour of dancing at their favorite night club, Kate and Angie took a break and wove through the crowds to get to the bar to get a drink and cool down. Kate grabbed a napkin and wiped the sweat off her face, while Angie groaned and stretched out her muscles.

A tickle went up Kate's spine. She glanced over her shoulder and saw him.

Agent Montgomery.

What a fine specimen.

Of course, she still had her doubts. She hadn't been able to confirm his identity. However, government agencies didn't always play well together.

Her heart raced for the first time ever — with *desire* instead of fear. He casually leaned against the wall in the middle of a group of people. He stood out, seeming alone. He appeared dangerous and powerful, yet intriguing and intelligent.

Kate used her abilities to search his aura and sensed no true danger, but she couldn't read his mind. That puzzled her. She tried to look away, but her eyes remained glued in his directions.

What is wrong with me?

His dark brown hair reminded her of creamy chocolate and ignited a craving deep inside. The strands were shaggy in layers, coming to his neck. He had broad shoulders with sculpted arms and a wide, muscular chest. She homed in on his amazing physique encased in a fitted black T-shirt. A vision of him without a shirt filled her mind and she swallowed to keep from drooling. His long, lean legs were perfection in his black form-fitting jeans. She had no doubt he could handle himself no matter what the situation.

He stood well over six feet tall and reminded her of a Greek god. Though she couldn't see the color of his eyes from where she was standing, she knew they were electric blue as they pierced a hole straight through her. *I'm not the only one interested.*

She told herself to breathe, as the pull of his energy tugged at her own. Her mind felt alarm at the ferocity of the attraction, while her body craved it. The battle between the two became intense, and she didn't know which would win.

A hand on her shoulder made her jump. "He's staring you down, and your hormones are off the charts," Angie said, broadly smiling. "I've never seen him here before. I know I'd remember. I wonder if they're still working a case."

"Yeah, tell me about it. Maybe they're tying up loose ends, since our team is here. They probably have tons of paperwork, too. I have to admit I feel drawn to him. How weird is all this? Maybe Trey and I have been waiting too long to ramp up our relationship." Kate let her gaze wander back to the stranger. She wanted to stop staring at him but found she couldn't. He was a magnet, drawing her in. *I'm in way over my head.*

Angie's smirk widened. *"You are too much sometimes. You never get flustered with the worst criminals on the planet and your life on the line, and yet here you are acting like a teenager over a guy. I never thought I'd see the day when you didn't have absolute control."* Kate glared. Angie continued, *"But I'll wait until you stammer your hello, before I politely disappear."*

"Funny. You're a real riot." Kate tensed. Agent Montgomery approached her from the side, making her slightly dizzy and nervous.

Angie stood with her hands on her hips and a mischievous grin covering her face.

Kate faced the agent, the perfect clear blue of his eyes engulfed her. Like getting lost in an ocean. She could stare into them for eternity. His sensual mouth had been made for kissing. She gathered her courage, trying to remind herself of her strength and independence.

"Hey, what are you doing here?" she boldly asked. "Shouldn't you be on a super-secret mission somewhere?"

Xander had watched and followed Kate for two days but couldn't get up the nerve to approach her. He was running out of time, and Gregory and Xavier were relentless.

It was now or never.

The demons would figure it out soon, and all hell would break loose, especially in the city. He had to quickly gain Kate's trust and get her out of danger — well, as much as possible. Being the Mystic, danger would always be on her doorstep. Plus, call him selfish, but he wanted to live.

He became more and more fascinated by her. Beautiful and glowing with her shiny blue shirt meant to tease. Those tight black pants with the silver belt resting at her waist invited lustful thoughts. He didn't need any help in that department, especially since he'd touched her blood. Her long blond hair was loose tonight and flowed halfway down her back. He had to resist the urge to bury his hands in it and throw her over his shoulder. No doubt that wouldn't go over well.

After an hour of watching her dance — her hips and waist moving enticingly to the beat — he was sweating again. Trying to restrain himself long enough to actually make contact was more of an issue than he'd anticipated. This new bond between them sucked, and he wasn't the only one feeling the sexual pull. She'd been fighting the attraction just as hard.

Their gazes met and he felt the instant connection. He wished he could fully read her mind, but her mystic powers protected her. At least he could still read her emotions through their blood bond, and right now she was accepting him. She needed his help, and he needed hers, but without her full acceptance, he couldn't breach her inner thoughts. Despite being humanized and losing power, he'd taken steps to make sure she couldn't read his thoughts either. At least not without her full powers.

Her voice infiltrated his entire being. How on earth were they supposed to work toward a common goal, when this stupid bond clouded their minds with sexual tension? *So much for being in control.*

What had she said? Oh, yes. What was he doing here? If she only knew. He smiled back. "Hello Agent Smith. It's good to see you again. Actually, my partner and I *are* here on a new case, but I can't say much more now. Would you like to dance?"

He held his breath, waiting for her answer. He needed to feed the pull between them without acting on it. He couldn't screw up this time. This was their first step into destiny.

Hell, yes! Kate thought, but said, "It's Kate, and I'd love to." She took his hand.

"Xander." He nodded and guided her through the large crowd.

They hit the dance floor and things heated up fast. Kate remembered going to amusement parks as a child. This felt like one of those times; at the top of the roller coaster. It suddenly dropped. Her stomach flipped. She finally understood the *having butterflies* concept. The brutal anticipation. He was a ship passing in the night, and she wanted a chance to feel the electric charge that had always eluded her.

He held her hand and reached for her waist with his free one. Fireworks erupted in her stomach. Heat traveled up her arm and through her body, and he'd barely touched her. When he pulled her completely against him, electricity jumped through her blood stream.

They were thigh to thigh, chest to chest, and melded together with her head fitting perfectly beneath his chin. She thought she might pass out from the sheer shockwaves pulsating through her. They moved to the music. He unexpectedly spun her out and back in, so she slammed against him. All rational thought went out the window.

A salsa came on next, and he immediately threw her into a quick Latin move — short steps and a lot of hip action. The man knew how to dance. *How sexy!* Their legs intertwined, and their hips gyrated. Not even a piece of paper could make its way between them.

"*Whoa, girl!*" Angie broke into her thoughts, which remained somewhat guarded. "*Who knew you could move like that? I'm impressed, but how did you put it: oh, that's right — be careful?*" Kate sent a surge of energy toward her that meant *butt out* and continued to focus on

Xander. Angie's laughter remained in her mind, but it helped bring a little clarity back to her wayward thoughts.

Xander's hands traveled up her sides, then down her arms. He encircled her waist and turned her around. Her back pressed to his chest, gluing them to each other. His hand blazed a path across her stomach and left behind a trail of fire. She inwardly moaned, astounded at how she responded to him. Especially since she'd never felt like this; didn't even know she was capable of this kind of combustion.

He spun her back around, so they were chest to chest, and only scant inches separated their mouths. Once again, he twirled her out into a full extension, then pulled her back in. He was trying to keep something from happening. She, on the other hand, was more than ready for something more. Passion consumed all her rational thoughts, and she was close to losing control. A red lustful haze consumed her; fire coursed through her veins.

He leaned down and kissed her. The world truly spun off its axis. Fire turned into lava and fireworks ignited. She could have sworn she exploded.

His lips were soft, exploring. He dipped his tongue into her mouth and she came unglued. She kissed back with all her repressed energy. They moved closer than she thought was possible. The kiss became wild and out of control. His hand slid beneath her shirt, caressing her stomach, then he eased it around to her back. Their desperation for a physical connection rose. For the first time in her life, she didn't care who could see them. Her only thought — calculating the time to get back to her apartment, or more importantly, her bed. She crushed the voice of caution in her head. She wanted to feel alive.

Xander broke off the kiss, as if reading her thoughts. She tried to stop a whimper from the loss of contact. He smiled and kissed her forehead. "Thanks for the dance. You're more impressive than I'd even imagined you'd be." He looked pained, and his blue eyes held a deep sadness she couldn't grasp.

He spun her, stepped behind her, and lightly hugged her. By the time she cleared the fog from her head and turned around, he was gone. *Vanished.*

Disappointment, embarrassment, and sexual frustration swamped her.

Angie walked up and put her arm around her. "What was all that? Where did he go? I guess you've got plans for later tonight." She wiggled her eyebrows, then took in Kate's bewildered expression. "Where *did* he go?"

"I have no idea, but I didn't know my body could feel this way. I guess that answers any questions of me being frigid. I'm shaking. Energy is shooting around my body. If I were to touch a light socket, I'd take the power out of the whole block." Kate shivered. Something irrevocable had happened tonight, but what? She shrugged. "I guess he had his fun and bailed."

Angie led Kate back toward their table. "If you'd been watching from the cheap seats like me, you wouldn't be saying that. He looked like he was going to devour you."

"Wishful thinking." Kate groaned and put her face in her hands. "I can't believe I did all that." Reality shined through. "Let's go home. I've done enough damage for one night, and I need a cold shower to gain some clarity." She stood and headed for the door.

Angie nodded and followed. "Sounds good to me. I wasn't able to find anyone remotely interesting. Not that

I would have acted easy to get like you!" She caught Kate's purse as it came flying at her head.

Laughing, they headed home.

Xander flashed into a deserted hallway and held himself against the wall. Two seconds longer, and he would have flashed them to her bedroom. Talk about a lot of explaining to do. He'd taken advantage of Kate, who he was supposed to be protecting. He had risked exposing his community's secrets and who he was. If Xavier hadn't broken into his thoughts and forced him to focus, he would have been royally screwed and a lot more satisfied. He groaned again. This shit wasn't fair!

He could still feel her lips on his, and the way her body pressed against his in a perfect fit. Nothing in his wildest dreams had prepared him for the reality of holding and kissing Kate. He finally understood what the connection between a Guardian and Mystic could become. He had known this was going to be impossible.

Growling at Xavier to vent his frustration, he snapped, *"What the hell do you want? You drive me to the brink of insanity to track Kate down and get to business, then you interrupt. I was kind of enjoying the moment. Since my days are numbered, I'd really like to know what was so important."* Electricity still swamped his system, and his raging libido was not helping. Thirty years attached to a phantom and not being able to connect with anyone else was beginning to take its toll.

Xavier flashed in and punched his shoulder. He bared his teeth and leveled an intense stare at his brother. "Sorry to interrupt your play time, princess, but I thought you'd like to know that a demon assassin team has breached the city, and they're searching for your girl. So, play time is over for both of you. Gregory is tracking them, and so am I. Right now, they've split into two groups. Gregory will meet you at her apartment. Tell the girl, tell her now." He faded back into the Shadows.

Well, shit. This conversation isn't likely to go well. Xander punched the wall and flashed to Kate's apartment building. She was definitely not prepared for what was coming. None of them were.

J.L. Lawrence

9

Kate pulled on her favorite black athletic pants and a blue T-shirt. She finally felt a little better and had most of her emotions under control. A cool shower gave her some space to think and helped her gain perspective. Her attraction to Xander was an aberration due to raging hormones and lack of sleep. It had to be. Hero worship was a common occurrence under the circumstances.

She needed to get her focus back on Trey and her five-year plan. She could do this. She could have a normal life with a man who cared for her. She refused to acknowledge the fact that she hadn't even seen him since she returned.

A heavy, hard knock at the door startled her. She grabbed her weapon from her nightstand and met Angie on the way to the door. Kate looked at the clock. "Who the hell has come here at this time of night?"

Angie shrugged and reached for the knob first, looking through the peephole. "Well, well, if it isn't our two adorable new agent friends."

"What? Why would they be here?" Kate wasn't ready to face her actions from a few hours earlier. Her heart raced with anticipation and fear. Hadn't she been humiliated enough? To make it worse, he brought a friend along. Whether she liked it or not, he made her feel desires and emotions that were best locked away. Her goal had been to *avoid* pain, not embrace it.

"I'm not the mind reader." Angie shrugged and opened the door. "Agent Montgomery and Agent Pierce. What a pleasant surprise at three in the morning. To what do we owe the pleasure?" Her sarcasm made Kate smile a little. They backed up to let them in. The two agents exchanged a glance, and dread formed a knot in Kate's stomach. Her *spidey sense* tingled, and that was never a good sign.

Xander walked in first and stood in front of them, while Agent Pierce walked over to the windows. "It looks like our current case has crossed paths with yours, so actually there is no easy way to explain this." His expression appeared agitated and he wrung his hands repetitively. He sat down on one of the chairs.

His anxiety brought an awareness to Kate. They weren't agents. She wasn't sure *why* she had the knowledge, but she'd bet her badge on it. *Who are these men, and what do they want with us?*

Angie pulled Kate over, and they sat on the couch opposite Xander. "You aren't with any federal agency, are you?" Kate patiently waited for his answer, but her own fear erupted inside. She closed her eyes and opened the door in her mind she always kept firmly closed.

With better calm, she reopened her eyes and focused on Xander, seeing a lot of gray in his aura. *Figures, he's hiding behind a wall.* She sighed and dug deeper to see his true energy field. He was accomplished at staying hidden, but she began to see shades of red for strength and passion, blue for calm and truth, gold for power and harmony, and many other colors swirling around him. They were vibrant and exuded a positive energy. She found no traces of evil or dishonesty.

Kate wanted this wretched night and her roller coaster emotions to end. "Just spit it out already."

Xander smoothed his hands over his jeans, obviously weighing his words carefully. Finally, he reached forward and took Kate's hand. "The world is not as simple as you believe. There are many more aspects and dimensions than you can imagine."

"Like what?" Doubt trickled into her mind. This couldn't be real. She tried to ignore pieces of her vision that kept popping into her head.

"Like the thing we killed in the alley. It was a demon, which is why it turned to ash." Kate stared in horror. These guys were crazy. They *had* to be.

"Demons, magic, dimensions. None of that's real. I don't know who the hell y'all are but stop wasting our time." As she said the words, she met his eyes, and a part of her recognized the truth in their story. .

Agent Pierce finally stepped forward and gaped at them. "Seriously? What the hell was kicking your asses back in that alley then? You both know you would have died that night. You saw how we killed it and what happened. Stupidity does not become you. Name's Gregory by the way. Guess we should all get to know each other."

"So," Angie retorted, "what does that make you, a demon hunter? Go back to your cheap seat over there by the window and butt out of our conversation if you can't be civil."

Kate took a moment to observe Gregory. He hadn't even flinched at Angie's comment. He always had a slight smile on his face like they were the butt of the joke in his head. His hair was short and clean cut, but black as night. His eyes were hazel, always varying on the hinge of blue or green depending on his mood, she guessed. His skin had a darker Mediterranean tint, but his build was tall and strong like Xander's. These men had obviously been training for a long time. Xander brought back her focus. Without meaning to, she gave a little growl.

"Quit looking as if you are ready to attack us, Kate. Do you think this is any easier to tell than to hear? Besides, you already know the answer. One, you saw it with your own eyes. Two, my guess is that you have been having weird dreams. Three, you have special abilities that average humans do not possess. That's why we're here. Demons have discovered who you are, and we're running out of time to get you somewhere safe."

Kate's first thought was to kill them. They had to be crazy and knew way too much. Reason settled in; her second thought forced her to wonder if this explained her vision. A warning. That's why she had been healed. She was so close to a normal life. She wouldn't just give up and go on the run with strangers. Truth or fiction didn't matter. Either way, she wasn't going to trust them, or go *anywhere* with them.

Xander jerked her off the couch, despite her yelp of protest. "Look, I don't have time for a detailed explanation. You are being tracked by demons much worse than what you saw in the alley. Gregory and I have been sent as your protectors. We have to take you somewhere safe. I know you have doubts. I can't imagine how overwhelming all of this is to you, and quite frankly, I don't care, but you have to trust us." He opened his hand, and a fireball appeared.

Kate gasped at the heat emanating from him. She couldn't allow herself to believe, because if she did, she'd never be able to return to a normal life. She held back her tears. The safe world she'd created for herself started to crumble underneath her.

Her mind spun. The best solution was to disappear for a while with Angie. They could take care of themselves and be done with all this craziness.

"That's a neat party trick," Kate finally said, "but I'm not buying. I decline your protection. I am *this* close to a normal life." She held her thumb and forefinger together. "I have a great guy I'm going to marry and a job I love. Nothing on this earth can make me choose otherwise." Sadness, anger, and pain flooded over her. She backed away. Everything spiraled out of control. Just once, couldn't she be allowed to find happiness?

Xander cut the distance between them in one stride. His own anger surrounded her. "Do you think I wanted to spend the last thirty years of my life searching for you?" he roared and grabbed her by the arm. "I haven't had a life from the time you were born! Now, you want to give me a sob story about all of this human shit? Get over yourself. It's your job to save the world, and that will be your only goal. Throw the rest out the window and don't expect pity from me." He released her and jerked back the sleeve from his forearm.

He stiffly pointed at an intricate tattoo covering his whole arm. It reminded her of a shield protecting an angel, but also had symbols she couldn't identify etched into a sword going down the center of the entire image. She had dreamed of this image every night of her life. What did it mean? Had she finally encountered her stranger in the mist? What would happen if she took his hand?

Gregory put a restraining hand on Xander's shoulder. "She doesn't understand our world or what has been sacrificed. We knew she would not easily believe."

Xander shrugged off his hand and fought for control. How dare she talk to him about marriage, when he hadn't been able to touch a woman since being branded with the guardian mark? She'd had a full life, while his had been reduced to that of a golden retriever. His whole mission was to fetch.

Gregory's words slowly sank in, and he realized some of Kate's resistance had been fear. She *couldn't* love the human. It wasn't her destiny. He needed patience and time. He'd screwed up once again and could feel the dread she carried. The panic wasn't because of him. He watched her and realized that she feared her destiny more than anything else. She knew more than any of them had believed.

"I'm sorry for yelling at you. This isn't easy for any of us. Our world is made up of many realms, but at some levels we all connect. Every four to five-hundred years, a battle called the Rising occurs. The winner of this battle determines dominion over the realms, or at least the majority of them. So far, the good guys have won — barely.

"The main determinant of the battle is the showdown between the Mystic and the Omega, or Demon Lord. Each represents light versus darkness. The Rising is not our main concern at the moment, and is not for several months, but finding the Mystic is. Without the Mystic, the world, including your human realm, will be plunged into darkness."

Xander could tell he had made progress. At least, she appeared to be *trying* to sort through the information. But, as quickly as she was processing, he also sensed new barriers she was erecting. Her eyes clouded over and he felt the denial raging inside her. She could hide her thoughts but not her emotions. Of course, she'd be afraid to accept and believe in her destiny. Any human would.

He tracked her thoughts through Angie to guide her to the truth. Kate wouldn't give in without a fight. After all, for the moment, her human mind didn't accept magic easily. Humans lived in ignorance of what they couldn't explain with science. Her denial seemed stronger than most like someone had purposely removed her ability to believe in the supernatural.

This next part was not going to go over any better, so he decided to get it all out in the open. "Kate, *you* are the Mystic. It's why you have the abilities you try so hard to hide. If you look deep inside yourself and conquer the fear holding you back, you'll find your destiny and know who you are."

"You *are* joking, right? I am *not* some savior going to do battle. I need you to leave and never come back." Kate walked to the door and opened it, inclining her head for them to leave.

He flicked it closed with a wave of his hand. Alarm streaked across her face. Part of him wanted to soothe her and part of him wanted her to suffer the way he had for so many years. "I'm sorry, but you *are* the Mystic. Whether or not you accept it right now is not my concern. We have demons right on top of us and must go somewhere safe."

Angie seemed unusually quiet, but her expression told a different story. To Xander's surprise, she didn't seem shocked by what he had told them. Instead, she seemed relieved. He decided to check her thoughts again and found that she'd been expecting something like this to happen. She'd felt something coming for a long time and had seen the ticking clock inside Kate.

He also discovered that Kate spent her life shutting down her true self and hiding behind the masks that she allowed the world to see. Angie spent hers believing there was more to Kate and both of their destinies. *How curious.* Angie would be helpful after all. He would take Angie with them to their first location, to help Kate move toward acceptance. Then, he'd find a safe place for her to hide. Demons could use her as leverage, and Kate would never allow her to be harmed. His life had gotten way too complicated.

"Pack a bag and let's go to a hotel outside the city," he said. "I'll try to answer more of your questions then. Right now, we don't want innocent people being hurt. Like an apartment complex full of them." He figured if nothing else, he could appeal to her sense of protection. She would not allow innocents to be harmed because of her. "Let's move."

"Too late." Gregory quickly moved toward Xander. They pushed the girls behind them.

Kate felt the presence of a third person but couldn't pinpoint where it was coming from. Xander opened his eyes and exchanged a look with Gregory that had her reeling from panic. Maybe she couldn't read his mind, but she could read his emotions. His heart raced and his protective instincts had kicked in. *Something was coming. Make that–something is here!*

"Xander," Kate started, but stopped when he motioned them to be quiet. He turned and reached out to squeeze her hand. He pointed for her to stay back with look of reprimand.

Mayhem erupted.

Three demons appeared in a triangle formation in their living room. *Talk about too much proof at once. I get it already!* Kate wanted to scream the words but knew this was real.

Xander threw Kate and Angie back against the wall. Kate hit with enough force to rattle her teeth. She got back on her feet and glanced at Angie to make sure she was okay, too.

The guys produced swords out of the air and faced the enemy in a manner worthy of the Romans. She sighed in relief. At least demons hadn't progressed to using semi-automatics. Xander and Gregory advanced, feigned, and dropped back. Both sides used incredible focus and techniques.

The men spun their swords and forced the demons to take several steps back. Xander advanced and Gregory stepped back. Then, Gregory moved forward and Xander sidestepped in front of the girls. Both men were determined to keep Kate guarded. Their movements were more restricted than the night in the alley. However, their speed had not diminished. Kate could barely follow the trail of the clashing swords.

Kate and Angie got into their own back-to-back formation, preparing to fight. Otherwise, they stayed out of their protectors' way. Kate watched the warriors and demons move with incredible speed and agility, and she knew the irrefutable truth. It terrified her.

The demons were hideous. One had red eyes, while those of the other two were completely black. Their skin was grayish, with scars of some sort, and tattoos covered them from head to foot. Probably symbols of some kind, but Kate had never seen them before, except the pitchfork which she equated to something evil.

The demons were dressed in black tanks and black leather pants. Their hair was cropped to the scalp, or completely shaven with tattoos in its place, and their facial expressions were full of hate and rage.

Kate met their eyes and her stomach rolled in revulsion. Horrifying images overloaded her psychic powers. They reminded her of evil creatures from the worst horror movies ever made. No one could doubt they were demon through and through, and their goal was to destroy her. Not the most pleasant thought she'd ever had.

She watched from the corner, Angie at her side. Xander and Gregory were careful with their movements. They continued to stay low and always placed themselves between her and the demons. She figured the guys could've killed all the demons but needed to stay close together to protect her. Their range of motion became handicapped because of her. Guilt swamped her. She watched them struggle between killing the demons and saving her. She wanted to help, but she also wanted to run.

She briefly read an image from Gregory's mind, that they were also concerned about how much power they could use, not wanting to attract another set of demons and become truly outnumbered. She shuddered and she helplessly watched furniture, collectibles, tables, and anything else in their path become destroyed. She kept her focus on Xander. Ready to help whenever needed.

Xander had the leader. He glanced at Gregory, who had the other two in his sights. Xander ducked. The demon's blade narrowly missed his shoulder. He returned a front kick that sent the demon flying. The red eyed demon recovered from the kick and charged directly at Kate. Xander intercepted. Their blades met in a battle of wills.

Xander tried to stay connected to Gregory to stay focused on all the demons. His main goal was to protect Kate at all costs, but he also had to conserve his powers. They had a long way to go, and he couldn't be weakened. Gregory was highly frustrated, avoiding kicks and punches, as well as fighting off their swords. Every time Xander or Gregory gained an advantage, the tables would turn before they could make the kill.

"Xander," Gregory's thoughts filled his mind. Xander ducked a sword aimed at his head and launched his own attack. *"We've got to go offensive and end this before we attract too much attention. We're not exactly being quiet or even winning for that matter. And where the hell is Xavier?"*

Xander blocked the next strike and swung his sword in an upward motion disarming the demon momentarily. *"He's protecting our magical traces and rerouting them, so we don't get any more visitors. You're right, we have to change the dynamics."*

Xander couldn't read Kate's thoughts, but through Angie he knew they were ready to fight. One thing he could do was open and project his own thoughts into Kate's mind. *"Kate."* He directed his energy so she could pick up his thoughts, while avoiding getting killed.

Kate briefly met his eyes "What can we do?" she whispered.

Xander paused momentarily to force his opponent back once again. These were some cocky little suckers. *"With limited movement, we can only do so much. If we move to kill these things, we run the risk of one breaking through. Can you handle it long enough, if you have to fight?"*

She stiffened. "Of course, we'll hold our own." Xander swore he heard the straight pride in her voice. She better be ready. It was time to end this.

Kate couldn't tell who'd been doing what at this preternatural speed. The fighting grew more intense. The clash of swords and grunts of pain overpowered everything. Xander had been right. When Gregory went for the kill shot on one of his opponents, and Xander went for his, the third demon slipped through and launched at her. Because Xander and Gregory had re-engaged *their* opponents, they wouldn't be coming to the rescue any time soon.

She'd already mapped out a plan while watching the guys fight, and she was ready. She connected mentally to Angie and sent it to her. They both had guns tucked into the back of their waist bands.

The demon approached, they drew their weapons, and Kate hoped for a miracle. The creature quickly knocked the weapons out of their hands. She ducked out of the way of his sword and aimed a strong kick at his midsection. It didn't slow him down. His ugly face revealed his surprise that she fought back. These idiots didn't know who they were messing with. With a smirk, he lunged at her.

She narrowly jumped out of the way and turned to take the demon's feet out from under him. Time stood still.

Angie grabbed her weapon. She shot the creature from behind, to get his focus off Kate. The demon turned to lunge at Angie. Kate grabbed her ceremonial sword from the wall and sliced through its neck. She never imagined she'd use her prized trophy earned during her summer karate tour many years ago for such a thing. The demon's body burst into flames, like it had been thrown into an incinerator and, with an explosion of smoke, it was gone.

Only a pile of ash remained.

Breathing hard, Angie looked at her gun. "Well damn! This is the first time I've ever wanted to toss my gun and embrace the sword. By the way," she glanced at Kate, also out of breath, "thanks for dragging me to the weaponry classes at the dojo." She exhaled and leaned against the wall.

She finally had time to put her attention back on the men and discovered that Xander and Gregory had also obliterated their opponents. Piles of ash remained. *Unbelievable.*

Gregory grinned at Xander and put his arm around Kate. "Your girl bagged her first demon." He sniffed and mockingly wiped at his eyes. "It's a Kodak moment."

Kate shrugged him off, but Angie glared at him. "A real smart ass, aren't ya?"

"Born and bred!" Gregory shamelessly grinned.

They took a moment to deal with everything and Kate sheepishly glanced at Xander and Gregory. They were covered in cuts and blood from the fight. She felt torn. Part of her wanted to apologize for being a pain *and* for being wrong, but part of her wanted to slap him for not telling her sooner. Pride. A huge sin to overcome, and she had it in spades.

She took a deep breath and squared her shoulders. "I want to apologize to everyone for being slow to believe and putting everyone at risk. A part of me knew you were telling the truth, and I could see the honest intentions in your aura. I wanted it to *not* be true. I'm afraid I gave into that selfish part of me and had a little denial going on."

Xander still didn't respond, so she walked closer to him and looked into his eyes. "Look, I'm still not saying I believe everything, but I *do* know I'm being hunted. We'll go to your safe location and sort all of this out. Truce?" She held out her hand and waited.

Sighing, Xander gripped her hand, but Kate knew she hadn't been forgiven. "These incredibly fast creatures are also highly skilled assassins. The Omega has sent out his best for you. Not a good indicator of what else is probably on the way. This was a small advance posse that got lucky. They may have communicated our position. We need to move quickly. Grab a few necessities and we're outta here."

For once, Kate held her tongue and didn't argue. She grabbed her emergency pack that she always kept in the closet and threw Angie hers. "So, what do we do from here?"

Gregory scanned the room, taking in the damage. "Scouter demons are basically assassins sent to find their mark — which is *you*, Kate. That's why I was telling you we had to get out of here."

Angie stabbed her finger into Gregory's chest, getting fired up in Kate's defense, but he held up his hands "I know, I know, back down, Cujo. This city is full of innocent victims, and the Scouters don't care if they kill every single one to get to the Mystic. We can't allow demons to run rampant through the city."

Xander's face clouded over, and he looked far away. "Xavier shielded the majority and threw off the scent," he said to Gregory. "But it will only buy us a little time before we get hit with the next wave. We've got to move quickly if we want to survive."

"Who is Xavier?" Kate wearily asked. She'd reached her breaking point.

"He's my twin. He keeps to the shadows dealing with his own personal demons but watches over us vigilantly and provides an extra layer of protection for you. He was blocking the energy we used, both ours and the demons, to avoid us attracting further attention. He's using our essence to lead the next pack across town, but it won't be long before they figure it out. These are highly trained assassins like we've never seen before, which just made our travel plans a lot more challenging."

"Of course, Xander and Xavier. There should be a law against naming twins almost identical names. As if looking the same wouldn't cause enough chaos." She'd been snide and a bit childish, but in her opinion, she'd earned the right to be a little pissy.

Gregory leaned back and stretched his neck, his own frustration evident. "Ladies, we've got to move a little faster, if you please. We don't want the second round of our beauty contestants coming to visit anytime soon." Kate and Angie rolled their eyes at his attempt at humor. "Let's go. We'll drive out of the city to a safe remote location."

After years of waiting and searching, Kate had finally started getting answers, and they were *not* what she wanted to hear. She learned that she'd eventually face a demon much worse than what she saw tonight, and it would be her responsibility alone, to win a demonic war, or plunge the world into darkness. That alone was bad enough, but first, she had to become the Mystic. How was that going to work? What would happen to her? And who the hell wanted that destiny? She most certainly did *not*!

Xander had basically told her she'd gain more powers, have to train for battle, and learn all these new things in a new world. She felt stuck in a Harry Potter movie, and someone had delivered her letter way too late.

She looked back at Xander "Where will we go, if they're tracking every move we make. How do we hide?"

"We'll travel mostly at night when the majority of the demons will be searching for us, so we are constantly moving and harder to track. We'll sleep as much as possible during the day. Scouter and assassin demons can only operate in the dark and are adept at tracking magical traces. Especially if they are confined to one area. We can't risk sitting idle and hoping they don't trace us. Although we can still expect some attacks during the day, they should be minor in comparison, and much easier to kill since they will mostly be humans under the control of demons.

"Xavier will be watching to give us a warning. We'll try to stick to large state parks, farmlands, and other less populated areas, to lessen the likelihood of innocents being involved. We may go into a city, if we need to get lost in a crowd, but we can't stay long and risk the humans."

"*I'm* human," Kate muttered. She took a deep breath; overwhelmed and defeated.

"Not for much longer," Xander said, and she glared back at him. Gregory rolled his eyes and grinned. "We have ways of getting other things you need along the way, if you forget anything."

Xander opened the door and glanced over his shoulder toward Gregory. "Is the car ready?" Gregory nodded in return.

Kate stepped out of her apartment, struck with an overwhelming feeling this would be the last time she'd ever see it. Her heart shattered. She finally admitted to herself that the normal life she craved was only a dream. She'd just been bitch-slapped by reality.

10

Xavier broke into Xander's thoughts while driving to their new destination. *"The demons have broken off the fake trail. They haven't latched onto your new location yet, but it looks like they're heading out of the city, which I honestly can't explain. I've never seen them break off from a trail this early."*

"That doesn't make any sense. Why would they leave a big city with a hot trail, without a solid scent to follow?"

"Beats me, it's like they were notified she left, but not where she's going. Weird. I guess it's possible they have a Seer of their own that the Council can't block."

Xander stretched his back and flexed his hands over the steering wheel, going over the possibilities in his mind. It didn't add up. *"Micah would know, wouldn't he?"*

"Who knows? Things have blocked his vision before, but something doesn't feel right. I'm leaning toward insider or possibly a spy that is tracking one of you. The demons are smarter this time," Xavier hesitantly said.

"That's impossible. Micah would definitely see that, and they wouldn't be able to enter the Meadows. No one else even knows her whereabouts to be that kind of an

informant." Xander knew Xavier was trying to look at all possibilities, but they had enough evil to fight without accusing the good guys.

"*Xavier, we don't need any more conspiracy theories. The battle has always lined up as it should, and there is no history of a traitor or spy. Focus on the demons and keep them off us or warn us. I know you've already read my thoughts from the fight. You saw what I saw, and so did Gregory. The assassins carried his mark. Fury is their leader, and my guess is he still holds a grudge that you and I condemned him. He can only serve the underworld now.*" Xander hated to sound so condescending, but his brother had been in and out of the shadows for over twenty years. He needed to come out and face reality. Fury was the threat, and a powerful one.

"*You stupid prick! I realize you think because I haven't been fully in your world for several years that I don't understand things. You forget all that can be seen in shadows, and how potent a weapon it can be. I've got news for you. You need to pull your head out of your ass and realize there are traitors everywhere. We are not immune any more than anyone else, and who are you to say there has never been a traitor? Maybe they've just never been caught. There's a difference. And I'm not stupid; of course, I saw the mark. He's still alive because we couldn't kill him the first time.*"

Xavier sighed and continued, "*I'm tired of dealing with your thick skull. Be careful. Your camp area is clear. Stick to the areas that have a camouflaging spell. Demons are still trying to pick up the trail, and you know Fury is very good. You should have the day to sleep. Most of the scouters are full demons and can't travel during the day. The others you can handle, and they won't be able to break through the protective spells.*

"When the sun starts to set, the demons will be ready to head your direction. Your site is in a state park two hours from here. By the way, don't forget I'm fully connected to you through our twin link, so I can read your thoughts at will. Try to keep your condescending crap better protected."

"Xavier, thanks for everything." Xander paused. "*I know I don't understand what you're going through, but you never gave me a chance to try.*" He inwardly sighed and realized Xavier had faded back into the Shadows and broken off communication. Xavier hadn't been *that* angry at him in long time. He guessed some emotion was better than none.

The rest of the drive, he went over and over what Xavier said. Could there be a traitor who had the ability to scrape the surface of evil and stay clean? Could someone have been tracking Gregory or himself, knowing they would be with the Mystic? He hoped not. If someone *could* stay off the radar, they would be nearly impossible to catch, and Kate would never be safe. If *she* died, *he* died.

He finally pulled into the parking lot. His head ached from all of the theories endlessly circling. His greatest concern was that it would be impossible to keep Kate and Angie safe from the most feared team of assassins in all the realms.

They had blocked Fury's entrance through the portals to most realms, so he had made his home in the Human and Hell realm, recruiting minions and torturing humans who held true traces of power. He possessed many powers similar to Xander and others that served on the Council.

Fury would be difficult to beat, but maybe they could contain him or get to the Meadows in time.

The moment he shut off the car, Kate sat straight up. She'd been incredibly jumpy, and not being able to read her mind infuriated him. He didn't need that particular power to know she wasn't planning to trust him anytime soon. He wanted to hate her but was drawn to her spirit and loyalty. If his damn tattoo would quit glowing and ripping apart his flesh, he'd probably be more tolerant to her mood swings and pigheadedness. Instead, he was a ticking time bomb, dependent on her ability to accept her new destiny. *Yeah, my future is looking bright.*

"Where are we?" Kate asked. She opened the door and stretched her body.

"At a state park in West Tennessee. Gregory called ahead and booked a room. It's pretty isolated, so not many bystanders, just in case. We'll hang out here for today and move to another site tonight. I realize you have a million questions, and that is completely understandable. But for now, I say we get settled and get some rest. I know the two of you haven't slept for nearly twenty-four hours." Gregory checked them in, and Xander led them to their room. All he wanted was a few minutes to clear his head.

"May I ask why we're all piling into one room?" Angie asked. "Also, it's pretty tight in here, but I guess we're just sleeping. She shrugged. She'd been unusually quiet, though he had kept tabs on her thoughts. She wasn't ready to run, but she wanted answers. He wasn't sure he had them all for her.

He had to admit the room didn't have much space, but it provided two full size beds and a clean bathroom. The paint was old and chipped in places and the faucets had a little rust. Overall, it suited their needs. Secluded and defendable. He noticed Angie still waited for his answer.

"Safety. If anything happens, we're all together and can run fast. Plus, as long as we stay close to each of you, we can use simple shields to confuse any of the minions that may try to track us. That being said, before you decide to throw any more hissy fits, you'll have to sleep next to us." Xander could have counted on one hand the seconds before the girls started mouthing. They didn't get the whole concept of dying by the demons' hands.

He watched their mutinous expressions and crossing of the arms. Something snapped inside him. He had endured enough. He flung back the covers, lifted both of them off their feet, and dumped them in the beds. They stared at him, too stunned to speak. He glared back. "Any questions? I thought not. Shut up and get some sleep."

He turned to storm off, but found Gregory standing behind the bathroom door laughing his butt off. "Nice. Real smooth delivery and excellent trust-building exercise. I was riveted."

"Shut up. I'm going to do a perimeter check and get some damn space." He didn't care if he was being a jerk. Although, it probably didn't exactly win him points toward her saving his life. He stepped outside in the cool breeze and pushed the emotions aside.

Furious, Kate jumped up to chase after Xander. Gregory caught her around the waist. "You actually *do* have the right to be a little upset this time. I'll give you that. But try to understand. He was given this mission to protect you at birth, which was one hundred and fifty years ago. Then, he knew when you were born, but not *where*. We've spent the last twenty-eight years searching for you and trying to protect our people along the way. He carries a huge responsibility, and so do you."

She took several deep breaths and tried to digest what he'd told her. Xander's resentment toward her made a little more sense now. He'd sacrificed a lot of his life. Still, she hadn't exactly asked for this. *And how old did he say he was?* "Xander mentioned earlier negative energy feeding the demons, what did he mean?"

Gregory shrugged, but finally answered as he ushered her back toward the bed. "Basically, all the crimes, evil acts, selfishness, all the negative things in the world produce a negative energy that demons funnel down and eventually build up enough to break through the seal of the portals. When — "

"So, you're saying," Angie interrupted, "all the bad crap that happens here in our world feeds the demons? Have you seen the news lately?" She shook her head in amazement. "Well, we're screwed every which way."

"When the seal is broken," Gregory went on, "only the Mystic can destroy the demon that opens it and reseal it. That's why the Mystic is crucial, and why our Council sent us to bring you home." He held up his hand and smiled. "Before you ask, the Ancient Council is kind of like your Congress. Luckily, with your career choice, you've already received a lot of training in fighting tactics at least. For now, please try to get some sleep."

Kate wanted to argue, to throw things, to make him take back what she knew was truth. No one had the right to tell her when to sleep, or that she was responsible for saving millions of people. Angie stayed silent, so Kate delved into her thoughts. As usual, Angie was trusting her to work through the information and make the right decision. Sometimes Angie's silence was more condemning than her words. For once, Kate wished she'd take the lead.

She tried to wait on Xander to return, because she still wanted to give him a piece of her mind, but the past twenty-four hours finally caught up with her. She drifted off, full of turmoil, hoping sleep would help clear her head and calm her nerves.

Kate woke with a start and tried to take stock of her surroundings. A man's arm lay across her abdomen. It hadn't been there earlier. Where was she? She tried to put all the pieces back together in her scattered mind. She slightly stretched, flexing in Xander's arms, and felt their immediate connection and warmth in the pit of her stomach. The butterflies flew, and she inwardly groaned at her wanton desire. She felt safe and protected for a moment, like she could let her guard down and be herself.

She'd dreamed of having these feelings all her life, but what a package deal it had come with. A horrible destiny and a jackass. Just once she'd like to do things the normal way.

Fast as lightning, the memories of the night before caught up with her, and she knew it wasn't a dream anymore. This was real. All of it. She didn't want to open her eyes and face reality, *or* the man sleeping beside her, but she'd never been a coward, and there was no reason to start now. *Okay, maybe I am a coward.* She forced herself back to sleep.

Xander awoke to Xavier buzzing in his head. He was the only one who could break his sleeping spell. *"Demons picked up your trail, and more have added to the search. They are desperate to find her."* Xander groaned inwardly. *"No use moaning about it. You have until sunset at most, and then move quickly."* Xavier slowly enunciated the last words.

"How many are coming?"

"Too many."

"Shit!"

"Yep, but I have a plan to slow them down. As for you, run!"

The demons had to be closer than he thought, if Xavier was already in position to spring the first trap. He'd have to wake everyone up soon and get moving. Now that Xavier was out of his head, he could focus on his current surroundings. Kate's sleeping face tugged at his insides and brought out his possessive instincts.

Her flawless skin held a scent all her own: strawberries and spice. Her mouth appeared to be smiling, like she was amused by his inner struggle for her. His gaze continued down her body, pressed so tightly against his own. The perfect fit. Even in a sweatshirt and athletic pants, she was the sexiest human female he had ever come across. A small piece of him wanted to reject her for the ticking clock on his life, but he grew more and more intrigued by her. He reminded himself that she was a means to an end. Her body heat made his own temperature rise. He scoffed. *Love is overrated anyway.*

His hand wandered down her arm and across her hip. He caressed her side and her abdomen on the way back up. Goose bumps arose in response to his touch. He wanted under that shirt so bad he could taste it. He was thankful they weren't alone, or he might not be able to stop. *Almost.* His strong arousal became painful in the confines of his pants. Damn tattoo. Damn destiny.

His gaze reluctantly went back to her mouth. A mouth made for his. His for eternity, or until she kicked him in the balls for lying to her. Though he shouldn't, he wanted one taste before he woke her. Leaning down, he brushed her lips, but it wasn't enough. The urgency to taste her was blinding. *Oh shit, he had opened the floodgates.* He wanted more. A *lot* more.

This time he held his mouth a little firmer, holding his lips to hers for several seconds. He moved to kiss the corner of her mouth. She opened her sapphire eyes and stared straight into his. He came apart. Losing control, he crushed her mouth. Her lips molded perfectly to his. Their tongues began the age-old dance and the temperature in the room skyrocketed. His hands grazed her sides, and his mouth plundered hers. His full erection strained against her pelvis. Her hips rose to get closer. A few more minutes, and nothing would stop them.

"Hey, hey, hey, girl. Stop that," Angie loudly protested. "I'm going blind over here." Angie's interruption broke Kate's trance.

She lightly hit him on the chest and brought him back to reality. His conversation with Xavier rushed to mind. He sat up and removed the protective spells sealing the room. "You up, Gregory?"

"In more ways than one thanks to your performance."

Angie jumped away from Gregory. Her flash of desire at his obvious interest glimmered in her face, before she buried it deep in her mind.

"Good grief," she grumbled. "Control yourself."

Gregory smiled at her reproof and leaned in toward her red face. "Don't lie to me, sweetheart. I felt your heart rate and breathing increase. Maybe you don't know what that means, but I'm sure I could teach you." He placed a quick kiss on Angie's lips, while her eyes were still wide open at his remark. He popped out of the room before she could fire back. She rubbed her lips, trying to wipe away the attraction between them.

Xander chuckled, reading her thoughts. "Flash your behind back in here," he called out to Gregory. "We have plans to go over."

Gregory popped back in, making sure to stay out of Angie's reach. Xander rolled his eyes. *What a fiasco.*

"Earlier you mentioned other beings or realms that were different." Kate changed the subject. A good thing. "If you take out those with powers like yourself, what else is there? Please don't tell me you mean vampires, werewolves, and all the other stuff we dream up in movies and books." She gave a half laugh, then froze.

He diverted his eyes from her penetrating stare. Xander uncomfortably shifted and glanced toward Gregory for assistance. His friend conveniently stared up into the ceiling, like he was working toward a degree in construction.

Kate bowed her head. "I'm not going to like this answer, am I?"

"Actually, most of your human ideas have some grain of truth, because we were once part of the human population, and stories have passed down from generation to generation. Vampire is a human term, and so is werewolf." Kate looked relieved, but he would change that. "But we *do* have sorcerers like us, gliders, shapeshifters, dream walkers, seers, elves, faeries, seekers, and many others in our world. There are more realms than you know."

Gregory ran his hands over his face in utter irritation. "Right now, we need to focus on the demons trying to kill us. We're never going to make it at this rate. As the number of demons increase, the less we can throw our scents and keep our shields invisible. Got any other friends, or do I pretty much round out the numbers?"

"We'll meet up with more help later, but for now we need to get out of here and keep it simple. The minions are easier to kill, so you should both be able to hold your own. Their strength is still inhuman, so you have to be careful. Decapitation always works best."

"Not exactly what they taught in the academy, huh Kate?" Angie dryly said. She stretched out her arms; psyching up for a fight. "But I'm down with it, how 'bout you?"

"Always. Who doesn't get pumped up to go for the obvious kill by taking someone's head off?" Kate's voice pitched higher than normal, and her overexcited cheerleader persona broke some of the tension.

Xander froze and tilted his head to concentrate on the shift in energy. He swiftly moved to the door and swore under his breath. "They sent a team in after us. I'm sensing eight to ten. We can't fight that many and protect both of you. We may have to make a run for it. As soon as we get in the car, we'll drive to a protected location." He decided to leave out the fact that they would be dropping Angie off at a safe house. The separation would not be easy. Angie was determined to see this through, and her connection to Kate was the strongest he had ever seen in humans.

They headed downstairs in a tight formation. They turned toward the lobby area. Minions surrounded them. The sun would set in a matter of minutes, and demons would be joining the fight. They would really be screwed.

Xander pushed the girls into the corner. He and Gregory placed themselves in front to deflect an attack on Kate and Angie. Minions weren't hard to kill or very skilled, but one moment of distraction and Kate could be killed. He couldn't allow it. The whole world would crumble, and millions of deaths would be on him. His heart nearly hammered out of chest. He refused to admit that part of the panic stemmed from his growing feelings for his charge.

He cleared the fear from his mind and focused on the task. Kill the minions. Save Kate. Fight another day. He brought his sword down taking off a head to his right and sent a front kick into the chest of another knocking the halfling back several feet. He pivoted and swiped his blade across the throat of another attacker. Gregory had taken several down as well, but they kept coming. He fought through the sheer numbers, but eventually they successfully separated him from Kate.

He rushed to get to her, but there were too many. They surrounded Kate and Angie. The women fought back. One of the minions picked up Angie and tossed her against the wall. Kate dodged an attacker blocking her path and ran after her. Kate rushed to her side and helped Angie up, but there was nothing left for them to do. Kate blocked a kick and ducked a punch. She delivered several of her own. Kate and Angie fought back to back but wouldn't last much longer.

Xander killed everything in his path. Still, he wasn't going to make it to her. Fear seized his chest and stole his breath.

"Kate, watch out!" he yelled.

She threw up her arm, and an energy shield emerged. From the shocked look on her face, she didn't understand how or what she'd created. Xander could make out the edges of the energy field denoting the boundary lines of the shield. If she could hold it, they might have a shot.

"Kate, try to hold the protection around you." He projected the message to her, but she struggled to maintain it. Gregory was nearly there. The shield began to weaken.

The cronies would have a direct shot at Kate within seconds. Angie threw her arms around Kate to protect her. Kate grasped Angie's hand. The shield emitted a solid white light, knocking the minions back at least fifteen feet. Xander and Gregory quickly killed the rest.

"Xavier intercepted several more, but they are pouring in." Xander said. "We have to get out of here. I've never seen an organized effort like this before." Fury had to be training more than his demon followers. He was building an army.

He glanced over at Kate, huddled with Angie. Both were still feeling the shock from Kate's new-found power. Angie had amplified Kate's powers threefold. Plus, the demons would definitely have her scent now. Whether he liked it or not, Angie would have to go to the portal with them. She might not be able to cross into the Meadows, but that was a problem for another day.

They snuck through the brush and neared the parking lot where they left their car. Kate and Angie froze. The minions looked like normal people, except their eyes were black and soulless. Their faces twisted into a look of torment and evil. They were all pacing and scanning the woods, waiting for a fight.

Xander stood in front, motioning them closer to the edge. *"A few more moments, and we make a run for the car."* He projected the directions to their new location into their minds. *"Gregory will drive. Ladies, you'll jump in the back while we hold them off. We'll have to fight our way there, so have your weapons ready and stay focused."*

Gregory came alert and stepped forward. "Shit, what are those dickheads doing to my car? That's a one-of-a-kind model I had special-ordered. They better get their hands off!" All of them leaned forward, squinting to see the car clearer. The minions were looking into it and doing something Kate couldn't see clearly. They continued to watch, not wanting to get trapped. That vehicle was their way out of here and to their next destination.

The explosion ripped through the darkness. The blast hurled them backward. Kate hit the building and pain erupted in her eardrums. The roiling fire washed over them and singed her clothing. They landed several feet back from where they'd previously stood. Shaken and injured, they scrambled to their feet and sank deeper into the trees, before being seen. Staying quiet was a challenge. All Kate wanted to do was groan and cough up a lung from all the smoke.

Once they were a safe distance away, Xander pulled her into an embrace, so tight she thought her ribs would crack. They were covered in cuts and bruises, but nothing too serious. He exhaled roughly in her hair, full of fear and relief. "Everyone okay?"

"Hell no!" Gregory roared. "They blew up my car, so no, I'm not okay. That was my baby. My perfect car. Do you know how hard it will be to replace it? Screw that, they're all dead." He started back toward the lot. Xander tackled him from behind and sent calming waves of energy through their mental link to subdue him, until he relented.

Kate was amazed at his reaction. *Good grief, it's a car.*

Angie's eyes were wide and her breathing heavy. She looked at Kate, and then turned to Xander. "They blew up the car. They blew up the damn car! What now, O fearless leaders?" Kate had thought modern weapons were out of this. *Guess not.*

She stepped forward and wrapped her arm around Angie's shoulders before everyone got out of control. She didn't want to die here tonight, so someone had to figure out an escape plan fast. Angie trembled in her grasp, and Kate found herself shaking. All of them were covered in bruises and completely miserable. On a good note, most of the idiots had blown themselves up in the blast.

"What do we do now?" she asked with more calm in her voice than she actually felt. "Anyone got a Plan B? Cause Plan A just went up in smoke." She added the last part to try and inject some humor in the situation and relieve some of the tension permeating the air. Gregory groaned and buried his face in the ground. *What a baby.* She met Xander's eyes. They were barely focused, and she could tell he was searching for a solution.

He told her he couldn't contact Xavier, so he didn't know where the demons were. They all knew they were out of time. The sun faded, and now it was time for the real demons to come out and play. At least Gregory finally seemed to be coming around. He was sitting on the ground sulking, but calm. The demons had to be closing in by now, and they had to move fast. The car was out. She hoped Xander would think of something.

Xander ran through all the possibilities in his mind, which were pretty limited with two humans. If they tried to flash out, they would be easy to follow with the women in tow. Kate and Angie would be sick at least a day, recovering from the shock it would cause their human bodies. At this rate, they didn't have any recovery time to spare. They needed a miracle to swoop down and take them away.

Wait a minute.

His pacing slowed, as an idea formed in his mind. *It might work.* Micah, the Council Seer, had said to travel and use limited magic, but he didn't give the exact mode of transportation they had to use. He grinned and sent his idea to Gregory.

"You can't be serious," Gregory muttered, looking straight into Xander's eyes. "They don't even exist here. Stop thinking about it right now. Xander, I mean it — *no!*"

Xander clapped Gregory's shoulder, with an even larger grin.

11

Xander turned toward Kate and flashed a smile. "How do you two feel about animals?"

"Depends on the animal, I suppose." Her response was hesitant. Xander admitted he loved the Southern drawl that seemed to deepen whenever she became suspicious or angry.

"I've always liked puppies," Angie added. She mischievously grinned and winked at Kate.

Xander braced himself for the arguments to come. "Look, we have to leave now, and our ground transportation went up in flames." He ignored Gregory's groan at the reminder. "Gregory and I can shapeshift and get you out of here, but you'll have to trust us unconditionally."

"That's easy for Kate," Angie snorted, "since she's the chosen one and all, but not so much for me." She glared. Gregory nodded in agreement with her. "Exactly what kind of animal? A horse?" She tossed a look over her shoulder toward Gregory. "Or a jackass ... if we're staying in character?"

Xander cleared his throat. "Not exactly. We can't travel on land. We'd be too easy to catch."

Kate stomped her foot. "Then what? Quit dragging out the inevitable and wasting time. What other way is there?"

Xander knew she regretted the question as soon as it left her mouth.

"A Dragon," Xander said and snapped his fingers. He disappeared, and a beautiful golden dragon stood in his place.

Kate's heart stuttered, and she gasped at the transformation. The huge beast had to be close to ten feet tall. The scales covering his body glistened in golden tones, but the head and tail were a deeper bronze. The tail was over eight feet long and had small spikes.

The dragon turned his head and came nose to nose with her and slightly nudged her.

His bright blue eyes had green rings around the outside. He licked her, and she finally came out of her stupor. He quickly turned back into human form.

She had to wake up from this nightmare, but no poke or pinch worked. *This can't be real. It can't be my life.* She shook her head hard, to get control. Thank God for her mental compartments, or they'd be dropping her off at the nearest mental institution.

She hated heights, but she'd be willing to bet she'd hate what the demons would do to her a whole lot more. "Tell us what to do," she said, gathering her courage and sucking in a sharp breath. "I don't want any of us getting hurt tonight."

Xander nodded. "Once we shift into dragon form, climb on, and we'll head out of here. We have shields to block from human eyes, but the demons will be able to see us, and will probably fire some weapons, since they can't reach us physically. We'll have to climb high, fast." Kate sensed the urgency building inside him. She gulped and nodded agreement.

Gregory shook his head and flashed into his dragon form. His was more of a silver color that glistened even at night, like lights bouncing off a mirror. It reminded her of ancient armor worn by warriors. His eyes swirled silver with rings of blue around the edges. He looked at Angie and lowered his front legs to the ground, to allow her access to his back.

She climbed on and glanced back at Kate. "Well, Kate, we sure as hell ain't in Kansas anymore," she quipped with a heavy southern drawl. Taking a deep breath, she wrapped her arms around the dragon's neck.

"No shit, Angie. We're riding dragons. We belong in the looney bin. At this rate it might be the preferable option." Kate grimaced and opened her mind for communication. Xander transformed into the golden dragon. His scales also glowed and seemed like armor. Kate reached out to touch it, hoping it was as tough as armor. They were slick *and* strong. *Amazing but insane.*

"*Trust me Kate,*" Xander whispered into her mind. "*I won't let anything happen to you.*"

A twig snapped in the distance. The demons were on top of them. She jumped aboard, tightly encircled his neck, and gave a tap with her heels to let him know she was ready. They launched into the sky, she held her breath and prayed.

Something whizzed by her ear, and she lost her grip for a moment. Bullets flew all around her and bounced off the invisible shield. She reached for her own gun, strapped to her side, but knew she'd be wasting her time and ammo shooting into the pitch-black forest below. The scales acted like a shield and deflected bullets. They climbed higher and higher. At least she'd found one positive in this whole situation. She'd become bullet proof for the moment.

The moon reflected off the water, trees, and open land. Breathtaking and serene, it all passed by in a blur. She relaxed and felt free and peaceful. She blended into the scenery itself and became one with her surroundings. An echo of energy fizzled through her entire body. She closed her eyes again and focused on her energy, for the first time admitting what was inside her. It was a beautiful moment of awareness.

They landed several hours later in a dense, dark green forest. Animals made light sounds in the deep woods, accompanied by the slight rustle of leaves from their footsteps. This place would have made a great, secluded, vacation spot, if only — She sighed and set her bag down.

"Where are we?" Angie asked as she stretched one way and then the other, trying to work out her sore muscles from the ride.

"In Kansas. Xavier found this spot of land that is rarely ever disturbed except by animals." Xander ravenously bit down on a protein bar. Kate figured he was restoring some of his energy.

"Kansas? Seriously!" Angie exclaimed, stricken at the news.

Kate laughed, remembering her earlier comment. "Are you really that surprised at this point?"

Angie shrugged, and looked a little forlorn. "Sure, why not? I would say stranger things have happened, but I'm not too sure on that one. I'm waiting for the tornado to take me over the rainbow and little strange men to burst into song. Or someone in a white lab coat to place me into my white padded room. Whichever." She sat down on a log, bemused. "So where are we staying this time?"

Xander tried hard not to laugh at Angie. This went far beyond the usual scope of the human mind. In most circumstances, he would find the humor in this situation. Unfortunately, having to use so much power to stay as a dragon drained him far more than he wanted to admit. "We get to sleep in tents this time." He walked over to one of the trees and pulled two tents out of hiding and an additional duffel bag of supplies.

"Thank the merciful Lord," Angie muttered, and started rummaging for food. Kate seemed to be trying to familiarize herself with the area.

After a couple of hours, Xander and Gregory had set up the tents and sorted their supplies. Xander put a meal together since the girls had only eaten snacks for the past couple days and needed real nourishment. He had to give Xavier credit; he had thought of everything preparing this site, including a bar of soap. The girls would appreciate that. He glanced up as Kate came stomping out of the woods.

"For the record," she grumbled, "outdoor plumbing is *not* a favorite of mine. I'd kill for a normal bathroom and shower."

Angie walked over, put her arm around Kate's shoulders, and playfully squeezed. "Weenie."

"Maybe so, but indoor plumbing is for me." Kate came to an abrupt stop and Angie ran smack dab into her back. "You *do* have indoor plumbing, right?" she asked Xander.

He tried to bite back his harsh remark and resisted the urge to momentarily make her squirm, but he went with the truth instead. He needed to keep her on task. "Yes, of course." He couldn't completely hide his frustration. "We have every basic thing you have, and then some. We've been over this. You think we'd have cell phones and Internet but no bathrooms?"

"It's a reasonable question," Kate fired back. "How do I know your kind even *need* bathrooms? Many of the books I've read mention they don't have those concerns, so stop assuming I should know everything." Her mouth twisted. "Besides, I panicked for a second."

"No problem. It will take time to adjust." He was still irritated, but he knew most of his frustration had to do with how little she truly knew about him or his community. It wasn't fair that fate had screwed with the natural timeline of the Mystic and Guardian. Not her fault, but still frustrating. He walked over to the fire to finish up their dinner.

Xander closed his eyes and turned toward the trees behind him. Everything got quiet.

"Umm, what's he doing?" Angie whispered.

"He's talking to Xavier," Kate and Gregory simultaneously spoke.

"We're in luck," he enthusiastically announced. "And, for once, something went our way. Both of Xavier's traps worked, and he slowed down the demons tremendously. He said they've dropped back to regroup and probably recruit more. But that means we'll have one or two days to rest and begin some proper training. We're not close enough to the Meadows to risk much magic but working on weaponry and technique is almost as important." They finally caught a break.

They quietly ate their simple but filling meal. Xander used energy funneled from Gregory and Xavier to recharge. He'd depleted a great deal, and his powers were waning. Toward the of the meal, they began chatting about interesting places they had visited and current events. From the outside, he realized that they probably looked like a group of friends on a regular camping trip. Not that he'd ever been allowed anything normal in his own life. Once everyone was finished eating, Gregory waved his hand, and everything disappeared, including the fire.

"Thought we weren't supposed to use magic." Kate poked Xander's shoulder gently, as she sat down beside him.

He wanted to live, so he had a decision to make on how much he trusted her. He wrapped his arm around her shoulders, trying to keep things light for now. "Gregory knows how to shield its presence. A little won't hurt because we can keep it from detection, but we have to be careful tapping into yours, since we might not be able to completely cloak it. No one is sure exactly how much magic is still inside you." *It would be a heck of a lot easier if they did.*

Kate smiled, making him feel a little guilty for his constant evasion of the truth. "You sure know how to lay it all out there. I'm not sure I want to know how much is inside me right now anyway. I'm taking baby steps so I can deal with everything."

He didn't have time for baby steps. He needed all out leaps of faith. If he could get her to fall for him, she'd willingly follow his lead and trust him, and he had the advantage of their built-in attraction. Neither of them had much control over its pull, once activated. First, he had to get her alone and find out what made her tick.

"We'll have to get a lot of rest tonight." Xander deeply inhaled and laced his fingers through hers. "But would you ladies like to take a look around and walk a little bit?"

Angie stood and stretched. "Actually, I'd like to read for a little bit and soak in the peaceful moment, while giving my brain a break from the overload. We haven't had many of those moments the last couple days." She laughed and grabbed her book, then moved to a quiet spot under a nearby tree.

"I wouldn't mind taking a walk, so I can clear my head." Kate smiled. She had broken their connection established during the dragon ride. It surprised him when she stood and extended her hand out to him. Maybe the whole situation wasn't as hopeless as it seemed.

"How about you, Greg?"

Gregory was checking the tents, separating the supplies, and reinforcing the protective spells. "Go ahead, I'll stay here and finish all this up. If the bookworm over there wants to go later, we'll catch up. After all, torture has always been my favorite pastime anyway." He smirked in Angie's direction, and she glared at him over her book. They went back to their mutual efforts of ignoring each other.

Xander led Kate through the thick trees and brush, until they came to a small stream. They walked silently, side by side for a few minutes, letting their thoughts gather. He needed some answers and wanted to know what kind of life she'd had. "What do your parents think about your career choice? Will you need to call them?"

He immediately noticed her hesitation. "My dad ran off not long after I was born. He couldn't handle my unique abilities." She whispered. "My mom remarried and he's a good guy, but we struggled to connect at times. I think he feared me a little, too. Mom tried her best to raise me, but early on I showed signs of my gifts. I know she loves me, but she didn't know how to deal with it all. Mostly I was raised by my grandfather. I called him Papa, and he was my stability — my *everything* — while I was growing up. He passed away several years ago."

She paused and dipped her hand in the stream. Xander watched the memories play across her face. It obviously had not been easy growing up in this realm, where her gifts were shunned, not praised. "To answer your question, I haven't spoken to my mother in a while. She knows what I do, and I can feel that she worries. A part of her expects this job to kill me, so I don't keep her in the loop. It would be nice to someday tell her exactly who she raised. If I survive all this, that is. And you?" He sensed she'd grown tired of talking and dredging up old memories.

"My parents are very different. I've only known them as protectors of our world and of all other creatures and realms. My oldest sister used to tell us stories. How they were before the last war. Full of life and traveling all over the dimensions.

"My older brother died during the last Rising, and then fate chose me as the next Guardian. The odds on a guardian's life aren't all that great. I can't imagine what they have suffered, and yet they still move forward. If I survive all this, I hope my parents will find some peace." He hadn't meant to say all of that, but once the words started, he couldn't stop them. Time to move on to another topic. One that had been bothering him.

"What about the guy you mentioned back at the apartment? I mean marriage is a serious thing to throw out there. Are the two of you engaged?" He worked hard to keep accusation out of his tone.

"Trey is a great guy, and we probably could have made a comfortable life together. I hate to admit it, Angie was right at least on one account. He would never have accepted this part of my life. I would have spent my entire life in hiding waiting for the day that he walked away.

"We both wanted simple, but I wasn't born for that. He doesn't even know that I returned from my last case. I think I knew — after everything that happened in that alley — it was over." Despite hearing the pain in her voice, at least Xander knew he had been right. It was convenience, not *love*, between the two of them.

He mulled over their conversation and came to the realization that she wanted acceptance for who she really was, and he guessed only Angie had given her that so far. It explained why their bond ran so deep, and it also left an opening for him to fit in. If he could show her what they could accomplish together, she would easily cross over to the Meadows. He might even be able to weaken her bond with Angie, so she wouldn't hesitate when the time came to leave her behind. His life depended on it.

He had no desire to fall in love, especially after he witnessed Xavier's devastation when his wife died. But as partners, they could conquer anything. He ignored the niggling at the back of his subconscious that he had already begun to fall for the brownish-blond, blue-eyed hellion.

He absolutely refused to feel the kind of pain he felt in his twin every day. Hell, he carried a portion of it. The tightening in his chest when Kate was near, the fear when she was in danger, and the mark of possession he was desperate to place on her, were all aberrations of his need to survive, and do his duty for his people. Nothing else. Nope. He wasn't giving in to feelings.

They continued walking and he asked her opinion on different cases, college, and other parts of her past. Kate hadn't had the glamorous life he pictured, but she had made the most of it and never gave up. He admired the steel in her, while noting the compassion and kindness that were second nature to her.

The moonlight gave her an ethereal appearance, and her eyes were bright as sapphires. Her steps were soft on the grass, as she continued to gaze in his direction. She studied him. He wanted to ask what she saw. Could she see the good in him, like he could her? Or was he too damaged to hold that kind of light?

Part of him wanted to invoke the rights of the guardian and take her right now. The images of her body wrapped around his haunted his dreams every night. Bound for eternity. The other part knew that even with a predestined fate, there was still a choice. Plus, if he completed the binding process, he would probably seal his fate as a human and die. Would it be worth it?

He wanted her in every way possible — plain and simple. Having patience was difficult, especially when he had been waiting for nearly thirty years. She was his, and he wanted her to know it. He had the insane desire to rear back his head and yell, *Mine! Mine! Mine!*

Xander tugged Kate's hand until she stood in front of him. His head slowly descended. His mouth captured hers in a deep, slow kiss. He broke contact long enough to place kisses on her forehead, cheeks, nose, and returned to her mouth. He quickly spun her toward the tree and pushed her against it.

She ran her hands through his hair. She arched toward him, fitting perfectly against his body. She made a purring sound in the back of her throat. Their tongues danced, and desire overcame sanity.

His tattoo throbbed, pushing him to complete the bond. He reached the edges of her shirt and steadily moved it up. The touch of lace was the only thing separating him from his goal. He flicked his fingers and accessed the beautiful mounds he dreamt about. She was his. Time to claim her. Consequences be damned.

12

"Guys, where are you?" Angie called out.

Kate connected, to warn her not to come too close.

She and Xander quickly straightened up, like two teenagers caught by their parents. Amazing how easy it had been to lose control.

"We're heading back toward camp. See you in a few," Kate hollered, but didn't expect a response. She sensed Angie was already gone.

Kate struggled to get her breathing under control. She kept telling herself that now was the time to stay focused, but her body demanded a different type of focus. Oh, how she wanted to give in to those desires.

Xander appeared even worse off than her. His angered expression and heaving chest gave away how much he wanted her, too. He still hadn't completely relinquished his grip on her, and for a moment, she wasn't sure he would. Then, he leaned down and softly kissed her lips. With a wave of his hand, he returned her clothes to their original position. He muttered an apology and grasped her hand. They started walking to camp.

Kate wasn't sure what to feel anymore. She should hate this man. He'd dragged her away from every dream of a normal life. So why didn't she? He certainly hadn't been warm and friendly. They fought more than they agreed. Maybe Angie had a point, Kate had never felt as alive as she did right now. One thing she knew for certain. She'd never go back to her old life.

She had called Trey from the hotel. She'd slipped into the bathroom and told him she was accepting an undercover assignment that could take months or years. He hadn't even seemed too upset. More like he'd been inconvenienced. Her boss had granted the extra time off but had hinted it would take her out of the running for the promotion. No, she could never go back. There would be too many questions. She and Angie would have to find a new way of life. You can't un-see what has been seen.

Xander was a hunter, like her. So, where did that leave them? No doubt in her mind, they had plenty of chemistry. If she couldn't have a normal life, then maybe in this new world she could find someone like Xander, who would accept all of her. Even if they only connected for a moment in time, would it fill her with enough memories for a lifetime? Tempted, she might have to give it a try.

Gregory and Angie had finished setting up camp by the time they returned. Everyone was still a little too pumped up to go to sleep, so they all sat around the fire. Kate wanted to know so much more but was afraid of the answers. So far, not many had been beneficial to her.

Silence made the time stand still. Like watching a clock that never moved. It didn't help she could hear the adrenaline pumping through their veins at what lay ahead. She opted to gain some more information and maybe bring some calm into the atmosphere. "Tell me more about your Ancient Council. When will I meet them?"

Xander seemed relieved when she finally spoke. "The Ancient Council is the governing body for most magical species. There are a few that have their own leadership structure. It has five members that rotate in and out as a current member steps down or dies. They are chosen by markings that appear on the palm of their hand, once they have proven themselves worthy and beyond corruption. Our current set have been in power for at least four-hundred years, some longer. The battle I mentioned earlier occurs every four to five-hundred years. Depending on casualties, the Council may change at that time."

"Who chooses them?"

"We don't know for sure. There are many different beliefs based on differing religions, but it comes down to a higher power or fate. Some believe that when the Mystic is born, several of our destinies are rewritten, and that determines the Council members. Some believe it's based on the success of the Mystic, and others believe many different variations. It's never been recorded in our history, despite many searching for the answer. So, it has become an unspoken agreement, to accept that it is done by a higher power and move on."

"So, who is the current Council?" Angie asked, perking up. "Why aren't they helping us?"

"Now there's the million-dollar question," Gregory grunted, and glanced toward Xander with a raised eyebrow.

Xander shifted and glared back toward him. "I guess they are helping in their own way even though I'm having trouble with that question myself. Micah, our Seer, said that in his vision we were meant to travel in the human manner. If we don't, our chances for success diminish.

Since he sees the future, most go with what he says. Especially the other Council members. Rowena is the only one who can contradict him.

"They are *way* too complicated to get into all of it tonight, but I will tell you over time, before we arrive, so you're prepared. We'll start with Marcus and Rowena, since they're the closest to us on this particular journey.

"Marcus is the Council leader. He may also be called the Alpha since the demons use Omega to denote their leader. He took over when his predecessor died in the last Rising. He's a wizard with extraordinary power. No one knows spells and potions better than him." Kate felt the admiration in his voice.

"Rowena is also a Council member, and she is a Mystic and over a thousand years old."

"Whoa, hold up!" Kate shook her head. "If there's already a Mystic, why the heck am I being drug all over creation to fight a demon to the death?"

"Rowena is great, but she has become weary and ready to leave this time and place. Everyone knows she was ready to step down and spend time with her husband, when Cassius was born as the next Mystic. Unfortunately, Rowena's spouse died in the battle. The day you were born was the first time I had ever seen true happiness on her face. I realized later, that was because it meant she had another chance to join her husband by crossing over into the Eternal Realm. It's her fondest wish. Only duty holds her here."

Cassius had forgotten to mention that he was a Mystic in her vision. Was that why he was able to connect with her? Why hadn't he told her? She focused back on Xander.

"She'll be a great asset to you and will teach you how to use and control your powers. However, she cannot show you how to embrace the light, because she never had to do it, which I found out recently." Kate realized there was a lot more to that story than he was saying, and she also sensed pain inside him. Had Rowena deceived him in some way? It wasn't a question she could ask at this point.

It was obvious from Xander's fidgeting, he was ready to call it a night. She'd absorbed everything possible anyway. They all needed a good night's sleep but not until she asked one more question. "Xander, I noticed that all of the demons and minions that have attacked us so far have a large tattoo covering their arms. The one with all the flames. The word *rage* comes to mind every time I see it. Is it significant or common?"

He froze and exchanged an uneasy look with Gregory. It took him a full minute to respond. "Actually, the word you're looking for is *fury*. The leader of this particular group of assassins is *called* Fury. He has created a small army of followers called Wrath Assassins.

"He may not get many points for imagination with words, but his fighting skills are damn near perfect. I have a feeling we'll face him before this journey ends." Xander ducked into the tent, ending the conversation. Kate sensed a deep connection between Xander and this Fury demon. Would what he was hiding get her killed?

She crawled in the sleeping bag toward the back. She didn't want to admit it, but her body screamed for sleep. Xander stayed toward the front and scanned their surroundings. She knew he searched for his brother. She could barely keep her eyes open, and she hadn't even laid down yet. She'd have to search for more answers tomorrow.

Xander watched Kate sleep for a long time. Beautiful, but dangerous. He hadn't even contemplated that she would catch the tattoos. She was much more intuitive than he gave her credit for, and he would do well to remember it.

He leaned his head against the side of the tent; fatigue seeped into his bones. He hadn't felt this much of a drain on his powers since he and Xavier had faced off against Fury over fifty years ago. He didn't *want* to remember but didn't have the strength to push the memories away.

Fury's given name had been Furyik, an ancient name of honor. He was a hundred years older than Xander and had been known to occasionally dabble with the dark arts. He proved to be a brilliant warrior, so the Council had allowed him access into the Meadows, on the condition that he never touch dark magic again.

Despite his past, Xander and Xavier instantly connected to him and were in awe of his skills in magic and fighting. Since their older brothers had died in the previous battle, Furyik had taken them under his wing and taught them how to fight and be excellent warriors. He hadn't kept his promise. He had become their greatest enemy.

His future was looking less and less lengthy.

Giving into exhaustion and trusting Xavier to protect them, Xander crawled over beside Kate. Obviously sensing his presence, she turned toward him and placed her hand on his chest. She snuggled closer to his warmth and tucked her head under his chin. For this moment, he could at least pretend that she cared, and that he had finally come home. He held on tightly to keep all his fears at bay and drifted into a blissfully dreamless sleep.

After catching a few hours' sleep, it was time for Kate to wake up, grab a quick bite to eat, and get down to business. She intended to be prepared the next time she faced a demon.

Kate and Angie quickly ate and cleaned up the food and trash, then they headed over to a nearby tree to stretch. Both were pretty excited to be doing some training. They talked about it all morning.

Gregory and Xander walked over to a decent-size clearing to set up the makeshift dummies and lay out the weapons for practice. Xavier had found time to drop off the supplies before dawn. Despite their training in law enforcement, they had little experience in handling monsters.

"We'll start with the basics," Xander said. "First, hand to hand. Gregory and I will fight as the demons, using their usual ploys and strategies. Both of you will try to get us in a position that you could take our heads off, but try to be careful. We don't have much time, so our sessions will be pretty intense."

Kate smirked. She and Angie both had their arms crossed over their chests, and their eyebrows rose in indignation.

"Do they really think we are that inadequate?" Angie huffed.

Kate sent her a smile and a mental shrug. *"Be careful Ang, we've faced these demons and know they have a serious advantage."*

Angie grinned. *"What do you want to bet they actually don't go full force the first time?"*

"I'd say that's a good bet, and we'll press our advantage." Over the past few days, Kate had learned how to block their conversations from Xander. It gave them a slight edge. Some days, it was great to be the Mystic.

They lined up in pairs, prepared for a showdown. Each side had something to prove. Gregory and Xander launched into offensive tactics, but the girls were ready for them. Moving quickly to the side, they got out of the way, so the guys caught nothing but air. Now, Kate and Angie took their turn and went full force into attack mode together, back-to-back.

Xavier watched from the shadows, impressed by their moves and agility. He had never seen humans quite as skilled. The guys still hadn't been able to pin them. Kate and Angie were perfectly synchronized; moving in and out, ducking punches, while exhausting the guys with kicks to the knees and shins. Then, the ladies took it up a notch.

He continued to stare in fascination and couldn't have turned away, even if he had wanted to. It was addicting to watch their fluidity and grace. Every punch, kick, or movement kept them out of danger and delivered blows to their opponent. Their biggest disadvantage was endurance. Despite their success so far, they quickly wore out. Physical training would be key, especially for Angie, since she would be fighting as a human.

Xander and Gregory gained the upper hand. They circled the girls and closed in for the final blow. Kate and Angie latched hands. Angie launched into the air. She kicked Gregory with such force that she knocked him off his feet. He landed with a hard thud.

Kate waited until Xander's eyes glanced toward Gregory and attacked. She vaulted all her weight toward him and landed the perfect jump kick into his upper chest. He fell backward and landed on his butt. Kate moved into position and pinned him to the ground. She made a slashing motion with her hand to denote the kill. A quick glance to her right showed Angie straddling Gregory in the same manner.

Gregory slowly got up and dusted off his backside. "Holy shit! Maybe *we* need the extra training. Our asses just got handed to us by a couple of humans. I've never even seen some of those moves before." He walked over to grab a drink of water, still rubbing his behind.

Xavier wanted to cheer but maintained his silence.

Xander approached Kate with his hands up as a shield. "Don't attack. I come in peace." He laughed and leaned forward, then kissed her on the cheek. "Great work. We weren't completely holding back, and you were able to take us in hand to hand. Now, let's try swords and see where your skills are there." Whether he wanted to admit or not, he was quickly falling for the blue-eyed Mystic.

"Before we start with weapons," Kate suggested, "I say we switch partners and work a little more on our technique. It looked like you guys could use a few extra pointers." Angie took a drink of water. Gregory shrugged and walked over. "We'll see about that. Let's try it one more time, switching partners. Ready, Kate?"

"Always." Kate stretched and headed toward him, keeping her stance confident and a little cocky. Xavier was a little more worried with this round. Xander wouldn't care, but Gregory hated to lose. Greg's behavior toward

Angie bothered him even more than his asinine antics. Xavier couldn't put his finger on it, but he didn't want him anywhere near Angie.

Xander growled a little, not completely hiding his possessive instincts. Xavier rolled his eyes. *What a dumbass.* He couldn't see that he had fallen for Kate during their first dance. When the whole truth came out, it was going to be ugly and heartbreaking.

Gregory raised his eyebrows and looked straight at Xander. "She will be sparring with everyone back home. Better work this out of your system now and get over it."

"Hope you can stay focused on little ole me over here." Angie didn't bother to hide her smile or knowing look as she taunted Xander.

Finally, looking and paying attention to Angie, he refocused. "Count on it!"

Xavier wasn't sure who he was cheering for but had a sneaking suspicion he was leaning toward the girls.

They went at it again. This time Gregory and Xander separated the girls. Kate and Angie weren't discouraged and still went into full force attack. After several minutes, the guys wore them down again. The girls held their own — barely. Xander and Angie called a draw and sat down to watch Gregory and Kate since neither seemed willing to call a truce.

Kate launched several feet off the ground and hit Gregory with a side kick straight to the chest. He flew off his feet and landed five feet away on his backside. Kate put her hand to his throat before he could react. "Gotcha." Xander's and Angie's mouths hung open.

Gregory jumped upright, furious. "No Fair! We're not using magic and you levitated." He sounded pretty agitated even though Xavier knew most of it was wounded pride.

"I what?" Kate asked in disbelief.

Xander rushed over and put his arm around her. "Are you sure she tapped into her power? She's not supposed to be able to do that yet."

"I felt the air shift until I got knocked on my ass." He got up and walked over to a log to get his breath.

"I certainly didn't do it on purpose," Kate fired back, defensive and frustrated.

Xander wrapped his arms around her shoulders and pressed her back against his body. "Of course you didn't mean to. It means you're gaining more of your powers. At least to a small extent. That's definitely something we need to explore. They'd be a great asset if we could develop them and find out exactly what you can do."

Xavier couldn't believe his eyes. The Council had led them to believe she was helpless in her human form. Had they not known all the powers she possessed, or were they still hiding information? It was time to start doing some research of his own. Could they tap into enough of her powers to buy more time for Xander? If they had to face Fury before the Meadows, Xander wouldn't survive without her help.

Xander kept his arm around Kate, while Gregory sulked. "Why don't we review weapons for a while and choose one that fits the girls best. Then, we can work on the dummies." He glanced toward Angie, grinning. "The *stuffed* kind."

Xavier wanted to be a part of the action. He hadn't felt this much happiness in a long time. He wanted Angie to kick Gregory's ass all the way back to whatever rock he'd crawled from.

"The dummies will allow us to illustrate demon weak spots and disabling techniques to reduce your active fighting time." Xander pointed to his left. Gregory mumbled but laid out the multitude of weapons that Xavier had provided.

He pointed to each as he spoke. "These are some of the different types of weapons and swords you'll encounter from both sides. As you can see, some are wider and heavier, while others are smaller and lightweight. But don't let size fool you." He picked up a long sword, then tossed it to Kate.

She caught it by the handle. "It feels like holding a feather." She easily tossed it back to him.

"The ones we're using today aren't sharp, just in case." Gregory pointedly stared at Angie. After a long-winded description of swords, axes, and athames, Angie and Kate picked the ones they liked best. Xavier assumed they'd chosen those that were the most lightweight, to assist their endurance levels, but Kate's was slightly longer than Angie's. They spent an hour with Gregory and Xander learning proper techniques and stances. Slashed to bits, the dummies would have to be replaced for tomorrow.

Xavier silently watched all afternoon. He had wanted to shout for joy when Kate knocked Gregory on his behind. So much elation had coursed through him he almost popped out of the shadows to congratulate her.

His concern grew when they started working with swords. Gregory hadn't mastered swords, mainly because he'd always relied too much on magic to see him through. Angie would need perfect swordsmanship to survive a demonic fight. Sighing, he rubbed his face and grimaced.

If only *he* could teach them, Angie's chances of survival would be much higher. For some reason, he'd become obsessed with Angie surviving the fight. Maybe she would be his redemption for Lily, if there was such a thing. He should have listened to Rowena years ago. Now, it was too late for him, but maybe not for her. The real world terrified him, and he couldn't find his way back. He had to start trying for all their sakes. He needed to save Angie and atone for his past grievous wrongs, so he swore to himself to make this right. No longer able to watch, he left to check in with Zane.

The sun faded into the horizon, the last of its rays filtering through the trees. The four of them headed back to camp and had a quick dinner. Afterward, they all laid down on the soft grass to cool off.

Kate had so many questions circling in her head. She knew they each had their own doubts and fears but continued to put on the brave front. She was sore in places she hadn't even known existed. Especially in her arms. Since the guys looked winded, too, she felt a *little* better.

Several of the questions floating in her mind became too loud to ignore. She sat up and leaned against the tree. "I understand who the Council is, and that they represent the governing body, but how do they keep control when they have communities all over the world and in multiple realms? It seems impossible."

Xander squatted down beside her and leaned against the tree. "You're still thinking with human restrictions. You have to begin to expand your mind beyond the obvious."

"I *am* human," she muttered, while playfully glaring. She sensed his frustration, but still couldn't accept the fact she *wasn't* going to stay a human. What would this big transformation do to her? He himself had said she was born as one but would change during this ceremony. She didn't want to change. She didn't want to die either.

Xander leaned his head back and stared up at the stars. "The Council is strict in their enforcement of policies.

"Rowena, Micah, and other Seers are able to discover numerous problems before they even occur. Or, at least they can see them as soon as they occur and act quickly. The issue is dealt with immediately, and swift justice is carried out to send the message that certain behaviors will not be tolerated. It's a hard cross to bear because many of the situations are initiated by humans. Their fairness and efficiency create respect and boundaries. And no one wants to cross Rowena or Marcus."

Gregory harrumphed and shook his head. "Or they get tortured if they do."

Xander glared a warning with his eyes. Kate felt the tension in the air rise. He silently told Gregory to shut up. "Yes, they do have forms of punishment, but the crime has to be severe enough to warrant it."

"What kind of problems or crimes are we talking about?" Angie asked, showing her curiosity. "I'm assuming they're different from the human world since everything else has been."

"Hurting or killing humans and magical beings are the worst crimes, and are sometimes punishable by death," Xander replied. "That's why Tristan, another Council member, has warriors searching constantly for rogues. He's in charge of our warriors. Some are given a chance for redemption, but most are given a death sentence depending on the severity of their crimes. Other offenses include exposing our magic to humans. We can't afford to start another crusade or war. We have enough to focus on with the Rising. We're much more dependent on each other than humans."

Kate scrunched her eyebrows together in concentration, trying to understand. "That actually doesn't sound too bad. It sounds like your justice works quicker than ours. Plus, you have the advantage of reading minds and predicting the future. That definitely helps. Our world has death penalties and different forms of punishment." She shrugged, not overly concerned with the whole idea.

Gregory grunted before Xander could answer. He stood up and walked toward the tents. Obviously, he didn't like this part of the conversation.

"Why does it bother Gregory?" she asked Xander.

"Some in our communities feel we shouldn't be punished if humans get hurt or get in the way. As I mentioned before, many magical beings feel superior and upset that they have to hide in another realm. The most typical punishment for human exposure is being stripped of our powers for a year and living in the human world. It's designed to teach us humility and respect and serve as a reminder about who we are responsible for protecting. It's our purpose in this world."

Gregory stalked back over to where they were sitting. "Basically, everyone fears the Council in a way. Wouldn't you? Together they have absolute power to do anything. The only thing that could stand against them and win is a full powered Mystic or the Omega on the night of the Rising. Ready for your glowing future yet?" Gregory's eyes glistened with resentment.

He paced back and forth. *Wow, he has some serious issues.* Kate certainly hadn't intended to open this can of worms.

"You don't realize the levels of power they possess," Gregory continued. "Yet all our hope resides in one single being raised in the human world. It's a lot to accept. No offense to you, Kate. But that's the reality of how many of us feel."

Xander quickly got to his feet, but Kate jumped up to intercede. "I appreciate your candor, Gregory, and must admit I even see your point of view. It must seem restrictive at times to feel like you're always in hiding. I *do* understand how you feel and have personally felt that way many times in my life. Maybe that's why I'll be able to do you justice. By the way, what do you mean a full powered Mystic?"

Xander raised his hand to silence Gregory. He'd heard enough from him for one day and still wanted to thump him. "He means that once the Mystic accepts the light, she is all powerful. Nothing can stand against her. We're dependent on her good judgment and purity of heart, to keep the communities safe and thriving. Our last Mystic, Cassius, received his mortal blow before the light entered his body, or he would be here today. Though many say he wanted to die, or possibly died on purpose. On the night of the Rising, the Omega, in your case, Braxus, will have a similar power based in negative energy or the dark light."

"Whoa." Angie sat back, wringing her hands. Xander recognized it as a sign of nervousness. He searched her mind and saw she was trying to find her place in this whole mess. "Has the Council ever allowed humans into your community?"

The instant tension of her question swooped in like a thick fog. Everyone, even Gregory, sucked in a breath. Someone finally asked it out loud. Unfortunately, none of them knew the answer. Xander spoke carefully, "No, their protective shield does not allow any human to cross, for their own safety as well as ours. We'll be traveling through a portal, but I've never known a human to make it through one. This situation is different though, and I don't know." He shrugged and looked at Angie apologetically, knowing he hadn't provided much comfort.

"That's quite a problem you've got there, considering Angie and I are human," Kate said with raised brows. "Didn't your precious Seer, or whoever it is, see this coming?"

Gregory took a step back. Xander glared at him and called him a coward through their link. "We think the portal will recognize you as the Mystic and allow access, despite you still being partially human. I don't know about Angie. She wasn't a part of our original plan, so we never considered it. Xavier is trying to research it, but he hasn't found anything yet." He looked ruefully at Angie. "But we're going to try."

"Try? What the hell?" Kate stood against the tree. "She goes or I don't. I will *not* cross over if Angie isn't allowed in the portal. Figure something out if you can. If not, lean over and kiss your ass goodbye!"

Kate went over to the tent and leaned her head against the side. Angie followed her and put her arm around her shoulders. Xander realized Angie was using their mental link to help comfort Kate. He rubbed his hands over his face and through his hair. He knew she wasn't joking. If he was honest with himself, he'd known it all along. He'd avoided the issue, because he didn't have an answer. If Angie couldn't cross and Kate refused, he was as good as dead.

"It's worse than you think." Xavier popped into his head. *"The two of them are irrevocably linked. Zane studied it himself. Their bond cannot be broken by man or magic, so Kate will not leave her behind. How are you going to get her through the portal?"*

Well hell. Xander closed his eyes and sighed. *"I have no idea. How about you?"*

"No, I don't. I'll try to ask around and see if Zane knows of a way, but his knowledge is more limited now. On another note, the demons have regrouped and are heading in your direction. They haven't picked up your essence yet, but it's only a matter of time. You'll have one more day, and then it's time to move on to the next location. I've already set everything up, and I also put an extra shield in place.

"Kate needs to start working on her magic. She has more abilities than anyone realizes, including the Council. I can feel it trying to break through, but she has phenomenal control. It may be her powers that allow Angie into the portal, so she needs to master them. Just a guess though." Xander felt Xavier's weariness of hiding, as he disconnected and returned to the shadows.

Angie grabbed her backpack and sat down, so he walked over to the tent and placed his arms around Kate, filling her with calming energy. The possibility of losing Angie had taken a toll on her usually unbreakable composure. He kissed her softly to get her thoughts moving in another direction. Distraction was his best weapon at the moment. Maybe it was selfish, but he had to keep her focused on the portal. "We'll find a way," he whispered in her ear. "Have faith." Goose bumps appeared on her arms.

Kate nodded and leaned into him, letting all the tension ease out of her.

He considered it a freaking miracle, that despite everything, she had started to trust him. He felt the bond between them growing. It created emotions both elated and guilty at the same time, because he didn't want to keep secrets. This was for her own good. Maybe if he told himself that enough, he'd start to believe it.

He stroked her hair and held her for a few more moments, until she had completely relaxed. "Gregory, how about you show Angie some more disarming techniques and some tricks that usually work with most demons. I'm taking Kate down by the river to work on meditation and focus. If she can tap into her powers, she needs to control them. Xavier thinks we'll be able to use some magic at our next location."

Xander sensed the unrest and worry inside Kate but didn't know how to help her. She had to come to terms on her own, to accept who she would become. "Kate," he whispered. "What's going on in that head of yours?" He tried to keep it light and not put her on the defensive again.

She leaned against his shoulder. "All these powers I'm going to have frighten me beyond belief. I could've hurt Gregory today, or someone else, and I didn't even know what I was doing. Or even that the magic came out of me for that matter."

"That's why we're heading down here to work with meditation and focus, so you can control it next time. You'll learn to become one with your abilities and pull from the energy surrounding you. You'll begin to accept the power as part of you, until one day, you'll realize it's second nature. Until you have complete control of your powers, your emotions can trigger all sorts of unpleasant responses. But I'll be here to help until you can contain it." Her tentative smile gave him hope that she was ready to embrace her inner self. He hoped so anyway.

They arrived at the river. He laid down a blanket and motioned for her to sit down. He sat behind her and rubbed her shoulders. After a few minutes, he believed she was ready to face the inevitable.

He turned her so they faced each other, linked hands, and closed their eyes. Their breathing synchronized moments later.

Kate found total peace within herself. It was like floating on a cloud. She let her conscious level drift away. She felt as if she were no longer bound to Earth but could go anywhere with her mind alone. She turned her face toward the sky, and her mind and energy soared free. Xander's mind connected with hers, and she reached toward him. She anchored her spirit to him, and a sensation of security washed over her. She explored her psyche and searched for her special abilities.

She observed the constant struggle between her mind and spirit over her powers. A mental wall that she couldn't quite break through. She'd erected the wall to be normal when she was young. Focusing all her mental energy toward that wall, she pushed to break through the barrier and unleash her gifts.

She wasn't sure if it had taken minutes or hours, but she finally broke through the wall and felt her powers course and connect throughout her body and spirit. It was mostly pure energy. Her entire being charged like a live wire. She examined several of her abilities like levitating and telepathy, and what each felt like on a subconscious level.

Each had their own distinctive flow of energy, so she could learn to control each one. She continued her search and saw many more waiting to be activated. She approached the many types of energy to sort them out. A jolt hit her system and flung her back into consciousness.

Disoriented and slightly groggy, her first thought was that something had happened and Xander brought her back. She realized *she* had broken the connection, not Xander. *What exactly had happened?* Sweat dripped down her face, and her hands shook. Something had terrified her, but what? Reaching for Xander, she sought his calming energy, so she could begin to sort through what had happened in her mind. He pulled her into his lap and held her tight.

Xander stayed quiet, while Kate worked everything out in her mind. He gently rocked her and surrounded her with calming energy. He was trying to soothe her enough to help her face what she had seen. He saw it, too. She was full of power, scarily so. Many she could already access, once she learned how to deal with them, instead of going into overload. Kate feared it.

He had been so proud when she broke through the barrier and tried to take control, but neither had been prepared for how many gifts and pure energy resided in her body. The magnitude of the release of magical energy had been too much for her human body to accept. They still had a lot of work to do before she released all her powers.

He honestly didn't know if her human body could withstand that much energy pumping through her veins. If it got released before she could control it, he wasn't sure he would be able to stop it. He had to admit he was pretty shaken at the amount of power inside her, not that he'd ever tell her that. He began to have doubts about the Awakening ceremony and what all they hadn't been told.

Kate's breathing returned to normal after a few minutes, and she stopped shaking. Xander was filled with relief, a little desperation, and a whole lot of hormones. The energy dose had set his sexual drive on fire, and he could feel the responding energy pouring from her. Not able to resist any longer, he tilted her chin toward his mouth and plunged into her waiting lips. The need to release their pent-up energy and fears overwhelmed him.

He pushed her down to the ground and onto her back without breaking their connection. His head roared. He couldn't get enough. He wanted everything right now. No more waiting. His hands slid under her shirt. He completely removed it using his magic. Fire caressed her skin, and his. He unfastened her bra and sent it flying. Her skin glistened in the moonlight. She tasted like heaven, and he wanted more. A lot more.

Kate moaned and strained beneath him, drawing him closer. He knew she needed a release for all her pent-up energy. She felt like a wild firestorm. He moved lower down her body, and she cradled his head. He totally lost it. His vision replaced by a lustful haze.

Xander rose up and plundered her mouth. He ran his hands up and down her sides and abdomen. He connected with her emotions, igniting a fire hotter than the blazes of Hell. He wanted her more than he wanted his next breath. He returned to her breasts. He slowly moved his hands down her stomach toward his goal. Tonight, she'd be his.

"Xander? Kate? Where the hell are you? It's been hours!" Gregory yelled through the trees.

Xander sent a couple of mental warning shots that quickly sent Gregory back to camp.

"Un-freakin-believable," Gregory mumbled.

Xander sent another small blast into the woods, so he wouldn't come any closer. He growled, trying to get control, when his body didn't want to leave Kate's. He breathed heavily and counted backward.

He had been about to fully merge with Kate, and once again they were interrupted. Maybe it was fate. The last thing he needed was to turn fully human and leave her with no protection from Fury. He would kill her for sure.

Xander refocused on their surroundings, and he came back to reality. He allowed his attraction to Kate to overcome his mind again. They were sitting ducks out here, completely oblivious. They'd have to finish this soon, if they were going to have clear heads, but tonight wasn't the night. *"Ok, Gregory, we'll be there in a few minutes."*

Kate moaned beneath him. She pulsed — painfully — with excess energy. "We have time. Let's finish this."

He groaned, took a deep breath, and pushed off of Kate, landing beside her. His body howled in protest. "No, I won't take you on the ground in desperation. I want our first time to be because we're both ready, not because we became lust-crazy and jumped at each other. And I want plenty of time to explore every inch of you — not a quick fix." He leaned forward and lightly kissed her, not wanting to set off another explosion. His chivalry could only extend so far, and deep in his gut he knew it wasn't time yet. He had to get her to the portal before his powers disappeared.

"Try explaining that to my body, which is on fire, by the way."

"I've got an idea." He lifted her up, removed the rest of his clothing with a wave of his hand, and jumped into the freezing cold river, taking her with him. "See, now we can cool off."

Kate glared, teeth chattering. "This is *not* what I had in mind." After a few minutes she had obviously gotten used to the water, and smiled at him.

Xander led Kate from the water and leaned his head against hers.

She laughed and wriggled her eyebrows. "Well, I see you're certainly interested in me. But do you want me for my body, or my mind?" She wiggled a little, and he jerked in response. He groaned, waved his hand, and they were fully clothed. "Both." He smiled, and they started walking back to camp. One thing he knew for sure, if he was going to die in this world, he would take this human and make her his before fate claimed him.

By the time they returned to camp, Gregory and Angie had already cleared up everything from dinner and their practice sessions. They all sat down around the fire before extinguishing it for the night and began to work out the details of traveling to their next location site. Even though they were tired from a full day, Xander wanted to make sure everyone understood the plan and to discuss the new glitch with the travel and rations that Gregory had discovered, while they'd been down by the river.

"We'll be staying in Montana for the next leg of the journey," Xander explained, leaning forward. "If we get a chance, we may try to rent a car and drive. But if the demons are getting close, it'll be too risky considering they have proven they know how to get rid of one. More than likely, we'll travel on motorcycles through some of the old trails. Especially ones that people tend to frequent.

"We need to mix the scents and blend in as humans, so we're harder to trace. The only thing in our favor right now is that demons don't want to be discovered any more than magical beings. They don't want to be hunted on both fronts. That idiot you fought in the alleyway in Boston was a rare exception of a demon so crazed, he didn't care anymore."

"So," Angie said, tapping her foot. "We're all going to be on bikes? Won't that kind of give us away?"

"Not exactly how you're thinking. I know it sounds bizarre and unprotected." He paused. "We'll be paired up on the bikes. If an emergency occurs, we can shapeshift into something else and fly away from the area quickly." Both girls groaned in unison.

He didn't feel the need to add that he couldn't sustain a shapeshift for that long anymore. He had to retain as much power as possible to face off against Fury. He could feel him searching for them. He wouldn't strike until he could see what each of them could do first.

"I'm still not sure about traveling during the day," Kate said doubtfully. "It seems much safer to stay on the move while demons are out, instead of being sitting ducks."

Gregory broke into his thoughts. *"So, she doesn't like the idea. Too bad. Don't get soft on me. I don't like staring down death every day because you stupidly touched her leg trying to help. It just is what it is, and we must adapt."*

Xander cut the connection and focused back on Kate's concerns. "Not if you're posing as humans. Zane has found a way to mask Kate's powers so it will seem like four humans riding a trail known to have human riders. Since he exists only in the shadows, it's impossible for demons to fully track him. It will take a few days to get to our next site, but Xavier thinks we need to stay off the radar for a while. The next site we're going to belongs to a magical family very loyal to the Council, and they're our friends.

"We need time and real rest, if we're going to continue serious training. They already have protections in place, so we'll hide under their shield. Hopefully, that will buy us enough time to start practicing some of your magic, discuss strategies, and answer more of your questions." Xander tried to hide his weariness. Nothing about this journey had been ideal, except the relationships they had built.

Kate frowned and still looked apprehensive. She wrung her hands, and her leg rapidly bounced. Xander recognized it as a bad habit, when she had a lot on her mind. "It still seems riskier than anything we've chosen so far," she said. "Trails are hard to secure like Angie said, and now we'll be involving other people in all this mess."

"We have to change up our ways every time to keep the demons and minions guessing. If they ever get one step ahead, we'll be toast. Hiding as humans is one option they won't even consider, because they automatically assume we'll always keep you hidden." Xander was actually impressed with Xavier's plan. It was the perfect disguise. He'd always been an excellent strategist. He sensed Kate was still not convinced.

"Makes sense to me," Angie said. At least she seemed to be coming on board. "But it'll be a lot of wear and tear on us all. We'll need a lot of rest along the way to make it work." Angie looked over at Kate, who begrudgingly nodded. "But I must admit I'm uncomfortable with the fact I'm going to be riding with Gregory for days." Xander watched her wince and shake her head, as soon as the words came out.

"Sounds entertaining to me and quite enjoyable," Gregory said. He walked over and put his arm around her. "We could put a whole new spin on the concept." He wiggled his eyebrows and leaned toward her, acting like he was going to kiss her.

"Puh-lease, you are so disgusting." She pushed him back and glared. Then, she cut her eyes and had a wicked smile. "Although, maybe you'll attract someone or something in a more attractive jackass form."

He walked away still laughing and went back to his seat on the other side of the fire. Xander caught his thoughts as he sat down. *One day she'll get her comeuppance for her smart-ass attitude. And I intend to be the one to do it.*

Xander hid his smile and shook his head. He didn't have time for a three-ring circus. He needed to stay focused, but a little comic relief was always welcome.

"Ok," Kate said. "I see the importance, but like Angie, I'm a little worried about endurance. And where are we getting all these supplies and food? We won't be able to use magic, because it would give us away."

Gregory cleared his throat and pointed toward the river. "That's why I was looking for you two earlier. I thought of the same thing. We don't want to establish a pattern of Xavier bringing us supplies, especially now that the demons know to track him. Zane can only cover so much. I was thinking I could go into town and stock up on whatever we can carry and pick up the bikes."

Xander sat there lost in thought, trying to look at all the ramifications that plan could bring. "That's not a bad idea. And it would also leave Xavier time to watch the demons more closely and set some more traps." He sighed in acceptance. What choice did they have? He sure as heck wasn't leaving Kate for a second. And Xavier wasn't strong enough to walk in this realm as an untraceable human. "When do you want to go?"

Gregory smiled mockingly at Angie. "I was thinking tomorrow afternoon, but early enough so we still have plenty of daylight for protection. Xavier will be close by if you need extra protection — right?" He couldn't quite hide the skepticism and distrust in his tone from Xander.

Xander rubbed his hands together and tried to work it out. The main priority was always the girls' safety. Should they take this risk? The benefits would be tremendous in keeping them hidden, but the cost could destroy the world. Although getting caught by the demons because they tracked them would have the same effect. And what about Xavier? Could he help if needed? Xander had his doubts, but mostly he was concerned he wouldn't be able to protect both girls. If they were attacked, he would have to make a choice. He knew what the choice would be.

Fury was the real problem. The time had come to tell Kate exactly who she was up against. She needed to know this wasn't only about her. It had more to do with him and Xavier. They should've known this would eventually come back to haunt them.

"Listen, before we decide on the final plan. I need to tell both of you what we're probably facing." He didn't want to add to their fear.

"For several years, Fury appeared to do everything the Council asked. Then, mysterious deaths began to occur within the Meadows. Unheard of, because most of its inhabitants were either immortal or had long life spans, as long as they stayed in the realm. The Council suspected someone had found a way through the portal, or someone had betrayed them.

"Eventually, it came to light that Furyik had been working both sides, but since he didn't actually harm the victims himself, his conscience remained clear. That's why he had been so difficult to trace.

"By this time, Xavier and I had become leaders of the militia for the Council. Our skills couldn't be equaled, especially if we were together. We were pulled into the Council hearing and told to capture and kill Furyik, by any means necessary. The Council also revoked his ability to enter the Meadows realm.

"When he was thrown out of the realm, it didn't take long for him to figure out that justice was coming for him. He changed his named to Fury and began recruiting others to help him escape. When he discovered that we were chosen to hunt him down, he went into hiding. He knew how powerful we were. He trained us.

"While he was hiding among the demons, Fury came across a unique set of armor that would deflect most magic. We finally found him, and even though we had heard stories of this armor, we had no choice but to try and kill him. He'd become an assassin for hire by this time and couldn't be allowed to survive. We fought for days using magic, sword, energy, and brute strength, but to no avail. The armor deflected any killing blow." Maybe they should have let him be, but he couldn't have lived with all of the blood on Fury's hands.

"Xavier finally convinced me that we may not be able to kill him, but we could strip his good powers that the armor didn't protect and revoke his ability to enter almost all of the realms. He would only have access to the Human realm and Hell realm. Even though some would still die, we couldn't find any other solution to save the majority of the realms that we had sworn to protect.

"We double-teamed Fury and blindsided him with the potion. He seemed shocked that a potion had worked, until he understood exactly what we had done. He'd been stripped of many of his powers and basically condemned to living among the humans or the demons. Most of his freedom had been taken. He vowed he would return and make us pay for what we'd done that day." Xander still woke often to the nightmares of Fury's screams, taunting him about what he would do to all of their loved ones, and to them one day.

Fury was patient and meticulous. Xander began to realize what a dangerous game they played. There was a reason his assassins had been chosen, and he would bet anything that Fury intended this to end in another battle. A bad omen, considering his strength was reducing daily, but Fury's only increased.

He also told them his suspicions that Fury requested this assignment and was determined not to fail. It put everyone at a higher risk, because Fury didn't want to just kill the Mystic. He wanted the Montgomery brothers to feel every kind of pain imaginable, and then some.

Gregory's astonished face spoke volumes, since Xander had never told the whole story to anyone except the Council. Xander silently apologized to him. "At the time, it seemed best to keep the whole thing quiet, but we're dealing with much more than a regular assassin team locked on the Mystic. This is full out military warfare, at least for Fury it is."

Kate decided the time had come for her to start acting more like a trained agent and less like a helpless female. She understood that Xander's biggest concern was their safety. She'd made plenty of tough choices and used unorthodox means to outsmart criminals before. It wasn't a different situation now, just a slightly different perspective. Crazy demonlords were not her usual cup of tea, but what in her life could be classified as normal?

She took his hand and squeezed. "It's a good idea Xander, and Xavier said they haven't found us yet. We may not get another chance, and we'd be prepared if Xavier got caught up trying to keep demons off of us. We can handle ourselves, especially with the minions, as long as he's back by nightfall." She brushed her hand across his cheek and gave him an encouraging nod.

Xander sighed. "Ok, we'll train in the morning, so you're as ready as possible. I'll work out the details with Xavier to make sure he's in place if needed." He turned his attention to Gregory. "Be quick. I don't want to waste much time with the girls not being fully protected."

Kate had never been a nail biter, but she sure felt like doing it now.

Gregory and Xander put out the fire and checked all the protection spells. Kate hung back with Angie. The four of them walked toward their tents to rest and prepare for training the next day. For once, there were no comments, jokes, or quips. The tension had become a heavy burden on them all. She couldn't even put a name on which part any of them feared the most.

Kate climbed in her sleeping bag and buried her head in her pillow. The emotions, fears, and uncertainties overwhelmed her. Sleep became her only escape.

Once Kate was settled and asleep against Xander's chest, he searched for his twin. He wasn't sure how Xavier would take this latest development.

"*Hey, what do you need? I was trying to get some sleep and felt you searching. I do still sleep, ya know,*" Xavier dryly said.

"Sorry to interrupt your beauty sleep. Lord knows you need it, but I want to run our idea by you." He proceeded to tell him what they had discussed over dinner and waited for his response. He could tell by his brother's hesitation, he was worried.

"*It's awfully risky,*" Xavier finally relayed. "*But I guess it would make a huge difference and leave me time, as Kate said. I'll be in the shadows right there with you while he's gone, but it will blind me somewhat to the demon activity. If I have to focus in tight on your camp, I can't see much past a thirty-mile radius. Make sure you check in with me before Gregory leaves. I want to check on their status and get in position.*"

Xavier had fully merged with Xander, so Xander could see he had a bad feeling about this new plan. Too many uncontrolled variables, but in truth, none of the demons were even headed their direction. The horrid fact was that Xavier didn't trust himself to come to the rescue. That was hard for a former — once considered–great warrior, to admit. Xander could only hope Xavier would find it in himself to overcome his past to save their future.

Watching Kate sleep, a sense of rightness washed over him. She belonged beside him every night of their eternal lives. *She's mine.* No one would take her away from him and live. He had fallen in love with his Mystic. Maybe Guardians and Mystics didn't have a choice with their destiny, but he would choose her no matter what destiny had in store for them. But would *she* choose *him* when she learned the truth? *"Thanks Xavier. Get some sleep. I'll catch you tomorrow."*

Xavier faded back in the shadows, and Xander held Kate tightly. *What will our lives be like if we survive?* What would their children look like? He smiled with that thought in his head and fell into a deep sleep, until the nightmares of the Rising replaced his cheerful dreams.

Kate awoke with the sunrise. The morning had come too quickly. After a light breakfast, they set up their plans and equipment for the day. In the back of her mind, she knew they were all worried how the afternoon would go without Gregory. She didn't even have to read any minds. It was clear with the somber faces, quiet atmosphere, and occasional fidgeting.

Trying to break some of the tension, she stood up and stretched. "What's on the docket for today, guys?"

Xander rose and began to clean the area and manifest weapons they'd need. "We're going to work with weapons for an hour, followed by a couple hours of martial arts. Then, we'll break for lunch and have a quick rest. I want everyone to be refreshed for tonight. After lunch, we'll finish up with some strength conditioning and a little light hand-to-hand, if there's still time. The important thing is for Gregory to leave in plenty of time to get back before nightfall." That was one point they all agreed on and couldn't afford any more of the *good luck* bestowed on them so far.

He'd decided to ask Rowena for help, but she didn't respond. Kate tried to understand their decisions but putting her in this much peril was plain irresponsible to their whole realm. If she was truly this all-powerful being, wouldn't they be sending out their armies to protect her? She was even more concerned about Gregory. He hadn't been his usual surly self this morning. His silence caused her more anxiety.

She walked forward and wrapped her arms around Xander's waist, and he pulled her close. She didn't want to admit it to herself or anyone else, but she needed him. She wanted his strength and his belief in her to keep from going insane. She liked having someone to hold her and help shoulder the responsibilities. He'd become as entrenched in her heart as Angie, but in a different way. "When are we heading out to the next site?"

"I figure after all we have to get done today, we'll need a good night's rest and head out early tomorrow morning." Xander tightly held onto Kate, as if he couldn't bear the separation. The stiffness in his back and shoulders revealed his attempts to hide his doubts and fears. Gregory rubbed his hands over his face and through his hair multiple times. He seemed more concerned than Xander.

Kate decided to listen to Gregory's thoughts and break her cardinal rule. If she could help ease his mind in any way, she would. *She's been watching me all morning, but what am I supposed to do? Give her a hug and say everything will be okay? This whole plan would turn into bullshit if Xavier couldn't pull his pansy ass out of the shadows and do something useful for a change. Twenty years hiding like a child, while I'm here busting my ass. I have to hide my own thoughts, so Xander won't get angry. We've already had too many fights over that piece of shit. Ok, just stay focused on the task at hand. If I can do that, maybe we'll survive. I'll protect Kate and Xander. If Xavier gets injured or goes crazy along the way, that'd be good too.*

Angie laughed at something Xander had said. A strange warm feeling went through his body. Kate struggled not to break the connection. *Great, I can't afford to start having feelings for her. I don't even like humans. They're always whiny and act entitled. But she makes me feel alive around her. The verbal sparring and physical training only make this stupid attraction worse. Was it them being thrown together in this situation or something more that sparked the interest? Was the Council interfering? I'll at least do a little investigating and maybe get to know her better.*

Kate broke the connection before he discovered her in his mind. There was nothing she could help him with. They all had personal baggage.

Weapons training was first. Gregory began with the swords and covered every other sharp weapon in the book. Angie and Kate could now use an ax better than ever before, and not for chopping wood. It was quite disturbing to be trained on how to take heads off. It would be worse when they were real.

The clash of the sword against the opponent's jolted Kate's body. Vibrations traveled up the entire length of her arm.

"Time!" Xander called out.

Kate breathed a huge sigh of relief and collapsed in the grass. Angie plopped down beside her. Feeling the sun warm her face, Kate sensed energy pulsing around her, and for once accepted its presence and tried to understand it. She relaxed and felt a little better, until they started the martial arts portion and pain took on a whole new meaning.

Xander and Gregory demonstrated crazy jump kicks and flips. By the end of the martial arts torture session, she'd learned many more take-down and disarming techniques than she'd thought possible. Feeling invigorated, she had a better understanding of her own skills. She connected with Angie and found she was exhilarated.

Covered in sweat and dirt, they all collapsed on the logs they'd set up in front of their tents. Kate wasn't entirely sure she'd ever be able to move or function in any capacity again. She would have preferred to magically appear and collapse in the sleeping bag, then wake up the next morning. *Next week would work, too.*

Gregory, the tyrant, would have none of that. If she didn't know better, she'd think he was punishing her for yesterday's kick. "Eat up, we still have physical conditioning to do before I leave. I thought we'd take a run by the river and then do push-ups and crunches. I don't want to risk bringing in a bunch of weights. We'll use what we've got for now."

"Don't work them too hard, Gregory." Xander cleaned up their supplies from the morning sessions. "We want them focused and energized while you're gone this afternoon."

Kate noticed that they always kept everything packed and ready to move at a moment's notice. Xander was covered in sweat and dirt, but still looked like he could run a marathon. Then with a wave of his hand across his face, he was as clean as if he just stepped out of the shower. Kate locked her jaw; it wasn't fair.

Kate winced. She stretched out her shoulders and tried to stand and extend her legs — both of which were still on fire. "I think adrenaline will take care of that. I imagine we'll be pretty amped up while Gregory's gone." She winced again as she worked more muscles that protested with every movement.

"Yeah, I think we'll be covered in that department. But I also don't want my muscles and bones to be jelly if I'm gonna have to fight." Angie worked the kinks out of her arms and legs, while wiping sweat out of her eyes.

Kate was grateful for Xander when he used his magic and freshened up both her and Angie.

Gregory held up his hands and smiled. "Okay, okay, I get it. We'll take a short run and only do a few other exercises for today, since we don't want to tire the *humans* out." They both glared at him. "But we're going to have to spend a lot of time working on strength and endurance at some point." He looked over at Angie. "Especially for you."

"I don't need the constant reminder. I know I'm human and will stay human. I get it, all right?" Angie moved directly in front of him. "Everyone doesn't have to keep reminding me how hard I'll have to work to fit in your world. I'll gain the strength I need and the knowledge to defeat the damn demons. I won't be put on the sidelines, so I'll learn to fight just like any of you."

She enunciated each word with a poke to his chest. She grabbed her bag and marched into the forest, with her arms across her chest. She leaned back against a tree, avoiding Kate's stare. An outburst like that was unusual for Angie.

Gregory whistled. "Touchy subject, I see."

"What was that about?" Xander asked.

"It's hard on Angie, knowing she'll be the only human in your world," Kate said. "She's a fighter by nature and used to being the best. Now, she constantly feels like the weak link." She could understand what Angie was feeling since lately she felt the same way herself most of the time. But, at least *she'd* gain powers at some point; Angie didn't even have that coming her way. She was stuck having to deal with the friction between her and Gregory. She missed their team and found it challenging to trust new people.

Xander pulled Kate's back against his chest and kissed her lightly. "She's good, and she'll learn how to hold her own and be that much better for it."

"Maybe, but she'll never be able to go back to a normal life after this, will she?" Kate didn't wait for his answer. She already knew it. "She'll always feel out of place like I have all my life. I don't want that for her, but I can't do all this without her. How selfish does that make me?" Kate sighed and tried to believe there was a special destiny out there for Angie in this new world. That way, she might feel like she was meant to be in the magical communities. It would never be a natural fit.

Xander tucked her head under his chin and rubbed her arms. "No, it doesn't. We all depend on someone to see us through. I need Gregory and Xavier. You need Angie. This isn't a battle that can be won alone. It takes hundreds of people, maybe thousands. We have to remember that we're doing this to save mankind from a fate worse than death. Angie wouldn't have it any other way, nor would you if you were in her shoes. In your heart, you know this."

Kate relaxed against him, letting his strength and belief in her convince her she was doing the right thing. She felt caught in a constant state of turmoil. Everything she had always clung to didn't seem to make sense anymore. The world was a brand-new place she didn't understand. She'd have to make new friends and create a new family in a place that couldn't be found on a map. She hadn't asked for any of this, but it was her burden to bear. Would she see it through? What would be the final cost? She needed to take a stand, but it was easier said than done.

Angie walked back toward them. Gregory finished stretching. He sauntered over to her and punched her lightly in the shoulder. "Let's head out," he said with a grin, then started running, leaving everyone else to catch up.

Angie groaned as she tried to keep pace. "Did I ever tell you how much I hate running?" she asked, panting. After a bit, she started massaging her side, but eventually moved into a rhythm.

Kate smiled, keeping a steady pace. "At least it's not five in the morning."

Angie harrumphed, and they stayed silent and focused for the rest of the run. Sweat drenched Kate's clothing and ran down her face, but she refused to quit.

They doubled back and finished at the riverbank, not far from camp. Kate and Angie sat down to cool off and stretch. Xander and Gregory hadn't even broken a sweat. *That's so not fair.* Kate's face burned red with heat and exertion. Her ears radiated fire. Once she became the Mystic, she fully intended to give them the workout from Hell. It was only fair.

Gregory laid down and rolled over on his stomach. "Push-ups and squats next, and not the *girly* kind either." He was enjoying himself.

Kate glared. They rolled over and endured yet another torture session. *Oh yeah, I'm going to make the guys suffer some day real soon.* Kate focused on those thoughts to get her back to camp.

Angie snickered when Kate used their link to show her the plans for her revenge. Once they got back to camp, the atmosphere filled with renewed tension. Everyone forgot about Gregory's departure during the workout, since it wasn't on the forefront of their minds. Tensions increased as the time drew closer.

Xander nodded toward Kate. "We finished a little earlier than expected. Why don't you and Angie catch an hour of sleep, while Gregory and I finish up details and get ready?"

For once, she didn't argue at all.

Not even a peep.

Preparing for the worst-case scenario, Xavier flashed into Xander and Gregory's meeting. Xander knew his brother was uncomfortable and hoped to stay in the shadows while Gregory was gone. Existing in a realm where emotions were muted, Xavier had difficulty coping with the clarity in *this* realm.

Xander reached out to help soothe him. He kept praying for a miracle. The emotions coursing through Xavier threatened to overwhelm him, but Xander could tell he held them back.

"Xavier, it's great to see you." They embraced. Xander held on a little longer. It felt good to actually feel his brother in the flesh, instead of only a presence in his mind. Xavier wouldn't be able to control his emotions for long. He had to relearn everything in this world. "Let's go through the plan before the girls wake up."

Xander watched his twin closely as they covered all of the information. Xavier's nervous twitches and the sweat on his brow proved he was shaken, but Xander could feel the strength in him wanting to break free. His greatest desire was to come out of the shadows and be the warrior he once had been.

"I'll take a look at the demons' position before you leave, Gregory," Xavier said. His voice held confidence and composure. "Then I'll be in the Shadow Realm right here at the campsite. If there is an attack, I'll try to bring them in the shadows. If need be, I can step out and fight."

Xander sensed Xavier's reluctance to have a fight in this realm, where his emotions were rampant and hard to control. He hoped his brother could handle it when the time came. Likely, he would have to fight sooner than later. "Hopefully, nothing will happen, and everything will go smoothly, but I'm counting on you if we *do* get attacked." Xander stared at Xavier, wanting a commitment.

"Have I let you down so far?" Xavier snapped, scowling. Xander glared at him.

"Ladies, pardon the interruption," Gregory said. "But I'm going to leave out in about thirty minutes. I'll break off communication so nothing traces me to you, and I'll travel at a high rate of speed to get a good distance away. That will leave a window of fifteen to twenty minutes when there is no communication. Our greatest weakness is in that time frame. The possibility of a traitor worries me the most. Have you or Zane been able to trace anything?"

"No," Xavier said. "But I've checked all around the campsite for any life forms and will again before you leave. Once I'm in the shielded area, it will be hard for me to see anything coming, traitor or demon." Xander noticed Xavier began to fidget and knew he wanted to return to the shadows. He merged their minds to siphon off some of the emotions.

Xavier took a deep breath. "One possibility that Zane discovered is that of a forced traitor."

"What the hell is that?" Xander growled and started pacing. It wasn't like they needed anything new to deal with.

"It's actually not as bad as you think. This means that the traitor might actually be a good person under duress. Their conscience would be clear in regards to how we search for evil. Maybe Fury captured a loved one or Braxus dreamed up something even more horrible. Maybe they were manipulated into believing they're doing the right thing. Any of these scenarios would make it much more difficult to find a traitor, because they simply aren't one on the conscious level. Zane has begun using everything at his disposal to target the subconscious." Xavier shrugged.

Xander decided to switch to their mental link. *"So basically, this person is impossible to track. How is this supposed to make me feel better? Could you not have told me these ideas after the girls are safe? Now, I have one more issue to figure out."* This whole mission had gone from bad, to worse, to miserable. Xander realized that he would probably not survive, but he had to make sure that

Kate made it to the Magical realm, where she would be safe until the battle.

"No, Xander, you don't get it. *If a person isn't evil, then there's still hope for undoing the damage. If we can figure out the problem, we can set them free. It's worth a try. Zane has it covered. All you have to do is stay focused on the task at hand and get to the Meadows. For now, we'll keep this between us, until we know more.*" Xander honestly thought it was a fool's errand, but maybe Zane needed something to hold onto, like him. He needed to refocus and worry about the next few hours.

After finalizing details, Xander felt fairly confident that they had everything ready. Gregory packed his backpack, while he and Xavier discussed last-minute signals and strategies that they could use in both realms.

Xander glanced at his brother and struggled against the doubt swirling in his gut. Would Xavier be able to fight off demons if there was an attack? He looked toward the girls' tent, and knots of dread tightened in the pit of his stomach. This could end very badly.

Kate stepped out of the tent and caught sight of two Xanders. She gasped. Her eyes darted back and forth to make sense. The initial shock subsided, and she noticed subtle differences between the two. She smiled. *Xavier*. It was the weirdest feeling, looking at a replica of Xander, with the exception of a small scar across Xavier's cheek and a dimple in his chin. Their eyes were an identical blue, and their dark brown hair had been cut in the same length and style.

Xavier wasn't as filled out as Xander, but Kate suspected it was because of all the time Xavier had spent in the shadows, not eating and sleeping properly. She caught herself staring and felt stupid, she nodded at Xavier and held out her hand. "Xavier, it's so nice to finally meet you. You've helped us tremendously and provided for us. Thank you."

He cleared his throat and shook her hand. A slight flush appeared on his cheeks. "No problem, it's nice to meet you, too."

Kate gently smiled, sensed his discomfort, and knew it was hard for him to stay outside the shadows. Angie stepped up behind Kate and touched her shoulder. Through their link, Kate noticed Angie's shock and instant connection to Xavier. Like a moth to a flame. She could feel the pull inside Angie to move closer to him. Kate turned and reached behind her. "Xavier, this is my friend, Angie."

"Nice to meet you, Angie." Xavier stepped forward to shake Angie's hand. Their hands touched. Kate felt the electrical current pass between the two. Her entire body responded to their energy surge; the draw of the power between the two.

Angie's head jerked up and she looked into Xavier's eyes. They stared for a few seconds before he broke the contact, clearly shaken. He backed up toward Xander.

Feeling the power of the connection, Kate nearly doubled over. She reached for Xander to stabilize the energy pulsing through her. *What the hell?*

14

"I'll be in touch and waiting," Xavier said. He cast a blank look at Xander.

Angie cocked her head. "What was that about?"

Xander shrugged, with a bewildered expression on his face, anchoring Kate's powers. "I have no idea. It's different than anything I have experienced."

Kate shook her head. Electricity still singed the air. "That was intense. I could feel the currents of energy moving through me." Her blood pumped from the energy at an alarming rate.

"You're the bloody Mystic," Gregory growled. "Energy is supposed to move through you. Don't you pay attention?"

Xander took a step toward him. "Hey man, what's your problem? Don't snap at Kate if you're having jealousy issues."

Gregory froze, and his pupils dilated to a solid black. "Jealousy — what?" He moved toward Xander, clearly looking for a fight.

Kate nodded to Angie enlisting her assistance. Angie stepped up and placed her hands on Gregory's chest to distract him. This was the last thing they needed right now. Kate wrung her hands to soothe her nerves.

"Chill Gregory." Angie grabbed his chin and forced him to meet her eyes. "It was probably nothing. People shock people every day. It's called static electricity. But right now, we need to focus on the task at hand."

Kate finally had control of her internal energy and knew Gregory needed to get moving. Angie's mind was still scattered from the encounter. Kate sent her calming energy and reached down and grabbed Gregory's backpack.

She had to get the plan back on track. "Are you ready, Gregory?"

"Yeah, I'm ready. Sorry about that, not sure what came over me. For some reason, Xavier always brings out the worst in me. We never could see eye to eye on *anything*." He slung his backpack over his shoulder and looked at Xander. "Sorry, man."

"We're cool. Get this over with quickly. I'll feel a lot better once you're back and we're on the move. I think we're all going to be strung tight until we get to the Meadows." He paused. Kate held her breath, afraid he'd start an argument again. "I also know at some point you and Xavier need to work out your issues. This battle is going to be a rough one, and your focus needs to stay clear. That will be difficult if you two still have unresolved crap causing problems. Maybe that's something we can work on once we're in a secure place." Xander grabbed Gregory's forearms. "For now, be careful and be safe."

Gregory nodded. "I know you're right, and we do need to at least call a truce and begin working together. Our focus needs to stay on the Mystic and the survival of the world. If only it was that easy." He walked through the trees and disappeared.

Kate tried to feel relief, but a sense of foreboding weighed heavily in her chest. She kept herself busy with small tasks around the campsite.

Xander watched Gregory walk away. Since he was still fully connected to Xavier, he picked up on his brother's hatred for his best friend. Xavier wanted to lock down the camp so Gregory couldn't get back, like a child pitching a fit because he didn't get his way. His bigger concern of the moment was his brother's reaction to Angie. He wasn't an idiot, and neither was Xavier. They both knew what it meant. Angie was a strong candidate to be his mate. When Rowena had refused to bless Lily and Xavier's union, she had told him then that his destiny lay within the human world, where he would be blessed with an incredible connection worthy of his lineage.

Xavier had been furious and refused to listen. He wasn't a huge fan of humans. Xander hadn't even known about the prophecy until Lily had died, and he had transferred part of the sorrow from Xavier to himself. Regardless, Xavier firmly believed he could never have a mate again. He wouldn't survive it, especially not a human one.

He also couldn't deny his possessive instincts or overwhelming attraction to Angie. Xander had his doubts and distanced himself from the connection as best he could. No one knew better than him that you can't outrun destiny. It knocks you flat on your ass and makes you its puppet.

Xander cleaned and packed everything in just a few minutes. He had to do something to make the time go a little quicker, or they would be basket cases by the end of the night. Xander turned back to the girls, hoping they had some ideas. "So, what do you want to do to pass the time?"

He never got their answer. Their protection alarms shrieked.

"The demons are here!" Xavier thundered into Xander's head. *"They've surrounded us! There must be an informant or a damn good Seer, or both, who informed them the second Gregory left. He felt the shift in power, but they have trapped him in some sort of magical prison. He's skilled enough to break through, but it will take time. They flashed straight into our location, and they're coming with a hell of a lot of power. Braxus is even lending his powers to bring in enough cloud cover for many of the demons to operate. We are screwed. The shields won't hold up if an Omega adds to their power."* Xander prayed the shields would hold. He wasn't sure if Xavier could fight in the Human Realm.

Xander positioned himself in front of the girls. He pushed his conversation with Xavier into Kate's mind and heard her responding, *Oh shit!* She sent the information to Angie. She immediately jumped up.

Xander scanned the area. They were surrounded —

The solid tree cover mixed with all of the clouds gave the advantage to the demons. Kate and Angie grabbed their swords. They stood back-to-back, ready to fight.

The clouds darkened. Rain poured from the skies.

The demons came closer, snarling and snapping their teeth

Rain soaked them and turned the ground into slippery mush. The weight of their damp clothes inhibited their ability to fight. Darkness continued to descend like an eclipse. There was no escape.

Kate looked at Xander. "Can they come through the shield?" She tried to keep her voice from shaking. "Why is it getting darker?"

"They shouldn't be able to. Our magic is absolute against demons. But if Braxus is using his power to bring in the weather changes, he'll probably break through the shield. He won't waste an opportunity. Your full mystic powers are the only thing that could hold the shield against him. Gregory is locked in some sort of spell, so I don't know how long it will take him to get here. I'm so sorry, Kate. We shouldn't have risked it." Xander circled them. His eyes darted in all directions, ready for the attack.

Guilt and sorrow etched across Xander's face, and Kate knew beyond a doubt that he'd die to protect her and Angie. They'd become a real team, like her old one, despite every obstacle and improbability.

She pushed her fear aside and focused on the fight to come. If she and Angie stayed back-to-back, they might have a good shot at staying alive. At least until Gregory could get free.

She'd also have to keep Xander from doing anything stupid. Like becoming distracted and getting himself killed to save her. She hadn't known him long, but she considered him a partner like Angie, maybe more. He'd become essential in her life, and she couldn't fulfill her destiny without his help.

The next few minutes were excruciating. Each second meticulously ticked off the clock.

The sky continued to darken. Rain drops the size of dimes stung their skin. The time for fighting fast approached.

She sensed the demon energy push toward the shield. The sword in her hand grew heavier and she tightened her grip. The rain had made everything slippery. Her boots sunk into the mud every time she held her feet still for even a few seconds, limiting her movement.

She heard every second tick off her watch. Tick tock. Tick tock. It taunted her.

Everything she'd learned the past two days replayed in her mind. She prayed it was enough to keep her and Angie alive. Angie linked to her mind, and they began working out several strategies to buy time and survive.

"Do you think Xavier will help us if it gets bad?" Angie was scared, *truly* scared, for the first time in her life.

"I'm not sure. His emotions were completely out of whack for the short time he was here earlier. I can only imagine how hard it would be for him to fight in that condition. It depends on his strength and ability to control those emotions." Kate tried to send calming energy to her, but she didn't have much to spare.

Malevolent energy seeped in and grew in power. The shield cracked. It was like watching an earthquake. A fissure formed and spread, weakening the entire invisible shield. The weight of the negative energy seeped through the cracks. To a weaker person, it would have caused a sense of helplessness or despair.

Angie's eyes held sorrow, like Xander's had earlier. *"I'm sorry, Angie, I didn't understand what I was dragging you into. Stay at my back."*

"I'm not sorry. This is where we were both meant to be. This is our time for whatever fate has in store. You know I'm a big believer in fate."

Kate attuned to the energy surrounding her. The demonic shields stuttered. Things were definitely *not* stacking up in their favor.

Kate shared Angie's nervousness, but also admired her courage. They would face this together, and it would work out — like always. She hoped. They linked hands briefly for solidarity, and the simplicity of needing the contact, and shared a smile of encouragement.

The shield fell. Xander's mind went crazy. Kate tried to connect with him, but he was all over the place. He tried over and over to reach Gregory.

Xander tried to stay calm. They were going to be surrounded, no doubt. He could feel Kate reaching out to him and did his best to calm her. *"Xavier, what the hell is going on?"*

"Zane says Braxus is giving up his energy to break the shield and bring in the stormy weather. It's probably a gift for his faithful servant Fury. We've never seen anything like it. In all of history, the demon leader has never been willing to use an ounce of power before the Rising. Fury did one hell of a sales job. This mother is either one cocky son of a bitch and using some new strategies to exploit our weaknesses or he has some inside information to make himself certain this plan will work."

Xander knew Xavier was trying to control his own panic. *"Get your ass down here and help. I can't fight a bunch of demons and protect the girls by myself."* Xander was on the balls of his feet.

"I'll do what I can." Xavier cut their connection but didn't come out of the shadows.

"Xavier!" Xander angrily yelled but received no response. "Damn it! I swear if anything happens to them, I will never speak to you again!"

Kate wasn't sure what was worse: the final seconds counting down, Xander's absolute fury at Xavier, or the fact she was probably going to get her best friend injured or worse.

The shield crackled. Energy levels waned, then popped. The demons burst through. They poured in from every direction.

She braced for the attack. *Here they come. I hope we survive.*

Kate stayed back-to-back with Angie. They danced in a circle, the demons surrounding them. The creatures were hideous. Many had razor sharp teeth, black soulless eyes, and an odor of decay. They tripped every alarm in Kate's body.

The energy inside her tried to battle back against the onslaught of negative energy. It took everything she had not to vomit from being in their proximity.

They challenged each other as if it were a choreographed dance. The demons advanced, and the girls retreated. Then *they* would advance, and the *demons* would retreat. Neither side attacked.

Why? There was no logical explanation. *Are they waiting for a signal? Toying with us? C'mon already. Get it over with.*

A massive, red-eyed demon charged to the front of the line. It stood over seven feet tall with bulging muscles and a tattooed face. Its crimson eyes looked at Kate and Angie. A smile curled around his green stained teeth. It cried out and pointed a massive fist toward the women. The demons quickly rushed in. They crowded around the trio, jostling each other, jockeying for position like they were late for a meeting.

Maybe this Braxus wasn't the all-powerful being they thought? Maybe he was only using his energy for a limited length of time? Without him bringing in the dark, would the demons go up in smoke? Kate's mind clustered with questions. *If only I knew how to bring in the sun.*

At least twenty demons surrounded them with swords and axes drawn. *Thank goodness they don't believe in guns.* Or maybe they didn't for the moment. Who knew what to expect with demons?

Kate held her ground. She kicked, punched, thrust, and ducked in constant movement. Sweat and rain drenched her body, weighing her down. Muscles burned with the double effort needed for her to move. All of her efforts only killed one. *Crap!*

Xander fought them off right and left, but he was covered up. They tried hard to hold their formation. The demons tried just as hard to separate them.

Xander killed as many as he could, but he couldn't risk moving too far from Kate. The demons realized this and he became a sitting duck. He was not going down easy. He ducked the sword of one and blocked a kick from another. A sword swiped his shoulder and pain radiated down his arm. The wound wasn't too deep and he kept fighting. Without help soon, they weren't going to make it out of this one. He abandoned his sword and focused on energy blasts to back them away. Magical traces and his power supply didn't concern him at the moment. The demons knew their location.

Xavier set up portals. Bright swirls of light bathed the combatants. Some of the demons aiming for the girls disappeared through the wormholes. Xander felt Zane trying to get rid of the darkness, but that would take too long.

"Xavier, get your ass out here now or she'll die!" Xander roared. He reclaimed his sword and cut off a demon's head. He was ready to kill Xavier himself. He checked on Kate again and found her covered with demons.

The air was smoky and thick with sweat and blood. Metal hit metal. Flesh struck flesh. It seemed hopeless. Kate couldn't hang onto Angie. They separated. She plugged into Angie's mind to keep tabs, but she had to stay alive, too.

She continued fighting but was wearing down. Her movements were slower, and she couldn't raise her sword as high or quickly slash. Pain radiated down her arm and her legs throbbed. The demons' strength was much greater than hers. Two demons headed toward her. She blocked the sword of one, but the second one knocked her feet out from under her. *Not good. Not good.* She kicked the first one back and tried to get up.

The second demon in front of her sneered and laughed. He swung his sword toward her neck. She rolled to the right and shoved her small sword into his heart. The sneering demon sunk to his knees, and she jumped to her feet.

Kate pulled it out of its chest and sliced the demon's head off. She tried to take in her surroundings, but there was too much smoke and fog. She couldn't see Xander anymore, and Angie was too far away.

She ran in Angie's direction and finally saw her in the haze. A demon came for Angie from behind. Kate froze. He was too close. She screamed at Angie to watch out, but the sword was already on its way down.

Kate's lungs shut down, and rage flowed through her entire body. Her mental barriers came down, and power flowed. For a split second, the sword froze in midair.

The demon's eyes widened in surprise. He quickly shook it off and took another swing but his sword met another sword. In the next instant, the demon's head went flying through the air, and he erupted into a pile of ash.

Xavier stood at the rim of the shadows, his face covered with fury, the sword he'd used to decapitate the demon loosely gripped in his hand. Angie swiftly turned to face her next opponent. Kate breathed a momentary sigh of relief, then faced her next battle. With Xavier now fighting by their sides, the odds changed.

The demon numbers dwindled and spots of light appeared in the dark sky. Zane was moving back the darkness. Still, they were only holding steady without the full light. She wanted to get back to Angie, but too many demons blocked her path.

Kate wished she could have stopped and watched the brothers fight side by side. What little she could see had been amazing. There were no missteps between them, only perfect synchronization. Their swords whistled, and their aim true. The fluidity in their motions was astonishing as they took down demon after demon. Unfortunately, there seemed to be a steady supply of demons coming at them.

She finally made it back to Angie. They used a lot of what Gregory had taught them to take down demons. What seemed like hours had, in truth, only been a few minutes.

A sudden bright flash of light appeared and Gregory arrived. Things turned in favor of the good guys. Gregory, Xavier, and Xander formed a triangle around her and Angie, so they could have a break. Once Gregory arrived and Zane started pushing back more and more of the darkness, the demons started retreating.

Just when she thought they were winning; another flash of light brought another group of demons. These were different. They were a military unit holding strict formations and had none of the demon madness she'd witnessed in the others.

The man at the front, their obvious leader, sneered in her direction. "Do you really think you can beat my army, little girl? As for you morons, it's been too long since our last encounter." His gaze was focused on Xander.

Oh shit!

Fury. It had to be. He was surprisingly good-looking, with shortly cropped, pitch black hair, and his eyes were a bright green. He had strong facial features and tanned skin. His appearance was deceiving. He might look like a movie star, but Kate sensed the evil that emanated from him. If Xander's stories were true, there was no way to defeat him. If Zane didn't remove the dark cover, they'd die.

Xander had blood pouring from the wound on his arm and a gash in his side. He stood tall and met his stare. "This is the Mystic. You cannot destroy her. For that matter, as I recall, you couldn't destroy *me*. Why don't you run back home to your master and give him a message for me?"

Fury's laugh was almost musical. He was nothing like the others. "What would that be, my old friend?"

"Tell him to go screw himself, and he's not laying a hand on the Mystic. She will kill him at the proper place and time, as have all of those before her. You may have him fooled but not me. You don't care about her. You want revenge. Sorry to disappoint, but your days are numbered. The sun is on our side. Even if you tried to launch an attack, you'd all burn."

Kate admitted she was impressed with his bravado. She wasn't feeling too sure herself. Fury looked like he could kill pretty quickly and efficiently. Kate decided to take the risk and connect to his thoughts. It might give them an advantage. His mind wasn't chaotic like the rest.

Without responding, Fury smiled with a lazy grin. *He never intended to fight this time.* He knew they'd take the upper hand. He'd been feeling them out to see how powerful they were, and what it would take to defeat them. He'd sacrificed his own army to test them. She could feel his silent message to all of them that they would meet again soon.

The sun started breaking through the rest of the clouds.

"By the way, Xavier," Fury smugly said. "Lily was gullible and quite the fool. Of course, if you had kept her happy at home, maybe she wouldn't have run across my path. She was a lovely little piece. I'll be seeing you."

Rage encased Xavier's aura but his face remained a blank canvas. He flung out his hand and a bright flash of light emanated behind Fury. Despite his radiating pain, he kept his focus. "Fury, I have no doubt we'll meet again."

Xavier gathered a force of energy and blasted Fury backward. He lost his footing just enough to fall into the portal. It sucked him inside as Fury howled in anger, but his eyes held astonishment. Xavier had taken the upper hand in this battle, and for the moment, they'd bought some time. The portal flung Fury to another place or realm.

The rest of the demons witnessed Fury flying through the portal and felt the light start to fall upon their skin, and they ran. Xavier and Zane were ready for them. Gregory and Xander herded them like cattle and Xavier opened another portal. Most of the demons disappeared. None of them would survive.

Kate caught a brief glimpse of one of the massive warriors on the other side of the portal. He gave her a respectful nod. The portal closed.

The fight was over.

"Who was that and what was that? And what the hell just happened?" Kate sat down on the ground and let the sun warm her soaked body.

"That was Zane, leader of the Shadow Warriors," Xavier replied. Though he looked devastated, he hadn't disappeared into the shadows with them. "They reside in what many call the in-between world. They can access portals to any realm and have incredible strength and power. They were once great warriors but suffered a curse that depleted their species and abilities. He has a great deal of respect for you and your destiny. He's remains powerful but bound to the Shadow Realm. Xander can tell you more about them later." He walked over to Angie to check her wounds. Gregory glared.

Kate couldn't endure any more drama. Guilt racked Xavier for arriving so late to the fight. She was impressed at the way he was holding it together for now.

The energy inside her pounded out of control again. Fury may not have won, but he'd weakened her. The moment Xavier and Angie came into contact, electricity roared again. They jumped apart in confusion. It hit hard; Kate dropped to her knees from the impact. She didn't know what to make of it, but it obviously upset Xavier.

His hand trembled as he reached down to heal Angie's more severe wounds. He made sure everyone was all right and looked once more in Angie's direction with a weird expression on his face. He stepped away from them and nodded. "I better go give Zane a hand." He disappeared, and so did the extra electrical pulses.

Kate felt Angie's confusion, but the most important thing was that they'd lived to fight another day. Sure, they all had cuts, scrapes, and bruises. They would be sore the next several days, but they'd survived. It wasn't perfect by any means.

They'd established themselves as worthy opponents, so Braxus would probably not waste that much energy again. He had to prepare for the Rising, too. From now on, he'd leave it to his assassins to keep trying. Not a great thought, but better than fighting Braxus until she was ready, much further in the future. She had to become the Mystic first.

Xander held onto Kate so tight she could hardly breathe. He kissed every inch of her face and cradled her head in his hands. Kate sensed his absolute terror that he could've lost her before the Rising even began. She also noticed his anger at the Council for allowing all of this to happen, and he was still irritated at Xavier for taking too long to step in and help. They were all dealing with their emotions as the adrenaline began to fade.

She wanted to believe he cared for her. She didn't want to be his responsibility. She needed more, but was that even possible with their current path? She'd begun to realize that it was worth the risk.

He continued to whisper words of encouragement. She gripped him tightly, trying to help dispel his fears and hers. She rested her cheek against his, the tremors inside him calmed. Overcome with emotion and energy, she pulled him forcefully down to her mouth, to help him see she was safe now, and with him for however long they lived. Peace seeped into her soul once again.

Gregory sat down quietly beside Angie and handed her a drink. He rubbed her shoulders, and for once she had no scathing remarks. She absently took a drink, still watching Kate, and wondered about her own fate and her crazy reaction to Xavier. Her face scrunched up, and she spit the drink out. "Ugh, what the hell is this?" She wiped her mouth and glared at him.

Laughing, Gregory rubbed his face and shook his head. "Herbal tea. Please tell me you've had tea before?"

"I'm from the South; we drink sweet tea, not this healthy crap."

"Drink it anyway. We use it a lot in the magical communities to help us heal faster, and we definitely have some rough days ahead." He paused and looked over at Kate and Xander. A small smile played across his face, but his eyes looked sad. "They're pretty great together, aren't they? Of course, they both have to admit it first."

"Yeah, together they'll be able to do anything. I truly believe that. She'll win in the end." Angie knew if there was any way for Kate to win and survive, she'd find it.

"You sound pretty sure." Gregory questioningly looked at her.

Angie sighed and shrugged her shoulders. "Can't explain it, but I know she'll find the way. Not for herself, but for mankind and for Xander. It's the way she's built."

Angie was finally connecting to Gregory. Above all, they loved their friends and would help them complete this journey. He always protected her. She couldn't completely dismiss the electric connection to Xavier, but what did it matter? He'd never come out of the shadows completely, and Gregory was here.

A warm and fuzzy feeling washed over her, weird, since she usually wasn't the sentimental type. As a human, she didn't exactly have a lot of years to waste. Setting animosity aside, she laid her head on Gregory's shoulder, and he wrapped his arm around hers. A truce had begun to take shape at last.

Xander came back to his surroundings and was shocked to see Gregory and Angie on friendly terms and voluntarily touching each other.

"I guess opposites *do* attract or maybe it's our situation," Kate said. "As long as she's happy, I don't care." She smiled up at Xander and kissed his cheek, but he knew she wasn't being completely truthful.

He tucked her head under his chin. He couldn't be more perplexed by the whole situation. Angie's weird reaction to Xavier and this turnaround with Gregory. Something didn't seem quite right, but now was the time for protection and getting to the Meadows. Crazy love lives would have to take a back seat. Everyone's emotions were all over the place, including his, so who was he to judge? Maybe Kate was right. Maybe the situation was making them all crazy.

Xander cleared his throat to address the group. "Xavier and Zane got most of the demons, but some escaped because they got around the portal. That means our location is compromised. We need to pack up and leave before we lose the light. Fury escaped through another portal, and he won't fall for that trick again anytime soon. But it saved us tonight. That's all we can ask for." Xander walked over to Gregory and tightly grabbed his forearm. "I'm sure glad you got here when you did. I'll always be in your debt."

Gregory shifted his weight and crossed his arms. "Actually, thank Marcus. Your mind was so focused on the fight that I couldn't tell what was going on. He sent me the counter spell so I could break free. I think they're watching us more than we realize, but those are issues for another day. I wasn't able to grab the bikes or supplies."

As soon as the words left Gregory's mouth, bags of supplies appeared in the middle of the camp, with a note that had the coordinates for where to find the two motorcycles. Xander laughed and closed his eyes.

"Thanks again, Rowena and Marcus." Maybe the Council was watching more closely than he realized. How else would Marcus know everything that had happened? He still couldn't understand why they were risking everything.

Kate separated the supplies. "What are we going to do now? We can't risk a vehicle or anything traceable if we're still going to hide as humans. Why didn't they pop in the bikes?"

Xander stored the tents behind the trees for Xavier to clean out later. "There isn't a great trail leading out of here, and we need some distance if we're going to pull this off. We'll have to travel as large birds, so we can travel high enough to mask our scent and magic."

Angie groaned. "Oh come on! Flying again, seriously?"

"It's the best way to get to our bikes undetected so we can keep our disguise and not put our hosts in danger."

"Uh-huh, big ass birds aren't suspicious at all," she muttered under her breath and grabbed her backpack. Xander rolled his eyes and prepared the supplies for flight.

He checked in with Xavier to make sure he was all right after the comments from Fury. Of course, they'd already known he'd been involved in Lily's death, but it didn't make it any easier to hear. Xavier was furious, but surprisingly more focused on Gregory and Angie. Jealousy burned through him, joined with guilt and self-loathing. Xander confirmed his suspicion that this love triangle could bring a whole lot more trouble to their happy little group. They did *not* need any more drama.

Once everything was packed, Kate and Angie climbed aboard their eagles. Kate rubbed his back and down his brown and white wing. The feathers were much softer than the dragon scales, but they probably weren't bullet proof. Xander had chosen the eagle so she and Angie would be more comfortable. *Maybe he really does care about me, but everything is happening so fast. At least I've finally found someone I can trust with everything that I am.* She leaned forward to anchor her position.

They were all sore and tired, but still held onto the hope of a brighter future. Kate thought of all the fairytales and silly stories told to children around the world. She'd never understood the point. In a way, it was cruel to build false hope and belief.

On the other hand, she thought as they left the ground, *I'm soaring through the night sky on my potential mate who happens to be an eagle at the moment.*

They flew farther into the clouds and Kate latched onto a memory from her past. She giggled to herself and felt a little like Santa Claus. "Up, up, up and away!" Maybe fairytales weren't so bad after all. They prepared the mind to accept the unacceptable and that it's possible to attain the unattainable.

Wasn't that the basic definition of hope?

15

Xavier rubbed his forehead, trying to alleviate the headache pounding through his skull. He wanted to pass along his updates and get some way-overdue rest. *"Xander, Zane thinks he briefly picked up on the traitor. He sensed a moment of intense anger and fear, but then it was gone. He agrees that this person is probably under some duress but is able to keep everything on the subconscious level, which to be honest, is harder than hell to track. It also makes it impossible to know whether they are being completely forced, or they intended to betray and made a deal with the wrong demons."* He wearily sighed. He went from years of no existence to this intense battle.

Fate sure wasn't showing much sympathy with his transition time. He guessed it was their typical trial by fire approach. He wanted so much to feel normal, or to feel anything except more regret, but guilt continued to consume him. His reaction toward Angie sucked. He refused to ever get involved with another female. He didn't trust them anyway, after what Zane had discovered about his late wife and her deception. Even Xander didn't know that.

He closed his eyes, but all he could see was Angie's face and her shocked reaction to his touch. Despite the fact he wanted nothing to do with her, he couldn't stop his body from desiring her. This intense attraction and electrical connection were a rare occurrence with potential mates. He had to find a way to get it under control.

It wasn't a problem until Gregory got near her, and every possessive instinct in his head tripped like alarm bells. Holy hell, he was in a big mess. The bottom line was that he never wanted to love again, so he never had to watch his love die for a second time. *Never.*

"Is there any way to track the signals or figure out who it is?" Xander popped back in his head, breaking up the pity party. *"Or are we sitting ducks until he or she decides to strike again?"* It was difficult to converse normally with Xander in an animal form, but this was too important, so he had split his energy. They needed answers above all else.

Xavier tried to be quick, to spare him any further drain on his powers. He had already used way too much. Xander had reached the point that he and Gregory couldn't restore his full powers anymore.

"Zane and some of his trackers are doing their best, but they are more limited now. He said that since he has caught a glimmer of the subconscious level, they should have better luck tracking. He believes it to be a male, but in the subconscious levels, the main person could still be a female, depending on how good they are. And I'd say this piece of crap is pretty accomplished to disappear from Zane. It's going to take a long while to get through all the layers, and it will not be easy." Xavier wished he had better news for him, but they were in short supply of that lately.

"At least it's a start. You can bet the Council is working on it, too. How far away are we from our first stop? We need to get a couple hours of sleep and to refuel, before we start on the next segment." Xander's energy levels were dangerously low. At least they would be switching to the bikes. He would have to transfer as much energy as he could to Xander to rebuild his power.

"Almost there. Zane will watch over you while you sleep, so I can get some rest. I think we'll be pretty safe at our next location but getting to the Meadows without getting tracked at all will be tricky. The Council picked a heck of a time to start believing in human forms of travel." Xavier felt Xander disconnect, to focus on keeping them safe in the air.

For the first time, Xavier got a wrench in his gut, fearing his brother may not survive this journey. If he could find a way, he would gladly take his place. What did he have to live for anyway? He closed his eyes but couldn't find enough peace to sleep.

Xander and Gregory landed softly, switched into human form, and immediately consumed a ton of food. They had a slight gray tint in their faces from their exertion, but otherwise were in pretty good shape. Gregory's color quickly returned. Xander's energy barely increased until Xavier transferred all he could into him. If nothing else was accomplished on this ridiculous escapade, at least he would die at peace with the fact his brother had returned to him.

Kate watched him closely since the transformation. He tried to cover it, but she saw the delay in *his* recovery versus that of Gregory. She was way too astute. At least she couldn't read his mind, or she would know he had no recharging abilities left. Gregory couldn't even help much anymore. Since Xavier was his twin, he could still transfer what he needed for now. If they had to fight any more big battles, he wouldn't make it to the Meadows. Part of him felt guilty for deceiving her, but he couldn't risk the cost of coming clean. Especially now.

Xander came up behind Kate and held her tightly. She leaned her head back against his shoulder. He'd made a massive mess of everything. He knew her trust in him was building, but she'd never forgive him for hiding his ticking clock and its impact on her future.

To make matters worse, he'd begun to realize how much he loved her. He decided at their next stop, they would finally finish what they'd started. The consequences didn't matter anymore, as long as he got to be with her *once* before he died. He kissed her on the top of the head. He didn't need his hormones to start raging again, so he avoided her mouth. "Go rest. I need to go over a few things with Gregory, and then I'll join you."

Angie had already crashed in the next tent and was sleeping soundly. Xander noticed she hadn't said one word about sleeping with Gregory, and the way she had reacted to Xavier bothered him more than it should. He knew what the connection meant, but he had honestly thought Xavier was unreachable. It was obvious Xavier had felt the link and responded, even though he tried to hide it.

Why would fate tie him to a human after everything he had suffered already? What did the blossoming feelings between Angie and Gregory mean? It was like someone had flipped a switch. He deeply sighed. This was one can of worms he didn't want to open. Not now. They could all have it out when they got to the Meadows and could adapt to a more normal pace and surroundings.

Gregory leaned up against the tree deep in thought. Xander approached him. "Everything okay?"

"Yeah," Gregory said, and scanned their surroundings one more time. "I can't shake the feeling that we're always being watched by good and evil. It's a freaky thought. For the first time, I feel like a little fish in a big glass pond surrounded by predators and spectators. I guess that's how the Mystic has always felt."

Gregory paused, then met his eyes. "You should tell her, you know. It isn't fair. Anyone can see she's falling in love with you. What happens when she has to leave you behind or watch you die? You think that won't cause as much disruption as her knowing everything and making a choice to save you? She's come this far, so hasn't she already made the decision anyway?"

Xander stayed quiet a moment and thought about his predicament. "Exactly, my point. She'll choose sacrifice and saving the innocent every time. And come on, she's been chased by demons every step of the way. She didn't exactly volunteer for the job. We also don't know what will happen with Angie, and that could change her course. Despite the cost to both of us, she has to make the choice to enter the Meadows with a clean slate."

"I disagree, since nothing on this journey has been clean, but I will follow your lead. Just don't say I didn't warn you when she beats the crap out of you for lying to her. 'Cause, damn, that girl is going to be furious." Gregory clasped onto his shoulder. "No man, I definitely do not want to be in your shoes. Now, go to bed and get plenty of rest to help restore your energy a little more.

Tomorrow should be a hell of an interesting day." Laughing, he went to his tent to join Angie, while Xander headed to Kate.

Gregory walked into the tent and saw Angie peacefully sleeping in her bag. He regretted the fact they could sleep in separate bags now. She always added extra warmth, whether she wanted to be there or not. He tried not to think of any feelings he had toward her, but he couldn't help the heat that always traveled up his entire body when he came into contact with her.

He watched the rise and fall of her chest and the wisp of dark brown hair that fell across her cheek. He wished he understood his protective feelings and other urges. He wasn't an idiot and hadn't missed the strong connection between her and Xavier. *A bunch of bullshit!*

They were potential mates. *How convenient.* Wasn't brutally losing one wife enough? He might hate him, but he still wouldn't wish what had happened that day on anyone. Shaking his bad thoughts away, he focused on Angie's flawless face, tight body, and her long reddish-brown hair. He remembered what he had said to Xander about small moments, and a smile lit up his face.

He was there with her every day and Xavier couldn't last ten minutes. He had time for many small moments, and he fully intended to take advantage of them with Angie, if Xavier would stay out of the way. He scooted his bag next to hers and fell asleep.

Xander joined Kate in the tent and slid into the sleeping bag beside her. She was sleeping heavily, but still turned into his warmth and rested her head on his shoulder. He brushed a kiss across her lips and felt his heart shift. He counted himself lucky for every night spent in her arms. He had screwed up letting the task of finding her spark a rage inside him that had almost kept them apart. Of course, his little white lie could also tear them apart.

If he was honest with himself, he hadn't told the lie for her benefit. He had told it for himself. He didn't want her to see his weakness or her power over him, while he guided her into falling in love with him. He'd been focused on saving himself and not building a true relationship. He hadn't wanted to like her *or* trust her. He'd wanted her to be a tool to save him.

Instead, she became everything to him. Their bond had brought more than his tattoo to life. Every minute spent with her was a gift. He'd been the one to fall in love, and deep inside he knew he was likely to lose her when she discovered the truth. Maybe that's why he wasn't fearing the ticking time clock anymore, or death. She had awakened him and given him a taste of life. Without realizing it, he had become isolated and emotionless just like Xavier. She had saved him, after all.

If they were human, they could plan their future, plan vacations, and children. He'd dreamed of their life together and had been fantasizing about his Mystic for years before Lily died. After she died and Xavier left, his sorrow, grief, and anger turned him into a man he didn't recognize.

Then the dreams shifted into nightmares, and he would break into a sweat as the woman in his dreams became the Mystic and sacrificed herself to save the world. Where would that leave him? Another barren existence?

Kate must have sensed his inner turmoil and turned toward him to comfort him. She lightly placed her hand on his cheek and brushed her lips across his. "Have faith in me, Xander."

He kissed her softly, needing the connection and wanting so much more. He brushed a strand of hair behind her ear. "I do have faith in you," he whispered. "But I can't stop the fear of losing you, before I've had any real time with you. The Awakening is closing in, and we must get you to the portal." He wrapped his arms around her waist and tucked her head under his chin. *Oh, what a tangled web we weave...*

Kate fell back asleep, while Xander focused on the traitor. Who was it? Where was he? Why would he want darkness to descend over the entire world? None of this made any sense. He finally fell asleep listening to Kate's even breathing.

Xander checked all of their supplies and turned to talk to Kate and Angie about last-minute instructions. "To keep our cover intact, we won't be able to telepathically communicate, but Xavier can break through to me if there's an emergency, or he can contact you, Kate, by following my link to you. Our focus will be on the shields. We'll ride most of the day and it'll be pretty physical. I know you'll need to take a break. Are there any questions before we leave?"

Kate and Angie shook their heads. Xander figured it was probably too late even if they did. "Ready?" Xander waited for their nod. He and Gregory started the bikes, and the girls mounted up. At least they had mics in their helmets if they needed to communicate.

Kate closed her eyes and imagined how beautiful everything would look in the fall. It had always been her favorite season with the reds, browns, and golds peppering the scenery. She wondered if she would live to see it someday on a real vacation instead of this craziness. Her number one rule would be absolutely no freaking demons.

Tired of the constant silence of the past hour and the heavy feeling in her heart, Kate decided to use her link with Angie. *"I'm not sure normal will ever fit into my vocabulary again. Can you imagine our team's faces if they could see us now?"* They both laughed.

Kate relaxed. She tried to enjoy all the scenery and peacefulness surrounding them but was always at the ready for a battle.

She took a deep breath and decided not to put it off any longer. She and Angie needed to talk about the future. She didn't need to spend a lot of time in Angie's mind to know that she doubted her place in the grand scheme. *"I want you to know that I value our friendship more than anything. Changes are coming and we can't go back or pretend it isn't happening. That's not how either of us works, but we can find a new way to move forward together."*

Angie gave her the thumbs up sign. *"You sound like a cheesy sitcom or girly novel but point taken. Thanks for trying to make me feel better, Mom."*

Kate tried to be patient with Angie's sarcasm, knowing it was her way of protecting herself from emotions. *"Let's be totally honest with each other,"* she fired back. *"You know you won't be able to return to a regular place in this realm and have a normal life or job after everything that we'll face and suffer to survive. You're the reason I'm here on this journey. You had faith in me when I didn't."*

Angie cocked her head back over her shoulder. The helmet kept Kate from seeing her face, but the intent was there. *"Really? I hadn't noticed. We have demons on our tail that are vicious as hell. I'm cut off from my job, other friends, and my life in general. We're riding on freaking motorcycles that appeared out of thin air, with men who have real powers. Come the freak on! I'm attracted to a man who lives in another realm and has issues beyond comprehension, and my other option is a jerk most of the time who doesn't like humans.*

"To add more insult to injury, I'm going to a place I don't have a chance in hell of fitting into, and you're talking to me about a normal life? I'm not an idiot. It doesn't make it any easier that I'll probably die on a battlefield with no one to mourn me, or even know what I died for. To be honest, I'm not sure what I'm dying for!"

Kate fully merged with Angie and took a deep breath. Not even Angie's famous sarcasm could bail her out now. Kate didn't want this hanging over their heads. *"Feel better now that you have all that off your chest? Is your little hissy fit over?"*

Kate opened her mind to stop the tirade and let Angie feel her sincerity and devotion to their friendship.

Angie sighed. *"I'm sorry. You're right, I know. I wouldn't have made any other choice. I can't move forward because I'll never be one of you with magical abilities. I'll never be able to go back. What kind of life does that leave for me?"*

Kate wished she knew, but no one seemed to have any answers. *"There are some moments when I wake up and hope it's all been a dream. I can go back to my normal life, normal friends, and not so normal cases. Starting a brand-new case, having my set routine, and being with my trusted team around me was how I survived and thrived."*

She paused. How do you explain your deepest fears and the possibility of something great? *"Then there are those moments that it feels like the pieces of an impossible jigsaw puzzle have finally come together, and a new light has been turned on inside me. In my heart, I know this is real and where I'm meant to be, but I can't erase my past and my memories. The closer we get to this new place, the more I feel in the depths of my soul that this is my destiny. Above all, I keep asking why me?"*

Angie's shoulders moved up and down in a shrugging motion. *"Why not you? Is there someone else you would wish this on? It's not in your nature. Even if the situation would have been different and someone else, let's say from our team, was chosen. You would have been the first to volunteer and try to take their place, so they wouldn't have to do it. So, I ask again, why not you?"*

Kate bowed her head but didn't respond, letting it hang in the air between them. They had finally reached a stretch where the guys could increase the speed, so it was easier to shut down and relax. Plus, she wasn't ready to answer that question yet.

She was ready to weep with joy when they approached their destination for their first break. Her muscles had stiffened up, and her back spasmed with pain. Xavier had found them a hidden spot tucked into a forested area that provided adequate cover. The guys quickly ate and leaned back to rest. While they were using normal human transportation, they still had to maintain shields.

Kate wondered if they would go through all their supplies this first stop. She was also terrified of an attack. They would be worthless in a fight right now. Everyone needed rest to recover. She sure hoped Xavier was out there somewhere, ready to help them if needed.

"He's there in the shadows keeping watch. Zane is with him, too." Xander's words came out as a whisper, but they were comforting to Kate all the same. She hadn't realized her fears were written on her face.

Xander leaned forward and squeezed her hand, but still moved slowly. Kate wondered why his recovery was so much more complicated than Gregory's. There was a missing piece here. She felt it, but his voice sounded strong and confident. Maybe she was imagining things.

"We made good time today," Xander said. "So, we will be able to get a little extra rest before we move on this afternoon. We'll sleep for a couple hours then stretch and get our blood flowing. Xavier says no demons have picked up on our trail, so we're doing okay for now." He leaned back against the tree and shut his eyes.

Kate waited until Xander woke a few hours later and asked the questions plaguing her mind. "You've mentioned several times about me transforming into the Mystic or some type of awakening. What is involved in that?" Kate felt guilty since he still seemed tired, but she needed to start wrapping her head around the facts.

"Mystics are predestined for a battle called the Rising every few hundred years, as I told you earlier. They're usually born within one hundred years of this battle. Once the Mystic reaches maturity, he or she is taken to the Ancient Council and a ritual ceremony is performed called the Awakening.

"I've never seen one, but my understanding is that it allows access to all of your powers and creates a permanent bond with your Guardian. You'll be stripped of your humanity and fully enveloped into all realms — in theory. We've never actually transformed a human." He leaned his head back again, but she wasn't done yet.

She wasn't sure if she wanted the answer to her next question, but it needed to be asked anyway. Basically, she'd be a guinea pig for these Council people. "So, if I'm not human, what would I be?"

Xander opened one eye to respond. She wanted to shake him to fully wake him up. After all, it was her life on the line.

"The only thing that would change would be your DNA. It would transform into something like mine or Gregory's. You would gain your full abilities. I don't know much else. Hopefully, Marcus and Rowena will be able to explain the whole process once we are there. All we were told is to make sure you arrive in the Meadows before the time of the Awakening ceremony. Apparently, there is a specific timeframe for the process to be successful. Mind if I just close my eyes and rest a little longer?"

Kate patted his arm in reassurance. She hoped he'd have enough patience for a couple more questions. He closed his eyes and turned his head away from her. Kate watched him, mentally working things out. Obviously, no one knew much about the ceremony. They probably kept it protected so demons didn't learn too much. *Smart but frustrating.*

She decided to move on for now, before he completely zoned out.

"I know Zane is a Shadow Warrior and is helping to protect us, but what exactly are they? I don't understand how he's helping Xavier and us, yet he's stuck in some other world."

"They're a bunch of dickheads that renounced their birthright, is what they are," Gregory venomously snapped before Xander could respond.

"Shut your ass, Gregory." Xander barked. *That woke him up.* "They've saved us several times, so quit your whining and be glad Zane doesn't take it personally when you run your mouth."

"Oooh, I'm real scared. Say what you want, but more of us will die because of them this time." Gregory turned away from them.

Kate glanced at Xander. Anger smoldered in his bright blue eyes. He glared at Gregory's back. Well, she'd certainly managed to touch a nerve with this subject.

Xander motioned for her to get closer. She scooted over and leaned against his shoulder.

"Shadow Warriors are a rare species," he said. "Extremely powerful and excellent at killing demons. They used to be guardians to humans. Their last leader made a grave error in judgment and locked them in the Shadow World. Their current leader, Zane, has not been able to find a way to get back to any of the other realms.

"Many magical beings blame the Shadow Warriors for all the demons we now have to fight. But more importantly we have never fought at a Rising without them. Zane hopes that once you are awakened, you'll find a way to help them. We need them in this battle. Once we get to the Meadows, I promise that you'll hear all the stories you can handle. For now, let's stay focused on your destiny and your awakening ceremony."

Kate nearly bit off her tongue to stop asking questions. He was tired, but she couldn't help it.

She decided to start a list of questions to ask him when they had more time. For now, she stood and dusted off her pants. She'd let him get some more rest and walked over to Angie. If they wanted to stay on schedule, a brief nap is all they could afford. She wanted to sleep in a bed tonight, and it wouldn't hurt if it included Xander and no interruptions. She was ready for things with them to move forward.

"Daylight's wasting boys and girls!" Gregory woke them after a few short hours of sleep. "Let's get a move on. I want to sleep in a real bed tonight if you don't mind."

Kate grabbed her pack and was surprised at her lack of reaction when the guys packed the bikes with a wave of their hand.

They hopped on the motorcycles and were off again. The wind rushed against her body. She wondered if one day this would all seem commonplace, and she would take this brief time in her human life for granted.

Angie adjusted herself yet again on the bike hoping for a moment of relief, but it was more and more fleeting each time. *"When do you want to stop for another break?"*

"I figure it's better for the guys if we keep going and make few stops. The sooner we get there the better."

"Amen to that." Angie focused on her surroundings. Her mind was always on alert and contemplating her future. After this last stop, things had gotten a lot more complicated. She was beginning to feel a strong sexual pull toward Gregory, and there wasn't any point in denying it. She wondered, *was it chemistry or circumstances?*

Then there was Xavier. Angie couldn't put into words the connection she'd felt to him. It wasn't just sexual. She considered it to be more spiritual. The absurdity of all of it made her laugh out loud.

On a good note, she'd finally begun to feel a purpose on this mission. Her job was to keep Kate grounded and help save innocents around the world. It was the same career she'd always loved, on a slightly different playing field. This was her destiny, and she'd see it through.

Kate sent her comfort through their link. Angie hadn't realized how closely Kate had been watching her thoughts and emotions. *Spooky* sometimes, but in a good way.

"All we can do is see how things play out. I think you need to spend more time with both of them before you decide anything permanent, sexual or otherwise. And it probably needs to be on more equal footing when we're better protected." Kate also passed Angie an idea that she had thought of earlier. They might feel attraction differently in their world.

Changing topics to lessen Angie's anxiety, Kate began talking about past cases that could have been signs or warnings had they known all this magical stuff existed. Angie wanted to laugh at her. She knew those tactics better than most.

"By the way," Kate asked, "were you ever able to reach any of the team?"

Angie couldn't stop the emotions as she passed along the updates. *"Yes, I talked to Teri briefly while we were still in Tennessee. I told her we were following a lead and would be out of communication for a while, and that we'd check in when we could. I feel guilty for the lies, but the truth would horrify them. That's why your ancestor protected you, he didn't want you to know. It gave you a brief glimpse of normalcy."* She replayed the conversation in her head for Kate.

Angie took a drink of water and stared ahead. They had entered a long winding side road. A forest stood on their right and to the left a ravine. It provided a smoother ride, but at this point the pain had become a permanent fixture in her backside.

She returned her focus to Kate. *"Why were you thinking about the Shadow Warriors earlier? I could see your brain ticking away, and I didn't want to intrude and mess up your flow."*

Kate sent the mental equivalent of a shrug. *"I'm not sure. Something triggered inside my head telling me to get to know the Shadow Warriors. All of them. I can't explain why. When I understand my powers, I intend to meet the warriors and try to find a way for them to help in the battle. It doesn't take a rocket scientist to realize that to improve our chances of survival we need them, and I do prefer to live at the end of the day."* Kate looked up into the clouds like she was searching for something slightly out of reach. Angie felt the constant anxiety she tried to hide.

"I'd prefer the living option myself." Angie adjusted her helmet and stretched her back. "What do you think of the brief information Xander provided?"

"That Zane is incredibly strong and gifted. I believe he has good intentions, but I'm curious to know the whole story. I hope he's trustworthy and will make a great ally, but we have to get him in the picture more." Kate grew quiet. Angie knew she'd slipped back into her reflections of everything she'd learned. Her own thoughts drifted as well. She contemplated what kind of future she could possibly have in their world. A place she didn't belong.

"Kate."

Kate jumped a mile at the new voice in her head, but immediately recognized it. *"Xavier, what is it?"*

"Everything is going well, so don't be alarmed. The demons are still randomly searching. You made good time and should be at the farmhouse by nightfall. By the way, I want you to know that I've decided to help more with the training and preparations than I have been. It shouldn't have been that close. I'm sorry."

He'd barely gotten there in time to save Angie, but he had, and that was the important thing. He deeply suffered every time he stepped into their realm. For him to offer his assistance demonstrated his resolve, and his way of declaring his allegiance to her. That's what struck her the most. He had come directly to her and not through Xander.

"It's wonderful you've decided to help us. We definitely need all the help we can get. But go at your own pace and comfort level, not ours. It can't be forced. Also,

I'd like to ask your help with Zane to get to know him better."

Xavier's laugh was hoarse in her mind. *"Maybe force is what I need to give me a wake-up call. I'll work something out with Zane. He welcomes the opportunity."*

"Xavier, I have a gut feeling it'll be something else that delivers your wake-up call." She had no doubt he understood what she'd referred to. Xavier broke their connection. What a crew they all were!

Kate answered Angie's questioning thought. *"Xavier informed me that we're only a couple of hours away from the farm, and we'll make it there by late afternoon. For the moment, we're still safe from the demons. It was a positive report considering our luck."*

They rode for what seemed like forever. Xander had maintained silence to keep the shields in place. In the distance, Kate felt relief seeing a massive white house sitting high on a hillside that reminded her of a Southern plantation home. Excitement overrode the unrelenting pain as she pointed toward the house.

"We're here."

16

Pain radiated up Kate's entire spine. *"Thank the Lord Almighty. I was ready to walk the rest of the way. We need to get somewhere safe for them to rest."*

"I know. Look ahead. There's a couple waiting for us."

Kate nodded at Angie's comment.

They cautiously approached the two story, white farmhouse surrounded by a wraparound porch. The afternoon sun warmed her skin. Beautiful flowers encircled the home and produced sweet aromatics. Kate felt a strange sense of déjà vu like she'd been to a house like this before. She shook her head to clear it and focused on the new people. The man standing on the front porch waved and ran toward them with incredible speed and agility. His wife, Kate assumed, followed close behind him. They stopped in front of her and Angie, to help them slide off, then grabbed their gear.

"Hi, I'm Joseph, and this is my wife, Lucia. Our home is your home. We'll show you to your rooms in a moment. The men will secure the supplies out here while the ladies can follow Lucia into the house. Security is our first priority." Excitement lit up his face. He rushed around to make sure everyone had what they needed. Lucia guided them to the back door.

Kate and Angie entered the charming house and everything became a blur. She wanted to make sure the guys were safe and then crash for a couple of hours. She finally understood the true definition of the word *weary*. Angie looped her arm through Kate's as they made their way through the rooms. Kate dragged into the kitchen and plopped down at the table. Angie sat beside her. The past several days had melded into what seemed like one extremely long endless day.

She glanced around at her surroundings, while waiting for the guys to come inside. She tried to distract herself from going back outside to check on them. It was insane how much she'd come to rely on their presence. Angie made small talk with Lucia allowing Kate to zone out.

The kitchen had an older style, with copper pots hanging from the ceiling over an island. The walls were half covered with an art-deco backsplash and neutral tan color paint above it.

In the center of the wall right above the table was a large hand-crafted frame with a beautiful farm scene. It appeared hand painted. Kate remembered her childhood home having a similar feel and found comfort sitting in the room.

Despite the older motif, she noticed their current appliances and some of the top-notch technology. These were not outdated or old-fashioned people, but they were probably a couple looking for peace and normalcy. Kate perfectly understood that notion, but all the decorating in the world couldn't fix everything or change what was coming.

The kitchen door flew open, catching everyone's attention. Angie gasped and Kate stood especially since it opened on its own. Anxiety tingled up Kate's spine.

Joseph stumbled through the door helping Xander and Gregory come inside. Xander's face was ashen, and Gregory only looked slightly better. What had drained them so badly? They were completely at the mercy of these strangers. It didn't make any sense.

Xander crossed the room to her and rubbed her shoulders, slightly calming her nerves.

Lucia brought over a ton of food and hot tea to the table. "Eat up. I know you must be tired. I carefully prepared all the food to be high in protein and vitamins. The tea is a special blend created by Xander's mother. She sent it this morning, when the Council discovered the change in plans." She touched Kate's shoulder in assurance. "They will be much better in no time."

Kate swallowed, feeling out of her league. "I'm new to all this and don't really understand everything. Xavier says we'll be safe here." She didn't want to insult the couple, but also wanted them to know she was still suspicious.

Lucia smiled and her brown eyes reflected understanding. "We know and have been waiting for you for many years. I have known Xander and Xavier for over a hundred years. Joseph grew up with them, but I moved there later. We trained every day and took many classes together before Xavier's tragedy." She looked off into the distance and pushed her long dark brown braid over her shoulder. Her skin appeared unusually pale, but her bone structure was strong. Her mannerisms inspired confidence, and Kate began to relax.

"We would stay up till all hours of the night, imagining what you would be like and how the Rising would play out. Once Xander's destiny was revealed at his birth, the Meadows became consumed with the Mystic and the

Rising." Her tone saddened at the mentioning of the future battle.

Joseph stepped behind her and placed a hand on her shoulder. Kate noticed that his looks were the opposite of his wife's. His hair reminded her of white sand on a beach, yet his skin had a dark tan. Maybe he worked outside a lot. His eyes captivated Kate the most. They were a golden color. He had a square jaw and an intense gaze. His demeanor screamed warrior just like Xander.

He bent down and kissed Lucia's cheek in reassurance then turned toward Kate. "After Xavier went into the shadows, and Xander began actively searching for you, we bought this farm and decided to have a few years of peace and quiet. We needed some time from all the talk of battle, but don't get me wrong. We always intended this to be a safe house and have been setting it up for years. We plan to fight by your side. We swear allegiance to you." Both he and Lucia bowed in her direction.

Kate wasn't sure how to respond.

"Should we survive," Joseph continued. "We intend to finally start the family we've been hoping for. But we have to help defeat the Omega first, so our children will have many years of peace before facing something so horrendous." He leaned forward and held Lucia's hand. Their eyes met and Kate felt the love and the strong bond they shared. He sat down beside her to drink some more tea.

Lucia wiped at her eyes, trying to hold in her emotions. "Forgive me for making a scene, but you being here starts the timetables that have seemed frozen for years. I can finally see a light at the end of the tunnel, and whatever the future holds, I'm ready. We'll hang onto this farm as a vacation home, but I'm excited to return to our true home in the Meadows." She went back to the stove to grab more food; the guys had already cleared the table — twice.

Kate finally began to understand the emotional impact of the upcoming war and how many people were placing all their hopes and dreams on her. It was a real wake-up call. She tried desperately to forget that the fate of mankind rested on her shoulders — at least for now. It could only be her. No one else could save them. If she failed, they all failed.

Thankful once again for her mental compartments, she pushed everything aside and focused back on Xander.

Xander focused on his surroundings. He felt like someone had ripped him apart and turned him inside out. His head pounded, but the pain began to ease as Xavier pushed energy inside him. Xander was careful not to accept too much and weaken his brother further. He could no longer absorb any energy from his surroundings. His time dwindled fast.

Xavier had chosen Lucia and Joseph for high magical ability and loyalty to the family. Joseph had always been one of Xander's best friends. He completely trusted him.

He leaned back and Kate's arm snaked around him. Her scent invaded him. With time running out, he intended to make some good memories for them here. Maybe one day she would be able to come back here and remember what could have been.

She met his eyes, and he smiled. She had feelings for him, but he wasn't sure how strong they were. He glanced toward Gregory and noted that he was making great progress. He knew they needed several hours of sleep to be fully restored. For now, he believed Kate was safe and well protected.

Xander glanced up at Joseph. "Could you take us to our room, so we can let the women sleep for a while? I could use a good sleep myself, and Kate is so excited about sleeping in a bed she can barely contain it." She shoved at him good-naturedly but nodded her head.

"Of course," Joseph said. "Follow me. Xavier wants you all deep undercover, so we've set up accommodations in our basement, which has an escape route built in for extra safety. There are a couple of bedrooms and a bathroom." He paused as Kate and Angie cheered. "I take it you're excited over the bathroom, too."

Both of them vigorously nodded. Xander smothered a laugh.

"You better believe it," Kate said. "Indoor plumbing was the greatest invention ever!"

Angie squealed in delight when she saw that the bathroom also had a shower.

He guessed they were more than pleased with these accommodations.

Gregory snickered and threw his bag down in one of the rooms. They were all still sleeping in the same area for safety, but at least they had separate rooms this time. Sleep was first and foremost on Xander's list. He was surprised, but pleased, when Kate chose to room with him instead of Angie.

Maybe her intentions were for safety, or this happened to be the room with its own bathroom. The sparkle in her eyes led him to believe that maybe she wanted to finish what they'd started at the campsite. Once he could actually function again, it was on.

Kate woke up before anyone else and finally paid attention to her surroundings. Joseph and Lucia had done a great job trying to make them feel at ease. The beds were big and comfortable with fluffy pillows and soft sheets. The walls were a pale blue, the sitting chairs were dark brown leather, and the furniture was all a beautifully polished cherry. There was a door leading outside for increased privacy and training.

She examined the trap door that Joseph had shown her. It led a mile away and had weapons and transportation for a quick getaway. It could only be opened magically. She wouldn't mind spending some time at this beautiful home but didn't want to put her new friends in danger.

Sitting in the nearest armchair to her bed, she watched Xander sleep. She tried to keep all her emotions at bay, but she could lose everything. Even if she defeated the assassins, made it to the portal, and survived the awakening, there was a high likelihood that she would die fighting this Braxus character in the near future.

Of course, this point was moot if she didn't transform correctly during the awakening. She couldn't see how a human body could endure a complete transformation. Maybe it wouldn't be too bad, since she'd been born for that destiny.

Death was a high possibility from her point of view.

She sighed and went into the bathroom, which was mostly plain with white walls and pale blue rugs and towels. It didn't matter, as long as it had hot water and a toilet. She'd never been this thankful for modern plumbing.

The warm water ran over her face, and the tears she'd been holding in for days mixed with the water. She'd tried to understand, needed to find her place, but no one deserved this destiny. Including her.

A small selfish part of her wanted to run away and not face her future. If she didn't have full confidence in herself, how could she ask others to believe in her or to fight? This would be a weakness the demons would prey upon.

No, she couldn't allow it. She had to save all the faces rotating through her head. Just like the relentless pursuits of her perps throughout the years. She had to win. She made the promise to herself in the mirror and saw determination take over. She smiled. Somehow, she'd found the way back to herself again. She found purpose. The reflection staring back at her was finally the one she recognized. It was time to embrace her new world, starting with Xander.

With a new mindset, she dressed in a silky gown Lucia had given her and walked out of the bathroom. It was still late, but Xander was awake and sat propped up in the bed. Grasping for courage, she made her way to him. There would be no interruptions tonight. It was time to declare the passion swirling inside them.

Xander met her eyes, and his demeanor shifted. Apparently, she gave the right signals. His chest moved rapidly, and he quickly shoved the sheets aside to move toward her. She loved him. At least she could finally admit it to herself. She'd fallen head over heels in love with this arrogant and overbearing man in a matter of days. More importantly, she knew he loved her, too. He hadn't said it, but she could feel it in every touch and glance.

Her eyes met his, and she held him close for several minutes, feeling and *accepting* the emotions. Xander kissed her softly and then plunged deeper. His tongue stroked across her lips, gaining access. After a few moments lost in each other's arms, he pulled back a little. Her eyes reflected in his.

He leaned in. "I love you, Kate," he whispered against her ear. "With everything I am."

She could see the love in his eyes, and he opened his mind enough so she could feel the depth of his emotions. She barely held her tears in check. She'd finally found the person who loved her for her, enabling her to completely trust him..

They'd never have lies between them. "I love you too, Xander," she rasped. "With all that I am." And for the first time, she opened her mind to him and let him feel her emotions.

Xander felt humbled and guilty all at once. Part of him knew he should tell her everything. The rest of him refused to lose her. Every minute was precious. The bond between them had solidified. She had given him her full trust, but he would eventually break her heart.

The feeling of cotton covered his tongue, and he couldn't speak. He loved her more than anything and would have to find the strength to eventually let her go. He pushed the emotions aside and focused on the beautiful woman in front of him.

After his initial reaction of self-pity, came the salivating and panting. He was truly pathetic. Her barely existent silk gown set him on fire. He'd always had a weakness for silk. The color was a radiant white against her tanned skin, and it was glaringly obvious she wore nothing underneath. Good Lord, he was already about to explode, and he hadn't even touched her. *Yet.*

Her electric blue eyes hypnotized him, and her hips swayed in time to the beat of his heart. Anticipation and longing surged. There should be a limit on how much torture he'd endured waiting for this moment. He desperately tried to hang on to his sanity for a few moments longer. There was one more thing he needed from her for tonight to be complete. In case he didn't make it to the Meadows, he needed to finish their bond.

Reaching out to pull her into his arms felt like heaven and better than any of his fantasies. Her skin was smooth like silk, and she smelled of strawberries with a light hint of spice. He combed his fingers through her hair and met her eyes with love and determination. He wanted the ultimate commitment from her. "Kate, there's something I need to ask you."

"All right." She nodded encouragingly, giving him her full attention.

"In my world, we don't have traditional weddings like many humans have, or at least that's not all we do. We have a bonding ritual to go beyond the physical into spiritual connections. It's a deep connection that can't be severed until death."

Her forehead crinkled in doubt. "What kind of ritual?" Fear crept into her voice.

This was not the way he had planned for this to go. He decided to jump in and hope for the best. "It's a promise to love each other eternally and have an unbreakable mental link. I've heard it also builds stronger attraction over time, so boredom doesn't become an issue when you're living for centuries." He smiled. She raised one eyebrow.

"We do this by connecting mentally and spiritually during our climax. It's called the *mating of souls* among my people. Essentially, we mentally and physically accept each other as soul mates, and it creates a special unbreakable bond between the two of us that will work no matter how far we are apart." He didn't add that it would also transfer all of his abilities and knowledge to her in the event of his death and give her an extra power boost for the future.

He took a deep breath and regretted not being able to tell her everything. "I'd like to create this bond with you," he added, "to be one with you. I want you to accept me for who I am, while you're still completely human. It's the way our relationship began, and I believe that this is the time for us to make our commitment."

At least that much was truth. It was how they began and quite possibly how they would end. He waited patiently for her answer.

"I love you," she finally said after what seemed like hours, but was only a few seconds. "And I want to be with you in every way possible. But I also want to understand what I'm agreeing to. You're saying this is a simple ceremony joining us together. No crazy blood rituals, weird soul-bonding, life-force sharing, or anything else right? I don't want you to automatically die if I do."

Xander laughed and pulled her in close. "You read too many books. It's simply making a lifetime commitment including a solid mental link, which we would sort of have anyway since I'm your Guardian. My life isn't physically connected to yours if you should die or vice versa. But I want you to choose me to be one true mate on your own. What do you think? Would you be willing to do this?" It was selfish, but he wanted to be with her completely.

Kate dismissed her initial feeling of fear. Xander offered total love and acceptance, and he was the one person who could see behind all the masks. Her eyes watered as she nodded and smiled. "Yes, I'll bond with you. I already know you're my soul mate, my heart. There's nothing I want more than to know you're by my side for as long as we both live."

She pushed up on her toes and pressed her lips against his. It started sweet and slow. Then deepened. She'd waited a lifetime to feel this way and to feel her heart soar free. She pushed aside the thought of how much time she had left in her world or his.

The temperature of the room skyrocketed, and Xander's hands began a slow exploration of her thighs and bottom. His tongue delved deeper. His hands moved upward, slowly taking her gown up as he went. She was on fire and wanted the clothes gone. Xander must have read her mind and removed all their clothing with a wave of his hand.

It went from hot to scorching, as bare flesh touched bare flesh. She wanted to take it slow and savor every moment, but also wanted the ultimate connection. His thumb brushed over her skin, and her core literally spasmed with desire. She ached with tension and pent-up need. If someone interrupted them now, she would shoot them dead.

She moaned as his hands massaged her sensitized body. Her muscles clenched with longing. She wanted more. She wanted to make *him* lose control.

She began her own exploration, wanting to learn his body like he learned hers. Starting at his shoulders, she slowly dragged her nails down his back and over his buttocks. He shuddered and gasped. Driving him crazy excited her.

He took it up a notch. He laced his fingers through hers, held her arms above her head, and his mouth slid down her throat to her chest.

She couldn't think. Couldn't breathe. She wanted more. She wanted all of him. She grabbed his hair and pulled him up to meet her in a passion-filled kiss.

They joined as if they'd been a part of each other forever. Tears came into her eyes at the sheer impact of their all-consuming connection. Once again, their eyes met. He leaned in to kiss her. "Don't forget to open your mind for me," he whispered into her ear, heightening the sensation of his movement all the more.

She felt like her insides were being torn apart from the pressure escalating inside her. The intensity built up from her toes. Using her last moments of sanity, she opened her mind and connected to him.

Instantly, emotions overwhelmed her. She felt his passion, desire, and need for her. She could see the two halves of a whole fitting perfectly together. She couldn't stop the tears, as she began tipping over the edge. They both completely let go and finished what they'd started. Their love exploded into something she'd never forget.

Her mind warped. *Wow! Holy crap! Wow!* Her body buzzed. She drifted, as if on a cloud, without a worry in the world. Her bones were like jelly. She wasn't entirely sure she'd ever be able to move again, and she didn't care.

She was addicted now, no doubt there. Knowing his feelings and how much pleasure he'd received, astounded her. She wouldn't need any of those fancy therapy books about women on one planet and men on another anymore. She could simply look into his mind and read everything she wanted to know. It was kind of scary knowing he could do the same, unless she invoked her Mystic powers.

He placed feather light kisses all over her face and smiled. He looked awfully proud of himself and very satisfied. She smirked and nipped at his chin playfully.

He pushed up on his forearms. "Are you okay?"

"I'm wonderful. That was amazing. Did I do the mental thing right? Did we bond correctly?"

"Search my mind and see." He held still and let her explore his mind.

She closed her eyes, trying to push her hormones aside. Connecting with his mind was amazing. It was as if it was hers. She could see his memories, thoughts, and desires. Everything was open.

She could even see he had compartments similar to hers where he separated and controlled his memories. This was fantastic! She could see their private link and how intense the connection was. They were — without a doubt — permanently tied together. The thought was comforting and scary all at the same time. She didn't have time to look at everything but would learn what all he could eventually teach her.

His hand glided down her cheek, and she laughed. Clearly, he was ready to distract her again. They both paused. The lights flickered slightly when she turned to face him. He kissed her gently, and their passion ignited. An electrical charge hit the air.

A shock slammed into Xander. He slid off Kate, assuming they were under attack.

Electricity bounced all over the room, and her back arched so high she nearly came off the bed.

His eyes widened as he saw hers begin to glow. He leaned down and peered into them. What he saw there resembled a storm brewing, with multiple shades of blue and flashes of lightning.

What the hell? Was she under attack or was it something else? He stared deeper.

He connected to her mind to understand what was happening. She panicked and started panting. She couldn't speak. He could feel the fire spreading through her, and her fear escalated. *What is going on?* All the energy rampaged inside her, unrestrained.

"Xander, what's happening?" Kate raged, out of control. She met his eyes. "I feel — like I've been — hit by a lightning bolt — or two." Her body undulated on the bed.

He'd never seen anything like this before and full-out panic set in. It was like she was drawing all the energy in from the whole state.

"I don't know," he said. "I'm going to dress you and call for Xavier. Hold on." The lights continued to flicker. Xander looked out the bedroom door and realized it was happening throughout the whole house.

Kate couldn't breathe, and her panicked state of mind made it more complicated for him to stay connected. An unrelenting pressure ran through her blood from head to toe. She reached out and grasped his hand. He could merely watch her thrash around on the bed and pray for relief. She needed a release, but what was she releasing?

He linked with Xavier.

Gregory pounded on the door. "What the hell is going on in there?"

Xander unlocked and opened the door. Gregory gasped, then charged into the room ready to fight. "What's wrong with her, Xander? What can I do?"

Xavier burst through the other door, with Angie right on his heels. "Let me see her." Running over to her side, he carefully looked over her. "Energy is pouring into her from an inner source that I don't understand. Gregory, put up a shield to block her powers from leaving this room. We sure as hell don't want to be caught right now." For once, Gregory didn't argue or make any comment.

"Angie, you and Xander try to keep her calm and comfortable. I'm going to Rowena and demand some answers. No way that they didn't see this coming. I can determine that it's something related to her mystic abilities but can't figure out the source."

Xander grabbed Xavier's arm. "Be careful. You're not their favorite person. Popping in on them is highly dangerous. I need you to come back with answers and not in a box." He turned back to Kate. After running his hand through her hair, he kissed her temple. Momentarily, everyone was silent.

"Don't worry," Xavier said. "They should see me coming, right?" He smirked and disappeared in a flash of light.

Kate continued to pant and thrash around on the bed, but at least the energy in the air had decreased a little. The lights had stopped flickering.

Gregory wiped her face with a cold cloth, while Angie held her hand. Kate's eyes rolled into her head and she lost consciousness. Xander held her other hand, trying to block some of the pain for her. She calmed and no longer thrashed. From the outside she appeared fine, but he could feel the agony radiating inside her. He would kill Xavier himself, if he didn't get back soon.

Xavier popped in. "She'll be all right."

Everyone breathed a sigh of relief upon hearing the most important information. Tears hit Xander's eyes, as his panic decreased. "So, what the hell happened? What did they say?" He was too focused on Kate to link with Xavier.

"I spoke with Rowena. She was waiting for me. As I suspected, she was not surprised."

Pure rage built inside of Xander.

"Wait," Xavier went on. "She said that this was necessary. That a level of trust must have been achieved for this to even be possible. She regretted that they couldn't warn you. She also asked that you forgive her, but it had to be this way."

Frustrated, Xander growled, barely holding himself back from popping in on the Council — especially Rowena — and telling them exactly what he thought about their interference. "What about Kate?"

"Ironically, it was her own natural energy stores. Remember you mentioned her having a lot of untapped abilities when you began teaching her meditation? When the two of you bonded, it released a portion of her energy sources. It was always the key and necessary for her to gain her powers in the Meadows. Without accessing her human abilities in this realm, she wouldn't have survived gaining her powers there. It would have been overload and destroyed her."

"What does *bonded* mean?" Angie's husky voice filled the silence. "You didn't do anything *kinky* to her, did you?" Xander tried to control his frustration. Gregory leaned over and took her hand.

"Bonding is like a marriage in our realm," Gregory said. "I won't go into the whole process now, but both parties must agree to share their lives forever. It's like soul mates. It creates an unbreakable mental, physical, and spiritual link between the two. It usually takes place for the Guardian and Mystic during the awakening timeframe."

"Oh, so y'all are like married now?" she asked, looking at Xander.

"In my culture at least. Look she's coming around." He leaned forward and reached for her.

Everyone focused back on Kate, who was drenched in sweat. She looked like she had run a marathon. Sweeping over her with his hand, Xander cleaned her and put fresh clothes on her. For a brief moment, they all sat there in silence waiting for their heart rates and adrenaline to return to normal.

Xander laid his head down on her stomach, relieved and still terrified all at once. "Thank you, Xavier."

"No problem. At least she's okay. That's all that matters. I'm heading out. We'll meet later tomorrow to set up everything. I've got to get the supplies and help Zane do all the prep. She'll need lots of rest to recover, especially with us being ready for a fight at any time. See you tomorrow."

He quickly faded into the Shadows.

Gregory draped his arm around Angie's shoulders and helped her to her feet. "She needs to rest. Let's go next door to get some sleep. We'll leave it unlocked in case she needs you."

"What happened to me?" Kate's weak voice couldn't have made Xander happier. Her eyes slowly opened.

"You received more of your powers." He sent the whole story through their mental link, to use less of her energy.

"Wow. You mean there's more of this to come? *Super*." Her sarcasm made him smile.

She remained weak, and he put her in a deep sleep, knowing she would recover by tomorrow. For tonight, she would be safe in the Dream Realm. She needed all the strength she could get. He hadn't told her yet what going through the portal would do to her human body. That wouldn't be pleasant either.

"Sleep well, baby." He tucked her against his body and drifted off into a fitful sleep involving hellfire and jets of lightning.

J.L. Lawrence

17

Kate dragged her eyes open and slowly sat up on her elbows. The fog lifted from her vision and she saw Xander. She remembered the information he'd given her last night before she'd fallen asleep.

If that was the human dose, the hell with the magical one. That Council of his would need to give her a heavy amount of morphine before she'd go through that crap again.

Xander sat at the table, looking perfect, sipping a cup of coffee. Of course, he had the advantage of waving his hand and being clean with a fresh set of clothes. She smiled. There would be some definite advantages to gaining powers.

Xander nodded. "Hey there, beautiful." He smiled up at her, his feelings for her shining through. He didn't try to hide any of it.

She went over to him and sat in his lap. "Hey yourself. How are you doing? You look much better today."

"I'm much better than yesterday and a lot more rested."

"I bet." She picked up her brush from the table to work through some of the tangles.

"How about you?" He took the brush out of her hands and began combing through her hair. He massaged her scalp and her head tingled in pleasure.

Kate leaned forward and turned to face him. "Good for the moment, but I'm sure you have a fun-filled day in store for us. My insides still feel a little hyped up. Nothing major." Not able to help herself, she placed her palm against his cheek for the contact.

"Actually, you're in luck. Today is mostly a talking and sitting day. At least for *you*. Angie will be working on training to build up her endurance and accuracy, but we have to start working on channeling your energy and mastering basic skills. This is the only place we can safely practice, before we enter the Meadows. Then, it will be full steam ahead with little time for basics." He leaned forward and buried his face in her hair. She could still see the fear in his eyes. Hell, *she* was still afraid. They had to move on.

"Will I be able to do much yet?"

"You have a lot of powers that couldn't be subdued. It's enough to perform simple tasks like levitating and manifesting weapons. You'll also be able to transfer and channel energy to some degree."

"Do I have to say rhyming spells and mix potions — "

"Well good morning," Angie broke in. "I certainly woke up at an interesting time. You're not going to start mixing things in a cauldron and wearing a pointy hat, are you? Kate, are you okay?" Angie gripped her hand. Kate swore their bones touched. Apparently, everyone had been scared by her light show. Gregory walked in and stared for a few seconds, evaluating her.

"I'm good now. A little extra energy, but the pain has subsided. As for the cauldron, I don't know yet. That's what I was asking when you interrupted me." Kate winked, then looked back at Xander. "Well?"

"I'd like to see the full image you have of the Meadows in that head of yours someday." Xander straightened his shoulders and cleared his throat. "Not everyone uses potions and herbs." He'd become more serious. "Some control energy itself and don't need those things to access their magic, while others do. All of us use herbs in some way, depending on what we need to accomplish. Especially in healing. Gregory, how about you go set up for training, and I'll explain a little to the ladies before we get started?"

Gregory shrugged and in a flash was clean and dressed for the day. "Sure, I don't mind doing all the manual labor. I know all the old stories anyway. I'll work with Angie on weaponry and demonic weak spots, while you work on tapping into Kate's energy field. Just make sure you keep it contained." He grunted and headed for the door.

"Don't forget, Xavier will be coming to work with Angie this afternoon. Like him, she's an excellent tactician. He'll be showing her how to focus on specific strategies to help us make it to the portal undetected and cross over into the Meadows. We need to remember to capitalize on her strengths."

Gregory rolled his eyes and ground his teeth together. "Great! Can't wait. That won't last but his usual ten minutes." He walked out and slammed the door behind him.

Xander rubbed his hands over his eyes, then down his face. "That went well. I can always count on my friends to act like adults."

Angie sighed and nervously ran her fingers through her hair. "I'm not helping an already stressed situation, am I?"

Kate didn't know how to help her with this one.

Xander looked straight into her eyes. "It is what it is. We can't help the way fate chooses things to unfold. For now, maybe it's better that you *can't* make a choice. That would only cause more hard feelings. We have enough of those. But eventually, you will have to choose. Make sure it's the right one."

Kate shivered at his tone and was unsettled to say the least. She reached out and squeezed Angie's hand in reassurance. "You'll know when the time comes. Trust your heart to decide in its own time. Until then, keep an open mind, but stay focused on our overall goal."

Angie weakly smiled back. "Always, the job first."

To dispel the tension, Kate glanced at Xander. She was struck momentarily speechless, as he waved his hand down her hair to tie it back into a complicated braid. That usually took twenty minutes to complete. Having powers would be so much fun but would be followed by so much pain. "So, what's the difference between using energy and spells?"

Xander leaned back and drew a line with his hand in the air. "You have three main categories in my realm. Since we're the home of the Council, we also have many other types of *people*, for lack of a better word. They consider our realm a safe haven of sorts. This leads to a lot of individuals with mixed powers, so it isn't as cut and dry as it seems.

"However, this may help a little. One group is the pure witches and wizards. Their power stems from nature, so they use spells and potions, tying in those components of nature to access their abilities. You'll hear them refer to chakras and spells a lot when channeling their energy.

"The second group is the sorcerers, seers, healers, and mystics. Their power stems from energy in the atmosphere. They learn to pool and channel the energy to access their magical gifts. The last group is kind of like a mixed breed, and where many of us fall now with the exception of gliders. Our parents are combinations of sorcerers, healers, wizards, or whatever. This doesn't include specific species such as faeries and gliders, but several of the different species have mixed together to some extent."

"Mystics are the exception," he continued before she'd even asked the question. He'd become much more adept at reading her. "Because despite their heritage, they can use any and all powers, especially if they embrace the light. They're put in the second category simply because of their control over energy. Guardians are also given more access to energy flows to complement the Mystic."

Kate rubbed her forehead. "Well, that's not confusing at all, now is it?" she scoffed.

Angie widened her eyes, staring at her. The more they learned, the more it became clear as mud.

Xander shrugged. "Just the way it is. We're all slightly different species, but the lines are more blurred than in the past. All humans have different talents, like we do."

Kate shook her head. "Are ya kidding? No, not like y'all. Very different, actually. Humans can't go around using mind control or shishkabobbing anyone! So, what exactly are you and Gregory?"

Xander pointed outside. "Gregory is a mix between a sorcerer and a witch. I'm a mix between a wizard and a healer. I also have sorcerer and seer in my lineage, which is probably why I was chosen to be the Guardian. I can control energy through spells and potions, or pooling energy from the atmosphere. Gregory tends to use spells more, but he can do both."

"Ok, so you're all mutts, and I'm some weird creature born every five hundred years or so. Perfect."

Xander glared, and she understood his frustration. "Yes, but you don't have to have any exact qualifications or a specific lineage to be a Mystic. In this case, you're a descendent of the former Mystic, Cassius."

Kate tried to process everything, but how could she possibly learn centuries of history in a few short months?

She rubbed her forehead. "So, what will Angie and I be learning when we get to the Meadows? I sure hope we're going to get plenty of training on understanding all this stuff. It's pretty important to know your people when going into battle."

"Angie will be learning spells, mostly protection spells, which humans with the right lineage can tap into." He turned to Angie. "With your level of psychic abilities, it is the Council's belief that you have some type of magical lineage. Probably a seer or something like that. Many magical beings have chosen to live human lives, which means there are many humans out there with above-average abilities. Camilla, one of our Council members, was once a human witch."

"What? I thought you said no humans had ever entered the Meadows." Excitement filled Kate. She asked for more information. If this chick had found a way, so could Angie.

"She's the first human-born witch ever allowed to serve on the Council. It's said she fought on the night of the last Rising with courage and selflessness, even though humans had never been allowed on the battlefield.

"She had discovered it due to her ancestors' records and wanted to help. She saved Marcus's wife, when she was trying to protect Marcus from a demon at his back. While his wife was focused on him, a demon came in behind her. Camilla picked up a sword dropped by a fallen warrior and sliced off the demon's head.

"Toward the end of the battle, Camilla was mortally wounded and was ready to die, feeling she had served her purpose. Then a bright white light encased her entire body. She was healed, and the mark of the Council placed on her hand. She was also granted immortality that day. The only time in our history that has ever happened. Many say that it was her bravery, some say it was simply fated, and others say it was her willingness to sacrifice her human life to save a supernatural being."

"But she survived the Rising," Angie stated.

"Only by divine intervention," Xander pointed out.

"But she survived," Angie repeated adamantly.

Xander nodded. "She did and has been a great asset and a wonderful leader in the world of human witchcraft."

Angie slipped away into the bathroom. This was becoming more and more complicated. The only way she could help Angie now was by sending her comfort.

Angie finally stepped back into the room with her shoulders squared. "So, I will have to do spells and make potions? Really? *I'm* going to be in the pointy hat?"

"Not quite. You'd have to have an incredibly strong magical lineage in your DNA to get into all of that stuff. Your focus is to learn basics, and for the immediate future you'll be concentrating on protection and strengthening spells and potions. This will help get you ready for the battle, and hopefully give you a slight power boost. Should you survive the Rising, you'll be taught more, if you choose to stay in our world." Xander was trying hard not to laugh at her comical expression.

Angie glared. "What the hell do you mean, should I live? I can't wait to be thrown into your world!"

Kate giggled, picturing Angie with a witch's hat, stirring her potions in a cauldron. She couldn't help it. Angie must have picked up the vision in her mind, because she kicked Kate's shin, hard.

"Ouch!" Kate yelled, doubled over, laughing. "You should have paid more attention to all those shows I watched for pointers."

Angie continued to glare, but the corners of her mouth tilted into a smile. Kate turned back to Xander. "So, what will *I* be doing?"

"Yours is actually a lot harder. Channeling energy is dangerous, and emotions can greatly affect the control you have on your energy levels. You'll learn to pull energy from your surroundings constantly, and then control it mentally to create what you want to happen. It's a lot less precise than spells and takes greater self-control. You have to be careful where you pull the energy from and not deplete the wrong source. Your main weapon will be energy blasts, or what we call *lightning*, that shoots from your hands or anywhere you direct it.

"As your Guardian, one of my jobs is to help anchor you and help you channel all your energy. As a Mystic, you'll be amped up all on your own, without needing to pull in a lot of energy." Xander appeared winded, trying to say everything before any interruptions came.

What do you say to all that? A panic started in her gut as the questions swirled in her head. She was *so* not ready for any of this.

Kate's silence concerned Xander. It wasn't like her not to question everything. He stared into her eyes and used his powers to read her emotions. He felt her panic and mostly her concern that others would get hurt accidentally, because she couldn't control it properly. *Good grief, she runs a federal team with precision and doesn't think she can control a little energy.*

The truth was that he felt much better. Kate's energy storm completely recharged him through their link. Granted, he couldn't sustain it himself anymore, but she was unintentionally supplying him power. If they could avoid any major battles, there was a slim chance he might pull this whole charade off and never have to let her down or cause her to doubt his love for her. Slim, but not impossible.

Laughing, he pulled her back into his lap. "I will anchor you, and you don't have enough power right now to hurt anyone. By the time we get to the Meadows, you'll be a pro. Stop worrying all the time. Let someone else do the worrying for a change." He kissed her nose, then her mouth. He couldn't resist but didn't want to start another energy war. He pulled back. "Trust me."

"Easy for you to say. You've been doing this since birth, but the rest of us not so much. You probably popped out with a fireball in your hand." Even though she spoke warily, Xander kept laughing.

"I thought *I* was the normal one," Angie said, still looking dazed.

The tension in the room eased. Kate laughed at the absurdity of it all. Xander realized they would have to take things one day at a time to prevent being totally overwhelmed.

Kate put her arms around Angie's shoulders. "You, girl, have never been normal a single day in your life. Don't start crying now."

Angie glared.

Kate continued to poke at her.

"What will we be working on today specifically and what is our timeline for staying here?" Kate asked, once the laughter had died down.

Joseph and Lucia had designed the basement with an entrance to the outside. It led into the back yard where their training would take place. Xander stood and walked to the window of the door, watching Gregory finish the training simulation setup. "Energy will eventually be your greatest weapon. More so than any of the weapons you've used so far. We'll be working on calling a weapon and casting a protective shield, like the one you were able to bring up to protect Angie. Xavier told me you were able to freeze the demon's sword for a few seconds. That was a type of shield."

"I meant to ask how I did that."

Xander noticed the fear still weighing heavily inside her. "My guess is that your fear for Angie gave you temporary access to your energy. Now you need to learn how to tap into it at will and control it." Xander rubbed his chin, and then his shoulders, working out some kinks.

"As for your other question, I know we'll be here one or two more nights at least. We're trying to work on a plan to get us to the portal, while providing a false trail. The demons are still searching pretty hard, and my guess is that Fury will try to launch an attack before we can get to the portal. He's an excellent tracker. We also have to prepare for the likelihood of one more battle if he finds us. We've got a lot more details to figure out first, which is why Xavier is coming this afternoon to strategize with Angie."

"How long until we get to the Meadows?" Kate asked, anxiety in her voice. "I thought we would be safe once we arrive."

"We hope to be there within a few days, give or take, depending on the false trail. Time is of the essence for the awakening, and we need to get you trained as much as we can. We also have to find time to recruit some of the best warriors to fight on the front lines. When the time comes — " Xander drifted off and ran his fingers through his hair. Frustrated, he began to pace. The reality of the time available versus what they had to accomplish made him extremely agitated. It was even worse knowing he might not be there to help her.

Clamping down on his emotions, he walked over, wrapped his arms around her, and tucked her head underneath his chin. "We'll get it all figured out. I promise. We'll find the way."

Kate smiled and lightly punched him. "What were you saying about me sounding worried?"

He squeezed her to him and rubbed his hands slowly down her back. He smiled and whispered in her ear, "I'll be worried until this is over, and I have you in my arms every night for the rest of our lives, preferably naked."

She snorted and raised an eyebrow. "Pretty sure of yourself, aren't you?"

"Absolutely." He gave her a cocky grin, then leaned down and kissed her deeply.

Angie left the room to give them some privacy.

Gregory stuck his head in the door. "If you're through telling tall tales and mauling the Mystic, Angie and I need to get to work, today."

"Oh look, my Prince Charming has come to collect me," Angie said sarcastically, popping her head out. She turned to face Kate. "Actually, I meant to say Grumpy, the annoying little dwarf." She walked to the door where he was taking up the entire doorframe and placed her hand across her forehead like a lady in distress. "All my dreams have come true. Pain, pain, pain. Yay me!"

"My lady," he smirked. "Your castle awaits your inspection." He bowed and gestured toward the obstacle course he'd concocted outside.

Kate felt Angie groan inwardly. Kate broke into her thoughts. *"Be careful, Angie, and try to be good."*

"No way, that's not my style. Merlin, here, will not get the best of me." Angie sent the impression of a sly smile and broke the connection.

Kate sighed. That's what frightened her.

"Are you worried?" Xander asked.

Kate gathered a few things in her backpack and slung it over her shoulder. "In more ways than one."

They headed out toward an open field with a big pentagram in the center, accompanied by various other objects, like a book and a feather.

Xander sat down opposite her and took her hands in his. She badly wanted him to kiss her, but the last time they tried tapping into her powers it became a sexual explosion. Clearing her mind, she focused on Xander's face.

"Are you ready to levitate?" he asked.

"As ready as I am to sprout wings and fly!" she fired back.

"Flying comes much later. We have to learn the basics first."

Kate was about to snap back another fiery retort, when she froze at the expression on his face. He wasn't kidding. *Seriously? Holy Crap!*

"When you meditate," Xander began, "You need to center your mind on a single energy source. So, let's start easy, with this feather." He gestured to the large white feather lying on the ground near her. "In your mind, focus on the fact that you want it to move up in the air. Then try to move it from side to side. It might help in the beginning to use your hands to direct the flow of your energy. Close your eyes and call the energy to you." Xander spoke softly and continued to hold her hands.

Her eyes popped open and she grunted. "I still don't get how to call it to me. I can see the flow but that's it. I doubt it has a cell phone."

He looked up toward the sky and took a deep breath. "Close your eyes and relax. Remember when we were beside the river meditating. You felt the energy flow into you. Grasp that thought and focus on how it felt. Everything has energy. Think of positive things like the wind blowing through a field, your friends and family, or anything that makes you happy. Use those feelings."

He ended and Kate became more aware of her surroundings. She continued to focus on her breathing. *In. Out. In. Out.* She listened to Xander's soothing voice; memories popped into her mind. Her grandfather twirling her around the room, laughing with friends, solving her first case. Relaxation encompassed her. A roaring started deep within her belly.

The memories spun through her mind and a sort of peace fell over her. She felt how the energy encased her every thought, feeling, and memory.

It was as if the energy had strings, and she had to mentally reach out and pull them to her. The colors of the world around her changed. She looked around in her trance. The hues were bright and beautiful like a kaleidoscope.

She reached out to pull more energy and more memories to her, then focused on the feather. She opened her eyes and stared at it, and as she lifted her hand, it rose. She moved it to the left, and then to the right. Down. Up. Sideways. The feather followed her every move. Elation coursed through her. She could feel it *and* control it.

Xander leaned forward. "Now, try the book," he whispered. "Keep progressing. You're doing great."

Kate switched her focus to the book and lifted her hand. Once again, the book immediately rose and moved in any direction she instructed. She felt the energy and paid attention to how it was working inside her. She quickly figured out how to send the energy to a specific spot, but she wanted to see her full capability. Setting her sights on something bigger, she refocused.

Xander startled. Her energy hit him square in the chest, but she kept her focus. "*What are you doing, Kate?*" He lifted off the ground, moving to her will. If she could do this with her powers incomplete, what in the world would she be able to do when they were set free?

She carefully moved Xander in various directions. His expression of dismay and a little fear made her laugh and lose focus. All of a sudden, her energy levels depleted, and her concentration broke. He hit the ground with a thud.

"Oops, sorry. I wanted to test my limits." She hadn't meant to drop him but was proud of what she'd accomplished.

"Bloody Hell!" He stared at her and rubbed the side of his hip.

She barely contained her excitement. She could move things with the flick of her hand. This was so cool. She couldn't wait to show Angie later. "What's next?"

Xander twisted his lips to cover his smile. Kate knew she looked like a fool jumping up and down on her knees like an excited child unwrapping presents. "How about manifestation? It would be good if you could call a weapon into a fight for yourself and Angie."

"Okay, tell me what to do."

"The energy process works the same for everything. This time you'll focus on the weapon you want and reach for it with your mind." He pointed to the ground beside him and several weapons appeared. "We'll start with something you see here, and like you did with levitation, try to expand from there."

Taking a good look at the weapons on the ground and committing them to memory, Kate closed her eyes once again. Focusing on her memories, she pulled the energy to her. She noticed that she didn't need as many memories this time. The energy came to her at will. She thought about one of the small swords she had seen and reached for it. It didn't work. She took in a deep breath and pulled in more energy to try again.

She was determined to succeed and tried to figure out how it all worked. Manifestation was much more complicated and took more energy to master. Her eyes were closed, and her eyebrows scrunched in concentration. The air rippled around them, as she continued with her efforts. She sure hoped Joseph's shields would hold up, because she was using a lot of power.

A small bead of sweat trickled down her neck from the heat of the day and her exertion. She felt Xander watching her and his sexual energy poured into her. He tracked a bead of sweat descending between her breasts and groaned in frustration.

Kate let a sly smile form on her lips. She refocused and used some of the sexual energy pouring off Xander and latched onto it. It felt like a power boost in her inner core. Concentrating once again on the sword, she called it to her. It appeared in her palm. She squealed in delight, not caring if she looked silly. Then she focused on one of the bigger weapons, and it appeared in her hand immediately.

She remembered what Xander had said. She needed to test her limits, so she observed her surroundings to see what to try next. She saw Angie and Gregory sparring with a variety of weapons. Gregory was about to pin Angie. A smile came across her face, as she focused all her energy. Gregory's weapon disappeared and popped into her hands.

Gregory scowled. Angie flipped him and pinned him. "Hey, Blondie, no fair! Stay in your own camp." He smiled and wiped the dirt from his pants. "But it was impressive. Excellent work, Kate. You, however," he turned to Angie, "will not always have Kate to bail you out. We have a lot of work to do."

Angie stuck her tongue out and snarled at him.

Kate turned away. She wanted to try one more thing before taking a break. If they were in a battle, she might need to call a weapon like Xander and Gregory had done in Boston and at her apartment. Kate breathed deeply and pictured the sword that hung on the wall of Joseph and Lucia's living room. She had seen it when they arrived yesterday, and its intricate beauty enticed her. She pictured its gold handle, sophisticated design, and lightweight steel. She opened her eyes, and there it was in her hands.

She gaped at it. She'd brought it from inside their house. She couldn't risk anything outside Joseph's shield, but she intended to try as soon as she could. It was amazing. Laughter washed over her. The enormity of what she was doing overtook her. Meeting Xander's eyes she flung herself into his arms. She could feel his happiness and hope. "I did it! I did it!"

Xander grabbed her in a big hug and held her in his lap, "Yes, you did! Congratulations. You can levitate and manifest. How about a break?" If she could learn everything this quickly, she could get ready for the battle. Maybe not for everything, but at least she'd be able to fight using her powers.

"Sounds good. I feel pretty depleted after all that. Will I always feel this tired after a battle or when I have to use a lot of energy?" Kate was a little concerned about running out of juice at this rate.

"Once you're the full Mystic, you'll have limitless energy. Not that you won't ever get tired or need to recharge every once in a while, but you'll pretty much always be amped up." Xander moved his hand, and their lunch appeared; sandwiches, fruit, and drinks on a blanket on the grass.

Kate leaned back onto the grass to feel the sunlight on her face, then turned her head toward Xander. "Do you know anything more about Fury or the Omega demon, Braxus? What will I be facing?"

Xander lay down beside her, lacing his fingers through hers. "The Council will be able to tell you more, I hope, when it comes to Braxus. Everything I know is from stories and seeing others' memories. We still have time to figure him out. As for Fury, I could tell you his story while he was in our realm, but it wouldn't do us any good.

"His damage came from outside our realm. He was a good friend and protected us in several battles, but over time the appeal of dark magic and power took over. He became obsessed with gaining more, until he no longer cared who he killed to obtain it. When the Council ordered us to kill him, it was the most difficult assignment we'd ever been given."

"Anything else? I know from experience that the smallest detail could change everything." She didn't want to push bad memories, but they needed to find his weakness.

"He wasn't happy when we banished him. My best guess is that he doesn't want evil to win. He likes playing both sides. He likes the power of existing between the two. I think he wants to find a way to take your powers and rule both sides. It's the ultimate high for him. That's why I think he is probably planning an attack soon. He didn't even try to fight at our camp and that isn't his typical behavior. He has to know that when we cross over, he loses. The question Xavier and I are trying to figure out is how to beat him. We'd have to remove the armor that protects his dark powers and his life."

"I agree that everyone has a weakness. We need to know more about the armor and where it came from.

Maybe Xavier and Zane have found something. There's always a way." She bet her life on it.

Kate chewed on a blade of grass, hoping divine intervention would strike, leaving all the answers in its wake. No such luck.

She hesitated, trying to correctly word her next question. "Where is Braxus now? I mean, he was able to help Fury and bring in the darkness, which nearly succeeded in killing me."

"He's trapped with his master in the Hell Realm. He can only enter the Human Realm on the night of the Rising. The other day we were unprepared, and he sent waves of energy using Fury to channel. The Omega has never risked using energy until the night of the Rising, but this is a problem for the future. We have to arrive in the Meadows first for your transformation." Xander drug his hand through his hair.

Kate could see that talking about their close encounter upset him, but what choice did they have? Finally, after she stared at him for a few minutes, he started talking again. "Trust your instincts. As a Mystic, they're impeccable. I don't think the answer will be simple. It never is with destinies."

Xander sat up and pulled Kate up from the ground. With a wave of his hand, he cleared all of the trash, and the props they'd been using earlier disappeared. "Are you ready?"

Kate couldn't hide her excitement. She felt like a puppy wagging its tail, but she couldn't help it. "What's up next?"

"Protective shields. These are a little harder because they require a consistent flow of energy, and sometimes you still have to fight, while continuing to maintain your shield. It takes a ton of focus, but you'll get the hang of it. I'm — " Xander broke off and met her gaze.

Uh-oh. What now?

18

Xander looked at Kate with a wry glance. "Maybe we ought to wait a few more minutes. Xavier is here, and we need to make sure there is a smooth transition." Kate heard the tension in his voice and admitted this didn't make for friendly times. He took her hand in his and smiled. "Then again maybe it's a good time to learn protective shields."

"What's Gregory going to do while Xavier works with Angie?" Kate asked while they headed over to Gregory and Angie.

"You mean besides pacing and going insane wanting to interrupt every five minutes?"

"Yeah that," Kate snorted.

"He'll work with Joseph on arrangements to the portal. But more than likely he'll be obsessing over Angie." He squeezed Kate's hand. His constant need to reassure her worried her a little. There was something nagging her in the back of her mind, but she couldn't quite put her finger on it.

Angie turned to ask Gregory a question, right as he took off his shirt. Her mouth watered, and her knees went momentarily weak. His chest was tanned and flawless. Forget the six pack, he had a good twelve. His skin glistened and his athletic pants sat low on his waist, so it didn't take much to envision the rest of him. She tried to keep her composure, walked over, and scowled at him. "Are we starting with a strip tease, or are we going to do real work sometime today?"

"Does it bother you? Feel free to join me anytime." He cocked one eyebrow in a challenge.

"Please, I've seen lots of naked corpses in my time, and you're not much better. So, I'll pass." He'd never know she was lying through her teeth. "What are we doing today anyway?"

He smiled and leaned toward her. "Kicking your butt!"

She snorted "Keep dreaming. You may get me at first, but once I learn, you're history. Now, how do I kill these things?"

"All demons are different. But there are three main tactics that work on every demon. Remove its head, burn it from the inside out, hence the flaming arrows, and remove its heart if it has one. This is not a stake through the heart, but an actual removal. I would suggest you stick to the first two."

"Excuse me, did you say removal of the heart?" Angie nearly choked. "Who gets close enough to do that?"

"Yeah, it is rare for us to get that close, but it does kill them. Shadow Warriors are the only ones who would use that tactic, because they have the power to turn them into dust in the palm of their hand. They also have the strength and speed to go in quickly, before the demons can react.

That was then. They're pretty useless now." Gregory's bitterness came through with every word.

"No worries there. I definitely don't intend to get that close." Angie looked the dummies over again and took a deep breath. "So, burn 'em up or take their heads off. I can do that. I think."

Several hours later, she'd never been so happy to see Kate in her life. Although Kate's expression showed trouble was on the horizon.

"Hey guys!" Kate cheerfully said. She walked over with Xander in tow.

"Hey yourself. Thanks for the assist earlier," Angie added.

Gregory rolled his eyes.

"No problem. I'm quite proud of myself. I feel like I've accomplished a lot today. I'm starting protection shields here shortly, but I stopped by to let you know it's time for your strategy lesson. Xavier's on his way with lots of scenarios, yada, yada, yada. I lost interest when he got technical. He's setting up on the veranda, so you're still out in the fresh air." Kate tacked the last part on hurriedly and factually. No emotion. No questions. *Yep, her fake sunny attitude had been a giveaway.*

Angie sighed. So much for peaceful relaxation or removing the burr out of the saddle. Every time she leaned closer to Gregory, Xavier made an appearance and confused her. Angie dreaded working with Xavier, and Gregory's reaction to the whole thing. She could already feel him stiff as a board, sitting behind her.

A sour look crossed Gregory's face, as she predicted. Whenever he got in one of his moods, Angie lost sight of why she was attracted to him. This dark temperament was not part of his natural personality, and she always felt guilty that she caused the change.

"Well, where is he?" Gregory growled. "Can't he handle being around us all at once?" He sneered, rolling the last words off his lips.

Angie watched his face freeze. His eyes met Xander's. She didn't need to read his mind to know he regretted hurting him.

"Shut your trap, Gregory," Xander snapped back. "I am *not* in the mood for your little girl games. Xavier has an excellent mind for strategies, and he has kept us alive this far. So, check your feelings at the door and focus on survival." He stepped closer. "And get over your jealousy issues!"

Angie felt a stab of her own jealousy as she watched Kate and Xander. He bent down and kissed Kate softly, then she leaned her head on his shoulder. At least Angie could be at peace knowing Kate hadn't settled for second best. She'd found the one person who accepted all of her. "Xander, one of these days you're going to have to explain all this animosity and pain."

Xander touched Angie's shoulder and gave a slight squeeze. "One day soon, I promise. It isn't an easy story to tell and tends to bring sorrow to whoever hears it. We need to focus on your skills for now without negative energy."

Angie patiently waited, feeling guilty for causing, or at least being part of, the reason for the whole scene. She also didn't want to admit she actually feared spending time with Xavier. He was a strong, dominant male and gorgeous to boot. The scar across his cheek and the haunted look in his eyes made him all the more appealing.

Why couldn't she simply commit to Gregory and call it a day?

Breathing deeply, she started walking toward the veranda. Kate squeezed her hand and sent her comforting energy. She stepped inside. Kate and Xander walked back to their training site and left her to face her own personal demons. She stepped in and faced Xavier; once again mesmerized by him. Her stomach jumped into her throat. How stupid could one girl be? She wasn't inclined to answer herself on that one.

Kate glanced back over her shoulder and watched Angie step inside. "Xander, I hope this ends well, but something will eventually come to a head between Xavier and Gregory. You can't contain it forever. Angie's not made for this type of entanglement and runs away easily."

He took her hand as they walked. He couldn't imagine having to compete for her affection. The simple thought alone made him sick. What would he do if she didn't forgive his deception? If he lived, that is. "In the Meadows, she *will* have to make a choice."

"I suppose we'll all be together a lot with nowhere to hide. Will the Council be able to help them since they approve matches or mates?"

"Not until she makes her choice and asks for approval."

"Great. By then she can't exactly go to the other one and say, *I've changed my mind.* This really sucks."

Xander chuckled and sat her back down inside their circle. "Okay, protection shields need a lot of energy. Your fear fueled it the last time to protect Angie, but fear is hard to control. This time, you want to call positive energy to have control over it. Breathe deeply, stay focused. It'll take some practice. Imagine a kind of bubble that protects all those inside it. You'll be able to see who's in it and everything it's protecting them from. Ready?" He linked their hands to help her channel the energy.

"As ready as I'll ever be." Kate closed her eyes and found her balance.

She pulled the energy inside her. She didn't have to use memories anymore. She felt the energy pulsing around her now and called it to her. She brought the bubble image into focus and imagined all the protective attributes she'd want the bubble to have. She blocked demonic energy from the shield and then decided to add in bugs. Since she hated bugs anyway, it seemed like a good choice, and it was something measurable to test her shield.

She opened her eyes. She blocked out everything but the shield, which started out the size of a quarter. *Great, unless I'm aiming to protect tiny faeries, I'd better figure out how to expand this thing.* Focusing all her energy on the little bubble, she envisioned it growing larger and larger. The bubble finally responded. It grew, until it covered her whole body.

She sighed in relief at mastering her first task and expanded it further. After a lot more effort, it finally enclosed around Xander. Once established, she took the time to test and understand her energy field. She watched bugs flee from her. She smiled. It was working to some extent.

She studied Xander and took notice of the pale light surrounding him that marked the boundaries. This is what it would look like when she wasn't using the bubble decoy. The same could be said for the circle surrounding them both. She was protecting their whole area.

Ready to test her boundaries, she tried to levitate a stick lying next to her, but she lost her connection and dropped the shield. Frustrated, she slammed her hands on the ground. "Dang it!"

Xander leaned forward and wrapped his arms around her. "Stay focused. You managed to cover our entire area with your first try. I was only able to cover myself my first time, and that was shaky. After a couple more tries, you'll be able to multitask. With limited powers, this isn't an easy undertaking. You've got this. Try again."

Kate refocused and pulled in her energy again. She wanted to prove to herself and Xander how much she was capable of doing. She didn't want to be a hindrance if they had to fight again.

After a couple hours, she managed to hold the shield and levitate or manifest objects. Nothing huge yet, but it was definitely a start.

She'd also learned how to control the light and envelop anything she chose. She could change the conditions of the shield without stopping and creating a new one. All in all, this had been a successful day, and the first time she believed she was going to have real powers. Even with sweat pouring down her face, she felt radiant. *I can conquer the world!*

She jumped forward and landed on top of Xander, knocking him flat on his back. Her excitement radiated through them, and her laughter was infectious. The laughter ceased a few minutes later. A new awareness pulsated through her. She became aware of his body beneath hers and felt his firmness pushing against her thigh.

She met his gaze and slowly leaned forward to trace his lips with her tongue. The first kiss was feather light, but the electricity still arced between them. They groaned in unison. Xander rolled her over onto her back and deepened the kiss. An electrical current started at Kate's toes and radiated up her body, slowly creating an intense ache.

Her need for him pulsed inside her like a bass drum. It overshadowed all rational thought. All she knew was that she needed him to complete her. It was like a strange primal need flowing through her blood. She thought she'd go insane from the whirlpool of feelings exploding through her. She wanted him. *Now.*

He ran his hands all over her body. She gasped, then sighed, every touch brought out new sensations. She whimpered with need. She wanted him. Only him. It was intoxicating. Her body exploded. It released the energy, excitement, and fears that had built during their training.

He continued kissing her until everything subsided, but he still held her close. Something inside her finally understood that this was her world and her future.

Xander glanced down at Kate's peaceful expression. The fates had given him a chance to experience true love. Their romantic interlude had cost them a little time but well worth it. He'd always remember this spot under the trees. Maybe they could have another picnic here when the battle was over.

A bolt of pain flashed through Xander's mind. He recoiled. *What was that?* At first, he thought he had hurt

Kate. All they needed was another energy storm. He should have remembered.

He realized it was Xavier and tried to push it aside. He'd have to deal with his own damn issues. Xavier pushed back in desperation, breaking through the haze in Xander's mind.

Xavier was having trouble; his emotions spiraling out of control. Xander connected to him and felt his conflicting desires. One part of him was ready to grab Angie and go somewhere private, and the other ready to run for the hills. What the hell had happened in the past couple of hours?

Xander slowly sat up to process the information. He waved his hand to redress and freshen up Kate and himself. Not only had he left Xavier when he needed him, but he had made love to Kate in a dirty field. When it came to her, he had no control. *Zero.*

The guilt of his lies weighed heavier and heavier. He wanted to tell her, but it was too late now. He couldn't spook her and risk her resistance to the portal. At least she didn't have the experience yet to navigate the many blockades in his mind. Without her knowing what she was looking for, he could keep his secrets well hidden.

Kate was still dazed and amped up on an adrenaline rush. "What is it?"

"Xavier is on overload dealing with Angie. Something happened between them, and he's having a hard time holding himself back from her, but at the same time fears getting close to her. He sent me a distress signal asking for help. He wants to stay and go over plans face to face, but all his emotions are swirling out of control." He took a deep breath to control his emotions. How many obstacles did the Council think they needed to endure?

"It's always something, but I feel confusion in Angie, too." She sat up and pulled her hair into a ponytail. "I guess we better head over before Gregory catches wind of something, and we *really* have a problem. We need to help Xavier cope, but I'm not sure how. He has to relearn emotions again."

"I don't think baptism by fire is the best approach. Add in Gregory's animosity to the mix and raging hormones, it adds up to a real big mess." Xander stood, pulling Kate to her feet. He kissed her deeply. "One day, we will get to spend uninterrupted time together." He hoped. "At least that much could be normal for you, and we could make love in a bed with candlelight and whatever you desire."

"All I desire is you and *no* interruptions. In a field or in a bed doesn't matter. Then again, maybe a deserted island should be our goal." Kate leaned on his shoulder. They walked to the veranda. "Let's go save Angie and Xavier, shall we?"

Xander gently touched her shoulders and looked into her eyes. "Kate, I want you to know that I've fallen deeply in love with you. Never forget that. Let's go, Mystic." He quickly pulled her along before she could question him.

"So," Angie said, "what you're saying is that the main goal of the battle is to bring the Mystic and Omega together. The quicker they meet, the quicker it's over, right? Why don't they meet in the middle and call it a day? Why all the fighting if it comes down to the two of them anyway?"

Xavier brought up a few painted pictures and handmade drawings from the last Rising that he had stored in a large paper folder. Ripped apart bodies and blood soaked the ground. One picture was of a woman who didn't look much older than a teenager. She held up her hands in terror while a demon ripped her heart out. Angie gasped in horror, but it was important for her to grasp the true concept of what she would face. He wished he could soften the reality, but her best chance to survive was to understand.

"When the Rising begins, the first goal is to kill as many demons as you can to protect the Human Realm. Without the Shadow Warriors, this will be more difficult. This also allows us to clear the path between the Mystic and Omega. After the winner is determined, many of the demons will be fighting to stay out of the Hell Realm or find a way to escape. The Shadow Warriors provided our best offensive weapon. Without them our greatest concern is getting Kate to where she needs to be."

She leaned forward to point at one of the pictures and her hand brushed across his. Electricity consumed them. *What the hell?* He wasn't sure if he wanted to laugh or cry at the absurdity. It didn't take any powers to see she felt the same.

Xavier grabbed his computer and pulled up more documents and plans in addition to the drawings. The one good thing about hiding for twenty years is that he'd had plenty of time to study technology. He pointed at the screen to refocus on their plan for arriving at the portal. The portal had been created as a permanent portal used for those exiting the Meadows. Only the Council could allow access to enter. They didn't want Fury or any other demons camping out, to kill anyone that exits. Keeping the portal secret was imperative.

"The only strong option is using blood. The demons can't resist the pull. The other options might work, but time would be limited and carry more risk for all of us. Also, that puts everyone in the Meadows at greater risk." Frustrated, he put his hands through his hair. "But Kate's not going to like it, and I still have several details to work out first. It requires an intricate spell that I haven't studied in several decades."

"You're right. Kate will most definitely not like it. You're wrong about why. It's not because of the blood, but because it puts you at such a great risk. She's a real pain when it comes to that sort of thing. And maybe the blood thing a little."

They had a plan to get to the Meadows. The time had come. Xavier felt the excitement in the air and was astounded at the emotions he hadn't felt in decades. Angie surged forward out of her chair and into his arms. She hugged him around the neck. Time froze. They both stopped breathing. A current of sensation swept through them. Xavier held her tightly against him.

He looked down and met her gaze. It was like two magnets pulling at each other, impossible to escape. His lips softly touched hers, and he felt her quick intake of air. His mind malfunctioned, and all he could think was that he wanted more. The kiss deepened, and she quietly moaned. His emotions spiraled out of control. His hands moved down her body, pulling her closer and closer against him. His mind told him to run.

He panicked and sent a message to Xander, asking for help. He pulled away, but the air in the veranda turned into a sauna. He couldn't breathe without pulling her scent into his nostrils and setting off another reaction in his body. She was lethal to him.

Panic and anxiety overtook him. He refused to fade and give Gregory the satisfaction of him running away from Angie. *"Xander, hurry the hell up."* He hoped Xander was paying attention. Right now, he wasn't sure whether he would fade or kiss her again.

He saw doubt and pity written all over her face, and that stung most of all. Whatever their connection, it would take two to make it work. He was definitely out for the count. So why did he still have the desire to get to know her? Why couldn't he let her go and have a chance at a better future?

"So, are you leading the discussion tonight on our decision?" Angie asked, breathing hard. Was she trying to dispel some of the tension? It didn't exactly alleviate his guilt.

"No," he managed to get out. "I'll pass the information to Xander and answer any questions that arise."

"How's it going for our top strategists?" Kate asked, and watched both Xavier and Angie sigh in relief. She and Xander stepped into the veranda.

"We came up with a couple plans," Angie replied. "So that's a start." She moved to stand by Kate, while Xavier walked over to Xander. Kate could tell they were transferring information.

"All right," Xander said. "Go ahead and fill in Zane. We'll meet to discuss details in two hours." Xavier immediately faded into the shadows.

Kate put her arms around Angie and Xander. "Let's go eat. I'm starving, and I'm sure Gregory is chomping at the bit for us to get inside." She glanced at Angie "We'll talk about it tonight." Angie nodded, looking a little better.

They had a great meal, mostly talking about random, unimportant information. An hour disappeared fast, and it was time to refocus on the battle. Kate was already tired from the long day, but this was necessary. She'd be entering the Meadows soon and permanently accepting a new role in her life.

Xavier popped in, and they all went into the living room to discuss the new exit strategy. Xander stood to address the group. "Xavier and Angie have devised a plan that will allow us to avoid detection leaving and arriving in the Meadows and protect Joseph and Lucia's home. We'll head out in the morning. All of us — including Joseph and Lucia — traveling together. It's reckless to stay any longer."

Kate scrunched up her eyebrows. "How will we be traveling this time?" It's a real shame that she'd gotten to a point that it was necessary to ask this question. Dragon. Eagle. Car. Motorcycle. Whatever the heck else.

Xander hesitated as if asking Xavier if he was sure. This didn't exactly inspire confidence. *Nope, definitely not a good sign.* She looked toward Xavier and Angie. "Care to explain the need for all the antics here?" She waved her arms toward everyone's wide-eyed, anxious expressions.

Angie took a deep breath and came to Kate's side. "Please stay calm and listen. Trust in me. This is the only way to buy us real time. *You asked for more time to figure things out and for me to trust you.*" She switched to their personal link. *"I'm asking for the same. This is the only way that keeps you safe."* Yep. From bad to worse.

Kate crossed her arms and leaned against Xander. He gestured for Xavier to take over. "Fine," she said. "I'm listening with an open mind. Lay it on me."

Xavier took a deep breath and glanced at Angie, who nodded for him to continue. "Traveling isn't the issue. We'll head out on the bikes. The problem is absolutely not being tracked.

"The best way to protect you and give you time to get to the Meadows is to set up a strong decoy. We don't want to hide, but to lead them in an opposite direction. This way, they are literally moving farther away from you. We're going to give them a trail they can't refuse."

"Okay, doesn't sound too bad so far. How do we do that?" Kate asked. Her hands constantly moved due to increasing anxiety. She couldn't stay still.

"You and I are going to swap essences, so the demons will come after *me* instead of you. Since they have no interest in me, they won't follow you if you're surrounded by my essence."

"Are you insane?" Gregory yelled, adding his own contempt.

"I'm sorry, what?" Kate asked, in complete shock. Dammit, did they not do anything normal in their world? "How exactly does that work? I'm not up for an out of body experience or essence of Xavier, no offense."

Xavier smiled and shook his head. She noticed his whole face lit up in those rare moments when he stopped grieving. "We aren't switching bodies. I have no desire to be a female." Kate glared at him. "It's actually a rare ritual. Zane has perfected it over time to protect his warriors from being tracked, and also to help other magical beings that are being hunted. It's a personal ritual and does include a blood exchange and energy swap. But the effects only last a few hours."

"Bloody hell," Gregory stormed. "Have you lost your mind? You can't take the Mystic's blood. It will kill you when it rejects your body." His face went slack. "Then again — "

Kate glanced at Gregory's red face and then back at Xavier. "What does he mean you can't take the Mystic's blood? How much danger will you be in if we do this?"

"It's illegal to take the Mystic's blood and highly dangerous. Except for the Guardian, no one can tolerate the power in the Mystic's blood. It drives them insane instantly. But you're not a full Mystic yet, and since Xander and I are twins and share DNA, it will allow me to accept your blood more easily. Zane tested my blood against Xander's yesterday and believes it will work for a few hours. Then, your essence will break free from me and return to you. In theory, anyway."

"In theory?" Kate huffed. "This seems a little dangerous to be saying *in theory*. I mean, I don't want to be rude, but can't we say *screw the Council* at this point, and you transport us there?"

"Technically," Xander said calmly, meeting her eyes. "I could probably bring you into the Meadows without the portal. Transporting and crossing over in the Meadows at the same time might severely damage your human body. Rowena could probably fix everything, but not Angie's. If we try it, and Angie is refused entrance into the realm, she wouldn't survive. The only way to test her entrance safely, is a portal based in this realm. If we tried transporting, your energy would be too depleted to help Angie cross over at the portal, and she would have to stay here."

"You've been adamant about not leaving her behind," Xavier said, taking over again. "I listened and want you to have every opportunity to pull Angie through the portal, but ultimately it's your choice, Kate."

Pushing her shoulders back, Kate whipped her hair and stepped toward him. "I will *not* leave her behind. She's a part of all this somehow. Maybe it's because of me, but I know she has to cross. I don't want to have this discussion again. So, back to your theory, Xavier."

"We need a lot more than a freaking theory for me to agree to put your life at risk." Xander finally spoke, with his voice full of agitation. "I'll do it. I'll perform the ritual and the demons can follow me. That's safer. Her blood won't hurt me. It will protect me."

"Absolutely not!" Xavier's adamant and forceful voice took them all aback. "You're essential to guarding the Mystic and must maintain your energy. I'm not."

Kate couldn't pinpoint the issue, but there was definitely something she was missing. Why would he mention Xander's energy levels?

"There's something the two of you aren't telling me. What is it?" She looked back and forth to each of them. Xavier wanted to say something but crossed his arms and remained silent.

"It's nothing. You don't need to worry." Xander pushed her question aside, hoping she would let it go.

She didn't. "Why are energy levels so important in this? All of you have been able to recharge. Why would it matter now?"

"None of us recharge easily in this realm." Xander tossed her an irritated look. "The longer we stay and the more power we use, the harder our energy is to restore.

Once we get through the portal, everything will be fine. Leave it alone for now."

"So, it's my fault, we haven't gotten to this portal?" She took a step towards him. How dare he act like her concerns were trivial!

"Enough!"

Xavier held up his hand to Xander and Kate, breaking up their argument. "This is the way it must be. She'll need her trust in you to be ready. Don't think that I haven't studied this from every angle." Xavier sat down. His face paled, and Kate felt his struggle to stay in the room.

"Gregory and I will take you on our bikes that have been sort of supercharged," Xander said. He'd returned to her original question. "Joseph will set up a shield, and we'll hide under it for a good distance away from the house. It's a couple hundred miles. We'll use our human forms but move a little more rapidly. Joseph and Lucia will travel to an alternate destination, and we'll combine our powers to create an untraceable shield. The shield still creates a void that can be found by some assassin demons, but it'll give us enough time. Fury will be the hardest to fool."

Kate took a deep breath, sorting through all the information. "And if not? How do we make a run for it? That's not a short distance. You said the portal is in Northern Montana."

This time Xavier stood and took center stage. "That's the tricky part, if we're to carry off this illusion." Despite his obvious discomfort, his voice still sounded authoritative and confident. "Please know I'm weighing all the options carefully. I will not choose a path that doesn't guarantee a successful decoy."

Gregory coughed, and Xavier and Xander both glared at him. He held his hands up in mock surrender. "Continue."

Xavier rolled his eyes and looked back at Kate. "Angie will be helping me as well, so you know the plan will be foolproof." Xavier raised an eyebrow, waiting for Gregory to challenge him again.

Xander cleared his throat and Xavier continued. "The only question will be how much time there is to spare, so we have to get you there rapidly. I talked it over with Zane at length, and he's willing to help."

"Assuming I trust a man that I've never met, who's asking me to place my life in his hands when we have a traitor on the loose!" Kate was tired and frustrated and wanted to be surrounded by her team again. People she trusted beyond a shadow of doubt.

Instead, she was in a room full of people, and most she didn't completely trust. Kate felt Xander's pinprick of pain when he picked up on her feelings. But this was too much.

Gregory stood and paced around the room. "I agree with Kate."

"Of course you do," Xavier dryly cracked.

"I don't trust the Shadow Warriors." He held up his hand when Xander started to object. "I know you trust Zane, and he does seem like a good guy. But we have to remember that they can no longer enter this realm because of their hatred for humans. I don't trust it, and I don't want Angie doing it."

"Angie chose for herself. She doesn't need you telling her what to do," Xavier snarled.

Before Gregory could respond, Kate jumped to her feet and held up her hands. "All right! This is getting us nowhere." She had everyone's attention and did what she did best. She assessed all the information and knew that this was probably the only way, or Angie would have never agreed to it.

She connected to Angie. *"What do you think? Is there another way?"*

"I don't think so, and we won't survive it without Zane's help. We'll need the Shadow Warriors help with the battle, too. I feel it inside you. This is a good time to start building trust."

"Why is it always our lives on the line when it's time to build trust?"

"Stop being a baby and be the leader," Angie snapped. *"Use your powers you have used for years. No one can sort the truth out like you. Have you forgotten who you are? You better remember quickly, or you'll get us both killed."* Angie disconnected, allowing Kate to concentrate.

Kate swallowed her guilt and frustration. She closed her eyes and studied each person in the room. Angie, she knew by heart, even if she was a little peeved at her for the moment. Gregory was divided between Xander and Xavier, and between his feelings for Angie. Xavier was broken, trying to hang onto sanity and rebuild his soul. The pain radiating from him was more than she could stand. She quickly broke the link.

Xander was rock steady in his determination and feelings for her. She didn't push that door too far for the moment, not wanting to become distracted. Even Joseph and Lucia appeared to have honest intentions and allegiance to her. She would have to trust her gut. It was time to meet the man himself.

19

Kate looked up at Xavier. "Can you open the portal? Will he let me connect to him–briefly?"

"I'll go ask." Xavier faded into the shadows. It was a matter of seconds when Kate felt a pop in energy and saw the air literally shimmering in one spot of the room. She walked toward it and realized it was a portal. Xavier stepped through. "I can't hold it for long. He's on the other side. I'll be able to hear everything because I am maintaining the link."

Stepping directly in front of the portal, she saw the man she'd seen the night of their battle with the demons. His appearance was blurred, but she could still see that he was handsome and absolutely huge.

Using her mind, she reached out to him. *"I want to trust you, but I'm hesitant."*

A deep laughter filled her mind. *"I don't blame you. That's smart. Our reputation is not the best. All I have are words. My race needs you to survive. I firmly believe that. All the Seers I have contacted say the new Mystic holds the key and that there is hope. I would do anything within my power for your safety."* His expression, while hazy, held honesty.

"*I believe you.*" She stared intently into his strange golden eyes. He was full of sorrow and badly wanted to rectify his father's grievous mistakes. Above all she felt his belief in her and his hope that she could save his realm and warriors. "*I'll help you in any way I'm able, if you give me the time to learn.*"

"*Thank you, my lady. By the way, I'm Zane.*" He gave a graceful bow.

"*And I'm Kate.*"

He threw one last thought in her mind before the connection broke. A secretive message sent directly to her, avoiding the link with Xavier. "*Kate, you need to know that Rowena is hiding something. I do not think she is the traitor. As I begin to study everyone more closely, I can see turmoil within her. You must find out what she is hiding if you are going to be successful. Keep this between us and good luck.*"

The portal closed before she could ask any questions.

What the hell? Could she trust *anyone*?

She turned around to find Xander handing Xavier a tissue to help stop the blood pouring out of his nose. She ran to him and placed her hand on his shoulder. "I'm so sorry, Xavier. I shouldn't have asked you to do it."

Xavier smirked, but his eyes were laughing. "Yes, you should have. It's only a nasty side effect. What did you decide?"

She knew he already had an idea of what her decision would be. It was time to start setting her own alliances and allowing what trust she could find to come first. The traitor would reveal itself in time and would be dealt with then.

"Zane has honest intentions and has sworn allegiance to me and our cause. We'll follow the plan and allow Zane to aid us in the blood ceremony until our arrival at the portal." She looked at Xavier. "You can fill me in on the ritual tomorrow morning. Go examine whatever else you need to work out."

She finally felt at peace for what she was becoming. *Sort of.* Acceptance was two-thirds of the battle, and she was ready. This would be her new team. She had to look forward and accept that. Her old life would become nothing but a memory. She fought back her sadness at the thought.

She watched Xander shake hands and clasp shoulders with Xavier. He faded and Kate realized her own fears made it more difficult. Everyone had banked on her, so she'd better put her game face on.

She grabbed onto Xander and brought him down to her, kissing him deeply. She didn't care if others were watching. She leaned back and looked into his mesmerizing blue eyes. "I do trust you completely. I had to remember to trust myself." Then she sent a silent thank you to Angie.

Gregory's face remained red with anger. He'd probably not quite made it to the acceptance stage yet. "Kate," he grumbled, "I can't believe you bought that crap."

"Gregory, all his intentions are good ones. He hates his father for what he did and feels trapped and wants to help. He believes in humans and in all supernatural beings." She met his eyes. "His intentions are clearer than yours."

His cheeks flushed red with embarrassment, but Kate let it go and changed the subject. Nothing would come from admitting feelings of jealousy or possessiveness at this point, and Angie didn't need any more confusion in her life. These issues would work themselves out in time. Tomorrow they would be in the Meadows.

It was almost midnight when they finally headed to bed, and Kate cuddled next to Xander to sort out her own feelings. It was foolish to deny she had fallen in love with him, and not because of a prophecy, but because of his patience, wit, strength, and intelligence. She knew it was time to make a deeper commitment to him.

Xander pulled Kate against his chest, and her head rested on his shoulder. He held her for a few moments, convincing himself that she was going to be okay with or without him. For the first time in a while, he allowed himself to believe they would both make it. "With all the trouble you caused last night and our busy day" — he smiled while she glared up at him — "we didn't get a chance to talk. I know you have questions. They're simmering in your eyes."

"Can you tell me a little about Rowena? Sounds like I have big shoes to fill."

The question caught Xander off guard. He never would have guessed she would care about the Council yet.

"Many say that she is a force to be reckoned with, and I guess they're right. As a former Mystic, her powers are pretty scary. When I was younger, she was like a second mother. Then, everything changed. She didn't approve of my brother's choice of wife but didn't stop them from making a terrible mistake. After his wife died and you were born, she informed me of your birth and that a spell had been cast to keep you hidden. She couldn't break it. I think I blamed her for Xavier's pain and my endless search for you."

"But not anymore? You sound like you're starting to forgive her."

"Forgive is a strong word, but let's say that having felt love for myself maybe I understand everything a little more now." He softly kissed her cheek. He had blamed Rowena for spending years of his life without his twin and the crushing pain that lived inside him. He had blamed her for many things that he now realized were beyond her control. Above all, she believed in free will.

Kate sat up, pushing the pillows behind her, and leaned against them. He could see she was still pretty wiped out from the energy spike and day's training. Her complexion was pale, and there were dark circles under her eyes. "Can you tell me Xavier's story? I've picked up that it had to do with a girl he loved, but his withdrawal is pretty extreme. There has to be more."

Xander hung his head and took a deep breath, then stared out the sliding doors, looking into the dark night. "It was much more. It was heartbreaking." He couldn't keep the sadness from his tone.

"Can you tell me? I need to understand."

"I promise I'll tell you the whole story once we get to the Meadows. It brings up a lot of bad memories for me, and I want to stay focused on getting you safely home today. The short version is that Xavier's wife died a horrible death and he had to witness it. We all did. Xavier and Lily were deeply in love, but the Council didn't approve their union. They defied the Council and bonded anyway.

"Lily got mixed up with a dark witch due to her insecurity over the Council's decision, and demons set a trap due to mistaken identity. I'll explain more later. We fought to save her, but we were too late. There were too many demons. Lily gave her life to save Xavier. He can't move past the guilt and heartbreak. It scarred us all."

Xander sighed. "That's what Gregory always references when he talks about listening to the Council. I also think he blames Xavier for not being strong enough to walk away from Lily. But he's never been in love like that. When Lily died and he watched Xavier's pain, he never got close to anyone again. Instead, he walked away from the love of his life. Angie is the first person he has connected with in a long time."

He paused. "I understand more now and know I could never walk away from you no matter the consequences. I'd go through Hell itself to follow you."

Xander lifted her off the bed and pulled her in close. His love for her was overpowering the memories, and happiness flowed through him again. He couldn't dwell on the past today.

He laid her back down across the bed and followed her, keeping them chest to chest. He needed comfort and the feeling of her love after the gut-wrenching memories and the fear from the night before. The kisses quickly deepened, and desire took over.

Xander felt Kate's energy pulling at her and the heat swamping her. He removed their clothes and an electrical current blasted from within her. The power knocked them both sideways.

Kate glanced at the bulge in his pants. "I could take care of that for you." She smiled slyly. He laughed and stuck his thumbs in the loops of his jeans to keep himself from making a grab for her.

"Yes, you could, and it would be fantastic. Still, we can't risk unleashing anything else until we are safely in the Meadows, and I don't want to be electrocuted. We were lucky the demons weren't anywhere near us last night or today."

He leaned back toward her and placed his mouth against her ear. "But rest assured, once we're in the Meadows, it's on! And I'm putting a spell on my room, so we have hours of uninterrupted time to play."

The phone rang at the same time Xavier broke into his thoughts. *"Some of Zane's men spotted Fury and a few of his assassins headed this way. According to Zane, their numbers are fairly low. He believes this is a personal vendetta for Fury and probably not sanctioned. Otherwise, we would be swarming. My guess is that after the last debacle, the Omega wants to let it be and pool his energy. Best get ready for a hell of a fight."*

Xander quickly jumped up, changed his clothes, and grabbed weapons. He blasted a message to everyone in the house. They only had a matter of minutes to prepare for a fight. *"Any ideas on how to strip Fury of that damn armor?"*

"Zane's brother told him that he ran across something similar at the last Rising, and only two things could strip the wearer of the armor. One, a shadow warrior can rip it off. Two, a Mystic can remove it with an energy blast. If you tap into Kate's powers, you might be able to remove it. My main concern is that you won't survive this battle."

Xander wanted to tell him everything would be all right, but he couldn't. What it would take to kill Fury would kill him. It also meant Kate would have to enter the battle instead of escaping. They would have to give Angie a post in the house for now. If he could get her to stay.

They met in the living room in full warrior dress and gear. Lucia and Joseph were completely transformed into full soldiers. They both wore black leather pants and protective vests including weapons belts around the waist and strapped across their chests. He smirked at Kate's surprise as they entered the once living room turned war room.

"How did they find us?" Kate adjusted her weapons around her waist and tucked her gun into her shoulder strap. Her face flushed, and fear radiated in her eyes.

If they fought Fury, he'd never have enough juice to hide everything from Kate. He'd be lucky to make it to the portal before the aging process began. Assuming Fury didn't kill him here and now.

Xander knew beyond a shadow of a doubt that Fury had tracked them through their friendship to Joseph. He knew them well enough to know the few people they would trust with the life of the Mystic. Score one for Fury. "Fury is the best tracker I know. That's how he found us. We should've been more careful."

"To make things worse, this isn't about you. This is a personal vendetta to cause us pain. My guess is that Fury is tired of serving others and sees this as his opportunity for the freedom from the hell we sentenced him to." *And he damn well might achieve it if Zane didn't come up with something brilliant.*

"It doesn't make any sense." Kate grabbed his arm to slow down his frantic movements around the room. "If his good magical abilities have been stripped, he's stuck with demons anyway. Why would he risk going against the Omega?"

"His powers weren't completely stripped. They were bound. If he kills either Xavier or me, he can get his full powers back. We can't allow that to happen. Our death could lead to your death, so it is a win-win for him." Fury seemed to have a hell of a lot more luck on his side than they did right now.

It didn't take a rocket scientist to understand the look on Kate's face. Instead of holding him back, she dragged him along while she paced the room. Her urgency spoke volumes. They had better devise one hell of a fool-proof battle plan.

Everyone took their seats around a massive table in the center of the room.

"What did Zane say about the armor?" Gregory was the first to speak, breaking the momentary silence hiding their inner fear. "You mentioned one of his brothers was researching it."

"According to Xavier, his armor can only be removed in two ways. One, a shadow warrior has the strength to reach past the protective shield and rip it off. Two, a Mystic can use an energy stream to disintegrate it." Xander wished he had better news.

It was apparent that everyone had done the math and realized that they were zero for two. The fear of losing the Mystic became suffocating in the small room. He had to give them a little hope.

"Zane believes that I can tap into Kate's current energy field through our bond," Xander mused. "Together we can send a blast strong enough to at least disable the armor for a short time." He decided not to mention how short of time Zane had predicted: a matter of minutes.

Kate would be tapped out of energy. Then, they all would die. Yeah, I'll keep that to myself.

Xavier was the last to enter the room, but Xander felt the relief at his appearance. He was known as the best strategist in the realm, or at least he had been. He was dressed all in black with his favorite sword on his side. He had come to fight.

Xander hadn't seen him like this since they had fought the demons to rescue Lily. Xavier's old confidence and poise fooled everyone but him. This was revenge, a way for him to lessen his guilt over Lily's death and to find a way to heal. He would kill Fury tonight or die trying.

"Fury and his most trusted followers are being careful according to Zane." Xander noticed Xavier's voice held a finalistic edge. "We probably have twenty or thirty minutes before the attack. The good news is that there are only ten or so demons. The bad news is that he's also using his own shield to prevent other demons from tracking him. He doesn't want interruptions. He wants revenge.

"If he overlaps our shield, it will render Zane useless at least for a while. It's not a surprising move given our last encounter. We have what we need to win, but it's going to take absolute precision and an assload of luck."

Everyone nodded toward Xander, waiting for their assignments. His mind raced. He felt as if he was leading them to their death. Kate would have to be near him at some point, but she couldn't defeat assassins on her own. Angie would need to stay near the house and keep their escape route clear. The odds were not looking good, but decisions had to be made.

"Angie, protect the perimeter of the house. Kate, you'll stick close to Angie in the beginning but will join me once we clear a few of the demons out of the way. Lucia, maintain our shield. Just in case Fury decides to let more demons in on the party. You also know the escape route and can lead Kate to the portal if necessary.

"Fury will hang back to let the demons weaken us. I will tell you when to join me but wait until I send the signal. If I give the order to escape, you must go with Lucia. We have to keep the bigger picture in our minds."

"But — " Kate seemed a little irritated at being told what to do. He knew it had to do more with her planning skills and OCD issues than anything else. They didn't have time to hash everything out or wrap it in a nice pretty bow.

"Not now," he cut her off. She glared but quieted. "We have one shot to defeat Fury tonight. All of you will have to trust us and follow directions. The remaining four of us will attack.

"Once we remove most of the demons, Joseph and Gregory will make sure that Kate gets safely to me. Then, Joseph and Xavier will create a distraction while Gregory drops back to protect Angie and Lucia.

"Xavier and I have our own plan to kill Fury once the armor is deactivated. Any questions?" Everyone probably had a question, but not a single person spoke.

Kate stood up. With her right hand, she grasped Angie's. With her left hand, she took his. Angie followed her lead, taking Xavier's, and eventually their circle was complete.

She met each of their eyes. "This is our circle, our team. Strangers and friends joined together with a single purpose. Tonight, there are no differences that separate us. Tonight, we are one. We will fight, and we will win." Her bravado inspired the confidence they needed.

Xander had never been prouder of anyone as he was of her in that moment. She'd managed to dispel the fears and reach for the warrior in each of them. Even if he didn't survive the night, he would die at peace. His heart had been touched by rare purity and light.

Pushing his emotions aside, he reached for his anger and hatred of Fury. He had to keep his head focused. To save Kate, Fury must die tonight.

The remaining minutes flew by. Kate glanced at the large mantel clock every few seconds. Her heartbeat pounding in her ears made the time move that much quicker.

Xander's face was unrelenting and fierce as he paced the front porch. She knew he was willing to die tonight to keep her safe, but something still didn't feel right. He expected to die for some reason.

With all of his powers and knowledge, it didn't make sense. That fact alone terrified her. Even if they all lived tonight, this would be her life. Living in constant fear of each new battle on the horizon and losing those she loved.

She focused on the current enemy to save her sanity. She closed her eyes and drew all of the energy inside her. She would be ready to transfer all she had when Xander called for her.

Torches appeared in the forest line. Demons advanced. Time was up.

Eight demons stepped out of the shadows. One more stepped into the moonlight.

Fury.

Kate immediately recognized him. His face was a mask of rage, but his overall demeanor appeared calm. He had a firm belief that he would win tonight and rule all of the realms. She hated to disappoint him, but that was not gonna happen.

Xander rushed the two on the left while Gregory, Xavier, and Joseph split the others. Fury was toying with them. He didn't even engage in the fighting. He used the demons as pawns to weaken them.

His eyes scanned his surroundings until they met hers. Keen interest, rather than hate, filled his gaze, despite his distance. She shuddered from the intensity.

She kept her mind open to Angie. Between the two of them, she could keep better tabs on the perimeter.

Fury shouted orders, and all hell broke loose. A sense of awe enveloped Kate as the warriors fought. Somewhere deep inside, she'd believed this could still be just a nightmare.

Time to wake up!

Everyone moved with incredible speed, and she squinted to make out most of their movements. Each individual had their own unique style, but together they functioned like a perfect military unit.

Joseph jumped at least six feet in the air and kicked the first demon in the throat. He zipped around a demon in a blur, hitting and kicking faster than Kate could follow.

He switched to his powers, and it was different from anything she had seen. Tiny red blasts shot from his hands and struck his opponent like bullets. She watched the red bolts travel through the demon's body. It went down and quickly turned to ash.

His next demon was savvier. They exchanged punches, kicks, and energy blasts, neither gaining the upper hand.

Gregory was the opposite. Xavier was right; he began with his magic. He threw curses and spells. They weren't blasts of energy like Xavier used, but light emanated from him. One spell blinded the demon. A thick vine encased another. He covered the first demon in a thick black substance, then manifested a sword and severed its head.

Xander and Xavier were the closest in their techniques. They worked together throwing energy blasts and using brute strength. Fury observed them more intently than the others. It was obvious he wanted to learn how they had changed over the years.

After several minutes of harsh battle, it was now four on four. Fury grabbed something from his back and flung it into the air. A strange orange powder surrounded his remaining demons. Their speed tripled.

"Watch out!" Kate cried out.

She grabbed Angie's arm and scanned for other threats. They backed up to avoid the orange substance.

Lucia moved into position beside them. Her features drew tight, straining to hold the shield in place.

Kate raised her new favorite weapon — a crossbow and magically flaming arrows. Time to provide assistance or at least a little distraction. She fired several arrows toward the demons.

A blast from one of them knocked Joseph down, his arm nearly blown in two. Xavier flashed over to protect him while fighting off two demons closing in on them. He released a bright white ball of energy and hit his target. The white fire engulfed the two demons and slowly burned them. Their horrific screams tore through the night.

Kate felt some satisfaction as they suffered. She pictured the demon they had tracked for months and earned a little justice for the victims.

Xander barked orders at Xavier and punched his shoulder. She took it as a warning that this was probably not a power that he should have used. She didn't see the big deal. A dead demon was the ultimate goal.

Xavier brought Joseph back to the house. He returned to help Xander and Gregory dispatch the last two demons. Fury was apparently waiting until the end.

"Kate, Gregory is going to set up a distraction for the other two, and Xavier will help him. As soon as I say now, run to me. We'll join powers and strip his armor. Once it's gone, get the hell out of here. Xavier and I will handle the rest. If you stay, you'll be a target and a distraction."

She didn't agree but didn't want to mess with his plan. She knew better than most that good intentions don't always work out well.

"Fine. I won't argue for now, but you can't keep me out of the fight forever. I have to learn and face my demons." The ultimate double meaning.

He didn't respond, but she didn't expect him to. He was used to being a one-man show. Who was she to judge? She'd been arrogant and self-assured once upon a time.

Patience was not her strong suit. She paced to soothe her nerves.

Xavier and Gregory conjured a mist that disoriented the remaining two demons. It also temporarily blocked Fury's view.

"Now!" Xander's command thundered in her head.

She ran to meet him at full speed. It took only seconds to reach him and grasp his hand. Fury began clearing the mist.

She transferred all the energy she could muster and sent it to Xander. Would it be enough? He literally glowed for a split second. The power surrounded him. Xander kept the connection open and sent a blast toward Fury.

The ground shook. The shock wave blasted everyone back five feet.

Fury roared with anger. "How dare you think you can defeat me with your weak little parlor tricks?" He angrily threw random blasts, but hit nothing.

"Did it work?" Kate gasped for breath, too drained to move.

Xander quickly helped her to her feet. "We didn't destroy it, but it's deactivated for the moment. We have to hurry. *Run!*" Xavier killed one of the other demons as she ran and stumbled to return to the house.

Heavy hands threw her to the ground. Xander landed on her a second later. "Stay down."

He threw energy blasts. Xavier joined him. They had Fury pinned, but he still deflected most of their power.

Xander's blasts began to lose strength, but with her face in the ground it was hard to know why.

"Poor Xavier," Fury taunted, desperation in his voice. "Setting up Lily wasn't enough, now I get to kill your brother, too. She was so gullible and sweet. She believed me when I said she would be safe. All she wanted was your eternal love."

He sneered and wiped a fake tear from his eye. "She would have been better off to have killed you in your sleep as she was told."

Xavier's rage hung on him like a second skin. "She had my love. You manipulated her right under our noses. We never thought you would stoop that low and be the Omega's puppet. That's all you are. Killing you will be my greatest accomplishment."

Xavier's blasts grew brighter. His eyes turned solid white. "You will *not* be taking my brother tonight, but you *will* answer the call of justice."

A whirlwind appeared around Xavier. He emanated a strange roar and directed everything he had toward Fury.

Xander lunged into the white tornado and connected with his twin.

Kate's heart stopped. The two brothers merged into one being. She stared at the scene, terrified and confused.

Fear distorted Fury's face. He moved left and right, ducking the energy balls hurling his way. She realized he was trying to teleport, but they held him within the shield.

The merged brothers flung him into a tree. His bones cracked with a loud snap. Fury fought back, but wind from the storm surrounding him tore off his clothes and peeled his skin.

He fired back with all of the power that he had. It wasn't enough.

Xander and Xavier's combined power was absolute. A massive ice blue ball of flames hurdled toward Fury. He couldn't block it.

Pale blue fire engulfed him. He didn't die easy. The fire melted his skin, exposing the muscle and tissue underneath.

"I'll find a way to come back and kill you all!" He cried out as flames engulfed his body. "You'll never know the truth about her or the one you seek!"

His final words.

Fury was dead. The fight reduced him to a pile of bones that quickly burned to ash.

Kate stood up and ran to Xander. He separated from Xavier and fell to the ground, a gaping hole in his side.

Tears flowed down Kate's face. She fell down beside him on the scorched dirt. Her heart in her throat, she prayed for a miracle.

Please don't let him die ...

20

Son of a bitch that hurts.

Xander gritted his teeth against the pain and tried to hold onto the fact that they killed Fury. He let out a deep sigh. He lay on the ground, his power and energy gone. He couldn't even heal himself. *I'm going to die right her in front of Kate. She's going to hate me for that.* He wanted to tell her everything and nothing all at once. He didn't want to leave her.

"Stop being so dramatic and listen," Xavier buzzed in his head.

Xander faded into darkness. He felt Kate's hands on him. Her lips on his cheek. Her distant voice asked why he wasn't healing.

Xavier ignored her. Brave man.

"Your powers are all but gone, so I can't recharge you. I can absorb your injuries and return your body to normal. However, this will only give you a day at best. Aging will take over. You have enough time to get her to the portal but won't be able to cross through it without her help. Tell her before it's too late.

"Once I absorb your injuries, I'll fade into the shadows. Zane will help me heal quickly. Tell her,

Xander. Take it from me, secrets destroy everything." He faded out of his head.

Pain, like hot lava, ripped through his side. Xavier saved his life once again. If he lived, he'd have to find a way to repay him.

Kate held his head in her lap, rocking over him. Angie joined her. What would he tell her? They were too close now. He couldn't risk deterring her from safety in the meadows. She would be safe and properly trained. Even without him, she'd have a strong chance of winning.

If she ran away, she would die. The hole he'd dug with his lies was too deep. He would tell her good-bye and let her cross over. He knew that, if only for a moment, he had experienced her love.

For now, he had to stop her fretting and get on track. "I'm okay. I'm okay. Help me up."

She watched him closely, her suspicions stronger. She searched his mind, but he knew how to hide the truth. Luckily, she wasn't trained enough to break through his barricades.

"What happened? Where's Xavier?"

"When we merged, it weakened us. He took my injuries because he can heal quickly in the shadows, and I'll have the strength to protect you and transport you to the portal. We should get to the house and check on everyone. Once Xavier returns, we need to be ready for the Essence ceremony." He hid the pain so she wouldn't question him further.

"They can wait a minute." She leaned down and grasped his chin, then pulled his mouth to hers and kissed him hard. He responded instantly. How on Earth could he be on death's doorstep and still want her more than his next breath? It was insane how much he desired her every minute of every day.

She must've decided he was all right, because she finally pushed herself up. She helped him off the ground, both of them breathing heavily from their passionate kiss.

She continued to sneak glances at him all the way to the house. She knew he wasn't being completely truthful. He guessed that she decided not to push. At least one thing had gone his way.

It was getting hard to keep up with the lies. He tightly held on to her hand and put his thoughts directly on her. Kate provided the perfect distraction.

"What did Fury mean by you will never know the truth about her or the one we seek?"

Excellent question. It would be even better if he knew the answer. "My best guess is that the first refers to Lily and the second to the traitor. Mostly, I think he was trying to distract us long enough to activate his shield. He may have known nothing at all."

They would never know. Regardless, he didn't regret that Fury was dead. They'd figure out the rest on their own.

They neared the house and he mentally prepared for the arguments that would come from their next adventure. The essence blood ritual was going to be extremely weird for her. After the last week, that said a lot. He didn't want her doubt to overpower her trust. One more excuse he was using to keep from telling her. *I'm such a coward.*

They entered the house, moved to the main room, and he took stock of the damage. Joseph quickly healed himself. He would be ready to travel in a few hours. Gregory checked and secured the shields. Little had escaped the double protection spells, but the other demons would have felt the loss of Fury and want revenge.

They had to move quickly.

Kate hovered beside him again, worried and afraid. His blood covered her hands and he sensed her thoughts; the reality of death began to settle in.

He wanted to make hot passionate love to her one more time. To feel her body wrapped around his until the world disappeared. It was not in the cards.

In a few short hours her love would turn to anger and pain. He would be saying his final good-bye.

He had to stay focused, get her to safety, and let go of the pity party.

An hour later, he felt Xavier return. Zane was damn good at healing.

Time for Round Two.

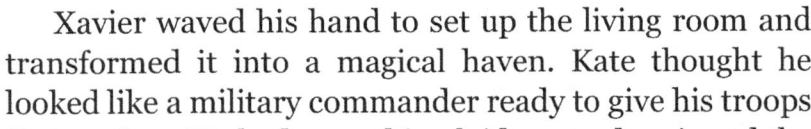

Xavier waved his hand to set up the living room and transformed it into a magical haven. Kate thought he looked like a military commander ready to give his troops their orders. He had everything laid out and reviewed the spells and rituals to ensure everything was precise.

Kate found it difficult to share authority, but knew she was out of her league on this one. She could finally see what a power trip she'd been on. Now she might not ever get the chance to apologize to her team. In her heart, they would always be hers.

At least she had Angie. Although at the moment, the way that Angie darted her eyes away from Kate's meant bad news was coming. *Great.* One normal day was all she wanted.

Strategically placed candles of various colors lit the room. A pentagram adorned the floor. Bottles of potions sat on a table to the side. Incense burned and filled the room with an acrid odor. A variety of crystals had been placed at precise locations throughout the area.

Angie stepped up beside him in support, ignoring Gregory's death glare. "I ran all the scenarios with him. No other options gave near the chances for success as the Essence Exchange." She turned and stared into Kate's eyes. "You know I'd never have chosen this path if I didn't truly believe in Xavier and this being our best shot."

That said it all. Kate knew Angie was an excellent strategist and so was Xavier. Angie understood all the risks and still believed this was best, even though it meant putting Xavier at risk. She felt that particular part of the plan ate at Angie, but still believed this was their best bet. Trusting her friend, Kate smiled and nodded. "Let's do this. How do we start?"

"What?" Gregory shouted. "I thought that at least you would use reason. Don't you realize the dangers of a blood exchange?"

"Actually, I'm beginning to. I read them in Xander's mind as he was processing this plan." Xander raised his eyebrows, but Kate ignored him.

"And I don't like putting anyone's life in danger, especially to save my own. But do you have a better plan that will work like this one? I'm willing to listen to any other options you have?"

Gregory's silence said all that was needed. There was no other way.

Turning back toward Xavier, Kate held her head high and gave a definitive nod. "So, how do we do the ritual?"

Xavier motioned to the pentagram in the middle of the floor. "I don't have time to explain all the components right now. You'll learn all that in the Meadows. For now, I'm going to use the easy-to-understand version, so follow my instructions. We will sit inside the pentagram and drink the potions Zane and I prepared." She ignored Gregory's muttering in the background and tried to focus.

"After we drink the potions, Xander will use an athame to make identical cuts on both of our hands. We will then latch our hands together to transfer blood. The potion helps the blood move rapidly into each other. Then, I'll chant an ancient spell to exchange some of our energy to completely swap our essence or energy fields. Questions?"

"Loads, but they'll have to wait, or we'll be here all day. It sounds pretty simple to me. Let's get on with it before I lose my nerve."

"Slow down, I need to go over the rest of the plan first because we're going to feel slightly disoriented after the change. I'll need to leave soon after to pull the demons and get them away from you, so you can make your move. Angie should be able to give you any more details or answer questions once I'm gone."

Despite the confidence in his voice, Kate had no doubt that Xavier was as nervous as her. He'd spent years avoiding people, and now he would have to exchange blood and energy with her. It appeared no one would be spared any feelings today.

Xavier went to stand by Xander. "Once I'm sure the demons are following me, I'll send a message to Zane who will then send a message to Kate. You'll drive outside the city limits to an abandoned farm. Gregory has made the transportation arrangements."

Gregory grunted and turned back around. "I still say this is ridiculous and risky."

"We have no choice but to make a run for it now. I'm not buying you hours. Only a few minutes. When you arrive, go through the portal." Xavier laid out all of the ingredients and lit more candles.

"How dangerous is all this?" Kate was sure that as the Mystic she would survive, but what about Angie?

"If you aren't tracked, it should be completely safe. That's why I have to ensure the demons follow me first."

"What happens if I can't get through the portal?" Angie asked the question on everyone's mind.

"I won't go without you." Kate met Xander's eyes in a challenge as he started to say something.

Xavier reached down and took Kate's hand, no small feat for him. "In the worst-case scenario, we won't leave her unprotected. Gregory and I will ensure that she stays safe from the demons." He looked toward Gregory, who nodded emphatically.

"I promise you that if Angie can't go through the portal, I'll keep her safe until you have your full powers and find a way to bring her into the Meadows."

He stared deep into her eyes, spoke into her mind, and she knew the pain it cost him, *"I swear to you, we will find a way to get her there. If anyone can find a way around the rules, it's you. Remember to listen to your heart."*

Kate still felt uneasy. She knew in her heart that all this happened for a reason and Angie was meant to cross over with her now — but how? She had to figure it out. Until then, she nodded so the guys would think she was agreeing with them.

She met Angie's eyes. Angie didn't believe that for a minute and knew she was up to something. They exchanged a quiet nod.

"Now, have all of you already discussed making it through the portal?" Xavier continued. "You need to be mentally prepared to go through and exit the portal with limited pain. There are also several techniques you need to consider to heal faster once you arrive, especially if Rowena isn't there to heal you. She probably will be though, maybe."

"Pain? What pain?" Kate groaned. She was greeted with silence. "I'll repeat. What *pain*?" Kate glared back at Xavier. Xander artfully looked away. He had a bad habit of that when he didn't want to tell her something.

Angie rolled her eyes. *"Have we managed to do anything yet from their world that didn't involve some degree of pain or danger?"*

"Come to think of it, no we haven't. By the way, this can't be good since Xander is avoiding me."

Xavier frowned and shook his head. After a final glare at his brother, he answered. "The portal uses energy and magic to transport. As you're going through, it will forcefully change your body composition to allow you to move between the realms. When you exit, it returns you back to normal. As a human this will be intensely painful, and you will probably be sick and have a killer headache."

"Can't you people do anything without sacrifice or pain?" Kate threw up her hands and flung her arms. "That's my first suggestion to your Council and something to remember when I'm a full Mystic."

She focused on Xavier. She had heard enough and was fed up with everything. "You mentioned timing being everything. I say it's time to get this show on the road." *Before I literally run back home with Angie in tow.*

Xavier gestured toward the pentagram on the floor. "After you."

She sat down and immediately felt the energy within her pulling in opposite directions. She took deep breaths and tried to rein it in. It was much harder since her recent power boost.

Xander leaned down, gently kissed her neck, and rubbed her shoulders, pouring comfort into her. "I love you, stay focused on that," he whispered in her ear. "Shove everything else from your mind." He kissed her one more time, then stepped back out of the circle and nodded to Xavier to continue.

Xavier sat down opposite her and grabbed the potions beside him. He handed one to Kate. "Bon Appetite!" She rolled her eyes and tossed back the potion before she could change her mind.

"Ugh!" she spluttered, "this tastes disgusting. Have you ever heard of flavoring?"

Xavier smiled and drank his own vile potion.

Xander pulled the athame from the air. He leaned over and sliced their hands. Blood railed down Kate's palm. Xavier cut the same design on each on them. A half-moon shape that — when connected — would create a full circle. He set the athame aside and clasped hands with Kate's.

She found it awkward and embarrassing to be intimately linked with Xavier. They were sharing blood, and nothing in her past had prepared her for this. Their blood mixed, and a powerful surge wracked her body.

She felt his guilt and a fierce determination not to screw this up. She hoped she didn't overload him with her own emotions.

Xavier pulled their hands apart, but the shape of the half circle remained on both their palms. His face showed total determination, but his eyes held fear. It couldn't be easy for him to establish a connection this strong. He took a deep breath and placed their hands back together. He practically pulled her into his lap. Talk about up close and personal. They were nose to nose.

Xavier softly chanted in a language Kate didn't understand, maybe Latin. She wasn't sure, but his melodic tone never faltered. The spell pulled on her energy, but she didn't know how to release it.

She tried to think of it as a gift that she was giving to him. All the while she could feel the stares of everyone around her, and their emotions amplified twenty times over.

Xander worried that something would go wrong, or she would bond with Xavier because of the blood. He could barely stand to watch their exchange without jerking them apart. It was hard to ignore his aggression and jealousy, but she tried.

Gregory, disgusted by the whole thing, thought that Kate was crazy for being talked into this foolish scheme or sharing anything with Xavier. He considered Xavier's blood tainted. He held an intense dislike for Xavier that didn't quite make sense to her.

Angie wasn't sure how to feel. Part of her was ecstatic that Kate had trusted her plan without much question, but scared that it might not work. Part of her was jealous that Xavier allowed Kate to touch him and didn't flinch or run away.

This was getting her nowhere.

Kate refocused her energy and removed the distractions; she pushed her energy toward Xavier. This time it responded and met his own through the connection on their palms.

Energy bounced around their palms. Everyone gasped and stepped back. It looked like lightning strikes jumping from one to the other. It had literally pushed their palms slightly apart so you could see it flowing.

Xavier's power poured into her. It created a shell around her, encasing her in his essence. Kate's skin tingled with his power and energy flowing through her, touching her own inner core.

The Mystic in her wanted to completely repel the invasion, so she worked on acceptance and allowed his energy to continue moving through and around her. It was her first realization that she had two separate beings inside her body. Half Mystic. Half human. Pure freak.

She opened her eyes when the chanting stopped and watched Xavier going through something similar, trying to get his body to accept the essence of the Mystic.

After several more minutes, Xavier sat her beside him and moved away. She followed suit, scooting back to her own side. Their circle was broken, and the half-moon shapes disappeared, leaving behind no proof of the ritual.

"That is some weird shit," Gregory spluttered, shaking his head. He looked totally freaked out. Angie didn't look much better as she glanced back and forth between the two of them.

"I'll second that!" Xander added, shuddering. "I know which one of you is which, but I'm still partially drawn to Xavier because I'm bound to Kate and still drawn to Kate though I sense Xavier in her. This is one hell of a head trip. Ugh, this is totally disgusting." He winced again, trying to get control.

"It will be easier when I leave," Xavier said. "Once I give you the signal, head to the portal. Gregory has the location if he can get over his shock long enough to be coherent. Be careful still. They are playing a different game this time, so be prepared for anything." He glanced toward Angie.

He was using her blood to have a brief moment with Angie, so she didn't intrude. Xavier offered Kate a nod and disappeared.

Kate walked over and hugged Xander to ease his inner turmoil. "It shouldn't take long for the demons to follow," he started rambling. "The daytime demons are usually pretty dumb and trail basic scents. They'll lead any others in the wrong direction. If you girls have anything last minute you need to do, better do it now." He went over to Gregory to work out any last remaining details.

She called her family, letting them know she'd be out of contact for a while, but she loved them. She needed them to know how much she treasured them since she wasn't sure if she'd ever see them again. She had written a letter to her family in the event of her death explaining a lot of stuff in case she never got the chance. Lucia promised to deliver it if Kate didn't make it. Joseph and Lucia had left during the ceremony to create another false trail. They would join them later.

"*Kate.*" A deep voice vibrated in her head. She recognized Zane immediately. "*The demons are actively tracking and following Xavier. Your scent is strong in him but does not seem to be harming him at the moment. Great work. I'll help all that I can. Be prepared for some surprises.*"

He disconnected before she could ask him what he meant. *Why did everyone have to be so cryptic?* She turned toward the others. "It's time. The demons are following Xavier, and Zane will be tracking them. Well, I guess this is it. Everybody ready?"

"As we can be." Xander grabbed the keys. They left the house and headed to an abandoned farm outside of town on two black Kawasaki Ninja motorcycles. Gregory had chosen them in order to move quickly and have the versatility to weave in and out of traffic if necessary. Their helmets had mics to stay in communication.

Kate decided since the trip would take a couple hours, it was time to have a deep discussion with Angie. There were so many unanswered questions, and both of them had avoided the heavy stuff for the last few days. She suspected the more they talked about it, the more real it became. *"I want you to know I'm working on a plan for us both to go through the portal. Don't give up on me."*

"I've never given up on you. But you already know that. You're afraid of the road in front of you. Hell, so am I. At least you know you have a place in this whole mess. Truth, you're scared?" She tried hard to hide the bitterness, but Kate still felt it in the back of her mind.

Of course she was nervous, or anxious, or scared, or all *three*. She still didn't understand the task she'd been given. *"Yeah, it's like taking the next step, but you can't see the path in front of you."*

Angie laughed. *"It's like the scene in that Indiana Jones movie where he had to take a leap of faith. Remember?"*

"Or like in Buffy when she jumped off the tower into the light — and her death. Come to think of it, we watch too much TV." Kate remembered watching all those shows *and* the reruns dozens of times, enthralled by the possibilities of what could be out there.

She should've stuck to the *Gilmore Girls* and *Grey's Anatomy*. "I don't like the feeling of not knowing what comes next."

"You never have, Kate, but some things can't be predicted." She'd always been a planner by nature. She couldn't accept the unknown.

"I wonder how they train there?" Seemed Angie had decided to change the subject a little. "Will there be sword fights or fireballs bouncing around? Or will it be like our training facilities back home?"

Kate thought for a moment. "I think it'll be a mixture of both, like we've seen so far. Physically we'll keep practicing and exercising, but we have a lot to learn when it comes to magic. It's one thing to watch it on TV, but a whole different story in reality. And there are no retakes. One shot is all we get. Did you see all that Xavier did for one spell? You know it all had meaning, or it wouldn't have been there."

"What's up with the constant morbid dialogue? Where are you hiding, my take no prisoners friend, Kate?" Angie sounded worried.

"Sorry, I'm being a whiny-butt right now," she laughed. The last thing she wanted was for Angie to tense up again. "I'm a little overwhelmed."

Kate hesitated. "I'm not sure I'm ready to give up humanity."

"What do you think it'll be like?" Angie wondered.

Kate searched for an answer, but the truth was that no one seemed to know. She sent Angie her best impression of shrugging and rolling her eyes. "I'm not sure, but I'd be willing to bet my life that there will be pain involved. We haven't done anything painless yet involving the Council." She'd added a bit of sarcasm to ease her friend.

"True that." Angie hesitated. *Here it comes.* "Kate, we have to discuss the possibility that I won't be able to go with — "

Kate tried to interrupt her, but Angie sent a blast of mental energy back to shut her up. *"I mean it. We've never ignored an aspect of a case or situation simply because we didn't want to face it."*

Tears pricked the back of her eyes. She wanted to argue, but facts were facts. Angie was right. The main reason they were so good and always got the perp was because they meticulously combed through every scenario.

Today could not be the exception. Kate nodded. *"At least give me time to figure it out. Promise me that much."*

"On one condition. That you swear when the moment comes and you have to choose, you'll go through the portal."

Seconds stretched into minutes while Kate struggled to make the promise. *"Okay, I swear, but know I'll do everything in my power first."*

"Agreed. Now what's the plan if I can't go with you?"

"Xavier and Gregory promised to look after you. I know they'll keep you safe. What worries me more is what Xavier said about pain, and how hard it would be on the human body."

"Don't wuss out on me now. If you find a way to bring me with you, I'll handle the portal and survive. I promise." For once Angie sounded completely like her usual arrogant self. Kate had missed that the past couple of weeks. Neither of them had been themselves since being thrust into another world.

"Enough with the heavy emotional crap. So, you and Xander are bonded now?" Angie smiled and sent a mental jab.

Kate nailed her right back. *"Yes. It was incredible. Our minds and bodies were linked, and there was this feeling of everything clicking into place. Listen Angie, Xander told me a little about what happened to Xavier. He was married — "*

A stab of pain flowed through Angie, momentarily jarring Kate. The girl was more attracted to Xavier than her conscious self would admit. *"And it was a rough go from beginning to end. To help you understand, I'm transferring the short story to you. Xander will tell us the rest later."*

Angie's flash of pain and sadness filled her heart. *"Don't try to decide anything right now. We'll sort everything out."*

Angie disconnected.

"Kate." Zane's deep timbre voice broke into her thoughts, startling her. *"You're almost to the site. It won't be long now. By the way, I think you are right. It's time for Xavier to love again, but he is more damaged than you know. I realize that's not much comfort, but I believe there is hope for him."*

"Thanks Zane. For everything." She passed along the message to Angie without the Xavier comments. Angie's mind was still quiet, but at least she'd reopened it to her.

They drove deep into the forest and finally reached a small clearing. She noticed a faint shimmer next to a large tree.

"What is — " She turned Xander. His face turned white, his eyes rolled back, and he collapsed on the ground. "Xander!" She lunged toward him and caught his head before it hit a jagged rock.

"What's going on? Why are you so weak? Xander, answer me!" She tried to plug in mentally but found chaos. He was swamped in regret and pain. Panic drummed deep in her chest.

She'd known something was off, but why wouldn't he tell her?

She kissed his cheek and wiped the sweat from his face.

He opened his eyes and smiled at her. "No reason for you to worry. Gregory will help you through the portal. He'll try to help Angie as well." The deep resonating pain inside him triggered a feeling of hopelessness.

"I can't go with you," he barely whispered. "It's time to say good-bye."

"Excuse me? What the hell are you talking about?" She forced the panic down and figured this had to be some kind of sick joke. Their gazes stayed locked. His mind blocked her searches. Panic turned to fear.

Hadn't she known that in some distant corner of her mind? She'd sensed it from the moment he'd been injured fighting Fury. Something had gone wrong. There *had* to be a way to undo the damage. This couldn't happen the moment she finally had a chance for happiness. Fate couldn't be that cruel.

"You have to get out of here. It's for the best. Everything will be okay. Hurry!" His skin grew clammy and his face lost its color.

"Like hell it is. You're lying to me. Why aren't you healing or recharging like the rest? Did Fury use some sort of spell?"

"I love you, Kate. Please remember that. No matter what happens, know there is nothing I have loved more in my life than you. But I can't give you the answer you seek. Go." He drifted away again.

She turned toward Gregory. He'd kept his distance. No shock on his face. He knew the truth. "Tell me what's happening."

"If I could, I would in a heartbeat. He swore me to secrecy using an ancient oath. I can't break it. I'm sorry, Kate." He avoided her eyes, but not before she'd seen the fear and pain. Panic gave way to terror. She knew exactly what they were saying.

"He's dying, right?" Still neither responded. Who could help her? Someone had to know.

She thought of the one person that loved him as much as she did.

"Xavier?"

"Yes, Kate?"

"Xander collapsed. What's he not telling me? He's nearly unconscious, and Gregory won't tell me anything. Please, help me save your brother." His silence seemed to last forever, like he was wrestling with his decision.

"Gregory can't tell you because he swore an ancient oath. To break the oath, he would forfeit his life. However, I didn't take a magical vow, so I will break my word and tell you. First, promise me that you will not let anger crowd your better judgment."

Uh-oh. The sting of betrayal began to worm its way into her heart. It meant something bad was headed her way. What had he done? Nothing could be that bad, *right?* Regardless, she loved him and pushed the doubts aside.

"*He's dying. Of course, I'll do anything to save him. Please, tell me.*" She'd never been one to beg, but she'd do it now.

"*Okay, when Xander touched your leg that night in the alley, he accidentally traded blood with you. It started the Awakening ahead of schedule. He began to bond with your human half.*"

"*What does any of this matter? We're fully bonded now.*" If he'd been within reach, she would've strangled him. He needed to get to the point.

"*Listen. He bonded with your human half. He started turning human.*" She gasped. He continued. "*He knew the clock was ticking from the beginning, but he wanted you to make your own choice. He thought there was plenty of time. Fury changed all that. Once you became the full Mystic, he would have been restored.*"

Something inside her froze. She sat back on her heels to digest everything. He'd lied to her this whole time?

Xander had known he was close to death and the only way to save himself had been to get her to the Meadows. He would've done anything and everything to earn her trust, yet he'd lied every step of the way. He hadn't trusted her enough. Not even at the end.

"*Kate, snap out of it. Maybe he didn't do things right according to you. Maybe at first, some of his feelings were superficial. But you've seen into his mind and know his feelings are real. Your bond with him is unbreakable. His side was blasted when he jumped in front of an energy blast to save you.*"

"*I'm the Mystic and that's his job. Why did he bond with me? I'd already agreed to go with him. Why didn't he tell me then?*" Even if he'd really fallen in love with her, he'd never trusted her. What kind of love was that?

"By that time, he'd already fallen for you. He was simply afraid to tell you. He didn't want to lose you. I know you're having trouble believing me at the moment but consider this. He knew the only way to defeat Fury and ensure your safety was to join forces with me. In order to do that, he had to be bonded with you. He knew if that happened, he would lose the rest of his power and die. The bond with your human half sucked the rest of his powers and will begin aging him within minutes. Still, he saved you."

Her heart shattered. Tears clogged her throat. She didn't know what to believe. Love didn't exist without trust, and she'd never be able to trust him again. It wasn't fair.

She pushed her emotions aside. Xavier was right about one thing. Xander had saved her life many times and risked his own. They couldn't afford to lose a Guardian. Even if she never spoke to him again, it was her duty to save him if she could.

"What can I do to save him?"

"It's not that simple. He's too far gone. Using your bond, you can link to him and hold him to you. In the Meadows, they can hold him in a sort of stasis until you are fully awakened. Stasis means that he would have his powers and age, but never be able to leave the realm again without restoration."

Kate flung her hands up in desperation, even though he couldn't see her. She yelled at the sky. *"What's so hard about that?"*

She closed her eyes and reached for him.

"Wait, that's not all, I'm afraid. I just learned from Zane that the only decent chance for Angie to enter the portal is if she is embraced by your essence. That means

that you would have to control it. Even then, there are no guarantees." He paused and let everything sink in.

Xavier flashed in beside her. He leaned over to check on his twin. The grief on his face said it all. They were out of time.

"You have to choose, Kate. Angie or Xander. You don't have enough energy or power to save them both." He briefly touched her shoulder and walked away. He informed Gregory and Angie of everything he'd told her.

Kate leaned over Xander and listened for his breathing. He was weak. She didn't know what to do. She couldn't leave Angie, the one person she trusted in this world. She knew what no one wanted to say. If Angie didn't go through the portal, the demons would use her as bait. She'd die. They couldn't hide her forever.

In the background, she heard Angie begging Xavier to find another way. She shut out the voices.

What was she supposed to do? How could she choose between the two people she loved the most? Even if Xander had been a complete jackass, she loved him. How could she even contemplate leaving Angie behind?

Tears streamed down her face. Xander had chosen not to trust her, she now had to choose who lived — and who died.

"Go!" Xander's hoarse and weak whisper startled her.

She gasped. "You're awake. I'm so angry with you, but you have to tell me how to save you. What am I supposed to do?"

"This was my choice. When I first met you, I didn't like you. I couldn't understand how a human would ever fit into my world. I was wrong. You taught me that. You helped me discover what love means. That discovery led me back to my brother and to you.

"I found my place. My only regret is not telling you everything from the beginning. I didn't trust you enough to make the right decisions for the right reasons. I can only hope you forgive me someday. I love y — " He faded out.

His skin was cold. She'd run out of time. Would she be able to trust anyone in this new realm? Would she survive without either of them? There had to be another way. She had to buy time and figure it out.

His breathing slowed.

"No!" She lifted him off the ground and rocked with his head resting in her lap. Something deep inside her moved toward him. "Ok, if blood began this whole mess, it can keep him alive while we come up with a plan."

She grabbed the dagger out of her weapons belt and sliced her hand open. She followed suit with his and she intertwined their fingers. Her energy field wrapped them in its arms. As long as her blood flowed through him, he'd stay alive. Their bond held him like life support.

So how would she save Angie? She ignored the stares of everyone around her.

"Xavier, I can't lose either of them. Please help me."

He sighed. He was hiding something. She stared him down until he finally spoke.

"Zane mentioned another possible option, but honestly I think it is ridiculous. It would be highly dangerous. If she doesn't cross with your shield, she simply gets thrown back into this realm. If we use Zane's other option, she will die or be trapped."

Shit. Her options were getting better and better. "Is there anything that doesn't come with a death sentence attached?"

"Wait a minute," Angie interjected and came to squat beside her. "What exactly is this other option?"

"You can't be serious?" Gregory tried to pull her up. "I'll hide you away somewhere."

Angie shushed him and turned back to Xavier.

"Zane can create a portal similar to the one he used the other night to communicate with Kate. He can merge the portals together for a few seconds to create a distortion with the portal. In that brief moment, it would be possible for a human to enter.

"The downside is, if it doesn't work, it would either cause immediate death or you could get stuck in the shadows. For a human, that would be a fate worse than death." Xavier looked down at his feet.

Kate realized that in a way he was choosing between the two. He could've lied and told her there was no way for Angie to cross. He cared about both of them, too — or did he?

Was this a way to make her choose Xander, and he'd simply take Angie out of the equation? Angie thumped her from behind. She'd read her thoughts loud and clear.

"Angie, neither option sounds good. I can't leave you. I know this sounds crazy, but I have this gut feeling that you have to cross through the portal." She met her eyes and could see determination taking hold.

"Damn right you are not using the shadows." Gregory jerked her away from Xavier. "Don't let him confuse you. His priority is saving his brother, not you."

Angie bitterly laughed. "Have you considered that's my priority, too? Don't get me wrong. I don't want to die. But I have to consider the big picture like all of you. This is my choice."

Kate grabbed her hand and used what energy she could spare to lock her into place.

"Kate, you're my sister in every sense of the word," Angie stated. "Despite Xander's screw up, you're meant to be together. I have to hope that you'll find your way back to him."

"I can't let you go. I can't let you make this choice. You've had my back for years and never lied to me. Who can I trust in this world except you? We'll find another way." Kate held her hand in a death grip. She'd honestly thought her heart couldn't break any more. She was wrong. She could lose them both.

"I'm sorry, Kate. I've made my decision. I'll trust Xavier to take me through the portal. This one's on me." Angie tried to pull from her grip, but Kate held on tight.

"I'm sorry to rush this along," Xavier interrupted, "but the demons are headed this way. They are only a few miles from this site. We can't risk them finding us or the portal. Kate, you have to choose. *Now.*"

Kate's grip slipped. She couldn't hold on to both of them. Sweat stung her eyes and rolled down her back. She was using too much energy to keep Xander alive and hold Angie in place.

"Kate," Angie said. "You've always believed in freedom. You're angry with Xander for not trusting you to make the right choice, but you're doing the same thing to me."

Within seconds, she'd lose them both and they'd have demons on top of them. Her gaze went from one to the other. *How can I choose?* Two lives were literally in her hands.

Using the last of her strength that she could spare, she let one of them go.

She broke her connection to Angie. She had to release the control and trust her best friend to make her own choice. She had to trust that Angie would find her own destiny.

Tears burned her eyes, as she watched her walk away. She refused to let them fall.

Angie walked over to Xavier despite Gregory begging her to stay. "Please Angie!" Gregory persisted. "I'll remain behind permanently and protect you!"

She met his eyes and stoked his cheek. "I know you would. See you on the other side."

She joined hands with Xavier. The portal turned a reddish color. Electricity hummed in the air.

"Now!" Xavier pulled Angie to him. He flung them both into the portal with his arms wrapped tightly around her. The red faded and the portal quieted.

Kate reached for Angie with her mind but found emptiness. The only way she'd know was to go through the portal herself. Red dots drifted into her vision. The energy drain tapped her dry. Fainting had become a high possibility. She had to hurry.

"Gregory, can you levitate us through the portal so I can hold onto him?" He had trouble focusing, so she asked him again.

"Yes, yes. Let's go." He lifted them up a couple feet in the air and slowly moved them toward the portal. Kate was careful to maintain a firm grip on Xander's hand and spirit. Her biggest fear was not only losing him in the portal, but also that Angie hadn't made it. Had she made the wrong choice?

Clutching Xander in a death grip, she felt the pull of the portal accepting them. They'd make it through.

A brief moment of triumphant elation for their successful journey was followed by an intense, excruciating and searing pain radiating through her entire body.

She burst into flames.

21

The burning started in Kate's toes and moved upward until it consumed her entire body. The pain intensified. She screamed. It felt like someone was picking the flesh off her body piece by piece. She thought it would never end — but prayed for it — and tried her best to hang onto Xander. Everything went pitch black, and she faded away to the sound of their heartbeats. She hit the ground with a thud and woke up.

It had probably been worse for Angie. Kate had never been afraid of burning alive before, but she would now for the rest of her life.

People surrounded her, but some didn't look quite human. She took stock of her surroundings. *As long as little people don't jump out and start singing about yellow brick roads, I'll be fine.*

She remembered where they were and breathed a sigh of relief.

They'd made it into the Meadows. She tried to cut through the massive pain overtaking her head and looked for Angie.

Angie lay on the ground ten feet away. She crawled or maybe rolled toward her. Angie groaned, and Kate sighed with relief. At least she was alive. They'd both made it.

Where was Xander?

She heard another thud and felt herself being lifted into someone's lap. Gregory held onto her, trying to soothe her. She should be pushing him away, but instead she relaxed. He rubbed her temples. The pain eased, but she still had a long way to go.

Barely opening her eyes, she saw Xavier rocking Angie in the same way. Dread filled her heart. She still couldn't move much. Using all the strength she had left; she ignored the pain and forced her head to look to her sides. She couldn't see him. Had he lived? Had he died? *Where's Xander?*

A moan turned her head. He was lying behind her.

"Move out of the way. Move out of the way. Coming through, in case you didn't hear me the first two times." A woman's voice cut through all the other voices humming in her head. The sunlight bathed her in a golden glow picking up the highlights in her brown hair.

She squatted beside Kate and laid a hand on her chest. "You were magnificent, my child. Absolutely ingenious. The whole Council was holding their breath. We are so proud of you." Her voice became hypnotic and put Kate at ease. The pain began to lighten, and her mind could focus.

Warmth seeped through Kate's entire body. Like warm honey flowing through her veins. It was heavenly. A few minutes later she felt normal again and sat up to thank the woman, but she was already healing Angie.

"Thank you," Kate called out. The woman nodded but stayed focused on her friend.

She looked up at Xander through glazed eyes. "What exactly happened? I'm still a little fuzzy on all the details."

Xander stroked her hair and brushed his fingers down her cheek. "We made it through the portal thanks to you.

Your idea was brilliant. The blood held me just as I was. When I crossed over, my life force was restored, and my mother had a potion ready to restore my powers.

"As for your pain, your human bodies aren't meant to change composition, so you literally felt changes that magical beings don't."

He kissed her cheek and then her lips. "I'm so sorry about before. I promise to always be honest with you. No more secrets. I let fear take over and it was not a pretty picture. I should have supported, not hindered you. I was the one who told you to trust your instincts, and then *I* didn't trust them. I'm so sorry for being a complete ass. Forgive me?"

She wasn't sure how to respond, but she wasn't ready to completely forgive him yet. "Since I experienced a brief moment with Angie and trying to control her decisions, I'll admit a better understanding of what you did. But over time and once we bonded, you still didn't tell me the truth. I'm having trouble forgiving that. You'll have to give me some time."

His eyes filled with pain, but she couldn't let it go yet. She had to find a way to trust him again if they were ever going to be true soul mates.

"I understand. Tell me what you need, and I'll do it."

"Let's take it one day at a time and try to rebuild." It was the best she could do for now.

Angie sat up with a groan and rubbed her head. "That was fun. Can't say I *ever* want to do it again! I'm stuck here permanently just so you know, because I'm never going through that thing again."

Xavier helped her to her feet. Gregory fumed.

Xander lifted Kate to *her* feet. She looked around the crowd and saw everyone's welcome gaze inviting her into their world.

She smiled and relaxed until she was rudely interrupted by a sneering, but gorgeous woman, who walked toward them.

"Well, isn't this sweet?" she said, tossing her long black hair over her shoulders. "Little humans have infested our world."

She was thin, but tall, reaching close to six feet. Slightly taller than Kate. Her skin was flawless and pale. Her eyes were bright green with flecks of gold that swirled around. A ring of brown also encircled her emerald eyes.

She would've been absolutely stunning if she hadn't looked completely evil. The sneer and glare ruined what could've been a very pretty face. She reminded Kate of one those faeries she'd seen on a *Tinkerbell* cartoon. *But much more bitchy.*

"Roxy, do you not have anything better to do than insult the Mystic?" Gregory taunted her. It was obvious there was no love lost between the two. "Soon, she'll be more powerful than you, so I'd watch that vicious little mouth of yours."

"Hmmm, you never had a problem with my mouth before, have you Gregory dear?"

Everyone looked at him. His face flamed.

"I wonder if she's even the real Mystic? Maybe she's only a pathetic human you picked up at the pound."

Her cruel gaze narrowed further when she spotted Angie. "Really, did you have to bring home two pets? They might have fleas."

Roxy laughed while everyone else glared.

"Roxy," Xander said wearily, "shut up before you cause hysteria or a riot. I'm too tired to deal with either. You know what she is, you saw her so — just — Shut Up!"

Kate didn't know what was wrong with this witch, but she was going to teach her a lesson real quick. She might not know much about magic, but she'd learned some very important things about being a Mystic.

Straightening her shoulders, she sent a blast of electricity toward Roxy and knocked her off her feet.

Roxy jumped up and spun around. "How dare you?" she spluttered. "How did you do that? I didn't see it."

Ah ha, she's a Seer. "I *am* the Mystic, bitch. You can't read my mind or see my intentions. Need further proof? I'd be happy to oblige and show you some other things this human happens to know in addition to knocking you on your ass." Kate winked for extra emphasis while adding in as much arrogance as she could muster.

Roxy stalked off with her face flaming and uttering a tirade of curses.

Kate looked up at Xander. "What's her problem?"

"There are too many to go into today. Let's forget her for now." He leaned to his side and gave the woman who'd healed her a big hug, then kissed her cheek.

Smiling, he turned back to Kate. "Now this is someone I want you to meet. This is my mother, Pam."

Kate's eyes widened. "Nice to meet you. Thank you for healing us. Xander told me you were a healer."

Pam's eyes were a warm and inviting chocolate brown. Her hair, light brown with streaks of gold, brushed the top of her shoulders. She wasn't tall but had an amazing athletic build. Kindness and love shone through her every fiber, especially when she looked at her sons.

The most surprising detail was that she didn't look much older than Xander. "We have waited a long time for you, but I can see you are tired from your journey. You need rest before you meet the Council."

Pam turned to address their whole group. "I have convinced the Council to wait until later to see you all. They have asked that the whole traveling party be notified.

"Plus, many are arriving by the hundreds to see their new Mystic. Rowena and Marcus are trying to clear them all in. This way you can see a little of where you will be living and get some good rest tonight, knowing you're safe."

She turned to walk away. Then she paused, looking over her shoulder at Kate and Xander. "And I mean let her get some rest, Xander dear. She will need it. It's going to be a long night for her."

She winked and turned back around. Her innuendo brought red to both their faces.

Clearing his throat, Xander smiled. "My mom is one who believes in saying what is on her mind. I think you'll get along great. She's right. Tonight will be a long one because everyone is going to want to meet their new leader."

Kate started to say something, when an excited squeal came from behind her. She whirled around. A woman skipped up to them, dragging along a man behind her. They were an attractive couple.

He was tall with a goatee, short blond hair, and strong build. His defined facial features made him quite handsome. He had unique-colored eyes, a liquid silver. Strangely, his companion's were the exact same color.

The lady was a good six inches shorter than him, but still around the same height as Kate. Her auburn hair tucked right under her chin set in an almond-shaped face. Her build was slight but emanated power.

"Hey guys, we missed you!" The woman hugged Xander and Gregory tightly.

The man calmly reached forward and shook their hands. "Maybe *she* missed you. I liked being in charge."

The woman elbowed him in the stomach. "Oh hush, you know it's not been the same around here. We've all been on pins and needles the last several years waiting for her to arrive." She smiled at Kate.

Xander grinned and hugged her again. It was weird to see him so relaxed and in his own element.

"It's truly good to see both of you. Kate, these are my good friends Illianna and Marco. Marco took over training along with Jeff once my mission was activated. Gregory was helping them until he had to come and help me search for you."

He winked at her. Kate scowled at him and shook her head. She reached her hand toward the couple and smiled. "Nice to meet you. I've been anxious to meet some of Xander's friends."

Xander watched the scene before him. Illianna looked insane from grinning so much. At least Marco acted more normal. Xander figured the first few introductions could have gone a lot worse. Except Roxy.

What crawled up her butt and died? She was a pain but usually not that forward.

"Guys, this is Kate, our new Mystic, and her friend Angie, who has come to help as well."

"I'm so excited," Illianna chimed. "I realize what's ahead, but it feels like a new chapter has begun instead of constantly waiting. Remember that we are your friends. You too, Angie. We welcome you both to our home and our world. We know the transition may be a little tough, but feel free to ask us anything at all." Illianna reached forward and took Angie's hand.

"More than that," Marco added. "We are your faithful servants. If you ever need anything, simply ask. We will follow your lead."

Kate started to refute the servant comment. A nudge from Xander stopped her. She quickly caught on, and instead took Marco's outstretched hand and smiled warmly.

Xander let out his breath. Many of the people here could be traditional and formal. He hadn't had a chance to tell her much about their customs yet, or how the power structure was regarded differently. She was like a queen to them. Their ultimate leader. Even if some were hesitant to accept her.

So far, he thought she handled it well.

"Thank you, but I consider you my friends above all. I have no doubt I'll need as many friends as I can earn and all the advice I can stand if we're going to be successful at the Rising. I look forward to spending time with you." Marco nodded in appreciation. Kate smiled.

Illianna wrapped her arm around Kate's shoulders. "Why don't you come over for dinner soon? It will be a nice meal for us to catch up. Also, I hope you don't mind, but Pam told us that you two were bonded. I know you didn't have time to celebrate, so I thought a small party would be better than nothing. Maybe we can put together something bigger later."

Xander's first thought was to refuse, but they needed to eat. Plus, he and Kate were in a dangerous place right now. She didn't hate him but held a lot of anger. He needed some quiet time to talk with her, but she needed opportunities to make friends and allies. Maybe if Kate knew more about their world and way of life, she could find a way to forgive him.

"That sounds great," Kate replied. "We'll see you again soon."

Illianna hugged Kate again, enthusiasm nearly bubbling over. "I'm so excited. See you at the Council meeting." She ran off, dragging her husband behind her.

Xander groaned. "I wanted to spend time with only you, but I know it's important to start working with friends. And they've gone to a lot of trouble for us." He leaned down and kissed her. Heat swiftly rose between them.

She stepped back and cleared her throat. He had to work hard to suppress the irritation inside him. He kept reminding himself that she had saved him. She still loved him, but they had to find their way back to each other. It was his fault. He would have to be patient.

They started walking down the street following Xavier, Gregory, and Angie. *This will definitely be interesting with them all living under one roof.*

"Welcome to your new home. It should suit all of our needs." He watched her eyes widen and a giant smile crossed her face.

They came to a stop in front of an iron gate and Kate's mouth gaped open.

"This is your house? I'd say adequate is an understatement."

They entered at the edge of a short driveway and she could only stare at the house standing before her. At least she liked his *home*. That was a start.

Holy crap. This wasn't a home. *It's a freaking mansion.* It was three stories and she assumed it covered several acres, although she couldn't see how deep the property went. The brick was a beautiful rust color, and the windows were all made of painted glass.

It had several wings and what appeared to be servants' quarters or extra rooms back behind it. The house was situated on a gorgeous piece of land with luscious green grass and the perfect number of trees to give the illusion of total privacy.

Angie's amazement equaled her own.

She glanced at Xander and gulped. "This is your house? Where you grew up?"

Nodding, he shrugged like it was nothing special. "Yeah, this is home."

"This isn't a home. It's an estate," Angie snorted.

"I take it you like it?" He lightly punched her in the arm and grinned. He used a remote that he had manifested to open the gigantic side garage.

Numerous cars and other vehicles were inside. *Show off,* Kate grinned. Angie drooled.

"By the way — " Xander wrapped his arms around Kate's shoulders and turned to address Angie. "You can choose any of these cars and it's yours. You can drive anything you like. I'll show you how to access the keys tomorrow. We have a small city, but we cover a lot of land

and some great driving strips should you ever feel the need to break some speed limits."

Her face lit up brighter than a Christmas tree. She barreled past Kate and hugged him, laughing as she looked around at all her choices.

Kate followed Angie, who lovingly walked by and touched some of the cars. Expensive cars had always been her greatest weakness, but she'd never been able to own one. She was in her own version of heaven at the moment. He received a few points for the sheer joy he'd brought to Angie.

She brought her gaze back to Xander and Xavier. "You both have a beautiful and amazing home. It seems so big for one family. Who all lives here? Surely you don't live here alone?"

"This is our family home. As you can see, it accommodates more than one family, but it's pretty empty. My parents aren't living here at the moment, and Xavier was living in Zane's home until now.

"Any visitors or family that come stay in the west wing, but right now we're pretty low there. When you begin recruiting, this house won't seem so big anymore once it is full of warriors. Enjoy it while you can."

Xander put his arm around her waist. They walked back to the front. "How about going inside?" She tried to be civil and not shake it off. He was trying, and she needed to as well. He held out his hand.

She pulled herself together, took his hand, and they walked back around front and up the porch steps. It was hard not to be impressed. Her chin hit the floor again as they reached the top of the porch. It wrapped around the entire house. She'd always loved wrap-around porches.

The front doors were the size of those old-fashioned massive doors she remembered seeing on churches and other historical buildings in other countries she'd visited.

Xander opened the doors and the shocks kept coming.

She felt like a princess taking a tour of her new castle. Cinderella or Snow White had nothing on her. She stepped into the foyer onto marble floors. A fountain in the center of the entryway flowed smooth and quiet. Soothing. Hypnotic.

A woman shouted behind her, jarring her out of her stupor. A woman a little taller than Angie, who looked to be in her twenties, came bounding at Xander. She launched herself into his arms, nearly knocking him over. She was uncommonly pretty and lithe.

He grabbed her up in a huge hug and swung her around.

She jumped into Xavier's arms next and kissed his cheeks. He blushed. Kate and Angie stared at the crazy woman knocking everybody over. Startled, Kate tipped back as the girl grabbed her in a crushing hug. At least she didn't kiss her, too.

"I couldn't wait to meet my sister-in-law. Mom told me to wait until later, but I had to meet you now. I've dreamed of you since Xander's birth, and you are everything I imagined. I'm Nikki Montgomery, by the way." The girl gushed and sat Kate back down.

Her smile could light up an entire town. Kate was looking at one of Xander's sisters and could see the resemblance, except she had her mother's soft brown eyes and gentle spirit. Her long dark brown hair was intricately braided and ended down around her bottom.

"Nicolette, please let go of Kate before you terrify her," Xander softly said, with no real censure in his voice and a smile full of affection.

"Oops," she laughed. "I'm so excited, discounting the Awakening thing and all that. I'm sure everything will be fine. You are even prettier and more powerful than in my dreams." She stared at her as though she would never stop.

Kate tried not to be creeped out.

"Nicolette." Xander tapped his foot like a frustrated parent.

She glared at Xander, and he shrugged. There was a moment between the siblings.

"Sorry, Nikki, could you calm down a little? No wonder Mom wanted you to wait a bit." He turned toward Kate and Angie. "Nikki is a healer and specializes in dreams and nature."

A what? Kate questioned him with a raised eyebrow.

"She can heal similar to Mom," Xander continued. "But she has the unique ability to travel through people's dreams. Or, she can use the dreams to learn more about the individual. She doesn't actually watch your dreams. I'll explain it later. It is a rare, precious gift, and she wields it beautifully."

Nikki flushed from the praise. "Aw shucks, little brother. I've missed you terribly," she added quietly. She glanced over at Xavier. "Both of you. Welcome home."

After the reunion, they continued to look around several of the rooms. Everything was made out of thick, hand-carved wood. She saw a music room on her left and a sort of den to her right.

She'd never get the hang of this whole house. She wondered if they had an App for her cell that would help her navigate. He'd said they had cell phones and all other technology.

The surprises kept coming as they proceeded down the hallway. Room after room of amazing and priceless art, decorations, and antiques covered every square inch. They stopped at a fork where there were three different hallways.

Xander pointed. "Straight ahead leads to the kitchen. To the left, there are two main sections. My parents' and sisters' quarters are in one, and visitors' quarters are in the other. We are going to the right. Mine and Xavier's quarters are in this section of the house. Although for the last several years, we've only used my set of rooms and will be using Xavier's as visitor rooms.

"As the time comes closer, everyone's house will be full. Many of the regular families here have large homes and house multiple or large extended families. We're the main training and education center for all supernatural beings, so it's easier to live and work together especially when we're nearing a battle."

Kate was amazed at how unified the communities and people seemed to be.

"Are all the communities set up this way?" Angie asked.

"Not all of them," Gregory finally chimed in. "Some are in between. And in some of the more concentrated areas, groups of warriors, covens, families, etcetera, might live together to maintain safety.

"With demons constantly hunting and rogues causing trouble, it makes more sense to band together so they aren't picked off. In less concentrated areas, or for those who have tried to mainstream with humans, they live in separate homes to avoid suspicion. Many will still stay near others of their kind and might have an underground safe house in case of attack."

Angie cocked her head to the side, with a questioning look. "It's weird to know that all of this exists, and humans are completely in the dark. I will say, I'm beginning to see how easy it is to hide and blend in our current culture that is starting to accept the unusual." She looked upward, hesitating. "Was it my imagination or did some of the people standing around us not look quite human-ish?"

Kate gave the conversation her full attention. She'd seen the differences, too.

"There are few humans who know about us except certain covens." Xavier, who'd been quiet since their arrival, reluctantly spoke. "On the whole it helps if we remain Hollywood legends. It was not your imagination earlier. There are lots of supernatural creatures that have banded under our protection to avoid human and demon persecution.

"They're all unique in abilities, or appearances, or both. Shadow Warriors have a tattoo on their backs. Elves and nymphs have slightly larger eyes and some of their ears are a little different. They can be different sizes and have other distinguishing characteristics. Shapeshifters, or Wereanimals, usually have markings on the back of their necks or sometimes down their arms.

"Gliders tend to be pale, but not always, and have unique eyes. They're usually warm, unless they've gone without blood too long, and then they may turn cooler and their skin becomes more and more transparent. The list goes on and on and gets much stranger.

"Wizards, witches, and sorcerers look much like humans except for distinguishing birthmarks usually on their hip, but sometimes in other places. Kate, you'll receive a mark as well — probably on your chest — that denotes you as the Mystic. This is supposed to be so all can see your power, but you can hide it at will. Especially when you're operating in the human world." Xavier took a deep breath.

He sounded winded. Kate wondered if he'd talked this much in the last twenty years. She tried to sort through all the information, but it overwhelmed her.

She was on information overload and not happy about getting some kind of marking across her chest. She'd never been one for tattoos.

It wasn't accepting other types of people but accepting several at once that was hard to grasp.

She had a lot to learn. How would she keep it all straight? "Are there any species that look a little more on the demon-ish side? I don't want to attack someone on accident due to a lack of knowledge."

Xander shrugged and shook his head. "There are some species that look a little more different than others, but most have learned how to blend in with humans to survive. There are some that turn into animals, so be careful attacking any animals, unless they're attacking you.

"Most demons are pretty easy to pick out. Legend says that it's due to their black souls and the torture endured in the Hell realm. I don't think this is something you need to worry about. Besides, once you're the Mystic you'll know who or what is evil automatically."

"Even the traitor?" Concern laced her voice. She thought of how much damage this entity had done so far. There was no way out now. Her only options were life or death. This traitor played a part in that outcome.

"Honestly, if Rowena can't feel the traitor, I doubt you'll be able to either. Once you embrace the full light, it'll be easy. At that point, I seriously doubt that it will matter anymore." Xander continued walking through the house until he came to another split.

"Xavier's old quarters are on the left. Mine are on the right. There are several rooms in each set with a large study. We've decided with everything going on that we will all stay in my quarters, at least until after the Rising, even Gregory. Right Gregory?" He looked pointedly at him.

"I remember, I remember. You don't have to keep reminding me every ten minutes. I gave my word, and I'll stay here until the Rising, or I'll at least give it my best." He looked at Xavier with severe distrust.

Oh yeah, we are one big happy family, dysfunctional and all. None of them would be speaking by the time this was over. She glanced over at Angie. She twiddled her thumbs, obviously trying to remain aloof.

She knew it was hard enough for her not to be magical. To be stuck between two magical beings that were your love interests and be stuck in the same house with them sucked. Big time. At least she'd be spending plenty of time with both of them and learning all their faults.

Xavier opened the first door on the left. "I'll be staying here for now." He waved his hand. All the sheets covering the furniture disappeared, and the bed made itself.

Gregory inclined his head toward the next door beside Xavier's. "I'll be staying here if you need me." He opened the door and followed Xavier's movements, clearing the furniture and fixing the bed.

"Xander," Gregory asked, "if it's okay with you, I'll take Angie to her room, so you can have some time with Kate."

Kate thought it obvious Gregory was trying to get Angie away from Xavier.

"Sure, but don't forget she needs to unpack and get ready for dinner."

Gregory glared. "Yes, master."

Xander sighed and Gregory took hold of Angie's arm and led her to the third room on the right. Xavier went into his own and slammed the door.

Xander rolled his eyes. "I am way too old for this crap."

"You are a little old, but I didn't want to say anything." Kate laughed at his mock look of indignation.

He opened the second door on the right.

Looking around the room he'd created for her, she froze. The laughter died in her throat. All of the colors were navy, cream, and brown. Her favorites. What caught her attention the most was everything else in the room. It brought tears to her eyes. Frames with her family pictures had been placed all around it. The clothes she'd missed hung neatly in the closet.

All of the items from her desk back home were now on her new desk. Quilts, mementos, photo albums, and many other personal items scattered throughout the room. She turned and saw her gun and badge lying in the top nightstand drawer that had been slightly left open. She could barely keep her emotions in check.

She looked above her bed and the floodgates let loose. Tears streamed down her cheeks. She stared at the photograph of Julie, Angie, and herself that day in the park during her college days before Julie had died the night before graduation. They'd been the best of friends. Julie's tragic murder provided the fuel for her own desire to protect the innocent. The reason she had joined the police force in the first place.

He'd put it in a beautiful antique frame that brought new beauty to the picture. She looked into Julie's eyes. Wouldn't she get a kick seeing them now? Kate closed her eyes and silently thanked her for the wisdom and creativity she'd brought into all of their lives.

Xander had done all of this for her. He'd listened to her stories and understood what mattered most to her. No one would spend this much time reconstructing a room if he didn't truly love her. Her heart squeezed. Forgiveness and love stormed the walls she'd begun to build around herself.

She gazed up at him. "Thank you," she whispered. "I do love you. This means so much to me."

He wrapped his arms around her and gently kissed her. "I love you, too, and I'm so sorry. I hoped this would show you that I did pay attention and I do know you. I want you to be happy here in your new home. I have to admit, though, my sisters helped me out a lot since I couldn't be here to do it all. They completed it before we arrived at Joseph's."

Her heart beat fast, and her chest tightened as she struggled to hold back tears. She refused to act like a total baby. Even if she felt like bawling her eyes out. His sincerity moved her.

Before they'd even bonded, he'd created this place for her. He'd trusted her to make the right decision even if he hadn't known how to talk to her about it. With demons chasing them constantly, she had to admit there had been little time for talking.

It all came down to the fact that she was safe with him. Cherished and important. He knew absolutely everything she was and would be. He loved her despite it all. Maybe it was time to honor that commitment and offer the understanding he sought.

If nothing else, he'd provided her with her innermost dream. To be loved for herself. Who knows, they might make a run at happily ever after. She wasn't kidding herself. It wasn't forgotten, but it was time to move forward:

Step 1: Forgiveness

Step 2: Healing

Step 3: Who the heck knows?

She placed her palm against his cheek and leaned against him. His warmth seeped through her entire body.

She leaned her head back to meet his warm electric blue eyes. "Since it's screaming inside your head," he said, "I want you to know that I'm ready for forgiveness. I may have moments of doubt, but we'll be okay. I know that you love me.

"I must admit, I'm surprised you didn't ask me to share your room since we're bonded and all now." She winked and squeezed his shoulders. She had to refocus and move them toward happier emotions. She didn't want to stay bogged down in the past.

He cleared his throat and focused on a spot right above her head. "Actually, I was hoping you'd volunteer to sleep in my room every night and allow this to be kind of like your private area or office space. But I wanted you to know that you have your own place. I know that's important to you. Also, your room happens to be in the middle." He pointed toward a door she'd missed earlier. "That room belongs to me." The door on the other side of her room led to Angie's.

Xander glanced over at the clock beside the bed and grumbled. "We better get going. The sooner we get there, the sooner we get back home." He turned toward her with a wicked smile. "Now that we've started down the road to recovery, I'm warning you that I fully intend to spend a couple of hours learning every inch of your body and every way to make you squirm with pleasure. Lightning bolts or not, we're going to have one hell of a night, Mystic."

His eyes darkened, gravitating to her, and Kate felt an irresistible urge to be with him. How could her emotions be so erratic? Would this get worse?

He fiercely kissed her. "Keep looking at me like that, and I'll have to make apologies as to why we won't be going tonight." He kissed her again as they slowly started making their way toward the bed. His hand slid under her shirt and spanned her waist.

She glided her hands up his chest and circled his neck. Her heart soared as she saw the love shining in his eyes. She wanted him more than anything else in the world. The fire between them burned bright and true.

Reality kicked in. Her sense of duty overpowered her rushing hormones. All these people were depending on her to lead them to victory. *Easier said than done.* She had to keep her focus on saving the world first, no matter what the distraction. She had to keep her balance and live through the Awakening.

She'd mustered all her energy to pull back, when Angie broke into her thoughts. *"Time to go, girl. You're not sending me alone with Gregory and Xavier. Suck it up and get your butt out here. Did I mention, now!"* She broke off before Kate could respond.

Xander took a deep breath and chuckled. "When this is all over, we're going to the Artic for a couple months where no one can possibly reach us. I guess we better put this on hold for now."

A part of her wanted to cling to the bed, but he was right. Fear held her back. The time had come for her to literally embrace her new destiny. "Not for long though. Let's get this over with, and I'd like to go someplace warmer than the Artic if you don't mind. I'm not much on cold weather." She didn't feel sociable at the moment either.

Xander pulled her into his arms and cupped her cheek. "Are you worried about tonight? I have to admit after your last infusion of power, I am."

Kate covered his hand with hers and couldn't resist teasing him a little by rubbing her bottom against him. He jerked in response. She climbed into his lap and put her arms around his neck. "Do you remember when you were teaching me to meditate by the river?"

He nodded and she continued. "The reason I became alarmed and backed out was because I could see the two parts within me. I didn't understand until later how strong the human part is inside me, or how much it wants to survive. But, so does the Mystic."

Xander's face contorted in confusion, and she tried again. "It's like having a dual personality. They're constantly fighting for control.

"However, that begs the question, which will win? There's quite a battle going on inside me as the Mystic gains more power." She shivered, saying her last few thoughts out loud for the first time.

Xander tried to alleviate her fear by encouraging her and telling her everything would be fine, but Kate could feel it inside him just as strong. "Rowena has never said how the mystic powers will be returned, only that she could return it once you entered the Meadows and completed the ceremony. She is quiet and keeps mostly to herself."

"Do you trust her?" She'd never shared Zane's warning, but the fact that this woman was a key ingredient in the ceremony worried her.

"Rowena? Of course. We've had our issues, and it became pretty bad between us when she sent me after you years ago. I always felt like she knew more than she was telling me. But she defeated her demon and is a Mystic.

"At the end of the day, I'd trust her with my life. The Council needs you and will not risk your life. I'm sure they know what they are doing. This isn't the first Awakening ceremony." He stroked her cheek, most likely trying to chase away her apprehension.

Kate kept her thoughts well-guarded. She didn't want Xander any more freaked out. Maybe it wasn't the first ceremony, but it was the first time for a human-born mystic. If Zane and Xander had both felt something, chances were Rowena was hiding something. But what? No one could breach her mind, so they'd have to find out the old-fashioned way — by waiting.

"I guess that's another thing that we'll find out later at the infamous Council meeting," Xander said. "How about it, my lady?" He held out his hand and pulled her into the hallway.

They stepped out as everyone else exited their rooms. Gregory was propped up against his door with a scowl on his face. Xavier had his arms crossed looking anything except friendly, and Angie glanced back and forth between both of them.

It was an unspoken fact that they were waiting for her to choose. Kate held out her hand, ignoring them, so Angie looped her arm through Kate's and walked with her through the maze back to the front door, leaving the guys to trail behind them. It was time to be Awakened. Whatever the hell that meant.

22

"Holy Crap! You weren't kidding. This is a castle. A freaking medieval castle!" Kate stood stock still and stared at the massive structure tucked into the mountains in front of them. Xander had told her how big it was, but she still never envisioned this. She understood that they existed on a separate plane to some extent but couldn't believe it was right here in the United States. A forest surrounded the backside of the property. Rolling hills were to the left, while a large field of flowers extended to the right. A stream flowed through the middle of the field and fed the moat.

They owned real land in the human realm, but their community actually spanned much more land in this realm. It would take years for her to understand how all this worked.

She'd seen castles like this in Europe, but they all seemed older and out of date. This one looked like it had come straight out of a Disney fairytale. The exterior was a grayish white with black accents and roofs. Several banners flew and had the same symbol. The Celtic Tree of Life stood in the center, but the top of the tree had burst into the wings of a phoenix. She'd seen similar designs in her dreams. The undeniable power emanating from the castle had the blood in her veins sparking in anticipation.

"There are towers, wings, flags, and even a freaking drawbridge and moat," Angie whispered, as Kate continued to gape. "I'd ask how this is all possible, but these days I'm too terrified of the answer."

Her apprehension wasn't lost on Kate, who had a touch of it herself. All her questions would be answered here. Whether she'd like those answers or not was a completely different story.

"I know, Ang, I noticed. This place is incredible. It doesn't seem real, and yet it seems right. I'm drawn to this place by some invisible force."

"I'll admit I'm a little nervous about what's going to happen in there," she added through their private link. *"I'll be different when I walk back out. I'll be the Mystic, and everyone will look to me for answers that I don't possess. I don't know much about this world and don't have much time to learn. Most of all I'm scared to lose my humanity and become some all-powerful being."*

Angie sent her the impression of a hug. *"You're going to be great. Just like everything you do."*

Angie's loyalty and Xander's love gave her the courage she needed to face whatever the day brought. Maybe that was why fate had led her into this mess.

She laced her fingers through Xander's. "Let's get a move on before I lose my nerve. We can admire the castle later."

They crossed over the drawbridge, entered the humongous doors that opened by themselves, and headed toward the foyer. The doors closed, sealing them inside. In her heart, she knew they couldn't leave now even if they wanted to. *Can't run. Can't hide. Here we go.*

They moved forward into the entrance hall and were greeted by the most beautiful woman Kate had ever seen.

She reminded Kate of a supermodel or Greek goddess. Her whole body had a faint golden glow, and Kate sensed the power radiating from her. It was suffocating with her mystic energy fighting for freedom. Being in her presence made Kate shiver with wonder and fear.

Her hair was the color of fire and cascaded halfway down her back. It was slightly wavy, and Kate's eyes were riveted by the brilliance of the color. Her face was oval but perfectly proportioned with high cheekbones, a straight nose, and slightly slanted pale blue eyes.

Her skin was flawless and glistened in the light. Kate finally managed to leave her face and take in the whole person. The lady exuded strength and athleticism. Not nearly as fragile as she'd first appeared.

Kate had never been jealous of anyone before in her life, but this could be a first. Clearing her head, she met the woman's eyes and held her ground, refusing to look down.

The woman broke into a dazzling smile that made Kate want to reach for her sunglasses. She tried to ascertain who this incredible being was, but it seemed impossible until she spoke and extended her hand.

"Hello, Kate, I'm Rowena. I've waited so many years to finally have you here. I know you have many questions, and they may not all get answered today. I promise we will have time to sit and talk about many things in the next few weeks."

In hindsight, Kate should have guessed but had been overwhelmed by the glamour. She recognized love, compassion, and what appeared to be a touch of sadness in her eyes.

"It's nice to meet you too, Rowena. I've heard many great things about you and your devotion to the magical communities." She hesitated, uncertain what else to say. "And I look forward to talking with you, since I admit that I do have many questions."

"I'll do my best to answer them." Glancing around the room, she began to greet everyone and take their hand.

"Nikki, it's been too long. You need to come visit me more often. Xander, Gregory, I'm so proud of you both for bringing our Mystic home.

"Xavier, I know how hard this has been for you, but believe me when I say it's time for you to come home. Your time in exile has ended.

"And Angie, my dear sweet girl, you have shown the true heart of a warrior, and I am honored to meet you."

Xander elbowed her to follow Rowena, but she still hadn't gotten past the fact that this was the woman Xander had been describing. She'd held a slightly different presumption of how a thousand-year-old woman would look. She'd obviously been wrong.

Second, she was amazed that, with a few words of greeting, Rowena had managed to mesmerize them all. Kate didn't possess that kind of grace, serenity, or confidence. *Oh boy!*

A voice inside her head still cautioned her not to believe everything she saw on the surface. Despite the power and confidence, she still sensed a great sadness and regret deep inside Rowena. This could easily add up to something dangerous. She'd have to stay on guard.

She still hoped that one day she'd build trust and be able to ask all the questions that burned inside her.

They walked down a long corridor filled with artwork and paintings of all sorts of magical beings. She wasn't sure how to express the influx of feelings flowing through her: Awe. Excitement. Doubt. Fear. Mostly fear.

They reached the two large wooden doors. They opened by themselves and the apprehension hit full force. *Doors seem to do that a lot here.*

Her first impression was that she'd stepped into a courtroom. This similarity didn't make her feel any better. Courtrooms had been a source of justice and rage in her past.

A platform in the front of the room held other people wearing black robes and serious expressions. Dozens of chairs were on her left and right behind two large tables she assumed were meant for them. They were directly in front of the raised platform.

She didn't like this one bit. It was like she was going to trial for something and began feeling uneasy with the inequality of the positions. Her only relief was seeing Marco and Illianna at one of the tables.

Rowena must have picked up on her discomfort. She waved her hand and the court transformed into a conference room. Surprise swept through the Council; all of their chairs were moved against the walls with the members still in them. A large conference table was placed in the front, leaving the marble floors mostly clear.

Now it looked more like a boardroom, which suited Kate much better. She couldn't believe this was real, and she was in it up to her neck. Snacks and drinks appeared on the table.

I'm in way over my head —

They all sat down at the table.

She started to reach for Xander, but one of the paintings caught her eye. She rose from her chair while every talked and caught up, and she drifted over to look at the painting and others surrounding it. They depicted past Risings and some of the fallen warriors.

Mesmerized, she followed the pictures down the wall. There was a painting of a battle from two thousand years ago, but it was pretty vague and the demon horrifying. It looked as if a child could have drawn it.

A picture of Rowena caught her eye. She appeared exactly as she did today and was plunging a knife into the heart of a demon whose startled expression told her he hadn't expected to die. This depiction was much clearer and more accurate. They must have started using professional artists.

Next to that portrait was another picture of Rowena with a man and a little girl. Kate read the plaque at the bottom and saw the dates of their deaths. The man's death was the same time as the last Rising, and the little girl's was nearly a hundred years later. Questions stuck in her mind to ask Xander later.

She continued on down the line. Her curiosity grew stronger when she saw Cassius plunging the knife into his demon with blood pouring down his side. Beside that was the picture of Cassius, Guinevere, and two twin baby girls. They all had dates of death.

For so many immortals, there was still a lot of death. Her eyes watered. She shivered from a sense of déjà vu. She was going to say something to Xander about the vision she'd had, when the next two pictures caught her eye.

The first was a depiction of the beast demons and Shadow Warriors along with other supernatural beings. Many of them were dying to save others. The second was a man who looked like Xander except he had soft brown eyes. Maximus Montgomery.

Xander's brother looked majestic as he fought off the beast demons, buying others time to save the world. Tearing her eyes away, she took a deep breath and shoved all she'd seen into her compartments for another time. *Too much death.* It surrounded her no matter where she went.

Wearily, she went back to her seat. Another shock slammed into her system just when she thought she'd reached her max. This day was never going to end.

A man walked in and stood in the center of the platform. She assumed he was the leader of the Council, but what stunned her was that he was the spitting image of Xander. Even the blue piercing eyes.

Angrily, she stared into Xander's eyes with a bewildered and accusing expression. "Did you forget to mention something along the way?"

He leaned close to her ear. "Sorry," he whispered. "We are bound by an oath not to speak of the Alpha, leader of the Council, outside of this realm. This is done for protection. It is usually the Mystic, but Rowena wanted him to lead us."

A look of guilt on his face, Xander turned his head and faced the man. "Hey, Dad, how's it going? I'd like for you to meet my mate and our Mystic, Kate. Kate, I'd like you to meet the leader of the Council, who happens to also be my father, Marcus."

Kate's mouth settled into a grim line. She was tired of all the secrecy in this realm. She would deal with him later. "It's a pleasure to meet you, Marcus. Although I must admit, I was not aware that you are Xander's father."

She heard a soft laugh as Pam walked in and sat beside Nikki. Marcus grinned as he stepped forward and placed his hands on Xander's and Xavier's shoulders. "We don't always see eye to eye on Council business, but I'm so glad to have you both home again.

"It's pretty common that they forget to mention that little fact even in places where they can. I try not to take offense."

She could tell by the affection in his voice that he didn't care or wasn't offended by the issue.

Xander leaned over and whispered again that he was sorry. She ignored him for now but understood how knowing his identity could have been extremely dangerous with a traitor on the loose. Still, he should have told her at his house.

Stepping back into his seat, Marcus focused on her. "I'm afraid we do not know much about you, either, or at least your future." He sighed. "I sincerely wish we knew more about what is to come but let us finish introductions first. Then we can get down to other details. We want you to feel welcome here. While I know you will choose to live with Xander for now, though I'm not sure why." Xander raised his eyebrow and gave him a wry look. "This will always be your home as the Mystic."

He pointed to his left at the man on the end. "This is Tristan, leader of the Gliders and, I guess, the Rogues. His main goal is to eliminate vampires killing humans, an increasingly difficult task given the world's current fascination with them."

Tristan rolled his eyes. "Yeah, apparently vampires are *romantic* and have morals these days." His voice dripped with contempt. *Yikes!*

She met his stare and saw through the sarcasm. The vampires of his kind were probably using the current pop culture to find easy prey while ruining the name of the entire species. She acknowledged he was right since she'd seen first-hand the stupid tendency, especially in females, to trust the unknown more times than she cared to remember.

Despite the scowl on his face, he was extremely handsome with those brooding silver eyes, black hair, and a straight nose. He had a lot of angles to his face, but they fit together perfectly on him. She'd expected gliders to be paler, but Tristan had olive skin that had a healthy glow.

His shoulders slumped slightly, giving her the impression of how much he had to handle. Nodding in his direction, she decided to create a rapport with him. "Hello, Tristan, I'd like to learn more about your people when you have the time. I want to understand and help you."

She must have said the right thing, he smiled and transformed his face from handsome to gorgeous. She could feel his entire energy level lift up. "Thank you, Kate. There are many that don't accept our kind, believing that we can be too easily swayed into darkness. I appreciate your willingness to learn the difference."

She chewed on her bottom lip. "All people of any species can be turned. Maybe it's easier for some than others based on what they need to survive. You're living proof that gliders can abstain from the temptation and hold onto their beliefs staying true to their kind and others."

Marcus cleared his throat. His smile seemed strained when he pointed to the man beside Tristan. "Kate, this is Micah, our Seer."

He beamed a sickly-sweet smile, and she sensed his interest in her pouring off him. His long blond hair was tied at the nape of his neck, and his blue eyes flashed at her. *Ugh!*

She didn't want to dislike anyone already, but he had an air of arrogance that was unparalleled. She hated misplaced arrogance almost as much as she hated demons. "Micah, it's nice to meet you."

She tried to keep her voice smooth but felt the tension radiating from Xander. Obviously, there were some serious issues between the two. That's what she needed today, more drama.

Micah stood and formally bowed. "It is a pleasure to meet you. We have long awaited your arrival. I have seen many visions of you over the years, but none compare to your actual beauty." He continued to stare at her as if she was a tall glass of water in the middle of the Sahara.

Pure anger flooded from Xander. She immediately laced her fingers through his and sent him calming energy. He settled back down and she saw the smirk in Micah's expression. Okay, definitely some issues there, but she didn't want to deal with that now.

"Okay moving along," Rowena said. Apparently, she didn't want to deal with him either. Micah locked his jaw but quietly sat down.

"The last member you haven't met yet is Camilla." Rowena laid her hand on the woman beside her. "She is a witch and will be supervising your training in the Wiccan arena."

Kate smiled and nodded. "Nice to meet you."

She seemed quiet and shy when she returned the greeting. She was pretty in a more traditional way. She had average facial features that gave her a simple beauty. Her eyes were a warm topaz, and she had a wide smile that lit up her entire face.

She exuded warmth and safety. Her hair was a light brown color that braided and looped to encircle her head, creating a type of bun. It looked intricate and suited her.

Camilla addressed Kate. "While you are not a witch, you will still want to understand the spells, potions, and power sources that exist. You don't need this form of power, but you will encounter it.

"Your training will be divided between Rowena and myself, so you can learn both. Rowena will handle most of your training in the beginning, so you can get control of your powers. That's the first goal.

"No offense, but we don't want you to accidentally fry anyone by lightning strike. So, first things first." Everyone laughed but realized the serious implications of the moment she became a full Mystic.

Introductions complete, everyone fell into a deep silence; there was nothing left to say. Kate gathered her courage to ask the all-important question that no one but Rowena could answer. "Rowena, how do I receive or embrace my full Mystic powers? What do I need to do?"

There, the question had been asked and everyone, including the Council, leaned forward on their chairs and held their breath, waiting on the answer. That meant only Rowena knew what was going to happen. *Curious.*

Rowena waved her hand and cleared the room of all furniture. Stunned faces glanced around the room. They had all been moved to create an outer circle.

Kate hadn't even felt the shift. She wasn't ready for this kind of power. Xander had a death grip on her hand. Xavier protectively leaned in front of Angie. They were the only ones left in the middle of the circle. Gregory had been moved to the outer circle. He scowled and crossed his arms in anger. *Guess he didn't like being pushed to the side.* Not that she blamed him.

Rowena joined them in the center. "My child, you were born a human and a Mystic. Your human half is dominant and must give way for the Mystic to rise. We know Cassius performed a spell to hide his future descendants. He wanted to spare them his fate.

"His wife was a Seer and probably had a vision of you. He never told us, and so, we weren't prepared for his actions. However, you cannot change a person's destiny. I think he knew better but had to try. In all my visions, it appears this spell was meant to be, just as you were meant to be the Mystic.

"Visions only give us the keys, but we still have to open the lock to discover the why."

Kate guessed she was telling the story for those in the room who never understood how everything had happened. She didn't mind hearing the whole story herself.

A fire glowed in Rowena's eyes. This was it, no going back now. "The weapon used by Cassius to kill the demon was the same athame used to seal the spell. It is a weapon of great power, thousands of years old. It has slain two Omegas. Some say it was made by the Angels themselves to help us fight the demons in our realms. Whether this is true, I cannot tell you. But its power is beyond question."

She walked over to her, and the athame appeared in Rowena's hands. Kate gasped. The weapon called for her, begging her to accept it.

She stepped forward, because she couldn't resist. It pulled her under its spell. She felt Xander move with her and felt comfort in his touch. She approached her new fate.

His hands sat at her waist, warming her and giving her confidence. Xavier and Angie moved closer but stayed at more of a distance.

Gregory and Nikki looked ready to jump in any second to protect them. Maybe Micah had been right about everything after all.

She was stronger with them near her. They were a part of her power and confidence.

Their journey had made them stronger, made them a unit, and made them a family. Despite all their issues within their group, they stood as an unbreakable force. Not that a single one of them would ever admit it to Micah. She knew they'd take that notion to the grave.

"Cadence Hope Smith." Rowena's voiced echoed through the air.

Kate flinched. *Uh-oh.* The whole name was never a good sign.

"You are the Mystic, leader of our People and all that exists in the realms. It is a huge responsibility, but the Council believes beyond a doubt that you are up to the task. You have demonstrated your great power even within human boundaries. You have already learned to control much of the energy pulsing inside your body."

Rowena raised her hand, and all of the Council members nodded their heads in assent.

"We, the Ancient Council, accept you as our new leader, and we will follow you into the Rising. It is time for your Awakening. Time to take your place within our Council. You have our allegiance always."

She took the knife, walked around the room, and sliced the palm of each Council member's hand. Pam followed behind her healing them. The athame soaked in the blood like it was a living entity. *So weird.*

Rowena turned back to Kate. "Once you become the Mystic, your fate is sealed. The need to fight at the Rising will be undeniable, and your views of the universe will change irrevocably. Know we are here for you, but some decisions will be completely in your hands."

She fought the desire to run away. *Great, all I need is more pressure.* She tried to refocus on Rowena, but her nerves were completely shot. *I'm not ready for this.*

Rowena raised her hands to the sky, and lightning popped from the ceiling into her hands. Her skin shined a brilliant shade of gold with silver specks circling within it from all the energy pulsing around her. The electricity had everyone's hair standing straight up; an electrical storm pulsed around them.

Kate picked up Rowena's feelings, and panic filled her chest. Pain. Secrecy. *She's hiding something and doesn't want me to find it.* The moment Rowena opened up her energy field, she lost complete control of her emotions. *What's she hiding?*

The athame spun in her hand. Kate held her breath, knowing the time had come. She wanted to shut her eyes but couldn't. She expected a lightning bolt to hit her any second. The athame launched into the air. Everyone's eyes were transfixed on the knife suspended all by itself.

Rowena spoke again, her voice ethereal and haunting. Her eyes became a pale bluish-green color. Her wild red hair fanned out like flames. Her clothing became solid white. "Return to your master!"

The athame plunged into Kate's heart. "No!" She gasped and fell back into Xander's arms. The dagger was cold, but the pain was excruciating. This wasn't supposed to happen.

She tried to grasp the meaning, but taking a breath became harder and harder. Her lungs filled with blood and stopped working. Her mind drifted away. Her vision failed her. Everything was a blur, including the noise surrounding her.

She heard the screams and weeping. Panic and fear engulfed the room. Despair wove its spell around the hearts of everyone there. Their emotions became hers. She was too weak to block them out.

Xander reached for her mentally, but her human half was dying rapidly. He couldn't hold her to him. And the Mystic inside wasn't strong enough to save her. *What happened? What did I do wrong?*

Did the traitor defeat us after all? She was supposed to help me, not kill me.

Using what little energy she had left, she told him she loved him. Her vision faded to black. She let go and took her final breath.

J.L. Lawrence

23

"Hang on, Kate!" Xander cried.

Angie fell to her knees, weeping. Xavier wrapped his arms around her. Silence and shock reigned, followed by an eruption of emotion.

Horrified, Xander watched the blood flow out of Kate. Her breathing slowed. He couldn't breathe. It couldn't be real. He couldn't save her. The ritual had failed, and she would die.

He glared at Rowena. He'd kill that bitch one way or another.

Tears filled his eyes, blurring his vision, but he could still see the red surrounding him. His hands were covered in her blood.

"I love you, Xander —" Her mental link lasted for a moment, then faded away.

Her heart stopped beating. Total chaos broke out and uncontrollable rage erupted. Xander launched at Rowena. Marcus and Xavier grabbed him and held him back. He struggled to break free. A red haze of pain replaced his vision. His powers popped out of control.

Rowena still hadn't moved.

Gregory ran to Angie and held her. Tears poured down her face. She rocked back and forth, full of fear and pain.

Tristan, Micah, and Camilla moved toward Kate.

Xander fought off his dad and brother, he struggled to break free from their grasp. His father magically bound him. He yelled and screamed but couldn't break free. *Why aren't they attacking Rowena? She's the traitor!*

His only goal was to kill her. He didn't care what his punishment would be. He'd gladly die as long as he got to take her down with him. He tried every spell he could think of to break free. He even begged Xavier to help him, but his own brother ignored him and helped their father trap him.

Rowena betrayed them all. For what?

Rowena raised her hands again and threw everyone, including all the Council members, against the wall. She pinned them there with sheer force alone.

Xander's rage vibrated through the entire structure. He fought to get back to Kate. He used all his strength to break through the invisible wall holding him in place. Agony and panic dominated his mind. His energy faded and he began to give up the struggle. He couldn't save her. He'd brought her here to die.

The invisible force waned and dropped them to their feet, but they couldn't come closer. He fell to his knees and hung his head to grieve.

A bright glow caught his attention. He raised his head and witnessed the athame pulsing radiant blue. Drawing everyone in, the brilliant light restored order in the room.

It grew brighter and brighter until he and everyone there had to turn their heads to stop the pain from the light. He shielded his eyes, while still trying to see what was happening. Questions formed in his mind.

Another strike of lightning came from the sky and struck the knife buried in Kate's chest. She jumped as if she'd been hit with resuscitation paddles.

He blinked rapidly to clear the tears from his eyes. *What the hell?* The blood flowing out of Kate had turned to a pale ice blue.

Is this the Awakening? A small thread of hope wove around his heart, which threatened to jump right out of his chest as it pounded away in desperation. The power holding him outside the circle diminished. He went to her side.

Gasping in air, she took a breath, but still seemed to be stuck in a trance.

His sweaty, shaking hands reached out to stroke her hair. Was she alive? Was she still his Kate? Even though he'd seen her take in a breath, he was afraid to give into the hope that everything would be okay. He wanted to scoop her up off the floor but didn't dare. He didn't want to cause her any pain.

Rowena's eyes slowly returned to their normal color. She walked over to Kate. The athame had stopped glowing, and she drew it from Kate's chest. She waved her hand and released the rest of her prisoners.

Camilla rushed behind her to quickly put a salve on the wound. The wound began to close.

Xander calmed; he believed deep in his heart that she'd be okay. He stroked her hair, but abruptly jerked backward.

Kate began to glow from the inside — the same color that had come from the knife.

It traveled from her heart throughout her body until light literally came from her head, fingertips, and toes.

Rowena no longer had to control the crowd. Shock and amazement took care of that now. Even *he* was back under complete control, believing her to be alive or *close* to it. He didn't care, as long as she still loved him. But what if she didn't? He had to believe their bond was strong enough.

The light got brighter and brighter until it consumed her body. It encircled Kate in a blue mist. An invisible force lifted her off the floor, and she floated in mid-air.

Surprise covered Rowena's face.

Not a good sign. Xander felt a new rush of panic. Rowena's frozen expression didn't help abate the fear of what was going on, or what had been unleashed. *What did she do to Kate?*

No one present knew exactly how you Awakened the Mystic, or maybe it was because she was human. Xander couldn't take his eyes off her. Kate floated in a sort of stasis that he'd only seen Shadow Warriors create.

The light continued to work on her body inside and out, changing her appearance.

Her hair turned to a white blond, her physique seemed to elongate slightly, and her muscles rippled with electricity. Her eyes opened. They were a bright, swirling blue and her clothes transformed into a long white flowing gown with a tight bodice.

She'd transformed into a Greek goddess, or at least it appeared that way. A faint golden glow emanated from her body like it was tracing the outskirts of her aura.

A tattoo designed by an invisible artist formed across her breast bone. Wings of a phoenix spread to the sides, and a bright light connected the wings and extended upward.

Two crossed swords surrounded by ancient symbols were in the center of the wings connecting the light at the top with something dark at the bottom—one red sword and one blue. It matched many of the symbols in his own Guardian tattoo, reminding him that they were soul mates.

A final blinding flash of light removed the mist and placed Kate on her feet. He immediately connected with her and found that she was stunned, scared, and confused. He transferred everything to her.

Kate raised her head and stared at all the faces gazing back at her. She remembered the knife flying into her heart. She remembered meeting Xander's eyes and telling him she loved him. She remembered taking her last breath, wondering what had gone wrong. Was Rowena the traitor? Was that the secret?

She recalled a soft welcoming blue light surrounding her. It wrapped her in a tight comforting hug, and she knew everything would be okay.

The light filled her as her human life relinquished its hold and the Mystic took control. She wasn't aware of her physical changes yet, but she could feel the soreness of her body from so much transformation. Xander's mental link filled in the rest of the gaps.

Her main concern at the moment was the massive level of energy pulsing inside her. She was afraid to move or speak. Afraid it might pour out of her and hurt everyone standing around her. No matter how hard she tried, she couldn't get control of it. She was frozen.

A constant hum prevented her thought process. She felt everyone's emotions even more so than she could before. What hurt her most was feeling Xander and Angie's fear of what she'd become. Granted she'd died and been brought back to life. *She* was afraid, too.

Rowena stepped forward and looked deep into her eyes. "Focus on my eyes, Kate. Push the energy down to gain control. Push your emotions into their compartments along with everyone else's that you're picking up."

Rowena placed a finger under her chin and drew her face in.

"Get control, Kate. You can do it. Close your eyes. Shut everything out and focus on my voice." She used Rowena's soft soothing words to push her energy down and take control. She felt herself come out of the fog and took in her surroundings. For now, she had a little control but wouldn't guarantee for how long. She owed Rowena an apology.

"Thank you, Rowena. I think I have it under control for the moment."

Rowena hugged her. "I'm so sorry for the way it had to be done, and that I could not prepare you. But this was the only way to guarantee the successful infusion of your powers. Cassius cast an intricate spell the night he died at the last Rising. I barely made a dent in it. At the last minute, I altered it slightly because I read his intentions. I will tell you everything later."

Tears shone in her eyes. Kate realized how heavily this weighed on her, to know that she had to kill her in front of the Council and Xander, whom she loved like a son. Her pain had been as great as theirs.

In addition, everyone had briefly thought that Rowena was the traitor. That had been her secret and her fear, Kate hoped. She didn't need any more surprises today.

Kate stepped forward and wrapped her arms around her. "I understand. I'm sorry you had to endure the reality alone, and that I thought for even a *moment* that you were the traitor. There is no animosity or disappointment between us."

Rowena seemed to brighten a little and smiled. It had been a terrible burden to bear. "I need your help to keep all this energy under control, before I tear down the whole town. By accident, of course." Kate winked.

Rowena sighed and wiped the tears from her eyes. "I now present our Mystic and Leader," she loudly announced to the Council and others in the chamber. "Let us welcome her to our world."

Rowena stepped aside, allowing Xander to come close. He wrapped his arms around Kate in a massive bear hug, then kissed every inch of her face. Once he'd finished, Angie hugged her.

Celebration broke out as the message was sent out to the community. The cheers and laughter exalted from all of the supernatural communities.

A large screen appeared on the wall and she saw the celebrations taking place in all the magical communities all over the world. All welcoming the Mystic home. She'd become their hope, their chance for a future.

Xander leaned down, nuzzling her ear. "I like the new hair and new look. Cool tattoo, too. We match." He softly kissed her lips.

Her head snapped up, and her heart raced. She had forgotten the physical changes. "What new look? What tattoo?"

Xander raised his eyebrows, smiled, and pointed at her chest. She looked down and gasped. She was not a tattoo person, and now she had a massive one spanning across her chest. *Holy Crap*!

"I see the tattoo. What about my new look? And what is up with this dress thing? It didn't come out of my closet." Panic settled into her voice. This was too much change at once.

Angie sent her a mental picture along with an encouraging smile. Kate studied the image of her altered appearance. Her hair was blond–*completely* blond. Her eyes were still blue, but it was like looking into the ocean and seeing several shades of blue rolling like the waves.

She appeared a little taller, and her skin glowed slightly like Rowena's. It could be much worse after dying and coming back to life. "Okay, I can live with this new look — I *think*. But the dress has got to go."

With a simple thought, she was back in her black athletic pants and blue fitted T-shirt. "Whew, much better." She turned back to the Council; they had returned to their original seats in the conference room setting. "What now?"

Marcus stood and straightened his shoulders. "First, tomorrow you will need to tour the training facilities and labs we use to practice witchcraft. You will also need to meet all of our warriors since you are now officially their leader – but not today. I'm sure you need some rest.

"And quite frankly, I think most of us need a chance to recover and find our balance after witnessing what we did. Despite feeling like we had the longest day ever invented, it's only been a couple hours." He smiled, and Kate admired his composure.

The council member's thoughts bombarded her. Tristan wanted her to begin training immediately to see her abilities and determine how much training she'd need to be ready. Camilla wanted to see her abilities with witchcraft and Micah wanted *her*, but he'd have to get over it and keep those feelings from Xander.

Kate felt exhausted and overwhelmed, but she addressed Marcus and Rowena. Everyone else could wait for one more day. As far as she was concerned, they hadn't died today, so she didn't care what the others thought.

"I appreciate the time for a little rest. I do want to see all of the facilities soon, and I will begin training and following Tristan's schedule tomorrow. I'm aware that time is of the essence and the Rising comes first." Her eyes flashed a brilliant blue, and everyone leaned back, ready to jump out of the way.

She turned to Rowena, knowing she'd understand. "Thank you, Rowena. My first concern is controlling my power and not hurting someone during practice. Can I meet with you tomorrow to get some mastery in that area first?"

"Yes, tomorrow will be perfect. I agree that getting your internal energy under control is critical to your success. And we can't afford to lose any warriors." She smirked and then resumed her more formal composure.

"Xander has prepared you well physically and with many of your powers," Rowena went on. "Angie will be learning the basics of chakras, spells, and potions but nothing too complex yet. But it is your mystical powers that will face off against Braxus in the end, so excellent idea to tackle that first."

Xavier stayed behind to meet with Rowena, and Nikki decided to wait for him. Everyone else walked out of the chamber and out of the castle. Kate stepped through the doors to the deafening applause and cheers of a gathered crowd.

Word had traveled fast, and many came to the Meadows to see the new Mystic. Astonishment overwhelmed Kate. Their outpouring of faith and trust wrapped around her existence and embraced her as their leader. *No pressure there.*

Her body ached terribly. She wanted all of these people to disappear and to feel normal again. Was that too much to ask? It would be a long time before she could walk down the street and not be accosted by well-wishers.

Some of them would even push their kids in her face, wanting her to touch them like she could bless them or something. This was getting ridiculous. It wasn't helping that her damn tattoo kept glowing like a beacon.

Marcus exchanged a few words with Xander and finally cleared the crowds, saying there would be plenty of time to see the Mystic over the next couple of months. The time had come to focus on training. He also told them there would be a great celebration after victory at the Rising.

Kate noted he didn't mention the Mystic as part of the celebration. She began to get the feeling that they expected her to win but also *die*. Oh well, she'd always liked a challenge and wouldn't die easily — the *next* time.

Approaching the Montgomery estate filled Kate with wonder. She'd probably get used to it soon. It was beautiful, and it was her home. She was a Montgomery now even if she hadn't had a traditional ceremony.

Secretly she would have liked to have some sort of official ceremony, but maybe they could do something after the Rising to celebrate both. Xander had closed off his mind, so she wouldn't pry. She also missed her family and team back home, but she wouldn't bring that up any time soon.

It was late by the time they returned to their rooms. They agreed to meet first thing in the morning. Xander and Kate rushed into their room, leaving everyone laughing behind them.

Xander laid Kate across his bed, taking in her beauty and strength. He wanted to take it slow, but his more basic instincts begged him to rush. Literally straining against the zipper of his pants, he tried to hold himself under control.

He wanted this night to be for her. Slowly, he lifted her blue shirt and spanned her waist with his palms. Then he skimmed his hands upward over her flat stomach, moving toward his goal.

They both had way too may clothes on, so with a simple thought he removed all of it and felt her sharp intake of breath. He paused to stay in control.

She smiled again and ran her fingers from his shoulders down his back, gripping his buttocks and digging in her nails. A little smugness filled her eyes, watching him struggle for stability.

Their tongues battled. Passion rose. Emotions collided. Breathing rapidly increased. Everything brought a whole new dimension to their lovemaking. He wanted her more than he wanted air to breathe, and he could tell she felt the same way. Her nails scored his flesh, and he nearly lost it.

Gritting his teeth and taking several deep gulps of air — that didn't help since they kept bringing in Kate's scent — he tried to regain some modicum of control. *Barely.* Grinning, he stared into her glazed eyes.

Kate was out of her mind with pleasure. Energy ricocheted in all directions inside her. His hands and mouth were doing heavenly things to her body.

She'd never realized how wonderful making love could be, until Xander showed her the way. *Jeez!* Her breath hissed out. Pure ecstasy. She never dreamed she could reach such incredible satisfaction. He deserved the same, and she'd never backed down from a challenge. If only she could convince her body to move.

She finally gathered her wits. She wanted him out of control and no longer able to hold back. She loved seeing his eyes light up with pleasure. Knocking him off balance, she reared up and locked her mouth onto his, fusing them together into one entity.

She attached their energy fields together. She continued to encase him in her arms and then focused on a lower target. He snapped his jaw together. *He's holding back.* Using their mental connection, she let him feel her deep desire for him. His focus snapped and he became a madman. She fell over the edge in a kaleidoscope of colors.

She couldn't move but felt intense womanly triumph having made him lose complete control. She wasn't sure they'd ever be able to move again, but at the moment she was fine with that. *I'm definitely fine with that.*

A surge of electricity hit her and she gasped. The lights flickered in the room, and she took deep breaths to get a grip on it. She saw it arch out of her and hit Xander square in the chest.

Xander jumped up. Panic covered his face. "Not again! Kate, Kate, are you okay? I'll get Xavier. We'll take you to the Council." He frantically rubbed his chest.

Kate placed her hand on his arm to get his attention and calm him down. She met his eyes and reared back her head. The light bulbs blew, and the energy subsided. "It's okay, Xander, just a little infusion of energy. It was much easier to control this time. Now that I understand more about the new energy inside me, I realize my body is releasing the excess. When we make love, it causes a major surge. Eventually, I'll be able to control it. Sorry about the blast." A little giggle escaped her, and he tackled her back onto the bed.

He silenced her with a deep kiss. "Now, where were we? I believed you challenged me to a long restless night. I never back down from a challenge and fully intend to deliver."

She arched her body toward him. "I'll let you know when you've arrived and met the requirements."

They filled the night with pleasure, love, and forgiveness. Two bruised hearts re-emerged as one. A true bond beyond any type of magic had been born.

24

Angie sighed. *Why can't Kate be here to referee?*

Xavier and Gregory had been arguing since the sun came up. The volume had intensified and caused her to have a major headache. Every word uttered deepened the animosity. Angie had no clue how to gain control of two powerful entities spewing hatred.

Nikki stormed down the hallway. "Okay, guys. What's going on between the two of you? I get you aren't the best of friends but come on — " She trailed off the second she noticed they both had their eyes on Angie. "Oh, I see."

Angie's face flushed. "With everything going on, it's confusing right now."

Nikki patted her on the shoulder and gave her a brief hug. "It's not all about you. I promise. So, don't worry. They still have issues from the past. Besides, they're men, they'll wait," she shrugged, "or kill each other." She smiled.

They headed toward their wing. Both guys took Angie by the elbow and pulled in the opposite direction.

"Stop it! Both of you. This doesn't solve anything and sure doesn't make me want to have anything to do with either of you." She glared back and forth between them. She wrestled out of their grasp.

Gregory growled at Xavier. "I still can't believe Rowena put your sorry ass in charge of training. It must be great to have your daddy on the Council."

"You son of a bitch," Xavier huffed. "Get your head out of your ass and see the bigger picture. I'm the better fighter and trainer. Remember who trained *you*. Would you like to tell everyone in the room?"

The red in Gregory's face turned to purple. She thought he was going to explode. "You think you're so great. Let's go prove you're so perfect. You might have taught me some basics, but Xander made me a warrior, not *you*. Never you!" he said through clenched teeth. "You're a weak, sniveling, worm that doesn't deserve to live. You couldn't even keep your wife alive and away from demons. Could you?"

Angie and Nikki both gasped in horror. Xavier's fist connected with Gregory's chin. It set off a brawl in the middle of the common area. Xavier threw Gregory across Xander's desk and knocked everything off. Priceless antiques broke into pieces. Gregory kicked Xavier in the chest. He smashed against a bookcase. Books rained down on his head.

Xander's going to be so pissed.

Xavier and Gregory rolled around on the floor. Punching, kicking, and throwing energy blasts and spells. It was definitely getting out of hand.

Nikki threw back her hands. Angie's entire body vibrated. Xavier and Gregory, caught off guard, were swept up in a gust of wind moving through the room. The maelstrom pinned them against opposite walls.

Wow, big sister had some power. She is obviously quite angry but controlled.

"You idiots!" Nikki yelled. "Have you both lost your minds? None of this is about you. Have you forgotten how many were lost in the last Rising and that they were amazing warriors with unparalleled power?

"Some of the best ever in existence, and I suggest you remember it. They died for us, and now the world depends on us to save them. It's our turn, so get ahold of yourselves and put your petty differences aside. You will both be leaders in this battle, so start acting like leaders and set an example worthy to be followed."

The wind gusts got stronger, turning into a tornado as Nikki's anger grew. Angie sensed the underlying pain of her brother's death and something more, but she couldn't figure out what.

With a final grunt of frustration, she waved her hands and both guys disappeared. Angie gasped. Fear flowed through her. She desperately wanted to call for Kate but didn't.

"Where'd they go?" She wasn't sure whether to be afraid or not.

Nikki had tears flowing down her face and walked over to the window. Taking a few deep breaths, she turned back around and smiled. "They needed to remember what was lost. They never met him, and that is such a disadvantage. They never felt the power or support of the Shadow Warriors. They don't understand how bad it is going to be this time. They're blinded by too many other things."

She referred to something Angie couldn't grasp. How does one comprehend the enormity of what they would be facing in only a few months?

"Max was quite wonderful and kind," Nikki said. "But a fierce and amazing warrior. So, I sent them to our memorial room where we have several pictures of the men and women who died for us to be here today. And allowed us to fight another round."

"Do you ever get tired of fighting? Just want to give up?" Angie wondered out loud.

"Not really, the alternative is death or a lifetime of torture. I don't care to go in either of those directions at the moment." She sighed and, with a wave of her hand, fixed most everything in the room.

Her smile turned into a full out grin. Xavier's and Gregory's bedroom doors slammed. She gestured toward the hallway. "Go ahead and get some rest while I finish cleaning up this mess. I don't want Xander having a stroke. He has enough demons to face, literally. By the way, don't rush to choose. There is a clear choice, but it isn't time for you to know yet."

Angie's eyes widened, and her mouth dropped open. "You know which one I'm supposed to be with, and you won't tell me?" Her voice went up an octave.

"I'm a healer. I see inner feelings of pain, love, hope, and many other emotions. I can also see the depth of those emotions and the more powerful connections. The problem is that so many things are in the way right now, and more healing and discovery is needed before I am absolutely sure.

"To tell you anything now could sway your decision before I have the facts. You and I both know the dangers of choosing love incorrectly in our world."

Angie hid her surprise and nodded in agreement. Nikki knew Kate had told her some of Xavier's story. Could Nikki read minds like Kate? *No such things as secrets in this realm.*

"Can he ever recover? Is it even possible for him to love again? I don't want to waste time on a lost cause and lose someone who is right in front of me and cares about me." Angie wanted to be hopeful.

She couldn't ignore the natural draw to Xavier, but she also didn't want her heart broken. It was easier to go the safe route. Maybe she should start focusing on Gregory and see if their attraction could be something more. She couldn't ignore the fact she missed not being around him as much.

"True love can conquer any obstacle," Nikki finally said. She seemed to be choosing her answer carefully. "More healing is needed by some more than others to move forward. Quick decisions can lead to pain and misery."

"Love didn't help much the first time, did it?" Angie sadly stated and walked toward her room.

"I was referring to true love like Xander and Kate's. Believe me, there is a difference. If it had been true love between Xavier and Lily, there would be no connection between the two of you.

"On the other hand, don't mistake an attraction or electrical surge for a connection. It takes so much more to be truly in love. It pulls at your soul. When you are ready, you won't have to wonder which one to choose. There will be only one choice."

This was the first indication that there was much more to this story than Angie ever imagined, and apparently, she was going to be smack dab in the middle of it, whether she wanted to be or not.

The look on Nikki's face made it clear that she knew more about the joy and pain of love than anyone realized. What was her story?

Leaving Nikki to her cleaning, she headed down the hallway. She paused to look at Xavier's and Gregory's doors on her way. She wished for the courage to go with her gut and make the commitment.

She stared at both doors, desperately wanting the connection. There was no question in her heart or mind which door she wanted to knock on. She raised her hand, then pulled back.

Sighing, she briefly thought of running away. Returning to her team and solving basic FBI cases involving humans – *plain* humans.

She thought about the total hell that would reign on Earth if Kate failed. No way was she going back through that portal. She couldn't leave and would stay by Kate's side until the end.

With nothing else to do and despair weighing heavily on her heart, she flung herself across the bed and for the first time in years had herself a real good cry.

"I got up early and slid notes under everyone's door, telling them we would meet in a couple hours." Xander had been thinking about everything all night and realized he hadn't focused on Kate's human side.

He'd been constantly pushing her to change and he needed to celebrate who she'd been. All of her. He sent a mental note to check in with Nikki. She sent back that she had everything under control.

Xander had intrigued Kate as she dressed that morning. He kissed her cheek and asked her to walk through the gardens with him. It was an odd request. She accepted.

He took her on a pathway that wrapped around the house. He'd always loved how it opened into a beautiful garden with lots of flowers, a fountain, a couple birdbaths, and benches placed in a circle around it. He hoped she'd like it just as much.

He pulled her over to one of the benches and hugged her tightly to him. She relaxed against his chest. He understood she needed some time to come to grips with everything that had happened yesterday, so he simply held her while she processed. She deserved a private place to let her emotions flow.

Kate briefly sensed animosity in the house, but he assured her that Nikki could handle anything. "She seems laid-back, but she can kick butt when she needs to. She'd tell me if she needed help. This morning is all for *us*. Put everything else out of your mind."

It sounded good to Kate, so she shut them out and snuggled against his shoulder. These moments would come less frequently as time progressed toward the battle. They spent several minutes enjoying the silence and peace of being together, like they were the only two people in the universe.

She could have sat there for hours soaking in the sun and relaxing against him, but Xander eventually shifted and turned to face her, cupping her cheek with his palm.

"Kate, you mean the world to me, and I don't want to lose you." He held up his hand as she started to speak. "Let me finish. *Please*?" His exasperated expression made her laugh.

She bit her tongue to keep from interrupting.

He placed a finger on her lips, smiled, and continued. "I want to do something special to celebrate your human and mystic heritage. Also, I'd like to meet your family. I guess I didn't think about it. They've become part of our family because they're your family.

"Honoring and learning your heritage is as important as you learning mine. I've been a little remiss in realizing that. Should we survive the Rising, I'd like to get to know them. They are family. I'm man enough to admit that I want to stake my claim in every way possible. I don't want any doubt in any realm that you are mine."

He turned and came off the bench to kneel in front of her. Her heartbeat ninety miles a minute. He pulled out a ring with a beautiful marquis cut diamond in the center surrounded by sapphires and took her hand. *It's gorgeous.*

"Cadence Hope Smith, would you do me the honor of marrying me in a traditional ceremony?"

She gasped at the love and sincerity shining in his eyes. He opened his mind to her. The depth and truth of his love surrounded her and fulfilled her every wish.

"Of course, I will." She launched off the bench and into his arms, knocking them both over. "I love you. You are my true soul mate for eternity."

He possessed her mouth with the sweetest kiss she'd ever known. He was her past, present, and future. His love was her fuel to fight the battle.

Training, recruiting, and battling were aspects of the near future, but at the moment, peace and contentment overflowed in her heart. A first for her. She got her fairytale romance. The dream she thought to be most elusive was hers because she'd finally accepted the hand of the stranger in the mist. Anything seemed possible.

Flashing into their bedroom, they made their pledges to one another in a more intimate way and reached the heavens of bliss. Tomorrow she'd deal with the world's problems. Tomorrow would wait.

With sighs of serenity whispering through all of the hearts in the manor, the electricity flickered, reminding them about love, hope, and a future.

The Adventure continues in...

Also from Jumpmaster Press

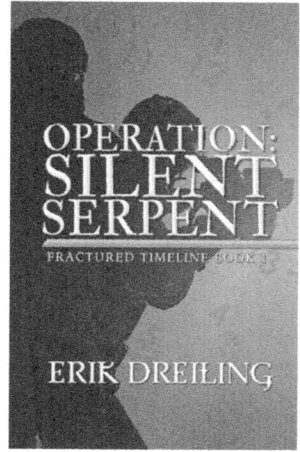

About the Author

J. L. Lawrence lives near Nashville, Tennessee with her family including three rambunctious teenagers. She loves reading and exploring new places. Her imagination has always provided her greatest adventures. She finally decided to capture some of the stories on paper to create the Mystic Series. Please explore the website and check out her Facebook and Instagram.

authorjllawrence.com

Made in the USA
Monee, IL
08 November 2021